THE FIRE ESCAPE BELONGS IN BROOKLYN

(A novel based on The Fire Escape Stories)

D1315522

Chuck Cascio

Bianca Rosa Publishing
Reston, VA

Author's Website:
Chuckcascioauthor.com

Author's email:
chuckwrites@yahoo.com
ISBN: 1546975837
ISBN 13: 9781546975830

Library of Congress Control Number: 2017910281

CreateSpace Independent Publishing Platform
North Charleston, South Carolina

DEDICATION

For Faye, whose support, courage, and love brought this book to life.

THE FIRE ESCAPE BELONGS IN BROOKLYN

(A Novel Based on *The Fire Escape Stories*)
by
Chuck Cascio

Time time time
See what's become of me
While I looked around
For my possibilities…
(from a "Hazy Shade of Winter" by Simon and
Garfunkel)

PROLOGUE

Dangling from the last rung of the fire escape, staring down at the short drop to the scruffy Brooklyn sidewalk below, afraid to let go, my ten-year-old brain raising fears in the night (Suppose I slip when my feet hit? Suppose it's further down than it looks? Suppose I land on my face?), my twin cousin, Sally-Boy, calling to me from below ("Come on, Mikey, I done it, so you can do it! It's easy! You just gotta let go, you drop, you land. Let go, Mikey! Let go!"), so I finally do it, I reluctantly release my fingers, I feel the brief emptiness of space and summer's suddenly cool air, I fight back a brief gasp when I fear the sidewalk has disappeared, and then my sneakers absorb the impact of the concrete, my knees bend slightly, I hold my balance, and Sally's laughter echoes, "Hahahaha! Mikey, we did it, Mikey, we did it! We made it all the way down! Hahahahaha! I knew we could do it, I knew it!" and I laugh with him as we punch each other lightly, and then the haunting blackness of the street hovers except for a few flickering lights in the tenements surrounding us and a distant street lamp shining its yellow-tinged glow, so I sit on the warm sidewalk with him, doing nothing, talking the idle chatter of two ten-year-olds enjoying the rush of having broken yet another rule, and I look up at the fire escape lining the outside of the apartments, all the way to the top and beyond into the starry sky, and suddenly I think, but I do not ask, "Where do we go now, Sally-Boy?"

CHAPTER ONE

Mr. Burger, my supposed guidance counselor during my senior year of high school, damn near had a heart attack when four colleges accepted me. He was certain I would not get into any school and had repeatedly urged me to join the military.

"Go fight the Vietnamese," he would say, glancing at his watch, his bloated belly hovering over his office desk. "Other kids will appreciate your service." When he saw the acceptances, he simply shrugged and breathlessly blurted, "You should still consider the military."

My older cousin, Harry, who was my real-life counselor, told me to ignore Burger and *not* to tell him to

1

go fuck himself, which is what my "twin," Sally-Boy Boccanera, would have certainly advised me to do... that is, if Sally-Boy hadn't disappeared more than a year earlier.

The previous spring, after my cousin Sally's disappearance the night before our seventeenth birthday, I struggled terribly for the remainder of my junior year in high school. I muddled through the last couple of months, my head bursting constantly with confusion and haunting sadness about Sally-Boy, where he might have gone, why he ran without telling me, how he could have left all of those days and nights on our Brooklyn fire escape behind so easily.

But with Harry's help, I slowly pulled things together during my senior year. When the acceptances came, I watched my parents visibly swell with pride and a new confidence grew inside of me. The acceptances reinforced my father's decision of a few years before, when he took a job with the Secret Service in Washington and moved us from my Brooklyn neighborhood to the Virginia suburbs. I was twelve when we moved, and I had done my best to try to understand the "opportunities" he kept talking about. In the early spring of 1966, when I sat down with my parents to discuss which college I would choose to attend, I had a better understanding of my father's decision.

"Pick any one of the four that you want," my father said, as I sat with him and my mother at the kitchen table with the acceptance letters fanned out in front of us.

Two of the schools were in Virginia, one was in DC, and the fourth, my favorite, was in New Jersey.

"The Virginia schools are less expensive," I said, "and the DC school would mean I could live at home."

"Right," my father said, "but this is your pick, Michael. If you want to go to Sinclair College in New Jersey, then go. You have earned it."

I nodded and thanked him. "Okay, then," I said. "I will go to Sinclair."

My parents stood and hugged me, and even as I enjoyed their warmth, I found my mind slipping to Sally-Boy again. I had purposely not applied to any schools in New York because I was afraid the proximity to the neighborhood where Sally-Boy and I had grown up would be too difficult for me, a constant reminder of the past, a persistent temptation to revisit those memories. But I also knew that I chose Sinclair, in part, because it was close enough to New York that I could go there occasionally, maybe look for Sally-Boy, maybe visit those places where we used to hang out, and maybe...just maybe...find him, or at least find out what happened to him.

And I did go to Brooklyn during my freshman year. Often. Quietly. Mostly at night. Always by myself.

I would leave the increasingly comfortable confines of Sinclair College—a place that just five years earlier

I could never have imagined becoming part of—get on a late-night train to New York's Penn Station, and take a subway to the old Brooklyn neighborhood, our neighborhood.

On those trips to Brooklyn, I told no one where I was going. I just disappeared from campus. I dressed inconspicuously, hid my face behind a turned up collar, or a sweatshirt hood, or a baseball cap. I peeked in at *Panificio di Boccanera*, the bakery my Uncle Sal, Sally-Boy's father, supposedly owned...but was really owned by the local boss known only as One-Eyed Jimmy. I watched Uncle Sal and Capricia—the woman Uncle Sal married many years after Sally-Boy's mother, my Aunt Maria, died within minutes of Sally's birth on the same day I was born—working in the bakery, playing with their little daughter, laughing...and, occasionally, I would see Capricia apparently comforting Uncle Sal in a corner alley or as they walked back to their deteriorating tenement, the one that held the fire escape Sally-Boy and I loved.

I quietly roamed the alleys, buildings, and parks, looking for Sally, hoping to see some sign of him, talking to people who did not recognize me, asking in passing about Salvatore Boccanera. But no one ever knew anything...or at least they said they knew nothing.

Then one night, just past midnight, while Angelina and Massimo Bortuzzi, the young couple who helped Uncle Sal at the *Panificio*, were closing up, I mustered the courage to step inside the otherwise empty bakery, to smell the wonderful aroma of fresh cannoli and coffee again, to hear the last bit of an opera aria fill the air just before the record was turned off for the night, to stand there amid memories that suddenly seemed so real that I wondered for a moment if I had ever left...if *he* had ever left.

Angelina saw me first. "Michele? Michele?" she said softly in broken English, uncertain, her beautiful brown eyes expanding. "It is-a you, yes, Michele?"

"Yes, it's me. Hi, Angelina," I said.

She rushed toward me and called to her husband: "Massimo, come-a here! Look! It is-a Michele! He come-a to see us!" Massimo came out, all muscle, black hair, and scruffy beard; he looked uncertain at first at the possible intruder who had entered, and then walked quickly toward me. "What the hell, kid, you're really here?" he asked. "We ain't seen you since...well, since you know when."

Together they squeezed me, looked me up and down repeatedly, made affectionate noises, grabbed my shoulders, muttered unintelligible Italian expressions, commented on my height, my muscles, and the length of my hair, and then...the inevitable question: "You hear something, yes? You have something to tell us?"

"No," I whispered, "no, I hoped maybe you did."

"Ah, *merda*!" Massimo said, punching a wall. Angelina made the sign of the cross.

We sat on the rickety wooden chairs around a scarred table, and in the dim light we swapped theories and hopes and questions, but no answers, until almost one in the morning. Finally, there was a long pause. Angelina wiped away a tear. "You were the good boys," she said, "such-a the good boys. I love-a you boys so much, you and the Salvatore."

And Mass, his own eyes moist, added, "You were the Delivery Men, remember, Michele? You did the deliveries. You and Salvatore, the whole neighborhood loved you knuckleheads."

And then my turn to fight a tear: "Sure, of course, I remember. I remember it all, but I wish I knew more. I wish I knew anything about him, how it happened, how he disappeared, where he is...why..."

With that, we stood and Angelina wept openly. She reached for me, hugged me, and said, "We all-a wish this, Michele." She paused, then said with piercing, brown-eyed conviction, "*Forse un giorno*, Michele, *forse un giorno*."

Massimo added, "She is right, Michele, someday we will know, but until then, it is also good that we remember, *la vita va avanti*, Michele. It does, you know, the life...it goes on."

Angelina backed up, wiped her eyes. Massimo put his arm around my shoulders again, squeezed, and said, "Strong, eh? The girls at the college...they feel how strong, eh?"

He laughed. I laughed. Angelina laughed. We walked out of *Panificio di Boccanera*.

I asked them not to tell anyone that I was there, not even Uncle Sal. They promised not to say a word. I knew I could trust them.

As I prepared to walk into Brooklyn's darkness, Massimo said, "If we ever hear anything, we gonna tell you first. You and Salvatore...*fratelli*."

I thanked them and said, "Yes, he was my brother," and then added with a forced smile, "*La vita va avanti*, right?"

Angelina nodded and said, "*Ti amo*, Michele" and Massimo whispered, "*Ti amo*, Delivery Man."

I said, "I love you, too, Mass and Angelina. I always will."

I walked away, fighting the swelling in my throat, riding the subway out of Brooklyn, taking it to the train in Penn Station that rumbled through the night to Trenton, where I hitchhiked in the darkness to the foreign land of Sinclair College, where I grew increasingly part of the college crowd and finished my freshman year, and where life definitely did go on, but in a very different way from the life I had known years before.

CHAPTER TWO

*Y*ou knew it, Sally-Boy, you knew it all those years ago, and you said it into the hot, black Brooklyn night on the fire escape we loved, the fire escape that reeked of rust and iron and our own sweat from wrestling on it, drinking on it, pumping iron on it. You knew it then, before everything changed, before the last boosted beer was drunk that night, before I left you and you left us all. You always seemed to know so much and you knew it then, and you said it, Sally, as we swigged the last can of Schaefer we shared:

"Remember this night, Mikey," you said, mysterious Brooklyn noises swelling around us like a concert of benevolent memories, "remember it because *it won't ever be like this again, never—too much going on, too much is, like, confused and gettin worse. So, my cousin, my brother, take it from me, take it for what it's worth and sip that beer real real slow...'cause Mikey, it ain't never gonna be like this again...never, not ever 'cause everythin changes...it just does."*

In my head, I see him sip, burp, smile. I know what is coming next, and I hear myself saying, *Don't say it, Sally. You scream it out, it means 'fire,' and the lights go on all over the neighborhood.*

I hear his laugh, his voice rising: *What the hell, do I know, Mikey? I am just Salvatore Fuoco!!! Fuck-a-you! Salvatore fuck-a-you!!! Salvatore Fuocooooo!!!* Lights flick on. People shout, *"Is there a fire? What's goin on, for crissake? Shut the hell up!"* Then I laugh and say, *"You always do it..."* but when I turn to see him, Sally-Boy is gone. The neighborhood slowly turns dark again.

Still, every dawn, the thought of Sally-Boy leads me to my Fire Escape Confession:

I committed a crime, but I know it was right.
I went too far, and then I stopped short.
I failed to speak, when words were needed.
I spoke, when words meant nothing.
I let people disappear, because confusion overwhelmed me.

And now all these years later, I still talk to you, Sally-Boy. You, who gave me fear and courage; you, who somehow knew when everything had changed for you, when nothing would ever be the same; you, who disappeared. And now I know when everything changed for me...and nothing has ever been the same...

For me, the changes began in January of 1968, the second semester of my sophomore year at Sinclair College. I can now see how the new me emerged as I left the old me behind, a time and a change that I could not have predicted...but that's how it happens, right, Sally-Boy?

CHAPTER THREE

My father pressed a five-dollar bill into my hand. I knew it was five dollars because he told me; he also told me what to do with it.

"Here's five bucks," he said. His breath puffed out in little white spurts as his words reached the January cold. "Get yourself a haircut when you get back to school."

His eyes narrowed as a slight breeze lifted my hair off the side of my forehead and left it dangling in my eyes. I brushed the hair aside with the hand that held the five-dollar bill as we entered Union Station in Washington, DC, where a large and loud group of anti-Vietnam War protesters were beating a huge drum and screaming repeatedly, "Peace now! Peace now!" stimulating my father's considerable pride in being a part of the government establishment they opposed.

"Spoiled, narrow-minded jerks," he said, staring at the protesters. Then he turned to me and said calmly, in the manner of a man who is used to having people do what he says,

"As soon as you get back to school, you cut the hair. You understand, right?"

My mother, perhaps the only person who could soften my father's naturally hard edge, tilted her head sideways and flicked her eyes sympathetically at the two of us.

The pervasive odor of diesel wafting up from the train platforms, and the loud drumbeats, and the chanting kept me from responding to him right away. I wondered if by opening my mouth I would swallow something harmful; maybe the air would turn solid when I breathed and I'd gulp down something that tasted like diesel-coated tin driven down my throat by the vibration of the hard-pounding drum. I stood submerged in diesel, permeated with it, suffocating in train stench, destined to smell like a locomotive forever and swept away by the anti-war spirit.

From somewhere above the odor and noise and benches studded with derelicts huddled for warmth against the bitterness outside, a nearly unintelligible voice on a PA pretended to give travelers information about their trains. But who could understand those garbled directions? You'd damn well better know where you were going, or figure it out yourself, or else you'd amble around aimlessly amid the noisome diesel fumes.

I forced out an objection. "I don't need the money, Dad," I said, the strength of my voice surprising me, encouraging me. "I don't even need a haircut."

My mother's small, gloved hands squeezed his arm, as if trying to grab a tight hold of his temper for him. We walked silently for a few steps toward my train. My hair really wasn't long, not compared to the shoulder-length waves, braids, and ponytails of kids back then. My ears were just half-covered, and the hair on the back of my neck scarcely crept over my shirt collar.

"Look over there," I said, spotting a guy about my age with red hair cascading down his back nearly to his waist; his hair bounced as he hammered at his drum. "Now that's long. See, my hair's not really long at all."

My father stopped walking and my mother automatically did the same. I put down my bulging canvas duffel bag and looked at my parents. I held the five-dollar bill clenched in my fist.

"To me, your father, it's long," he said with typical terseness. "To me, the one who supports you and your escapades in college, your hair is long. Too long. You should have had it cut while you were home on break. It looks ragged." He paused, then added as an afterthought, "And so do you, almost as bad as some of those knuckleheads." He nodded in the direction of the drumbeat.

"You do look a little tired, Michael," my mother confirmed, reaching to flick a stray thread off my ski jacket. She took the five-dollar bill out of my fist and stuffed it into my jacket pocket. "You didn't get enough rest at home, did you, working late so many nights?"

"Sure I did, Mom," I lied, while forcing a smile. "It was fine. I had a good vacation."

My father knew I was lying, of course, and I guess he kind of liked the fact that I was trying to comfort my mother. He smiled at me, one side of his mouth sliding back a little further than the other, and I relaxed momentarily as I recognized the smile I used to try, without success, to imitate. He put a hand on my shoulder.

"When you come home in April for Spring Break, we'll all go to a ballgame," he said. "See the Senators play. Maybe I can get the Presidential Box. It's been a while since we all went together. Anna, you'd like to go, wouldn't you?"

"Sure, Kev," my mother answered. "Why not? Washington is so lovely in the spring." She stood on her tiptoes and pecked my father on the cheek.

"So what do you think, son?" he asked.

"Yeah sure, Dad, it sounds great," I said, but the words were so flat they sounded as though they had been squeezed out instead of spoken. I could hear the protesters' drum pounding in the distance, and the damn train chose that moment to hiss, as if laughing at my feebleness, snickering and spitting its stinking diesel-powered smoke at me.

How could I get worked up about baseball? It was, after all, winter, and I was cold, tired, and worried—about school (no major yet); my hair (my father's Crusade); my future (bleak, as 1968 opened with President Lyndon Johnson and General William Westmoreland renewing "commitments" following the Tet Offensive bloodbath in Vietnam); my sex life (non-existent for a couple of months); and, of course, the constant fight to keep from "talking" to Sally-Boy. The fact that I was now ruining a good-bye for my parents didn't make me any happier.

The PA crackled with another fractured message and we started walking again. The grimy platform grew crowded with people preparing to board the trains. My duffel bag banged into my thigh every other step, forcing me to zigzag as I walked. That, in turn, threw my parents off balance, and though none of us said anything, we all tried to adjust our strides to provide some coordination of movement. The result was that we walked like three drunks, wandering hopelessly out of synch.

I put the duffel bag down in front of the entrance to one of the train's cars. My mother frowned at my lumpy baggage and tried smoothing it with her hands. "If you'd fold your clothes, Michael, your bag wouldn't bulge so," she said.

I shrugged, then hugged her and kissed her good-bye.

My father nudged back the sleeve of his gray trench coat and glanced at his watch. The cold always seemed to make his naturally sharp features turn rigid. That's how he looked standing on that platform—chiseled, solid, self-assured. He nodded with obvious satisfaction, rubbed his bare hands together, and said, "Fifteen minutes to spare. That's what I like. The Green Bay Packers call that 'Lombardi time,' you know?"

"Yeah, I know, Dad, but I just call it early," I said, reaching an arm around his shoulders and squeezing. Even the depressing reek of diesel couldn't obliterate the familiar smell of his aftershave, and I was annoyed with myself for feeling comforted by that whiff of Old Spice.

I picked up my bag. My mother turned her coat collar flat against her neck. The winter air had tinged her nose red, and she gently rocked from side-to-side to keep warm. My father put an arm around her. They looked so familiar, so comfortable, so stable—a little hub of security, neat and proper and always on time. I couldn't wait to get away from them.

I climbed into the stuffy train car and found an empty seat toward the back. They were waving to me—Mom with her palm out, fluttering her fingers like a bird ruffling its feathers, Dad with an angular, two-fingered salute and just the smallest hint of kindness around his mouth. I could still hear the protesters' drum beating surprisingly strong outside. Maybe I *will* get my hair cut, I thought.

I waved good-bye once more, and as I did, my father focused his eyes directly on mine, turned his two-fingered salute into a scissors, and mouthed, "Get your hair cut."

On second thought, I said to myself, maybe I *won't*.

CHAPTER FOUR

The train pulled out of the station, and my parents were quickly out of sight, though I could still hear the drumbeat. For a childish instant, I wondered whether I'd ever see my parents again. Inside my head, I blurted, *People and things disappear, right, Sally? I mean, we know they're real, but then, they're gone. You. The fire escape. Brooklyn. What is real goes away…and somehow, la vita va avante…but how?*

A group of soldiers bound for somewhere stood rigid and tense on a distant platform, and I wondered where they were from, and where their parents were, and my thoughts kept shifting to Sally-Boy, and the scene at Brooklyn Hospital Center when we were born almost simultaneously to the DeRosa sisters in 1948, Sally-Boy's mother dying within an hour of giving birth to him. My mother lived, and Sally-Boy and I grew together like twins, sharing our lives for many youthful years as though we were one person. But I have always believed that Sally-Boy reacted to a reality filled with an emptiness that he struggled mightily to understand.

Sally-Boy and I used to spend every day together, walking to school, exploring the streets, working at Big Sal's *Panificio*, and then, after my family moved to Northern Virginia when I was twelve, I spent school vacations and many summers with Sally. I would go to Brooklyn to stay with him, his father and, later, his stepmother, Capricia. Sally and I had become well known as the Delivery Men, the two kids who delivered baked goods by wagon at dawn to Brooklyn row houses and tenements. Eventually, as we got older, we started delivering mysterious envelopes for a man named One-Eyed Jimmy, who had loaned Big Sal money to start the *Panificio* in exchange, apparently, for a lifetime of payments.

After Sally vanished that night before we turned seventeen, I had to fight to bury Sally deep inside. Over time, the urge to talk to him dissipated, but it never left completely and now, as the train pulled away, I succumbed to that urge and reached for him again. I pictured Sally-Boy, sitting with me on the rail of our gritty fire escape, and I began muttering, my lips actually moving slightly:

> *I'm on a train, Sally, going to New Jersey, at least that's where they say it's going. Suppose it goes someplace else? Someplace no one knows exits? I mean, everyone just eventually disappears, right, Sally? Isn't that what happens? Those soldiers—they'll disappear, won't they? I won't ever see them again, and they never even saw me. It happens. I know it happens. You know it happens, Sally, you know it best of all. The fire escape was real, Sally, it was real. We would throw pennies off of it at night, remember? Then in the morning, when we looked at the sidewalk, the pennies were always gone. But the fire escape, it was always there for us, and when we were on it, you were real, and I was real, and we were safe there together. That's where you needed to go, Sally, instead of disappearing—you just needed to go to the fire escape.*

A soldier waved at the train and blew a kiss toward it, and I wondered who was on the receiving end of that gesture, and whether they would see it, and whether they would take it with them wherever they were going. I started to ask Sally-Boy what he thought, but I fought back the impulse and said to myself: You know, maybe disappearing for a while wouldn't be such a bad idea.

CHAPTER FIVE

As the train clacked along, slowly narrowing the distance between my home in the Virginia suburbs and Sinclair College in central New Jersey, I wanted my life to calm down so I could just be a College Joe like Harry had been, and I wanted to put Sally-Boy back into the quiet place in my head where my childhood was forever safe, where we would sit on the fire escape and fantasize about Angelina Bortuzzi and where we would make up nicknames for ourselves, Sally's favorite being Salvatore Fuoco, and how he used to sing out operatically as "Salvaaaaatoreeee Fuuuucka Youuuu!" But everything everywhere seemed so muddled, as though nothing was safe, as if I was looking at the world through murky water that changed the shape and depth and texture of all that I could see and remember.

I just wanted to attend a few classes, drink lots of beer without getting a pot belly, party all night, and eventually set up a leisurely but lucrative life.

The simple life, the good life, the simply good life was all I wanted. On rare days, I'd know just how the new me should act. But on most others, I couldn't even decide what color socks to wear. And now, sitting in a dank train car, I was turning to Sally-Boy again, a sure sign of my rising insecurity.

So I rode alone, feeling the evening's cold, a little depressed, a little curious about what this semester would bring, and I turned my *Time* Magazine to a story about Senator Eugene McCarthy's chances of winning the upcoming New Hampshire primary. The story didn't give the poet/politician much hope, but the part about him advocating a pullout of Vietnam sure appealed to me with the draft of 1968 becoming the prevailing focus of every young male's life.

Bouncing along on the train, a diesel-tinged depression swamped me as I watched an elegant African American woman wearing a flowing black dress try to hand sandwiches from a worn picnic basket to her two sons. The older child was about twelve, but a tight-skinned, tough twelve. He refused to eat, pushing aside the sandwich, his wide brown eyes staring ahead vacantly. His mother would occasionally whisper to him and then pull his head to her billowing bosom, but the boy hardly responded.

At one point, the younger child nibbled at his sandwich and then accidentally spilled a can of grape soda in front of a Marine who was walking down the aisle. Purple seeped into the threadbare carpet, creating a dark, expanding circle. The Marine picked up what was left of the child's drink, handed the can to him, rubbed the boy's hair, and walked on.

The little boy looked up at his mother and said with certainty, "That man, he a soldier, Mama."

"Yes, baby, he is," the mother said gently.

"He fight the bad people, Mama, right?"

"Mama doesn't know that, baby, and we don't know if the people are bad, but he is a soldier, baby, and he might have to fight. Now, don't you want to eat the sandwich that Mama made for you?"

"Mama, Cousin Junior, he used to fight the bad people, didn't he?"

The older boy turned his eyes toward his mother, who now offered the younger boy a biscuit while saying, "Shhh, shhh." But the little child continued innocently, shaking his small head vigorously, asking, "That soldier, he going to heaven like Cousin Junior, Mama?"

"Mama doesn't know that, baby."

"Not see Cousin Junior no more," the child said, still shaking his head.

The older boy stood quickly, stepping just beyond his mother's grasp. "I'm going to the bathroom,
Mama."

"Gerald, honey..."

"Mama, I have to go to the bathroom, that's all, I'm
okay," he said quietly, getting up from his seat.

Gerald rocked from side to side with the rhythm of
the train, and as he walked slowly up the aisle I noticed
his brown pants cuffs fell about two inches short of
meeting the edge of his worn, high-top black sneakers.

The little boy nibbled without interest at the biscuit
and then handed it to his mother. "Cousin Junior..."
he started to say, but his mother interrupted.

"Honey, that's enough about Cousin Junior now,"
she said gently, placing the biscuit into the picnic
basket and replacing the lid. "You take a nice rest for
Mama."

The child patted his mother's knees and looked up
at her kind face. "I love you, Mama," he said, resting
his head on her lap.

CHAPTER SIX

The train's gentle rocking lulled me to sleep, and I dreamt about walking toward a basket filled with fried chicken placed in an open field, kind of like the farmland in the Virginia countryside close to where I lived. A man and a woman were sitting next to it, and I thought they were my parents, but as I got close to them I realized they weren't. I walked up to them anyway to see if maybe I could buy some food from them. As I got closer, one of them reached into the basket and flipped a piece of chicken to me. I caught it, but as soon as I did, Sally-Boy appeared next to me and said in his usual cool way, barely opening his mouth when he talked, *"That ain't chicken, Mikey, unless it's the kind that explodes, blows you off the fire escape, and turns you into yesterday."* The chicken turned into a grenade, and I threw it across the field; out of the corner of my eye, the couple transformed into Vietnamese who laughed at me. There was an explosion, and I sat straight up, awake and safe in my seat as the train screeched to a stop.

"Philadelphia!" the conductor shouted.

I thought for sure I had screamed, but no one around me seemed to notice. In fact, everyone in the train car seemed different—the African American family was gone, and so was the Marine. I began to wonder exactly where my dream had begun and whether the people I thought I saw on the train had, in fact, been real.

As I cleared my head and looked out of the train window at the dreary 30th Street Station platform in Philadelphia, a woman helped an elderly gentleman with a cane onto the train. The woman looked slightly older than I was, and she was completely focused on helping the man, smiling as she talked with him. He looked straight ahead, walking carefully, bent slightly at the waist, and taking mini-steps. The woman carried one small suitcase. They disappeared from sight, only to reappear at the front of the train car. The woman whispered something to the man, and walked him back toward me. She smiled at me, and said softly as she approached, "Can he sit with you?"

"Sure," I said.

"Oh, thank you," she said. She wore a camel-colored topcoat that set off her long brown curls perfectly. A brown-and-white striped scarf added to her sophisticated appearance. She made sure the man could not hear what she was saying, as she explained to me, "I know there are a lot of empty seats, but I'm afraid to put him in a seat by himself. Sometimes he gets a little confused. He won't talk much if at all. And it's only one more stop. Only to Trenton. My father will pick him up there."

"No problem, really," I said. "I'm going to Trenton, too. I don't mind."

"Oh, thank you *so* much," she said with sincerity that immediately made me think that she must be much older than I had originally thought—this was a distinguished, classy woman, not someone just a couple of years older than my still near-juvenile stage of life. She turned to the man, and said, speaking just a little louder and more slowly, "Zaidi, this nice man says you can sit with him. He's getting off at Trenton, too, so he can make sure you meet Abba." The woman realized that she hadn't mentioned that, so her face reddened slightly, and she turned her mouth down just a little: "Oh, I was presumptuous. I'm so sorry. I hope you don't mind. I mean you're so kind, but I don't mean to take advantage."

"No, of course, I'll make sure he connects with—is it *Abba*? That's Yiddish, right?"

"Actually, it's Hebrew."

"Oh, I'm sorry, my roommate is Jewish and on occasion he sprinkles some Yiddish or Hebrew sort of indiscriminately into our conversations."

27

"Oh, no problem at all. It can be confusing. I still say *Abba*, kind of a childish thing," she said, rolling her eyes, making her even more beautiful.

"Sure, well, anyway," I said. "I'll make sure we find your father."

"That is so kind of you," she said. "Thank you. My Abba's actual name is Aaron Lieberman; he'll be waiting on the platform in Trenton. And this is my Zaidi, Morris Lieberman."

"I'm sorry," I said. "What's the word you used before 'Morris'?"

"Oh, *Zaidi*," she said, smiling.

"Let me guess—Hebrew?"

"No," she chuckled, "Yiddish. For 'grandpa.'" Then she turned to the man and said, "You're my Zaidi, right?" and she kissed his cheek.

The man sat down next to me and stroked the woman's face gently. "You bet I am… and you are… my *shayna punim*," he said haltingly, pausing often for breath. But his voice was clear and his eyes glowed as he turned to me to explain: "*Shayna punim*…beautiful face. You agree, right?"

I felt myself blush slightly, but I said, "Yes, definitely, sure."

"Zaidi, you are a smooth-talker, but don't go putting words into this man's mouth," she said, kissing his head and then almost effortlessly lifting his suitcase onto the rack above our seat. She turned to me and said, "Shayna is actually my first name—just a tad pretentious, don't

28

you think? I'm Shayna Lieberman." She laughed warmly, displaying perhaps the most beautiful smile I had ever seen. She extended her hand to me; I shook it and was immediately surprised at the strength of her grip. She turned to her grandfather. "I have to go now, Zaidi, but let's find out this nice man's name."

"He's Jewish or Italian with...with all that black hair," Mr. Lieberman said.

"Well, my mom's Italian—Boccanera was her maiden name...translated, that's considered 'Blackmouth,' not the most beautiful name, I know—but not my dad, he's Irish," I said. "My name is Mike Burns." I shook Mr. Lieberman's dry hand.

"A good name," Mr. Lieberman said, his thick, white eyebrows lifting. "You can burn...with lots of things, no? Love, intelligence...knowledge, beliefs, commitment... rage, eh?"

"It's a great name," the woman said, "but I have to get off the train now, Zaidi. I love you so much, and I loved having you visit me. Promise you will visit again soon." She kissed his cheek this time.

"God willing...that I live," Mr. Lieberman said, "I will visit you again... my *shayna punim*." He reached up, they hugged, she kissed his forehead, and then she said good-bye and walked off the train.

CHAPTER SEVEN

As the train pulled away, Mr. Lieberman adjusted his glasses and looked across me and out the window, searching the train platform for his granddaughter. He spotted her waving and said excitedly, "Look, there she is...there she is!" He waved to her and then sat back and looked at the train ceiling.

"Would you like to switch places with me so you can sit next to the window?" I asked.

"No...that's not...necessary. There's not much...to see along here...but leftovers. Besides, I'll probably... have to pee twenty times between here and Trenton!"

"What do you mean 'leftovers'?" I asked.

"These factories...and tenements along the train tracks. They're what's left over... from what used to be important...vital. Now...now...they're just straining to mean something, anything...just to find a use. Leftovers. But...they don't have to be that way." He shrugged. "That Shayna of mine. She is the light...of our family. She could take one of those tenements," he reached across my body with his cane to tap the window, "and...and make it live again. Don't get me wrong. I love all eight...of my grandchildren, but she... she is the light. You could see that, right?"

"Well, yes," I said. "She seemed very caring."

Mr. Lieberman peered directly at me from behind his horn-rimmed glasses. "Caring? Oh, you have no idea. This is a woman...who graduated NYU in three years... and became an attorney...two years later. Can you believe that? Do you know...what determination that takes? What brains? She works...in inner-city Philadelphia, I mean the toughest parts of that city...and...and she helps the poorest of the poor families...families where the parents have to cover their children with cardboard boxes because the rain...it comes right through the walls and ceilings of their tenements. She...she could have worked in any law firm, *any* big firm...but she is so very very good in the heart...that she works with the poorest of the poor. That is her; that is my Shayna."

He looked at me, waiting for my reaction to his story, and I sat there for a few seconds realizing that I had no experience in responding to such emotion, particularly from a virtual stranger. "You have a lot to be proud of," I said. "She's an exceptional person."

He nodded and then struggled to take off his black topcoat. I reached across the back of it, and held it as he pulled his arms free. "Thank you, Michael," he said, sounding as though he had known me for years. "You say Shayna…is exceptional?"

"Well, yes, sure, from what you have just told me, definitely exceptional."

He nodded approvingly at me. "You're a gentleman, Michael. I like that. You don't see that…in some young men today. I see how they look at my Shayna… and my Aviva and Shira—my other granddaughters. We need gentlemen…we need them, you know?"

What could I say? You can't tell a man that you were attracted in some way to his granddaughter, can you? If he wanted to believe that I was a pure gentleman, then why should I do or say anything that might change his opinion? So I said, "Well, I try to be a gentleman, Mr. Lieberman. Do you want anything to eat or drink? I'd be happy to get you something."

"No, thank you," he said. "I'm fine. I'm going to eat…at my son's house in Jersey… and then tomorrow…tomorrow he will drive me into Manhattan, where I live."

"Do you live by yourself?"

"Yes, yes, I do…in the same apartment that I lived in with my beautiful wife, Tzipora—Tzipi—for twenty years…until she passed two years ago. After our children were grown…Tzipi and I moved into a small, one-bedroom place…it's on the Upper East Side…We had lived in that same general area…but in a little bigger place—two baths, two bedrooms—when the kids were growing up. Tzipi…she loved our little one-bedroom. I still try to keep it just the way she left it…so it's almost like she's still there…Do you think…that's strange?" He tilted his head a little in anticipation of my answer.

"No," I said. "Not at all. It makes you feel like she's with you, right?"

His eyes lit up. "Exactly!" he said. "Yes, it provides me with…with a… a permanence, a piece of my life that remains in place…no matter how much other things change…kids grow, they leave you, they make their own lives…the neighbors move…brothers and sisters die or just naturally…just naturally drift to their own families. But I have my apartment…and I keep it like it was when I was with my Tzipi, and—don't tell anyone—but sometimes, sometimes…sometimes I talk to her…and I hear her talking to me…You get that, Michael, right?"

"Oh, yes, I definitely get it," I said.

"Shayna, too; she gets it, she understands," he said.

He stopped talking abruptly and then stood with his cane. "Pee time," he said, rolling his eyes. "If I'm not back in twenty minutes…the emergency cord—pull it." He smiled and walked with his cane carefully up the aisle.

I looked at the lights now glowing inside apartments along the train route, and I wondered about the people living there—about the lives unfolding, the family sitting down to eat, or people with perhaps nothing to eat, the couple who might be making love, the student studying, the parents worrying if they will be able to feed their family, the soldier getting ready to ship out—and the reality that there is probably some elderly gentleman like Mr. Lieberman trying to keep a piece of his life intact.

I glanced back around the train. The grape drink spilled by the little African American boy had left only a faint stain; I had to think hard to convince myself that it had even happened. In fact, the few passengers in the train car all seemed like they had somehow boarded while the train was running and others somehow exited simultaneously. And just before Mr. Lieberman sat back down, I narrowed my gaze and saw a reflection I didn't recognize for a moment—it was my own, but the scattered lights of the "leftovers" seemed to be shining inside my head.

"Almost in Trenton," Mr. Lieberman said.

"Yes, just a few more minutes."

"Shayna always tries to find someone…for me to sit with," he said. "Most of the time, after she leaves the train…I make an excuse to get up…and I go sit somewhere else on my own."

"I'm glad you sat with me," I said.

"You're a gentleman, like I said. You know…I owned a small shop in Manhattan. Made clothes; worked fifteen…sixteen, twenty hours a day. Had four kids…two boys, two girls. Lost one of the boys…Ari…to TB…he was twelve. My Tzipi, her pain over losing him, it was…it was so much to see and lasted forever. But she persevered. This is what we do…what people must do. Persevere." He stopped abruptly, and then said, "I talk too much."

"Not at all," I said. "I understand what you're saying."

"Well, you are a *mensch* to say so—do you know this word, *mensch?*"

"Yes, the man who owned the bagel shop in our Brooklyn neighborhood called me that sometimes."

"So, the man knew you were good guy, a gentleman. And it's true…you are a *mensch*. But also it's true…I do talk too much to some people, but I have such…such *nachas*—pride, good fortune, the things that keep us going. I…I lost family in the camps. I had times where I didn't know when…or what…I would eat. I lost my son, my Ari. But all in all…*nachas*. Like my Shayna. Goodness. You must always…always think about the *nachas*." He paused again because he realized that in his intensity, he had gripped my arm tightly with one hand. He let go, turned his head, his eyebrows arched in slight embarrassment, and said again, "I talk too much."

"No, that's a great way to live," I said. I meant it too, but I didn't really understand how anyone could live with that philosophy, how you continually find comfort after all the shit life dumps in front of people...and some more than others. The camps, the loss of a son, poverty, disappearance, war...and this man talked of *nachas*?

"You are kind to an old man," he said. "What do you do?"

"I'm a sophomore at Sinclair College," I said.

"Oh...good school that Sinclair. What do they call it...a 'Small Ivy,' right?"

"Yes, I guess so."

"I know all these New York...and New Jersey schools. My *kinder*—my children—looked at all of them. But they all went to City College. They didn't want me... and their mother to worry about finances. But I told them...'Go wherever you want.' For your kids, you find the money—a few more hours of work for a little bigger dream...Small price...Whatever it takes, you do... What's too much for your kids, right?"

"Sure," I said, picturing my father's scissoring fingers in my mind.

He nodded his head quickly as if punctuating my affirmation. Then he adjusted his glasses and said, "Maybe you would like to meet...my Shayna again? You know...how do you kids put it? You could look her up?"

"Well, sure," I said, surprised and unsure, "but I'm certain that she has a boyfriend, right?"

He laughed in a short, phlegm-coated chuckle. "No boyfriend...but you can't even count how many men beg...beg to see my Shayna...Beautiful, successful, single...and twenty-eight. You are how old?"

"See, I'm only going to be twenty," I said, thinking the eight years difference would certainly change his mind about having me meet his granddaughter.

"Why do you say 'only' twenty? What? Age should make you not seek to know my Shayna? Should age keep you from something...something you want? Something that might change your life? Be careful, Michael...a word like 'only' can become an excuse for not trying...for not succeeding. Her number— I'll have Aaron give it to you when we get to Trenton. Me...I don't remember it so well. Okay?"

"Sure," I said, but I wondered what it would be like to call a woman like that—eight years older, confident, sophisticated, already in a career. The thought was intriguing, but something I could not imagine doing.

The conductor called, "Trenton! Next stop Trenton!" Mr. Lieberman started to wrestle with his coat. I helped him, and then I said, "Let me step into the aisle, Mr. Lieberman, and get you your suitcase."

"Okay," he said, pulling his feet in so he almost seemed to shrink into the train seat, "but you must call me Morris."

"Okay, Morris," I said, stepping past him. I pulled down his suitcase, and I noticed that I seemed to struggle with it more than Shayna had. I grabbed my duffel bag and extended my arm to Mr. Lieberman. He gripped it, stood, steadied himself with his cane, and started shuffling forward carefully with me. The train stopped with a slight jolt but Mr. Lieberman scarcely moved.

We walked off the train and on the platform, we spotted a bald man wearing a long leather jacket and gloves and holding a hand-written sign that said, "Welcome, Abba."

"That's him!" Mr. Lieberman said excitedly, pointing to the smiling man just a few feet in front of us. "That's my son…my Aaron. Dr. Aaron Lieberman."

Dr. Lieberman stuffed the little sign into his pocket and extended one hand to me while the other rested on his father's shoulder. "Thank you so much," Dr. Lieberman said to me. "Shayna called and said you agreed to help with, as she calls him, Zaidi. May I give you something for your trouble?" He reached for his wallet.

"Oh no, no, it was my pleasure," I said. "No trouble at all."

"He's a real *mensch*…this one," Mr. Lieberman said, nodding his head sideways toward me.

"I can tell," Dr. Lieberman said, shaking my hand again. "But please go on ahead of us. It will take us a little time."

"I think I will," I said. "I have a bus to catch. Goodbye, Mr. Lieberman...I mean, Morris."

"Goodbye, Michael," he said, waving with his cane. "May your life be filled with... *nachas!*"

"Thank you!" I called over my shoulder. Then I realized that I had never gotten Shayna Lieberman's phone number. I thought about turning back and asking Dr. Lieberman or Morris if they would give it to me, but then I saw my bus pulling up, and after all, I told myself, it's the only bus that stops at Sinclair College. I exited the platform, and the train belched diesel into the night as it left the station supposedly headed for New York, but I really wasn't certain where it was going. As I stood and watched the train's lights and stench disappear in the distance, I heard Sally-Boy say, *"Could be goin anywhere, Mikey...once it's gone, you don't really know where."*

CHAPTER EIGHT

I arrived on campus in darkness. The bus from
Trenton stopped at the top of the hill, and Sinclair
College sprawled in a random pattern of black and
gray shadows in front of me, the outline of its trees and
buildings forming a hazy skyline. A sanctuary seem-
ingly apart from, and untouched by, reality except for
the growing presence of anti-war posters and graffiti.
The school insulated me from so much, including the
wind, which had felt biting at first but now sent a pleas-
ant tingle across my cheeks and ears. The sky, lightly
streaked with the remnants of dusty clouds, formed a
protective dome over the grounds. I crossed the large
oval rimmed with bare trees in front of the school and

walked past the administrative buildings, behind the towering Mountain Hall, and several hundred yards to Cunningham House, a high-rise dormitory that stretched black against the sky. I breathed the cold air deeply; *nachas*, I thought. Few lights shone.

Then I spotted the red paint and shining chrome of Darrell Bingham's Austin-Healey glistening under a yellow parking lot light. I cringed. The car, like its owner, looked arrogant.

I stopped. I looked around. I did not want to see Darrell, and I knew he'd be in the dorm. I felt a definite need, the need for more time to think about the words of Morris Lieberman, to imagine the life of Shayna Lieberman, to think more about the Leftovers, to picture the cardboard boxes covering children, to wonder if the soldiers waving good-bye would disappear. And, yes, I wanted to talk with Sally-Boy, not Bingham, a guy who suddenly seemed so wrong—as wrong and empty as the typical college life that, for some still incomprehensible reason, I felt slipping away, even though I had strangely started to grow comfortable with it.

Darrell embodied the college life I had aspired to originally and had begun adapting to. He lived just two doors down from me and my roommate, whose name was David Fishbein (I called him "Fish," a nickname he said he had embraced since childhood even though his parents hated it). While our room looked like a war zone, Darrell's bordered on elegant—pinstriped draperies with a matching bedspread and a hand-woven (so he said) throw rug of varying shades of brown. A color console TV sat in one corner and a huge stereo, which he never seemed satisfied with although it was the best that I knew of in the dorm, was mounted on the wall next to the bed. The wall across from his bed (he called it "My Chick Wall") was covered with photographs of girls who (he said) loved him and who (he said) he had fucked (doubtful...but maybe). Darrell Bingham lived alone.

Darrell's stories about his adventures during semester breaks and vacations were the stuff of movies. After all, he was about six-two, well-built and good looking in that carefully groomed, fully confident way. He referred to his Healey as "My Sweet A-H," flaunted money like a Vegas high roller, and oozed certainty about himself, his status, and his capabilities.

At that point in our sophomore year a freshman named Juliet Starlipper had imprinted herself to him. What particularly grated on me was that I had taken Juliet out myself twice during the first week of school. She wore blue jeans and sandals and smiled sweetly at all the right times. I didn't try to hustle her with the kind of Brooklyn "charm" Sally-Boy and I used to practice on the fire escape; in fact, I only kissed Juliet once—on the second night after walking her back to her dorm. I never asked her out again; I don't really know why, but I do remember that our conversations, such as they were, struck me as particularly vacuous with neither of us seeming to have much to say. In October, I heard that Bingham had her lined up for a motel after Homecoming. That bit of news was delivered, of course, by Bingham himself, who made the announcement during an invasion of the suite where Fish and I lived:

Fish and I were sitting around watching a late night movie, one of my all-time favorites—*The High and the Mighty* starring John Wayne—in mid-week. It was about the fifth time I'd seen the movie (as kids, Sally-Boy and I had strutted around for days imitating the way Wayne whistled the theme song). Wayne played a rugged loner, a commercial airplane pilot who had to land the plane safely. Bingham came in just as Wayne found out that his plane had engine trouble and had passed the point of no return.

"What the hell is this?" Bingham asked, nodding toward the television. He tossed a piece of bubble gum to me—that was another of his habits, always flinging around gum or mints or little bottles of booze or something.

"It's a movie," I said, unwrapping the gum.

"No kidding. But what the fuck is that?"

"What?" I asked. Fish hadn't flinched. He always made a point of ignoring Bingham until he was ready to insult him.

"That thing the movie's coming out of. What the fuck is it?"

"What are you talking about, Darrell?" I asked, chomping hard on the gum and snapping off an aggravated "crack." "We're trying to watch the movie. It was quiet in here, wonderful in here, until you blew in." A commercial came on. "So exactly what do you want, Darrell?"

"You guys call that goddam thing a TV?" he asked, bursting into forced laughter. The TV was an old portable black-and-white that Fish's parents had discarded. "Hard to watch that black-and-white. Come on down to my suite. I've got a big color console."

"The movie's in black-and-white, Darrell," I lied. "Or does your set change black-and-white movies into color?"

Fish had reached what he called his "Bingham Limit": "Look, what'd you come here to tell us, schmuckface? Tell us quick and then slither back into Darrell World."

"You really ought to trim that 'fro of yours," Darrell said, pointing at Fish's mass of ever-expanding curls. Darrell fumbled around in his pants pocket. "Gum, Fish-man?" he offered, flipping a piece that Fish swatted out of the air and back at Darrell's head.

Darrell shrugged and looked at his own reflection in the mirror as he blew a huge bubble that he pulled out of his mouth and held between his index finger and his thumb.

"Some fucking bubble, eh, Burns?" he said, staring in admiration at the pink circle he held.

John Wayne was back on, coolly trying to calm his passengers who were near hysteria at the idea of plummeting from twenty thousand feet. Bingham made three consecutive pops with his gum.

"C'mon, Darrell, will you please..." I started to say.

"Sorry," he said, "but I bet you can't guess who the old Bingo is going to see sheets with over Homecoming weekend." His jaw muscle clenched and loosened like a mechanical vice as he chewed slowly and deliberately. "She's a friend of yours, Burns, not a particularly close friend, but a friend." He snapped his gum to accentuate what he had said.

"What the hell are you..." I stopped suddenly, almost swallowing my gum, and then blurted out with more surprise than I intended, "Juliet?"

"Fuckin-A yes, man," Bingham grinned. "Shocked, eh? Yeah, a nice fresh freshwoman for Old Bingo." He unwrapped a new piece of gum and put it into his mouth as he moved toward the door. "I'll let you know how it is, Burns. Or can you tell me?"

"You'll never know," I said weakly.

"Right," Bingham said, flashing his obnoxious grin. As he walked out of the room, he blew another tremendous bubble, held it between his fingers, and said, "Some fucking beautiful bubble, eh, Burnsey?"

For me, Homecoming had just been a typical college weekend, an empty string of parties and booze. I did have one of those vintage hormone swaps with a nice girl named, incredibly, Monalisa. We got very worked up at a fraternity party I'd been invited to after the Homecoming game, so we slipped upstairs in the frat house. We screwed while a band blasted away downstairs and some drunk and his date screamed at each other in the room next to us. At the end of the night in front of her dorm, Monalisa told me to be sure to call her soon, and we both got worked up again. We eased our way around the corner of the building and started with her standing with her back against the wall and somehow finished with her on top of me and my blazer picking up grass stains.

I called Monalisa the next weekend, but she had a date. And she dated the same person—some wrestler, built like a Coke machine—the whole rest of the year. The thing is, I didn't care in the slightest that she was dating someone steadily. In fact, whenever we saw one another after she started dating Coke machine, neither of us even acknowledged the other. Strangers together for strange night. That was it.

But that had all taken place in the fall. Now, as I approached the entrance to Cunningham House, I figured Bingham had Juliet in his room; they'd probably been there all break. I could see Sally-Boy shrugging and saying, *"The bigger they act, the smaller they are; the hell with that jerk. We handled bigger assholes than that every day in our neighborhood."* I took a deep breath of the cold night air and muttered to myself, "Persevere persevere," and wondered if Bingham wouldn't test even Morris Lieberman's superhuman will. But then I veered away from Cunningham House toward the Bendorff Student Union, where I walked in and found a phone booth. I dialed the operator and asked for information in Philadelphia.

"Information. Can I help you?" the operator said twice before I answered.

"Yeah, I'm not sure, but yeah, I think so," I said.

"Well, whose number are you looking for?" The operator sounded annoyed.

"Yeah, I um, I'm trying to find someone."

"Oh really? Look, I think I know that. You called 'Information' for a number, I assume. I need to know the name of the party you're looking for in order to give you a number. You understand that's how this works, right?"

"Shayna. Shayna Lieberman."

"What's that first name?"

"Shayna."

"And that's the *first* name? Are you *sure?*"

"Yes, I'm sure. It means beautiful."

"Oh really? You're looking for someone beautiful? Please don't be cute. I'm busy."

"No, that's actually her name."

The operator sighed in exasperation. "Okay…and the last name?"

"Lieberman."

"How do you spell it?"

"L-i-e-b-e-r-m-a-n…I think."

"You *think*?"

"Yeah, no, I'm sure that's it…I think."

A long, silent pause. I could hear students laughing loudly in the Student Union. Another reverberating sigh and finally the operator said, "No one by that name listed in Philadelphia or the Philadelphia suburbs."

"You're sure? I mean, I know she lives there. She works with the people in the tenements. She…"

"Not listed. And listen, you're calling from a booth on a college campus in New Jersey, right?"

"Uh, yeah…but, but how do you know that? How do you know where I am?"

"We know about campuses, let's just say that, okay? Trust me. Drunks and druggies like you call all the time with threats or stupid requests…like looking for 'beauty' for god's sake. Sober up or come down off your druggy high and try getting a job instead of going back to your protests and your little college life. Some of us actually have to work for a living. Your little beauty—well, assuming you didn't just make up that name, she's not in Philly." The operator hung up abruptly.

I held the dead phone receiver in my hand and stammered some incoherent objection before just sitting there in the phone booth until a few students walked toward it, spotted me, and waved. So as they approached, I started to talk loudly into the empty receiver in order to discourage them from stopping to say hello to me.

"No, Sally-Boy, nah," I said, "I'm not gonna do that, man." Pause. "Look, you shouldn't do it either. I mean, what's so bad?" Pause. "You always say that, you always say, 'There's gotta be more.' And there is, there will be, but you don't just get it that way. You don't take off not knowing where you're going. You gotta think about things, what you're getting into, Sally." Pause. Fake laugh. "Ha! That's more like it, Sally. That's it. Sure, there's time. You'll be ready." Pause. Laugh. "Yeah, man, yeah, of course, always—me and you are brothers so let it all happen."

The students had passed, so I hung up from Sally... and from Shayna Lieberman.

CHAPTER NINE

I left the Student Union and walked back to the dorm wondering: Why was I unable to locate Shayna Lieberman? How did the operator on the phone know that I was calling from a college campus? Why did it seem as though I had actually talked to Sally-Boy?

I entered the dorm and saw Tomato Thompson sitting behind the intercom desk. His constant companion, a girl I knew only as The Thatch, bounced jollily on his lap. Tomato's real name was Ted, but no one, not even the professors, called him that. His body was round and soft, and his skin had a distinctly reddish tinge—thus, "Tomato." His fleshy jaw shook whenever he talked, and whenever several intercoms buzzed the main desk at once, his skin rippled in tiny waves and he'd complain, "I just can not do this all by myself! I just can not do it!"

That's usually when The Thatch, a girl with an explosion of hair the color and texture of cooked, but cold, spaghetti (with sauce), would jump up and growl something like, "Honestly, Tomato, you are so helpless!"

The Thatch wasn't thin either, but her skin did appear slightly tighter than Tomato's. Faint but thick hair dotted her forearms and, yes, the bet was that her less visible areas looked the same way—hence, her nickname.

Tomato and The Thatch embraced as I approached. While The Thatch struggled to get her arms completely around Tomato's body, his florid face looked perilously close to exploding. When he glimpsed me out of the corner of his eye, I think he was thankful for the chance to break loose.

"Hello, Tomato," I said. "Any messages back there for me?"

"Hmmm...what is your name again?" he asked.

He knew damn well who I was because—besides the fact that he saw me and talked to me every day—he had lost his lit book once and he had a test the next day, so he called practically everyone over the dorm intercom to try to borrow one. I loaned him my book, and when he returned it to me the cover was soiled and reeked with the spicy smell of garlic-soaked pickles. When I asked him about it, Tomato just whined and said it was like that when he got it. On rare occasions, when he didn't feel like being a prick, he'd call me by name.

"Come on, Tomato, you know my name," I said.

He huffed: "Look, there are over a thousand people in this dormitory. Do you expect me to know everyone? Now you just have to…"

I couldn't stand the whining, so I said, "Mike Burns, room 409B."

Tomato's forehead started twitching as he stared and squinted repeatedly at the small message boxes behind the desk. I looked across the room and saw two students hanging a large picture of President Lyndon Johnson wearing prison garb, giant black letters above his head proclaiming, "**WAR CRIMINAL!**" Peeking out from around The Thatch, who was futilely attempting to primp her hair, Tomato sighed enormously and repeated, "Burns, 409B," several times. He shuffled some papers, blew his nose with The Thatch still perched like a huge stuffed animal on his knee, and finally looked up and said, "No messages."

"Thank you," I said, and I walked to the elevator wondering why I so often thanked people who simply seemed determined to annoy me. Even The Thatch wouldn't hesitate to cut Tomato to the quick with a vile comment on occasion; sweet Juliet Starlipper would have looked hurt enough so that even Tomato would feel rotten; Bingham would have squashed him with a word; and Sally-Boy would have given Tomato what Sally called "The Italian Eye"—a look so menacing that people literally stammered when confronted with it, so Tomato might never have spoken again. God knows I wanted to lean over the counter, try out my own version of The Italian Eye, which I called "Crazy Stare," go all-out Brooklyn, and say to him, "Listen, you...my name is Mike Burns, and you better remember it from now on." But, no; in those days, I often said thank you to assholes.

As the elevator doors closed, I glimpsed Tomato and The Thatch kissing messily behind the intercom desk, and I noticed that in the hovering mug shot of Lyndon Johnson, the president seemed to smile down at the words "War Criminal!"

CHAPTER TEN

My room, with its comfortably haphazard décor, sealed me off from the chaotic world outside, but I was only able to enjoy the quiet loneliness for about twenty minutes. Shortly after I unpacked my suitcase, put a Beach Boys album on Fish's old stereo (it just happened to feel like working), and plopped down in one of our two Salvation Army easy chairs to read The Sunday *Times*, Darrell Bingham showed up at the door. He must have been waiting for me to get comfortable.

"Mind if I come in?" he asked, walking into the room and flopping across Fish's unmade bed.

"Why are you back so early?" I asked.

"What the hell are you listening to?"

"Darrell, that's the Beach Boys. I think you've heard of them."

"Hard to tell."

"Hard to tell? Oh, I get it, Bingham. You're driving at something. Let's have it."

"That fucking record player is assaulting that record, Burns! God, I can't listen."

"So leave."

He reached underneath his sweater into his shirt pocket and produced two chocolate kisses. "No hostility, okay?" he said, tossing me one. "I just brought back a brand new set of Fisher stereo components and set them up in my room. Why don't you do the Beach Boys justice in my place so you can hear what they really sound like?"

"Is that why you came back early?" I asked, unwrapping the aluminum foil from the candy. "To put up a new stereo?"

"That's a minor reason. But the major reason is I've got a blue-chip prospect waiting for me."

"Oh yeah, who's that, and why should I even care?" I immediately regretted asking. I figured he was going to start telling me about Juliet panting breathlessly in his room.

"No one you'd know...this time." He looked at me as if he were sizing up my worthiness for the conversation. Then he went on. "High school senior.

Hot. Lives in Moorestown. Hot. Did I already mention that?" He unwrapped the candy and placed it on the crotch of his pants. He grinned, popped the candy into his mouth, and stood to comb his razor-cut hair, though it never seemed to move out of place. He leaned very close to the mirror and gave himself an approving half-smile.

"So why are you here instead of out making her dreams come true?" I asked. The cool chocolate filled my mouth with a sweetness that made my empty stomach rumble.

"She called earlier and said her cousin is staying with her. She wants me to round up a date for cuz. Interested?"

"Nah," I said immediately. The thought of being in the same car as Bingham at work nauseated me.

"Come on, Burns. What the hell do you have to lose? I'll pay for everything. If you stay here, all you'll do is read all that junk in the papers about Vietnam and get so depressed you won't even be able to jerk off. Come on."

"Blind dates just aren't for me," I said.

Bingham picked up some of Fish's Jade East cologne and sniffed it. "No wonder that Yid smells like gefilte fish," he cracked, making no apparent sense, but then he splashed it on his face and neck. "Listen, if she's not fine, I'll play like I'm sick and we'll come right back here. I'll even throw up on my date for realism."

"Chances are good that she'll beat you to it," I said. Bingham somehow took that comment as a sign that I was weakening, and he attacked like the rabid dog he was.

"Man, you're gonna love this. Picture: We pull up in my A-H and then once we get there, we all pile into her car. She said she has a Camaro, and you *know* they have really cozy back seats." He winked at me. Then he unzipped his fly, picked up the cologne again, and dabbed some between his legs. "I swear, you goddam guys never want to do things that are fun. I'm always offering my things—TV, stereo, clothes, and now a chance to have an all expenses paid trip to nook-ieland. Let's go." Then he zipped up his fly, rubbed his hands together and stroked more cologne across his cheeks.

So, of course, what I didn't say was, "You're a repugnant asshole, Darrell, who reeks of Jade East," which is what I was thinking, but, "Where would we go, Bingham?"

"Who knows? Drive-in movie maybe. Yeah, first we'll go out for some food, then to the drive-in for something good to eat." He grinned widely and winked to make sure I had caught his lousy attempt at a joke. "Come on, Burns. How long will it take you to get ready?"

"Who said I was going?" I said unconvincingly. The lingering taste of chocolate reminded me of how hungry I was.

"You're going, Burns.You're not as dumb as you look with that long hair, thank god. Even you know when there's a chance to strike gold. You're definitely going. When will you be ready?"

"I'm ready now," I said, glancing into the mirror and running a hand haphazardly through my hair.

"Dressed like that?"

Bingham scanned me from head to toe. I wore the college-issue wardrobe for the still slightly pre-radical crowd—light blue shirt under a white tennis sweater, blue jeans and desert boots. He had on khakis and one of those thick white turtleneck sweaters that would have made any other guy sweat his ass off from having it pick at his neck. Not Darrell Bingham, though; in his own mind, at least, he was just too cool to sweat.

"You're kidding, right? Gotta change your shoes," he said, nodding to his own soft leather penny loafers as an indication of what I should wear—shoes that looked similar to a pair I had thrown out months ago.

"No, Darrell, this is me and this is how I go."

He shook his head and said, frustrated, "Okay, have it your way. Jeans, desert boots, hair's growing long. I suppose your the next step is to—what does your crowd say—tune in, turn on, and drop in or some bullshit. Don't you know Draft Boards search and destroy pseudo-hippies like you?"

"I guess there's only one thing you don't know, Darrell."

He thought for a second. "What's that?"

"When to shut the hell up."

Mysteriously, he produced another chocolate kiss and handed it to me as we walked out of the room.

CHAPTER ELEVEN

For about twenty of the thirty minutes or so that we spent on the ride toward Moorestown, Bingham rambled about things like the "new A-H" he would get when he graduated, his family's new vacation home in Cape Cod, and the many different kinds of rubbers he had used—and which ones he preferred. And, of course, he casually mentioned that he had been at Juliet's for part of the semester break after which, he said, "I was off to Stowe, just me with the ski-bunny crowd—no hippies acting like jackoffs there, none of those mangy war-protesting bitches." Finally, as if he had reached a point where he was out of important things to prattle on about, he said, "How about you, Burns? What'd you do over break?"

I thought about Silhouettes, the nightclub my cousin Harry owned right on M Street, Georgetown's main drag, where I had worked during break and any other time I was at home. Silhouettes had soft spotlights along the floor that shone upward, casting shadows throughout. A small, hardwood stage extended outward in front of a brick wall. Harry had the hottest club in DC, and his wife, the African American folk singer Sparrow, opened for acts like Richie Havens, who gently lisped through his melodies and punctuated his lyrics occasionally by rapping his fist on his guitar; Peter, Paul and Mary raised questions like, "Where Have All the Flowers Gone?" or made penetrating statements such as, "If I Had a Hammer"; and Ian and Sylvia, sang their sensual Canadian folk music, she with her waist-length hair and penetrating eyes that devoured Ian while she held her microphone sensually with her long fingers.

My job was to take reservations, organize the people who waited in line, and eventually get them all seated. Harry paid me twenty-five dollars a night, plus tips, but I would have worked for free—there was something about the smallness, the sense of belonging to something unique that pulled me in. It felt special to sit around a nightclub at three in the morning, stacking chairs, joking and flirting with the wait staff, watching Havens sketch a scene based on his lyrics with a pencil on a napkin, or humming to myself as

Sylvia softly ran through a new song with Ian. Plus, Silhouettes allowed me to put Sally-Boy in the back of my mind for a while.

I wasn't about to tell Bingham any of this, but especially not about the night a year or so earlier when Bob Dylan had performed at Silhouettes for a weekend. Dylan and Harry were close friends from the early, struggling years of their respective careers; in fact, Harry referred to Dylan simply as "Zimmerman," Dylan's real surname, even when talking to Dylan. I had sat there one night when Harry said to Dylan, "So, Zimmerman, why the hell do you call that song 'Positively 4th Street,' man? You never even mention 4th Street in the song."

And Dylan turned to me, scratched his shaggy head of curls, smiled and said, "Kid, your cousin is about as unhip as a club owner can be, ain't he?" Then he turned to Harry and said, "Just like I say in that song, man, 'You got a lotta nerve to say you are my friend.'" And then the two of them laughed and raised a fist to salute one another.

So Dylan occasionally played Silhouettes as a favor to Harry, and one night, an hour or so after Dylan's final set, I went to tidy up the Green Room (another of my executive responsibilities), which I thought was completely empty. But as I opened the door, I heard a gruff voice singing softly in near darkness. It was Dylan sitting alone facing a wall in a corner, a black knit cap pulled down over his ears, his back to me. He didn't seem to hear me enter, so I stood there straining to decipher the lyrics.

Was it "Chimes of Freedom"? I listened, but did not hear any lyrics like, "Tolling for the rebel, Tolling for the rake/Tolling for the luckless, the abandoned an' forsaked…"

Was it "My Back Pages"? I listened more closely, but, no, he didn't sing, "'We'll meet on edges soon,' said I/ Proud 'neath heated brow/Ah, but I was so much older then/I'm younger than that now.'"

I moved a little closer, and then I heard it more clearly. It wasn't Dylan's own song; it was Buffalo Springfield's. He hoarsely sang, "There's battle lines being drawn/Nobody's right if everybody's wrong…"

Suddenly, he stopped playing, and without turning his head said, "Great, ain't it, what the Buffalo Springfield's done? Just fuckin genius is what it is."

Surprised that he knew I was in the room, I stammered, "Oh, hey, yeah, but I'm sorry, I didn't mean…"

He turned and pushed back his knit cap so his full head of curls uncoiled. "I sure wish I wrote that one, but goddam Steve Stills beat me to it," he said, picking at a chord.

"Really?" I said. "I mean, after all you've written, you still…"

"Oh, hell yeah, yeah, sure," he said. "There's always gonna be something you wish you'da done, man. That song there? That one, man? That one's a news report, a poem, and a premonition all rolled into one cool fuckin song."

He turned back toward the wall, and sang loud this time, "I think it's time we stop, children, what's that sound/Everybody look what's going down..."

And then he just kept picking and singing with his face to the wall, so I walked out. As I closed the door, I think he said, "See ya, kid," but I'm not sure.

But those were *my* experiences, not ones to be shared with, and ridiculed by, Bingham, who would also have needed to top the experience (and most certainly would have), so I didn't tell him about Silhouettes at all.

"I just worked a little," I said.

"Worked!" Bingham snorted. "I hate that fucking word." As he sped down a straight highway bordered by block after block of homes that looked like cut-out copies of one another, many with American flags proudly on display, he reached around behind his seat and pulled out a bag filled with candy. "These remind me of me," he said, shaking the bag. "Good and Plenty." He winked and offered a handful of the pink and white candies. "Worked! Jesus. Why? Where?"

"In the projects."

"What? What projects? What do you mean?"

"The inner-city, dumbass. I worked reconstructing tattered apartments where little kids have to cover themselves up with cardboard when it rains because their apartments leak so bad they don't have any shelter from storms."

"What the fuck? Why would you do that? Are you some sort of Commie? Who'd you do that with?"

"Me and my cousin Salvatore Fuocco and his girlfriend...nice Jewish girl named Shayna."

"Jesus, that sounds terrible! That's no way to spend your vacation, walking around a bunch of shithole apartment buildings, helping people who won't help themselves. You're a weird guy, Mike, you know that?"

"Maybe I just seem that way because you're so fucking normal, Darrell."

"Calm down, will you? I just don't get you; you need to relax. You never go out of your way to have fun. Like tonight. If I hadn't practically begged, you wouldn't be here right now."

"Don't remind me."

I looked out the window. The houses weren't similar any longer; each one was unique, and the road we were on now was bent with turns that Bingham accelerated and squealed the Healey into. I concentrated on the scenery and counted the American flags, anything to avoid thinking that Bingham just might be right about some things.

CHAPTER TWELVE

The house was long, almost semi-circular, with the rooms on the ends half above ground and half below. A floodlight above the garage door cast a pale tinge on a carefully landscaped stone garden, neat pine trees, and naked maples. The garage was large enough for three cars, but only one, a gray, primer-spotted TR-3, was in it. A blue-hulled cabin cruiser named *Happy Times* occupied another space.

"That's what I like," Bingham said, speaking in his usual pompous tone. "Lots of signs of lots of money."

"Yeah," I agreed, "but no sign of any car big enough for the four of us."

"Can't wait to hit the back seat, eh, Burns?" he said with his aggravating wink.

Actually, I was more hungry than horny, and I wondered why I was doubling on a blind date with a guy who would definitely mock the Brooklyn neighborhood I loved. We were about to enter the home of a girl whose house looked like it sprouted into reality directly from some three-dimensional cardboard fairy-tail cutout. In my narrow mind, a mind trying to kick and scream its way out of stereotype, I pictured female Binghams. As we walked up the flagstone walkway to the massive wooden front door, I ground a handful of Good and Plenty between my teeth. The cold night air pierced me, and for an instant I contemplated feigning sickness—pulling a Bingham—anything to avoid confronting the uncomfortable and unfamiliar.

"Remember now, Burnsey, stay loose," Bingham advised. "If things aren't working out, if you can't handle your date, or if she's berserk and goofy beyond hope—" now that would be my luck, I thought—"I promise you, I'll give an Academy Award-winning puke scene that'll clear out the house. But remember, these are high school seniors we're talking about. You should be able to handle it."

We stood on the doorstep. Darrell winked again. He poised his finger in front of the doorbell but, suddenly, I grabbed his arm and yanked him toward me. I could feel Brooklyn's streets rising inside me. "And *you* remember *this*, Bingham," I said slowly, "you wink at me again, I promise I will put your lights out. Got it?" My breath smelled of licorice.

Bingham stepped backward and tried pulling his arm free, but my grip tightened.

"Take it easy, goddamit," he said. "Just fucking relax, Mike. I'm only kidding around. Whatever you say, fine, no more winking. Anything to loosen you up." I let go of his arm. "Christ, let's have some fun; get some pussy, right, man?"

I stepped in front of Darrell Bingham and knocked on the enormous door myself.

The girl who answered had a confident, friendly smile that revealed cutely crooked teeth. Her name was Katie McGee and her brown hair swished around her shoulder blades when she walked. Not the gum-snapping high schooler I thought might be attracted to Bingham, which sort of depressed me. Here she was looking smart and sweet and there was Darrell striding into the softly lighted house with me trailing obediently behind. He flashed his smug smile at Katie, but her eyes went a little flat when she looked at him. And as he draped his arm around her and asked, "Where's the chick for my good friend Mike here?" she coolly slid out from under his arm and replied, "I'll get her; the *chick*"—Katie's sarcasm tinted the word—"is upstairs, no doubt plucking her feathers." An impish flicker danced in her green eyes.

As Katie went upstairs, Bingham kept repeating, "You must agree, that's fine. Oh yeah, old Bingo is gonna enjoy..."

The sight of the girl coming down the stairs with Katie stopped Bingham in mid-sentence. Katie introduced her cousin, Erica Wakefield, to us, and my fascination with the older, more worldly and mysterious Shayna Lieberman was relegated immediately to the past and replaced with a range of juvenile thoughts: That girls who look like Erica never wear braces or have smudges of dirt on their jeans or little pieces of salad stuck between their teeth...nor are they ever likely to be seen in a place like the *Panificio di Boccanera*, or a Brooklyn churchyard dance. To me, in my simplistic imaginary world, their lives flowed perfectly from one day to the next, one uninterrupted stream of good fortune.

Until that moment, I had never felt my breath actually hitch at the sight of a female, but hitch it did, and I had the oddest sensation that something actually fell out of me. Erica Wakefield's hair was a full burst of black curls, no hot iron had befouled that hair. The blue of her eyes was so deep that it almost hurt to look at them, and she smiled with a mysterious tension at the corners of her mouth that made it clear that she was no baby doll. She was real, as real as the shakiness that pounded out from my heart and into my arms and legs, shakiness that simultaneously served both to weaken me and strengthen me.

As Katie led us all to a rec room carpeted in thick beige shag and filled with lush plants, she deftly avoided Bingham's claw-like grasp. I walked behind them all, desperately trying to compose myself. I had simply said, "Hey," during the introductions, and then I forced out a cough just to make sure I was capable of making some other sound. I felt spasmodic, walking in jerky little steps, my arms a bundle of twitches instead of smoothly swinging by my side. Katie turned on the record player, and Bob Dylan filled the room; she lowered the volume and "The Times They Are a-Changin'" (Oh yes! I was hoping it were so!) settled comfortably around us.

"Don't say it!" Katie said with a grin, leaning toward Erica. "I know you're about to say it, but don't do it!"

Bingham and I shared a confused look.

"Okay," Erica said, pausing briefly as Katie leaned toward her, laughing. "I won't say," Erica said, shifting into a deep, professorial voice "that I find it 'counterintuitive' that a song can be *about* change…but can't really *force* change. Rather admirable, but still…counterintuitive, if you ask me."

"Arrrrghhh!" Katie yelled though she was laughing. "She uses that word, that 'counterintuitive,' all the time now!!!"

"Yes," Erica admitted in the same voice, standing erect and looking straight-faced at Katie, "for I believe firmly that if you use that word—'counterintuitive'—people automatically think you're smart."

"Well, I think you're a dumbass, but I love you anyway," Katie said.

"There, you see, that is rather counterintuitive, proving my point," Erica said, now using a British accent.

"I think you're smart, Erica," I somehow blurted.

"Thank you, Michael. My point exactly," Erica said, still in her British accent.

"I think it's fucking stupid hippie music," Bingham snorted. He walked toward the record rack and rifled through it.

Suddenly, Erica turned and faced me directly. "Floor or sofa?" she asked quickly, sounding a bit like a prosecutor.

"Excuse me?" I responded, but I said it so fast and so clipped that it sounded to me like I might have said, "So sue me."

"Do you prefer...sitting on the floor...or perching on the sofa?" she asked slowly with a slight smile and a tilt of her head as she gestured somewhat dramatically with her hands.

"Oh, well, uh, it's, uh, it doesn't matter, you, uh, you pick."

I would have sat on a spike if it were next to her. Erica stretched out on the carpet and looked up at me. As I eased my spasm-riddled body, snapping and popping to the floor, I surprised myself by wisecracking, "I kind of wanted to sit on the sofa, but..." Erica laughed quickly, genuinely, a reaction that, along with the comfortable plush carpeting, seemed to settle me somewhat.

Katie brought out some beer and pretzels. Bingham griped about the brand of beer—Budweiser—and asked Katie if she didn't have Michelob; she said no and quickly returned his can of Bud to the kitchen unopened until he finally was reduced to asking her if he could have it back.

Erica leaned against the leather sofa and we listened to Dylan without talking much; I briefly considered telling her my Dylan stories, but decided against it. I watched her carefully, but inconspicuously. She nodded her head only slightly with the music and closed her eyes whenever she mouthed some of the lyrics. And when Katie put on the Beatles' *Rubber Soul*, Erica said, "I love this album," but not gushing like some Beatles-crazed teenybopper, but just a simple, honest statement that I believed instantly.

The song "In My Life" came on and Erica looked straight ahead at some vacant space in the room, narrowed her eyes in concentration, and softly sang along:

"Though I know I'll never lose affection
For people and things that went before,
I know I'll often stop and think about them,
In my life, I'll love you more…"

She scanned the room intently, as though she expected to see something the rest of us would miss, or perhaps she actually *could* see something that none of the rest of us could, and her lips tightened, and with one hand she pulled her thick dark hair behind an ear. I grinned faintly (idiotically?) just looking at her. She held a small pretzel to my lips and I took a bite. I muttered "thanks" like a naive-waif who might equate nibbling a pretzel with the early stages of foreplay.

Engrossed in examining every pore of Erica's that I could see (and imagining those I couldn't), I forgot about my hunger and Katie and Bingham until I heard Bingham say loudly, "Hell, I'm hungry! Where's the car you said you had? We can't all just jump into my A-H, you know."

"Oh, trust me, nobody wants to do that," Katie said.

I laughed out loud at the high school girl's wisecrack.

Bingham crushed the empty Budweiser can he held.

"What are you laughing at, Brooklyn boy?" he said to me. "You've never sat your ass in a nicer car than my A-H." His voice, extra clear, blatted like a long blast from a car horn, but I detected an underlying weakness, like the horn's connection was going bad.

I just grinned at him and gave my best impression of his wink. He got up to go to the bathroom. Without him, the room grew quieter, more relaxed. Katie noticed me looking at several oval-shaped photographs of two young men who, she explained, were her brothers. The younger one, Tim, was a junior at Dartmouth, she said, and the older one, Brian, had graduated Dartmouth the previous June and was now a Marine at home for a short time before his departure for Vietnam. Brian was running the house while her parents and Erica's parents were vacationing together in Florida.

"As soon as Brian gets back with the car, we can go out," Katie said. "He's at his fiancee's house."

Then Katie talked excitedly about a three-day ski trip she and Erica would be leaving for the next day. "We have the whole week off for Winter Break and almost the entire senior class will be on the trip," she said.

"Sounds like fun," I said without conviction. I conjured up a ski resort, though I had never been to one, loaded with High School Harrys, College Joes, servicemen on leave, the entire follow-the-snow crowd. The more I looked at Erica, the more I envisioned her in tight ski pants with a line of male skiers sashaying down the snow behind her. I was fading into the plush carpet, a big ball of dust returning to dust, thinking that ultimately the Binghams of the world win girls like this.

Then, in that shaky moment, he popped into my mind; I remembered Sally-Boy grinning at some girls who had walked into Big Sal's bakery; he offered them a free tiramisu, and then turned to me with a sly smile and a shrug as the girls blinked their eyes and thanked him. "Nah," Sally said, "it ain't nothin. It's just what I do. What *we* do," he nodded, motioning toward me, "just the kinda guys we are."

Then I smiled at Erica and gently held a piece of pretzel to her lips.

CHAPTER THIRTEEN

B rian arrived, a Marine poster come to life, six-one, muscular, sides of his head shaved clean, fuzzy patch of hair brushed to one side on top. His face was angular and tough, but you could tell he was Katie's brother by the kindness they shared around the eyes.

"Sorry I'm late," Brian said. "I know you guys were waiting for the car." He held out the keys. Bingham took them.

"Well, we are getting a little hungry," Bingham said.

"Sure," Brian said, looking at Bingham with a quizzical smile. "Have a good time."

Katie and Erica asked Brian a couple of questions about him and his fiancee, Karen, and he responded courteously before saying, "Hey, you two, your dates are waiting. Get going."

Katie hugged Brian. Bingham rolled his eyes in my direction, which aggravated me, so I decided to aggravate him. I said, "Hey Brian, why don't you come along with us to get some food? We don't mean to just run off with your car."

Bingham glared, but Erica and Katie smiled at me and urged Brian to join us. "It's a-gonna be fun, Brian, *molto bene*," Erica said in an Italian accent that immediately made Brian smile and made me think of so many people from my childhood in Brooklyn. "You come on-a with us, eh? It will be the good times." Brian declined with a laugh and a hug. Bingham rolled his eyes again, but I wouldn't have minded. Here was Brian, maybe twenty-three, just a couple weeks away from being shipped off, back from his fiancee's in time to loan his car to two unknowns from college so his sister and his cousin could go out for a while.

In the car, I wondered how Brian would like Bingham driving to some hamburger place with one arm draped around Katie's shoulders. Erica and I rode in the back seat in virtual silence for several minutes. Then, either the car turned slightly or Erica purposely moved in my direction, but she was suddenly closer to me in the conveniently cramped seat.

"Tired from your trip?" she asked.

For a moment I didn't respond; instead, I continued to study the trucks that are the hallmark of industrial New Jersey. Even on a Sunday night their grinding gears and popping air brakes dominated all other sound.

"Not really," I said.

"How long have you lived around Washington? All your life?"

Now I turned and looked at her as I began to talk; I stuttered slightly. "Uh, no, I was born in New York. Brooklyn...ever hear of it?"

She pushed lightly on my shoulder as a reproach for my tease and said in a Brooklyn accent reminiscent of Gina Falengina, one of the girls Sally-Boy and I had a crush on from elementary school days: "Course I heard a it! Waddya think? I'm some sorta dumb broad?"

I laughed, and said, "No, I sure don't think that."

"Good," she said, easing out of her accent. "So... tell me."

"My parents grew up there, in Brooklyn," I said, my voice steadying. "I lived there until I was twelve. Then we moved, but I spent a lot of time there with one of my cousins helping out in his father's bakery. Every vacation, just about."

"Why did you move to DC?" she asked.

Maybe it was the contrast of gentle understanding in her soft blue eyes with the taut toughness around her mouth, but she seemed to have no penchant for insincerity. She wasn't just making small talk; she was actually interested.

"Well, my father took a mid-level government job in Washington to get us out of Brooklyn, to give me more 'opportunity,' as he always puts it. Now he's higher level. Secret Service."

"Really? You mean he guards the president?"

I could not recall a single time that I had ever discussed my father, much less his work, with a date before. Yet here I was, actually enjoying it with this mysterious, beautiful high school senior.

"No. He works in public information. He says he makes reporters feel like they've got a lot of information when, really, he just tells enough to keep everyone happy. He seems to be good at it."

Erica paused for a second, then said, "Is that a good thing to be good at? I mean, it's just so...I'm sorry..."

"No, I know exactly what you mean," I said. "But I think my father is pretty fair. He knows his roots. Brooklyn kid. World War II. Taking care of family and country."

Erica nodded and hair fell loosely on her light blue ski jacket. Headlights and streetlights provided varying glimpses of her face, glimpses that changed as the lights accented the contrast of her mouth and eyes.

Bingham pulled into a parking lot and blared, "I am fucking starving!" We piled out of the car, and he said, "Hey, everyone, order whatever you want. Bingo's buying!"

I gritted my teeth.

Burgers Made In Heaven was a preppy place with a pulsating jukebox. We walked in amid the creamy smooth lyrics of the Four Tops: "You're sweet, like a honey bee..." A long row of tables stretched down the middle of a bright informal dining room with vinyl padded booths along the walls. My stomach growled at the aroma of pizza and burgers.

Erica seemed innately aware of the attention she stirred, the long looks guys cast toward her from every direction of the restaurant as we all walked toward an empty booth in the back, but instead of encouraging more attention, she discretely took my elbow and walked closer to me, talking quietly, her hair brushing over my shoulder. Now I was John Wayne whistling; the guy who makes small talk with Bob Dylan; the person who sits down with his father and talks sensibly, maturely, convincingly about why hair length, of all things, should not be the major issue it has become in so many families, including ours; the cousin who talks his "twin" out of vanishing.

With my heart thumping so powerfully (was its pounding visible?) what could go wrong? We ate hamburgers with exotic names like Hawaiian Surprise, where a piece of ham was cooked inside the hamburger and a slice of juicy pineapple garnished it.

Erica sipped my beer, flicking aside her hair quickly before lifting the frosty mug to her lips, and then she ordered one of her own, all of us flashing our fake IDs. A pickle slid out of her burger and onto her plate, splattering ketchup onto the checkered tablecloth. So, I thought, things like that actually *do* happen to girls like Erica. I laughed. She looked mortified at first, but then she laughed too, tilting her head sideways. Suddenly, she picked up the ketchup bottle, gripped it tightly, and implored to it in her mock-British accent, "Why? Why, ketchup bottle? O, ketchup, how couldst thou? Why hast thou forsaken me?" Then she stared eerily at me, her eyes slowly widening until they looked like they would burst before we simultaneously started laughing.

Obsessed, stricken, my insides short circuiting, I noted her every move—the long fingers pulling her hair back from her smooth cheeks, the angular eyes studying the room, the face living and knowing and promising a life that Mike Burns could never imagine. Odd desires consumed me—I wanted to dab at her mouth with a napkin and maybe brush away that hard tinge that lingered around her lips, I wanted to trace her face with one of my fingers, I wanted to know about her when she was five...eight...ten years old, and what time she woke up in the morning, and exactly when she realized how beautiful she was. What do you do with your life if you're Erica Wakefield?

And interrupting me was my own voice, droning repeatedly in my head, a stuck record saying, "Remember, you're Mike Burns, a guy who still has his daddy's five bucks in his pocket to get a haircut, a guy who wouldn't even be here if it weren't for Darrell Bingham's insistence, a guy Tomato Thompson gives a bad time to, a Brooklyn kid who talks to a missing person and yearns for a fire escape."

But then I looked at Erica looking at me. I thought about the interest she showed in my mundane life, how she had laughed at my not-so-funny wisecracks, how just hours earlier Shayna Lieberman had picked me to watch her Zaidi, how Dylan had talked to me, and how Sally-Boy always boosted my confidence, and I wondered if perhaps a different Mike Burns might finally be struggling to the surface.

CHAPTER FOURTEEN

When we finished eating, Bingham whipped out twenty-five dollars to cover a twenty-dollar tab and handed it to the waitress.

"Keep the change on that, fox, but remember old Bingo's face," he told her.

Damn if she didn't touch Darrell's hand and fix him with a long stare as we prepared to leave. He winked at her.

Katie and Erica went to the restroom, and as soon as they were out of hearing range, Bingham began talking quickly, earnestly. "You gotta help me out, Mike," he said. "I got a great chance to get laid tonight, but I need your help."

"Come on, Darrell, Katie doesn't want your body."

"Not Katie, dumb ass. The waitress. That fucking waitress, man. I can bang that stuff tonight. Look." He held out a crumpled piece of paper. It said: "Off at eleven. Ditch that date. Stop by...for dessert. Amber." It had her address and phone number on it; she had slipped it to Bingham when she touched his hand.

"That doesn't say anything about getting laid," I said stupidly.

Bingham rolled his eyes. "You wouldn't know a come-on if it sat on your face, Burns. Look, Erica seems to be buying your act a little, and if you don't take advantage of that, you ought to turn in your worthless pecker." He handed me a red-and-white mint wrapped in cellophane. "Here, wipe the hamburger off your breath." He popped two into his mouth. "Now here's what I want you to do. When they come out of the bathroom, tell them some relatives of mine came by and asked me to go home and spend a couple of days with them. Tell Katie I could see she wasn't having that great a time, so I didn't think she'd mind—you know, it's good to downplay yourself like that occasionally with the chicks. Anyway, here are my keys. After you drive them home, take my A-H back to campus. It's all yours for the night. I'll call you at school tomorrow and let you know where to pick me up. Okay?"

"You expect them to believe that?"

"Who gives a shit? You have to go after what's hot, right?"

Damn if Amber didn't walk by and whisper, "How does it look?" Bingham gave her a thumbs up sign, and I thought she'd wiggle out of her mini-skirt right there.

"Will you do it, Burns, goddamit!"

I nodded.

Bingham handed me two more mints and patted me on the shoulder. Amber squeezed his arm and hustled him into the kitchen where he would be out of sight.

Erica and Katie came out of the restroom and Katie said casually to me, "Has Darrell taken off with that waitress yet?"

"Waitress?" I bumbled.

"Come on, Mike. They sat there goo-goo eyeing each other the whole time we were here." Katie smiled. "If you and Erica had stopped talking to one another for a second or two, I might have been able to get rid of him earlier."

Erica punched Katie gently on the shoulder.

"Well, then I'm not sorry," I said. "Mint?" I opened my hand.

"From Darrell, right?" Katie said.

"Yes."

"Why do guys like him always think minty breath covers up the smell they leave?" Katie asked matter-of-factly. "No thanks."

"I'll pass too," Erica said.

I put the mints on the table and said, "May I escort you ladies out of this establishment?"

Erica grabbed one arm and Katie the other. As we walked out, the Rolling Stones sang:

"Let's spend the night together,
Now I need you more than ever,
Let's spend the night together now..."

Oh, how I wished!

I drove the Camaro back to Katie's house with Erica riding next to me. From the back seat, Katie ordered the radio turned up to nearly full blast. Janice Joplin was singing about Bobby McGee ("That's my Family Song!" Katie shouted) and Erica surprised me with a hair-flying Joplin impersonation, changing the lyrics from "Bobby McGee" to "Katie McGee," so I chimed in with my best Bob Dylan voice.

"Holy shit! It's Joplin and Dylan!" Katie said. "What an act you two could put together!"

When I found myself quickly imagining what it would be like to be in a band and on the road with Erica, I knew my mind was hopelessly working overtime.

"Do you do any other impressions?" Erica asked.

"Let's see... how about Bobby Kennedy?" I asked.

"Oh, I just love him," Erica said. It was the same simple, sincere tone she had used in talking about the Beatles' song "In My Life."

I jabbed my right forefinger in the air and said in my best nasal stammer, "I would just like to shay...uh... that if you feel...uh...that way about him, then it's...uh... worth it for me to...uh...try to impersonate him."

"Not bad, not bad at all!" Katie said. "It's like RFK is here in the car with us, isn't it E?"

Erica made a mock squeal and shouted, "Bobbyyyy!" Then she quickly turned serious and said, "I think Kennedy has character, something that makes you believe in him, and he seems so empathetic to people less fortunate than he is...which is practically everyone, of course. But my parents sure don't think much of him."

"Oh, my parents can't stand him either," Katie said. "Dad says, 'Bobby Kennedy's a shanty Irishman born under a shamrock.' I try to stay out of it myself, but I like what Kennedy says about Vietnam. It's a shitty mess there, I don't know if anyone can really stop what's going on."

"Or anyone *could* stop it," Erica said flatly.

"Maybe, but not soon enough," Katie said. "Not before Brian gets there."

They exchanged a few more thoughts about their fears and their anger, and I turned off the radio as they spoke so I could listen more closely. When they stopped talking, Katie hummed to herself, Erica looked out at the black New Jersey night, and I drove, thinking about the words of two high school girls—two girls I barely knew, but two girls who clearly had thought about the war, its impact, the politicians leading our country—speaking personally, passionately, and I found myself considering, probably for the first time ever, how anonymous soldiers are to the people who are not fighting, to the people safe and secure in college classrooms, eating at burger joints, driving around in Austin-Healeys, sitting on fire escapes, and how blank the faces are that cross the TV screen—until you see the face of someone you know and love preparing to leave his home and family to go into battle for them and for millions of people he will never know.

CHAPTER FIFTEEN

The house seemed eerily empty and cold when we entered. A Tiffany swag lamp gently illuminated the chamber-like hallway between the foyer and the rec room, but a thick noiselessness—like humidity before a storm—smothered the house.

"Bri?" Katie called, and a high-pitched ringing filled the hall as her voice disappeared into the corners. With smooth detachment, a grandfather clock clicked off time. A chill ran through me, as I remembered the many times I had walked through Sally-Boy's apartment in Brooklyn after he disappeared. I was trying to help Sally-Boy's father and stepmother make sense of his disappearance. My parents were there, too, and everyone followed me around the tiny apartment and onto our fire escape, holding one another as we looked futilely for clues in each little room, sobs echoing, and me stammering repeatedly as I found nothing but emptiness and could recall no clue, no hint of where he might have gone.

Katie called for Brian again and tilted her head quizzically as she looked at Erica. "Where did he go, E?" Katie asked.

Suddenly, Erica's eyes lit up. "I bet I know where he is, Kates!"

"No, do you think so, at this hour?" Katie asked, shaking her head doubtfully.

Katie and I followed Erica through the rec room toward a door that looked like it led outside. As we approached, we could hear a steady scraping that made both girls smile reflexively.

"See, he's in his shop," Erica said.

Katie looked relieved. "God...he is *so* determined," she said, tapping once on the door and then opening it.

"Hi, you two," Brian said without looking up from a work table. He scraped sandpaper over a small wooden object. "Have a good time?"

"With that asshole? Are you kidding?" Katie said. "You're working now? It's after midnight."

"I only have a few days to finish up," Brian said. "And don't be so rough on that, what was his name—Big-Ham?—guy. He might become a terrific person... some day."

Katie snorted and said, "Yeah, and Erica might grow some boobs some day."

Erica straightened, pushed her chest out toward Katie's face, and said haughtily, "I find you offensive in every respect, and given your own lack of physical attributes, your comment is…counterintuitive."

"You set yourself up for that one, Sis," Brian said, laughing at Katie who had thrown her hands over her face while muttering, "Oh god," repeatedly.

Erica smiled and then turned to Brian and asked, "Are you almost finished, Bri?"

"Yep, almost. Want to see?"

She nodded and Brian held up a minutely detailed replica about a foot long of the *Happy Times* cabin cruiser. Even the name was hand-painted in flawless blue script. Brian offered it to Erica to look at, and she held it as carefully and affectionately as she might hold an infant. With an index finger, she traced the smoothly varnished side of the hull.

"Think they'll like it?" Brian asked.

"It's perfect," she said. Then she handed it to me. "It's for his parents. He carved it himself."

"He's giving it to Mom and Dad before he leaves," Katie said.

I breathed shallowly, half out of fear for the delicacy of the small ship and half out of a closeness I felt for a reason still too embryonic to understand.

"Look, Kates," Brian said, reaching out with a finger and flicking the ship's miniature captain's wheel while I held the model. The wheel spun freely, and Brian smiled broadly.

Impulsively, Katie hugged her brother, and Erica joined her. I admired their openly mutual affection even more than the intricate woodwork of the fragile *Happy Times* I held in my hands.

Then Brian said I could spend the night, an offer I accepted partially because weariness began to smother me and partially because, inside myself, I groped for any chance to be a part of the house and the people in it. Somehow I suppressed a mild, child-like hysteria that arose at the thought of sleeping anywhere remotely close to Erica. The girls left for bed, and I stayed with Brian while he cleaned his workroom and examined *Happy Times* while blowing gently at particles of dust.

"How long have you been interested in this kind of work?" I asked.

"Since I was a kid, maybe five or six. It started with little clay figures."

He pulled out the bottom drawer of his worktable and opened a clear plastic case. In it were mini football players sporting the red and blue of the New York Giants, complete with helmets, facemasks, and jersey numbers.

"I'm a huge Giants fan," he said a little sheepishly.

"How long does it take to make things like this, or the boat?"

Brian shrugged and snapped shut the plastic case containing the football figures. "I don't know, really.

I'm not that conscious of the time when I'm working. Whatever it takes to reach a point where I'm satisfied, that's the time it takes. But I'm not easily satisfied. Time just doesn't matter."

He placed the *Happy Times* model on a shelf and then slid a wooden panel, which he locked, over it. "I'm pretty protective of my stuff," he said, smiling.

"It must take a tremendous amount of patience; I'd be protective too."

"I like working with very coarse wood, ugly wood really," he said, flicking off the light to the room as we walked out, "and then making something delicate and beautiful out of it. Flawed wood has a little, I don't know, sturdier quality; a lot of times it winds up being prettier and stronger in the end than higher-quality wood."

Brian turned off the den lights from the bottom of the stairway. In the darkness of the foyer, Brian's features sharpened, his jaw line grew more rigid, his neck muscles more clearly defined in the shadows. But then, despite the obvious physical power he possessed, a thought struck me so hard I almost swayed with apprehension—he's a creator, not a killer.

Brian talked casually as we walked up the steps. "Hard for me to believe Tim will be graduating in June. I know I'm going to regret not being home to see it."

"Don't take this wrong, Brian," I said, "but I don't get it—why the Marines with your Ivy League background?"

Brian had reached the landing at the top of the steps. He turned toward me and said, "That's what Tim always asks, too, but you know, it's funny—Tim thinks he's such an individual, but really, he's like a lot of other people." He reached into a linen closet for some bath towels. "Tim only likes to do what he wants to do. But when it comes to others, me and the Marines in particular, he wants me to do what *he* wants instead of what I feel I *have* to do." Brian handed me some warm, fresh-smelling towels. "Tim's room's right there. Make yourself comfortable, and we'll see you in the morning." Brian motioned to the end of the long hallway, which suddenly seemed drafty, as if someone had opened a window in one of the rooms.

I could barely see Brian as he walked away and faded into darkness, but I blurted into the night, "But don't you ever worry...?"

"What, me worry?"

"Seriously..."

From out of the darkness Brian said, "Look, Mike, Vietnam is a place, right? It has grass and roads, trees and flowers, forests and rocks, sky and clouds...and people like me, like you, like Erica, Tim, my fiancee Karen, Katie, people like that guy Big-Ham...well, maybe not like him." I could hear the smile in his voice. "There are so many similarities between any one place and any other."

"But that sounds like a good reason *not* to fight." A realization flashed through my head: I had never seriously articulated any sentiment like that before. But now I was worried...for myself as much as for Brian.

"Not to the people who live there and are trying to lead normal lives," he said steadily. "To them, protecting what they perceive and value as their individuality is a reason *to* fight."

From the room directly across the chilly hallway, Katie shouted, "Quiet down, dammit! It sounds like the start of another Brian versus Tim battle."

"Hardly," Brian called out. "Mike's enlisting."

"Bullshit!" Katie shouted from out of the darkness. "He has more sense than that."

With a sudden war whoop Brian dashed into her room, shouting, "And you seem like a little sister who needs to be dumped on her young ass!"

Erica, who was sharing the room with Katie, turned on a light, and I walked over to see, well, to see Erica, really. Brian tilted Katie's bed while she shrieked, and he shook it until Katie rolled onto the floor in a heap of covers and blankets, laughing. Erica, with parts of her body tantalizingly accented by a thigh-length Dartmouth nightshirt, bent over to help Katie up, while calling in a deep, authoritarian voice, "Truce! Truce! Make peace, not war! I command you!" Brian pulled her down too and hugged them both. He stood up and stepped back into the chill of the hallway with me.

"I enjoyed talking with you," Brian said, shaking my hand. "I'll see you in the morning."

Erica called out, "Good night, Mike."

I clutched the towels tighter for some warmth in the chilly hallway, and to steady myself from the sound of her voice. "Good night," I said, turning into Tim's room.

Suddenly, I was extremely tired, and I felt alone, misplaced, and cold in the darkness, thinking of war, miniature ships, and these unusual people, and I thought for a moment about the beautiful Shayna Lieberman, a woman I doubted I would ever see again, a woman who was there for a few minutes just hours ago and then gone, reduced to a memory not even as permanent as a phone listing.

CHAPTER SIXTEEN

A train's single headlight roared toward me, cutting a swath of steadily expanding yellow in the darkness. I tried to scream for help, but I couldn't with the light hypnotizing me, its engine roaring and shaking me until, seconds before it crushed me, I shielded myself from the light, wrenched myself free of the tracks, and leapt to the side. I stumbled against Sally-Boy, who steadied me, stood me up tall, and, in the instant that I took to brush myself off, vanished. The train sped behind me, spewing the smell of diesel and another sickening odor, one that was unfamiliar to me.

My eyes sprang open from the dream, and I breathed in soft, rapid gasps as I sorted out my surroundings. The sun shone brightly, a yellow beam bathing the room. I picked up my watch from the floor; almost nine o'clock. I rolled out of bed and shivered. The towels Brian had given me were on a dresser that had a large yellow peace sign painted on top of it. I looked in the mirror over the dresser, approvingly pulled my hair down to the tip of my nose and then saw a Jimi Hendrix poster on the wall behind me, Jimi staring from beneath a true explosion of hair. In the shower, I concentrated on washing my dream down the drain.

By the time I got downstairs, Katie and Erica had left to shop for last-minute items to take on their ski trip. Brian sipped coffee and waited for Karen to pick him up. On the breakfast table, next to some cereal boxes, was a note: "Mike, sorry I missed you at breakfast. I'll cook one for you some other time (that is, if burning an English muffin counts as cooking!). Erica." I felt like a child who has discovered a new talent, like whistling or riding a bike. I folded the note carefully and put it in my pants' pocket. Instead of eating, I thanked Brian, wished him well, stepped into the cold sunshine and got into Bingham's Healey. I revved the engine, flicked on the radio to ABC in New York, and wheeled recklessly amid the bread trucks, small service trucks, and carrier rigs that jam the Jersey highways.

About halfway to campus, with the rumble in my stomach nearly drowning out the roar from the highway, I spun into a truckers' diner and sat on a cracked stool at the counter. Halfway through my eggs, potatoes, and coffee, a big driver wearing a plaid flannel shirt sat down next to me. The trucker stared at me and breathed noisily, his chest expanding and contracting like a mammoth accordion. With surprising ease, I brushed off a feeling that maybe I didn't belong there. He continued to breathe and stare, a sort of living gargoyle. Instead of just quietly ignoring him, I opened my eyes wide, went into my "Crazy Stare"— the look I would share with Sally when he used his "Italian Eye"—and said enthusiastically, "Try the eggs and potatoes; they're great!" I flaunted a forkful in his face.

He made a noise that sounded like air brakes, then said out of the side of his mouth, "Been eatin here six days a week at this hour for eight years. Never seen you here before. Think I need you to tell me what to eat? I suppose you drive a rig?"

The whining gears from the highway were beginning to sound like high-pitched laughter directed at me. But I answered, still in full Crazy Stare, "No, just that little Healey out there, man."

"Fuckin sports car, eh? Hate 'em. Gnats. Pains-in-the-ass. Fag cars. Run 'em off the road whenever I can. My truck's got fourteen gears. Handle that sometime, sports car driver."

Though he hadn't ordered, the waitress put a golden mountain of pancakes on the counter in front of him.

"Thanks, Myrtle," he mumbled to the waitress.

Myrtle batted purple-coated eyes at him. Her bleached hair had the green tinge of swamp weed in it, and it was so teased and sprayed, it surrounded her head like a football helmet. The driver said to her, "Got a fag-car driver here, Myrt, a weirdo, bug-eyed, fag-car driver."

"I think he's kinda cute, Angie," she said flatly.

Angie considered that witty. He roared in noisy laughter. "Yeah, a cutie, especially with that hair all over his head like a hippie. Hey, are you Ringo, Bingo, or Jingo?"

I ate just a little faster, but purposely expanded my Crazy Stare. An unusual desire overtook me—a desire to antagonize the big bastard, to push him toward, or over, the edge. He had a couple of inches and about seventy pounds on me; I wasn't eager for a fistfight, but I wasn't afraid, and I was pretty strong for a 170 pounder due to all the time I had spent in the weight room as part of my high school football training pro-gram...and all the summer nights Sally-Boy and I had spent pumping iron on the fire escape while sipping cans of Schaefer.

I noticed that Angie was the Picasso of Pancake Houses, an artist who dripped syrup delicately over his pancakes, buttered them individually with smooth careful strokes, and then made three neat diagonal cuts and three horizontal ones. Just as he moved his first forkful up to his mouth, I said, "Angie, excuse me, but pass that cream," though I really had no use for it since I was preparing to leave. He stopped in mid-forkful and slid the cream toward me. As he moved the fork back toward his mouth, I said, "Angie, do you always eat like that?"

He placed the forkful carefully back on the plate. "Like what?"

"You know, all those neat little squares of pancakes lined up just so?" I pointed my fork menacingly close to the pancakes and opened my eyes extra wide.

"What's it to you?"

"That's real nice, Ang, you know?"

Wrinkles of confusion lined his heavy face as he blurted, "Whatthefuckyamean goddamit asshole?"

I stood and paid for my food with the five-dollar bill my father had given me for a haircut the day before, enough to cover the check and provide a tip for Myrtle, who winked at me when she picked it up. Then, with Crazy Stare more fully engaged than ever, I turned to face Angie and called up the Brooklyn street-voice of my youth: "Ya know, Ang, someone sees you eatin like dat...they might just think you're one a them sports car drivers, know what I mean, eh?"

It took Angie a moment to digest my words and swallow the forkful of pancakes he had shoved into his mouth, and by then I had walked toward the diner's exit. I heard him yell out, "Long-haired bug-eyed

faggot hippie, I'll run your ass upside down and sideways if I see you on the road!"

"Bye bye, Angie, honey," I shouted in falsetto as I
left, and I heard the few other truckers in the diner
start laughing and calling out, "Angie honey, oh Angie
honey..."

Truth is, I kind of liked being called a hippie—sort
of a cocky, fearless hippie. Even the thought of facing
Tomato at the desk was almost bearable. I wheeled
onto campus and spun into a space next to someone's
glistening black MGB. I walked into the dorm, and
Tomato—in an odd Thatch-less moment this time—
peered at me from behind the desk. I decided not to
ask him about messages, but he fooled me and said,
"Aren't you Burns from 409B?"

"What was that?" I said. I had heard him, but I
wanted to hear him repeat it.

"Burns from 409B? Isn't that you?" A wonderful
trace of exasperation welled in his voice.

"Right, Mr. Tomato."

"Well, Darrell Bingham wants you to call him right
away at this number," he said, holding out a piece of
paper. "He sounded quite angry."

"No shit?"

"Yes, he's called several times."

"Really? Well, next time he calls, ring me, okay,
Mr. Tomato? I'll be in my suite reading. You know the
number."

"409B?"

"Pardon?"

"I said 409B," he whined.

"Call me, when he calls," I said.

Tomato brimmed bright red. "But Darrell Bingham said..." The elevator doors shut, slicing Tomato in mid-whine. I waved to him and gave him a dose of Crazy Stare.

CHAPTER SEVENTEEN

Fish wasn't in the suite yet. Though he only lived about an hour away, it generally took Fish a while to return to campus because of all the arguments he had with his parents. I sank into the isolated safety of a Salvation Army chair and looked around happily at the cluttered comfort of our room. We were starting our third semester rooming together, but during our first semester of college in the fall of 1966, we both had different roommates. My original roommate had been a ministry student named Gary Leake. To say that he was modest is as much an understatement as saying that Lyndon Johnson was homely. Gary either changed clothes when I was out of the room, or, if I happened to be there, he'd casually hop into a closet and then pop out wearing something different.

Soon it got to be a lot of pressure, an unnatural atmosphere, to worry about walking in on Gary with his pants down or shirt off. So before leaving the room I'd casually say something like, "Gary, I'll be gone for about ten minutes." I figured that gave him enough time to make a change if he wanted to. But one time I returned a minute or two earlier than I had said I would, and Gary stood decked out in a pair of blue-and-white checked pajama bottoms. His shirt, however, was off, exposing his naked chest.

"Boy, Mike," he fumed, turning red from hairless face to hairless chest, "a guy can't have any privacy around here!"

Then there was the matter of swearing. Gary never did, and every time I swore, which, I admit, was nearly every sentence, Gary looked at me with his head cocked to one side and a sympathetic little grin across his lips, like he understood that I had just lost complete control of myself again. I started saying things like, "No stuff!" and "Doggone!" so I guess Gary was probably a very positive influence on me in that respect—or at least he should have been. But I didn't feel natural around him, and that whole first semester of college I constantly filled my discomfort by imagining Sally-Boy was nearby.

Fish's original roommate, George Hairston, was a large, very talkative guy. A sports freak, he decorated his side of their room with countless pictures of his sports heroes, and he would often carry on at length about their career statistics. George grew morose whenever one of his favorite teams lost a game, and then he'd eat to quell his sorrow. He loved the San Francisco Giants and, after one particularly devastating loss, Fish and I watched, amazed, as George ranted and cursed at a small radio, while devouring a couple of Devil Dogs and a dozen or so chocolate chip cookies.

Fish and I met during orientation week of our freshman year at a six-man flag football meeting for freshmen on the oval in front of the school. About four hundred pseudo-jocks massed together with half of them trying to direct the show. Finally, an upperclassman in charge of intramurals stood in the bleachers with a bullhorn and shouted, "Listen up, you pack of dumb fucking frosh! Break into teams of between six and ten! In five minutes, if you're not on a team of between fucking six and fucking ten, then you're not playing in the fucking intramural season!"

A guy with massive curly hair, a goatee, and a football tapped me on the shoulder and said, "I'm Dave Fishbein, world's most unusual being—a Jewish quarterback. You look fast. Run out for a pass."

I sprinted out about twenty yards and looked back over my left shoulder. The pass was a little long and to my left, but I jumped, stuck my right arm out and felt the ball smack into my hand. I cradled the ball against my chest as I hit the ground while simultaneously rolling onto my back, a little trick I learned while playing receiver on my high school team, and never lost control. "You play with us," Fish announced, pointing to a few other guys who looked like they might be on the FBI's Most Wanted list, and we had our team.

We played well against some of the fraternity teams, and I drew the attention of the college coach, Ev Tinkers. My high school coach, who had been a teammate of Tinkers' at the University of Michigan, had apparently told Tinkers that I was a decent receiver and defensive back. Tinkers watched me play intramurals, and twice in my freshman year he talked to me about playing college ball. Sinclair was hardly a football powerhouse even in its small college division, but it did offer some financial aid, which Tinkers tried to use to lure me onto the team.

One day, in a driving rain, Tinkers, wearing shorts and an open windbreaker revealing his bare chest, watched us play in the mud against HAWKMEN, a powerful team of right-wing war supporters known for their animalistic attitude on and off the field. Students from the activist group STEP, which stood for Students Toward Educational Priorities, picketed all the intramural games because they felt intramurals in general grossly detracted from political issues.

And STEP equated football, in particular—even flag football—with, as they put it in a letter to the student newspaper, "another sprocket of conflict reflecting the war machine mentality, a hostile game honoring violence."

We kicked off to HAWKMEN in the downpour, and after the whistle to end the play two of their players rammed into our biggest lineman, Andy Lambert, and sent him sprawling for a mudslide of about ten yards. He limped off the field. On the next play, the HAWKEMEN's quarterback threw a long pass, clearly out of bounds, but in the direction of the pickets. Someone yelled, "Heads up!" and as the pickets looked up, a HAWKMEN player leaped head first into their line, knocking over two girls and a skinny guy with a beard. The entire HAWKMEN team laughed, including the receiver who wound up about fifteen yards from the ball. But the HAWKMEN receiver stopped laughing when the skinny bearded guy struggled to his feet and cracked him over the head with a plywood sign, while screaming, "Fascist! Fascist!" In an instant, HAWKMEN players were all over the protesters, flinging them and their signs in every direction, ripping up posters, tearing at clothing and hair. I watched with the rest of my team from across the field. Someone behind me chuckled; it was Coach Tinkers.

"These games sure can get out of hand," he said, smiling and shaking his head.

"I don't really think that's part of the game," I said, as I watched the HAWKMEN players pounding away at the STEP members. Game referees and a couple of campus cops were trying to break things up across the way. Tinkers just stood there.

"Hell, I bet if you were to tell the truth, you wouldn't mind getting in a few licks, would you?" he said.

I thought he was referring to us getting even with the HAWKMEN players for what they had done to Andy Lambert. "Oh, we'll get them for what they did to the big guy there," I said motioning toward Andy, who limped tenderly along the sideline.

"No, I meant those hippies. Wouldn't you just like to take a crack at them? I would."

If I had any real guts I would have told Tinkers he was a fascist moron, but I only thought it—and, actually, I was proud of myself for even thinking it. But I simply shrugged foolishly and said, "I just enjoy playing the games, Coach, that's all."

The refs and campus cops calmed things down, a couple of HAWKMEN and a couple of STEPs were pushed into a campus van, and the game started up again. I jogged through the mud onto the field, and Tinkers called out, "Come out for varsity, Burns, where you can enjoy some real hitting."

Despite the miniature monsoon, Tinkers stood and watched for about half the game, mud splattering his bare legs, rain soaking his chest. He never seemed to move, standing straight and still in the furious rain, bareheaded, windbreaker unzipped. In the huddle, Fish stroked his goatee and said to me, "That fucker's nuts to stand out here. He's a spooky asshole, one very wet, very spooky, very big asshole. But let's entertain him."

On the next play, Fish threw me a sideline pass that I caught right in front of Tinkers. I spun past one of the HAWKMEN for a couple of yards, slipped out of bounds into a puddle the size of a farm pond, and another HAWKMEN player landed on top of me, sending a fresh coat of mud all over Tinkers.

"Beautiful, Burns, beautiful!" Tinkers cheered, not even flinching at the mud that now caked him. "Come play varsity and save your parents some money."

I stood to go back onto the playing field, and Tinkers planted a stinging wet slap on my mud-caked backside. When I got to the huddle, Fish grinned and said, "Very wet, very spooky, and very very strange."

The next day, Tinkers stopped me on my way to a class and said he wanted me to play for Sinclair, no financial aid right away unless I made the first team. He'd give me every chance, of course.

"Not interested, Coach," I said flatly.

"We'll be in touch," he said intently. "Got a uniform just your size, Burns."

The sad thing was that I used to think about playing at the college level—Sinclair was a small enough school that I thought it would have a relatively pressure-free program so I could stay sharp competitively, keep in shape, and have some fun. But Tinkers made the thought of playing seem inconsequential, unimportant, even silly. And the growing intensity of protests on campus, actually made me question priorities—mine and the school's.

"Where does a guy like Tinkers go from here?" I asked Fish one day in our freshman year as we rode into town in Fish's 1962 Chevy wagon to pick up some townie dates.

"Same place he came from—nowhere," Fish said. "Someday he'll watch one-too-many games in the rain, come down with pneumonia, croak off, get cremated and have his ashes spread all around the locker room, where he can watch guys dress and undress for all eternity. Asshole to asshole and putz to putz."

Even though we weren't roommates that first semester, Fish and I spent most of our free time together playing intramurals, double-dating, griping about our parents (Me: "My dad and mom say rosaries that my hair will fall out." Fish: "Mine too, well, I mean, no rosaries obviously, but they actually want me to speak to our rabbi about my 'attitude'...like his opinion would matter to me.") and swapping roommate antics. Inevitably, Fish and I figured we should room together, and the end of the first semester seemed the perfect time for making the change.

"Which of us tells his roommate to get lost?" Fish asked one evening in the Student Union. I had told Gary I'd be gone for a half hour, giving him enough time to change clothes if he wanted.

"I hadn't really thought about it," I said.

"Well, let's settle this intellectually," Fish said.

We flipped a coin; I lost. There were a couple of single suites vacated by kids who flunked out mid-year, so I knew there would be a place for Gary. I tried to make myself feel less guilty by rationalizing that in his own suite he wouldn't have to worry about someone walking in on him while he changed. But all the way back to the dorm I worried about breaking the news to him. When I got there, Gary was sitting in a pair of flannel pinstriped pajamas, sucking an unlit pipe, and reading The New York *Times* at his desk.

"Bad news, bad news," he muttered. He was referring to something in the paper, of course, but for a moment I thought he was predicting what I was about to unload on him. Still looking at the paper, he said, "I do believe sometimes that people are incapable of fully understanding the Vietnam situation. People protest the war, but they forget the essential truth behind it."

"What's that, Gary? What's the essential truth?" I asked, trying to sound casual and sincere.

"They forget that the Lord has his reasons, and we must follow the Lord's way. He has sent us on a mission, and we will prevail for it is the Lord's will, and the Lord protects the righteous." Then he looked up at me and said, "Gone longer than you expected?"

"Uh, yeah. Got to talking to Fish, you know, just bullsh...just blowing off steam. Actually some of what we talked about had to do with you...and his roommate, too, sort of, only more about you."

Gary munched his pipe with his head tilted to one side.

"Really? I didn't know David even knew me that well."

"Oh, sure he does, he really does, and he thinks you're a good guy and all."

Gary nodded as if to indicate he agreed completely with the last statement, which, of course, he didn't know I had made up. Then a plan for justifying the news sprang into my head. "Yeah," I said, "but poor old Fish—David, I mean—has been having problems with his roommate."

"That rather large, talkative young man named George Harrison?"

"No, that's the Beatle—George Harrison is the Beatle. Fish's roommate, I mean David's roommate, is George *Hairston*."

"Oh right! Of course, I have heard that name before—Harrison, George Harrison, the Beatle. But Hairston is the large boy's name, yes? Must be difficult to have a name so close to the name of someone famous. You know, some people have made fun of my name—Leake. Lewd comments. So odd what people do, isn't it?

"Yes, it is odd," I said, and then tried awkwardly to steer the conversation back to the news I had to break. "So much is so odd that Fish—er, David—needs a change."

"David probably can't leave any food around the room, can he? That would be a real strain on a relationship. No comfort in your own room."

"Right...exactly...David isn't comfortable...so he wants to move out and get a new roommate." I looked into Gary's face to see if my point had registered. He put his pipe and newspaper down, brushed at his pajamas, and looked blankly at me. How come sometimes a plan can seem so good in your head and turn into a shitfest in reality? "So you see, Gary, David wants out of his room and into here."

Gary breathed deeply and said incredulously, "You mean David wants to live with me?"

I thought he was being sarcastic, but of course he wasn't, which made me feel even worse.

"No," I said.

Gary chuckled and tapped his pipe on a glass ashtray shaped like a duck. "Whew," he said, "I was afraid he wanted to live with me, just when I have started to reach *you* with the way of the Lord."

Suddenly, Gary grew animated, as if ash from his pipe had fallen down his pajamas. He sprang to his feet and started drawing in deeply on his pipe, and without looking at me he said, "Oh, I see...yes...That's it, isn't it?...I'm the one who's going...I get it...The two of you, social carnivores...Fine, I'll move. I'm used to it. Actually, you're the first roommate I've ever had for any length of time; even in prep school I chose to live by myself—the carnivores all made lewd comments about my name. I can't adapt to the vagaries of you social animals."

"So...you'll do it?" I asked.

"Surprised, Michael, or hurt that I don't feel rejected?" he said coolly.

"No, neither, I just didn't want to tell you this, I mean..."

"Oh, I see, I see. 'Michael The Sensitive' can't imagine that someone wouldn't mind living without him." He still didn't face me, speaking toward the only window in the room.

"No, hey, Gary, that's not it at all."

"You and your profanity, your atheistic nature, your strutting in underclothing, your lack of concern for my privacy."

"Lack of concern for..."

Now he turned and faced me. His lips parted in a razor-thin smile. His pipe and head jabbed at me in unison like a double-billed woodpecker, and he said, "You haven't even noticed that I've had to change clothing while in the closet to maintain a modicum of modesty. If you had ever noticed maybe you would have been more considerate and left the room just before bed time."

"Well," I said quietly, "in your own room you won't have to worry about it."

I walked toward the door.

"And neither will you, Michael, not that you in your singular self-indulgence ever did."

Out of habit I said, "I'll be back in about an hour, Gary." I walked out of the room.

From the hallway I heard him shout, "The Lord sent me to save you, Michael, but He shall not blame me for your lost soul! How dare you cast ME out for a JEW! A Christ Killer! The Good Lord SHALL NOT BLAME ME!"

When I returned several hours later Gary, to my surprise, was already gone. He had packed and I didn't know where he went, but I was sure it was better for us both. I stood there wondering how you can live with someone for nearly half a year and still understand so little about one another. And then I noticed the pictures on my desk, nude shots torn out of some porn magazine, photos of men and women in a collage of twisted body parts. Gary left a note saying, "Feast your heathen eyes on the parts I've encircled, Michael, and yield to temptation as your kind always does. The Lord is watching you!"

"Jesus," I said aloud. I looked around the room, half expecting to see Gary jump out of the closet. I balled up the pictures and turned to toss them into the trash can, but first I had to pause for a few seconds so my hands would stop shaking.

CHAPTER EIGHTEEN

From the time Fish moved in with me, he and I were practically inseparable. The Salvation Army chair I sat in, the dartboard we had set up, the closets bulging in disarray were all part of our comfortably cluttered existence. There was something safe and secure about the friendship and the suite—there was no pressure between us, nothing forced. We felt free to share—or not—whatever we wanted. I didn't tell him about Sally-Boy—I kept those cherished stories to myself—but still, in our dorm room, it seemed that Fish and I had established a fire escape of our own.

Fish griped about his parents a lot, and he seemed eager to escalate the conflict. His gigantic hair and sharp goatee were a constant focus of his parents' phone calls, calls that Fish often simply ignored, angering his parents even more. When he refused to go home for the Jewish High Holidays, his parents had threatened several times to cut off his tuition.

"They won't do it," Fish said confidently, casually, after one particularly tense call during which I could actually hear them yelling at him through the receiver. "The last thing they want is for their only son to go off to Vietnam, and that's what'll happen if I'm not in school. After all, then I would never be a doctor—that would be such a shame, a *shonda*, in their eyes. Oh, so terrible! Not that I'm going to be a doctor anyway. But they don't know that." Fish seemed intent on angering his parents, rebelling against all the straight-arrow life he had led until going to college.

I knew Fish would be interested in my escapade with Bingham, but before Fish arrived, Tomato was on the intercom to the room.

"Michael Burns! Michael Burns! This is the desk," he squawked from the speaker.

"Really?"

"Darrell Bingham's on the phone for you. I'm going to transfer the call to your suite."

In seconds, the phone rang. Before I could even say hello, Darrell said, "You fucker! Where have you been?"

"Who is this please?" I asked.

"It's the guy who got laid so many times last night he can hardly move! Get the hell out here now. I've got a date later and I need to wash my dick off first."

"A date with the waitress?"

"No." He paused. "Someone else. Hurry up, dammit!"

"I'll leave as soon as the tow truck returns your car to campus."

Bingham didn't even acknowledge my attempt to rattle him; he just blurted out the address and directions and then hung up. I left the suite and bumped into Fish, who was coming out of the elevator as I prepared to step in. When I told him where I was going, he said, "Let Bingham sweat it out. He'd fuck you over anytime he could."

"Yeah, but he did introduce me to a really great girl," I said. "Besides, it is his car."

Fish threw his suitcases into the hallway. "Didn't have to get your haircut I see," he said. "Good for you! You will soon be my Fro-Bro!"

"Had to. Didn't," I said, resisting the urge to say, "yet." I stepped into the elevator.

"You absolute rebel!" Fish said. The elevator doors started to close and he called, "Hey, did you get the beach info from your cousin?"

"Yeah, I'll talk with you later," I said as the doors shut.

I had almost forgotten about Harry's offer. He was going to promote a series of concerts in Virginia Beach in the summer, and he wanted me and Fish to live there and to handle the grunt work—hanging posters, passing out handbills, selling tickets, and even shuttling the acts back and forth from the airport. Fish's parents, of course, hated the idea, but he simply told them, "I'm doing it." Harry would pay us each $100 cash per week plus rent on a beach house that we would share with assorted vagrants and groupies who followed the acts around. Fish and I agreed that it had the makings of a well above-average summer.

Just before I opened Bingham's car door, Donna Sanders and Kerry Tindel, two active partiers who had spent the break in the Bahamas, stopped me. Their tans looked like smooth, perfect layers of beige paint. I pictured them and others like them adjusting their bikinis along Virginia Beach in the summer. They asked what I had done over the break.

"Not much," I said. "I'm afflicted with a plain, average life."

"Oh, I will bet that you are anything but average, Mike," Donna said.

Kerry laughed at Donna and said to her, "Slut."

"I am a slut, and proud of it; that is so true," Donna said sexily, "but can you blame me? Don't you like the new, long-haired Mike?"

"Oh, yes," Kerry said, pulling the curls that touched my jacket collar. "I declare him 'Mike, Maker of Sluts.'"

"Ouch," I said, as they both grabbed playfully at my hair. "You'll just have to get in line, ladies."

I got into the car.

"Driving the A-H?" Kerry said.

"Taking it to Darrell," I said.

"Just don't let the old A-H make an a-h out of you like it does out of Bingham," Donna said as they walked away.

"Never happen," I said, "because I know how to treat people, especially women. After all, I am 'Mike, Maker of Sluts.'"

"Anytime you want to, you can make me your Slut for a Day," one of them called out, laughing, but I couldn't tell whose voice it was, and I realized that I really didn't care.

CHAPTER NINETEEN

The car was cold, reluctant to turn over before finally sputtering a little and then starting but still trembling. Jimi Hendrix's "Purple Haze" blared through a jumble of feedback and a crackling buzz from the radio. As I pulled off campus, the car jerked slightly, and the news came on the radio:

Increasing death counts in Vietnam; a cafe in Saigon blown apart by a bomb attached to a Vietnamese busboy; Senator Eugene McCarthy, supposedly carrying a folder with his newest poems, renewed his pledge of peace to a group of students in New England.

The car bounced along the rutted highway, and I felt curiously out of place in the Healey—like a busboy with a bomb, or a poet with a political plat-form. Something my father said to me, prompted by the length of my hair, ran through my mind: "No one has any right to be anything other than what they ap-pear to be. Anything other than that is a deceit."

Why did the Healey's rough whine grate like the nagging cry of an infant? Weren't things going well? Wasn't that a cleaver, sexy exchange with Donna and Kerry? And Erica had promised me breakfast...well, a burnt English muffin anyway...and then my mind shifted to the telephone conversation with Bingham:

Him: "I've got a date in two hours."
Me: "With the waitress?"
His calculated hesitation: "No...someone else."

I pictured Bingham trying to make me sweat as he said it: "No...someone else."

"Son of a bitch!" I said out loud as I arrived at the address Bingham had given me.

Bingham burst out of the front door of a paint-chipped duplex. I got out of his car and slammed the door shut. My cheeks stung in the cold air. He looked smug and a little tired, but he glowed with confidence. My eyes focused on his, and I ground my teeth. My face flushed slowly.

"Hop back in," he ordered with his fucking wink. "I have to go back to campus and freshen up before my, uh, next date." I stood in front of the door on the driver's side, blocking his way into the car. For the first time, he looked carefully at my face. "What's wrong, Burns? Get in, will you, or I'm gonna be late." He reached into his jacket pocket. "Tootsie Pop?" he asked, pulling one out.

"Who's your date with, Bingham?"

His eyes darted toward mine but didn't hold. He stepped backward, looked at the Tootsie Pop, and motioned toward me with it silently.

"Hey," he said cautiously. "I didn't know you laid a claim to her after one half-assed date."

"I thought she was going away on her trip?"

"Yeah, well, she has just enough time for old Darrell." He put the Tootsie Pop on the outside of his crotch.

"Don't you..." I paused involuntarily, blindly, and then said, "don't you ever talk about her around me, do you hear me?"

The index finger of my left hand jabbed the air inches in front of his face. He turned his head slowly to the side. My jaw tightened.

"Burns, you're fucking crazy, she's..."

The streets of Brooklyn rushed up inside of me. I grabbed the collar of his ski jacket and felt the cool nylon rip along the seam. I whipped him sideways and bent his back over the top of the Healey. With his head flush against the car's hood, his face looked straight into the clear sky. "I said...*not*...to mention her...

around me, you *asshole*!" I bit off each word from between clenched teeth. "Do...you...understand...me?"

He tried saying something, but he choked on his words. I bounced him hard against the car, turned my back and walked away. I could hear Bingham coughing, then spitting, and then settling into his car. Incredibly, he drove up next to me.

"Tootsie Pop?" he asked again, holding one out the window.

"Fuck you."

"Come on, Burns. No hard feelings. I'll drive you back to campus. You don't really want to walk all that way."

"Go to hell, Darrell. Leave me the fuck alone."

"Okay okay, have it your way, Burnsey," he said.

When the Healey hummed out of earshot, I stuck out my thumb and depended upon the sheer, random chance of a stranger to get me back to school. Several cars and trucks whipped up road trash on me as they sped by.

After about ten minutes, an elderly truck driver, who looked like a textbook pro-war sympathizer—perhaps an older version of Angie from the diner—drove me nearly all the way, talking the entire trip about his three teenage grandsons and how he hoped they never had to go to Vietnam because "it ain't logical. Defend a village during the day, take a bullet in the head from a villager at night. Where are the boundaries, the good guys and bad guys? We might as well be fighting ourselves, for chrissakes. The people sending you kids to war—most of them don't have kids going themselves. Where's the logic in that? I want the war protesters to win; I want them to shut the war effort down; they should blow up all the goddam Draft Boards. I want you kids to keep showing the rest of the country that there's no logic to entering a fight where you don't know what the outcome *should* be let alone what it *will* be. A logical person in an illogical argument can frustrate himself to death because not only can't he win, but he can't even make himself understood...and I don't want my grandkids in an illogical fight..."

When I climbed out of the truck, he flashed me a peace sign, and I self-consciously raised my fist in the air, an involuntary—though not illogical—posture. I held that pose momentarily as he drove off. I paused to determine the direction back to campus, and in that instant, a car full of girls drove up slowly next to me. They rolled down their windows; two yelled, "Hippies are queers!" and then another one gave me the finger, while still another mooned me from the back seat.

CHAPTER TWENTY

Several days later, I watched a fine snow falling outside our dorm window smoothly and quietly blanketing a small wooded area. The white crystals sparkled deeply, their softness promising comfort, not the cold they actually possessed. That's how snow is, I thought. From afar it excites, commands attention, promises pleasure. But when touched by warm hands, snow chills first, melts quickly, and then changes form. On the fire escape, the snow always looked clean...until we picked it up to make snowballs and saw the dirt and rust it held.

Fish was out somewhere. I was alone in our room tormenting myself by playing *Rubber Soul*, thinking of

Erica, and reliving the night when we had met. I tried unsuccessfully to keep from having a conversation with Sally-Boy—I kept hoping I had left that piece of juvenile behavior behind, but he and I had spent so much time together, talking about everything and nothing, I found myself saying, *What do I do, Sally? She's not like the girls at the outdoor summer dances in the church parking lot in Brooklyn, not like the girls we met making deliveries for the Panificio. This girl makes me think—and no, not just with my dick because that's what you're about to say. Now it's cold and there's war and protests and school and then there's her—she shows up in my life and I am feeling different—but then this asshole beats me to her. How does shit like this happen? Morris Lieberman talks about 'nachas' and persevering, but what the fuck, you just know how these things will turn out. Ah, Sally, where the hell are you?*

And then I heard Sally say in that way he had of being not exactly on topic but near it: *Remember that time at the Panificio—Christmas time—that kid come in and we seen him slap his girlfriend across the face? It was you who jumped in, not me; I didn't do shit, Mikey. You did. You threw him to the floor, then chased him out, made sure she was okay, walked her home. You done it, Mikey. You done just like that. And then when you came back to the bakery, Massimo and Angela Bortuzzi came out of the kitchen and hugged you...Angela even kissed you twice right on the forehead, and I know you liked that. You did that, Mikey, by yourself.*

Outside my dorm room, shrieks pierced the night as college students played in the snow; I couldn't actually see anybody, but I continued to look into the darkness. Soon it was hard to remember what things looked like without snow covering them. But snow doesn't really change anything, I told myself; it just covers things up. Then again, if things look different, maybe they are different.

The door opened, and I turned from my desk to see Fish speckled with snowflakes.

"Let's cruise," he said.

"What?"

"Let's cruise. It's Thursday night. Weekend time. Cruisin time."

"No thanks. And since when did weekends start on Thursdays?"

"Since we became wise sophomores and stopped scheduling Friday classes. Come on. You've got no excuse. You've been sitting around moping since last weekend when Bingham buddy-fucked you again." Fish walked over to the record player and turned it off. "Listening to the same album still? Again? Christ, it's time to drop it, Mike."

Fish yanked some papers out of my hands. It was the syllabus for a writing course I was taking. The professor hadn't shown up for the first class; instead, he had just left a syllabus and a stack of readings for us to begin on.

"I've got all these readings to do for this writing course," I said.

Fish scoffed. "Reading for writing—doesn't make sense. Neither does getting a head start on your work. The first week of classes and you're working. Bad for your health, not to mention your image—not that you have an image. Come on. Let's cruise. Let's tune up with this." Fish unzipped his jacket and revealed a six-pack of Budweiser. He removed one can and tossed it to me. "There's another sixer in the car. Bobby Matson's keeping it company."

"Is he going, too?" I asked, opening the can and taking a long pull.

"Oh yeah, and he's already wound up pretty good. Says he's been drinking all afternoon. He was out in the snow bitching at people for not building any black snowmen. He says snow is racist and this is a racist institution. See, this promises to be a fun evening."

"He belongs in an institution," I said, grabbing a heavy coat and a pair of gloves.

Fish did a couple of quick dance steps. "All right!" he said. "Cruise time!"

Fish's car engine was running and the radio was blaring so loud we could hear it fifty feet away. Snow fringed the outer edge of the windshield just beyond the sweep of the wipers. Bobby Matson grinned from behind the steering wheel, his Afro teased into full bloom. We opened the car doors and saw Donna and Kerry sitting in the back seat sipping beers.

"They insisted on going on the cruise," Bobby said in his nearly falsetto voice. "So I told the mamas to come to papa."

Fish and I piled in next to Bobby, who stayed behind the wheel. Bobby floored the old Chevy and it spun across the parking lot, skidding recklessly through the snow. "Hey, is this car gonna hold up, Fish, my man?" Bobby asked.

"Steady as a rock," Fish replied confidently.

I wasn't so sure about Bobby driving. He was definitely tanked up, and I'd seen him in manic moods where he would charm everyone by doing a dead-on Smokey Robinson impersonation one minute and, in the next, describe in morbid detail how he would die in Vietnam, bleeding to death with his arms blown off or from a hand grenade somehow dropped down his pants. But no one else in the car seemed concerned; they drained their beers and started new ones.

"It's lonely back here, Mike," Donna said.

Fish jumped head first into the back seat.

"I believe the lady said Mike," Bobby laughed shrilly.

"Really?" Fish said, the picture of innocence. "I thought she said Fish. You know, Fish, Mike, Fish, Mike—if you say them fast they sound the same."

"'Yeah, sorta like *horse*shit and *bull*shit," Bobby said, turning all the way around momentarily to look at Fish in the back seat. The car swerved, but Bobby quickly straightened it out.

"Okay, if I'm not wanted back here I'll leave," Fish said. He began to dive into the front, but Kerry grabbed him firmly around his hips and pulled him back, causing Fish to squeal, "Bobby, Mike—oh my god, she wants me, oh god, she wants me!"

Bobby said in a high-pitched slur, "Sheee-it, Fish, Uncle Sam's the only one who wants your white ass, and he ain't exactly what you'd call choosey 'cause he gonna kill us all; we all gonna be butchered into chopped meat."

Bobby slammed on the brakes and bounced the car off a snow bank in front of the Bendorff Student Union. We chugged another round of beers while sitting in the parking lot and then tumbled out of the car. Bobby staggered, slipped, and fell, landing flat on his ass in the snow. He sat there laughing crazily like a child who's being tickled unmercifully while his arms are pinned. Kerry kicked snow on him, the flakes glistening like stars on his black skin. When he stood to run after her, he immediately fell again, this time skidding a few feet on his chest. As Bobby picked snow out of the top of his jacket, he laughed such a wild laugh, I couldn't even laugh with him. I could only stare.

"Lord, I do love that beer," he said, finally standing but wobbling. "Kerry, I'm going to dance with you so long and hard tonight that those big beautiful honkers of yours are going to be bouncing for the next three days."

The Tombs in the basement of the Student Union was crowded and smoky as usual, but we found a table. Chuck Berry singing "Johnny B. Goode" blared out of the sound system, and Bobby immediately pulled Kerry onto the small dance floor. Fish wandered to the bar. Donna stuck close to me, but it was Erica who was on my mind, as she had been all week. I tried to recall a word, a look, an instant where Erica had shown even a mild interest in Bingham. I came up with none.

Fish had said, "Hey, what do you expect? A high school girl is easy meat for a vulture like Bingham. You should've knocked Darrell asshole over A-H just for the hell of it. Then she'd be easier to forget."

But Fish hadn't seen her. He didn't know how I lay awake at night that week picturing Erica's blue eyes turning soft and submissive while a smug Bingham, instead of me, studied her face.

Fish returned and put a tray of beers and some chips on the table. "The cruise is smooth," he said.

Bobby and Kerry, back from the dance floor, looked sleek with sweat.

"To cruising," Bobby said, staggering a little as he raised his beer mug, "where every stop means another good brew!"

"Sounds like a goddam beer commercial," Fish said.

We drained the mugs just as the Four Tops burst into "Can't Help Myself." Bobby grabbed Kerry again. "C'mon, girl," he said, "you can't let those beautiful things rest now."

Fish looked at Donna who was looking at me, waiting for me to ask her to dance.

"Next round of beers is mine," I said, getting up from the table.

Fish shook his head at me and took Donna to the dance floor.

I walked to the bar and looked around the hazy room. "Five draughts," I said to the red-haired girl behind the bar. Maybe Erica will come looking for me, I thought, ready to tell me it was all a mistake. Yeah, she'll come right through those doors, fresh from her ski trip, where she'd met no one to compare with me. But, of course, Erica was not in the Tombs—she didn't even know it existed. The Tombs was loaded with typical college people sectioned off into groups of drinkers, talkers, and dancers.

"That's two-fifty," the red-haired girl said.

In a corner just off the dance floor sat a white-haired man who talked animatedly to a small group of about fifteen attentive students, many of them wearing the peace sign or the letters STEP on their sweatshirts, hats, or jackets. On the wall behind the white-haired man, the STEP students had hung another "War Criminal" poster, this one with Defense Secretary Robert McNamara's picture on it. The room was too noisy for me to hear their conversation, although I walked close to their table as I returned to our place. Next to the man sat a woman in her mid-twenties with ass-length black hair, who was at least thirty years younger than him, flicking gently at his bright red sweater, touching his arm, stroking his hair. The students who surrounded them were fully engaged in whatever the man was saying, and they would occasionally thrust their fists into the air and cheer loudly at his comments. Though I tried, I couldn't make out his words, only his intensity.

I returned to our table as the Four Tops were finishing.

"Hit me with a new brew, brotherman," Bobby said, dabbing his brow with a handkerchief. "You know how that sweet soul music drives my black blood crazy!"

He smiled, but there was something false about it; it almost looked as if he were gritting his teeth instead of grinning. "Get down to Motown!" he shouted several times in his piercing voice, drawing attention from nearby tables as he swiveled his narrow hips to the rhythm. Bobby danced his way up to the bar and back, beer sloshing out of the mugs and onto the tray.

"Hey, hey, look here!" Bobby shouted to everyone in general with a wave of his hand, his voice reaching a new shrillness. "This here is the good life. Typical college scene. Music, beer, fine women, oh my god how *fine*, **fine**, **FINE** they are!" Bobby rotated his hips while gazing at several young women with their dates at the table closest to ours. Then he turned to us, took a huge gulp of beer, and said, "This makes the world go round, so drink 'em down! Oh, yeah, this is the life! College, where we all safe...for now! We all brothers and sisters! Ain't that right, Kerry, baby?"

Bobby leaned over and licked her neck. Kerry pushed his sweating face away.

"Dammit, Bobby!" Kerry said, wiping her neck. "That's just gross!" At that moment the records stopped spinning and Kerry's voice rang out across the Tombs. People at the tables around us looked up.

"Well forgive my mother-fucking black ass," Bobby said loudly. He turned toward the table nearest ours and said, "No, no, no problem here. Go ahead and drink." He raised his mug, gesturing for a toast. No one from the table joined him, so he drained the mug himself, his head jerking back toward the dark ceiling.

By the time he lowered his head and his mug, Bobby's eyes glistened fiercely. He turned to the people at the nearby table and said, "None of you brothers and sisters gonna drink with this drunk black boy, are you?" They shuffled uncomfortably in their chairs. "Come on, let's see a little of that old college liberalism," Bobby squeaked. He raised his fist into a salute and thrust his jaw toward a student in a dark crewneck sweater, and said, "Black power there, brotherman! I mean, we *are* brothers, right, my man? Or you just like to say we brothers?"

The guy started to grin in hopes that Bobby was kidding. But Bobby's voice raised another incredible notch as he said, "Don't you fucking grin at me! This ain't Amos and motherfucking Andy! Now, I want to know if we're all learning to be good liberal-minded children at this school. We are, right?"

With that, Bobby rested his hand on the shoulder of a young woman sitting next to the guy in the crewneck sweater. The guy grabbed Bobby around his skinny wrist. Bobby jerked away and grasped the back of the guy's chair, trying to pull it out from under him.

"Get up, motherfucker!" Bobby wailed.

Fish grabbed Bobby's shoulders; I jumped between Bobby and the guy in the crewneck, who was now standing, fists clenched.

"Sit down, Bobby, come on," Fish said quietly.

Bobby released his grip on the chair and turned his eyes toward the floor.

"Cool off," I said as he relaxed. "We're cruising, remember? Good times, Bobby."

He sat down and said softly, "Why don't they want to drink with brother Bobby? They drink with you guys…even with Fish, and his fro's 'bout big as mine." His eyes lacked focus and his head rolled involuntarily in small circles from side to side, as if his huge mass of hair caused him to struggle for balance.

"Don't worry about it, Bobby," Fish said. "Relax. Typical college scene, right?"

"Sure, fuck yeah," Bobby said, exhaling loudly.

Kerry and Donna stared blankly at their nearly empty mugs. Bobby jumped to his feet, clumsily banging into the table as he walked toward the bar. He returned unsteadily with enough beers for both tables. "Sorry," was all he said to the group at the other table, handing them the beers. They took the beers and said nothing to him.

Even Bobby drank this round more slowly. Kerry breathed normally now, though she said little. In fact, no one spoke much. Bobby continually dabbed at his brow with his handkerchief in a futile attempt to stem the perspiration. Fish yawned once, then stifled another, and Donna stared vacantly at her half-full beer, occasionally lifting her eyes to mine. I watched the white-haired man across the room leave with the dark woman by his side, while the students he had been talking to stared at him with something bordering on awe, some of them raising a fist as though it were a salute.

Our cruise was stalled, the steam missing, the engine blown. The Supremes finally came on with "Baby Love" but the record skipped from the start at "Oooooh hoooo" so Diana Ross just repeated the sound without reason or rhythm or purpose until it became a wail, "Oooooh hoooo, oooooh hoooo oooooh hoooo oooooh hoooo oooooh hoooo," knifing through our typical college scene, howling at the fact that our cruise was destined to be wrecked, piercing as a siren signaling a rescue...or an oncoming attack. Someone finally lifted the arm off the record and silence swept the room, only a few soft murmurs and tinkling of glasses could be heard. The crackle of a record scratched through the speakers; then came Simon and Garfunkel softly humming the opening to their song "America," and by the time they sang the opening line, "Let us be lovers, we'll marry our fortunes together..." the entire Tombs seemed to listen as one.

Even Bobby was quiet through the whole song, his head rolling, his eyes wandering. Just as the song ended, Bobby put his head down on the table.

"Is he falling asleep?" Donna asked.

"I don't know," I said, "but let's get him out of here, Fish, before he gets sick."

Bobby lifted his head with what seemed like a great effort. "I'm okay; everything's cool with Bobby," he said, his voice like a radio signal breaking up. "But I'm thinking that what it is, you see, is like that song says, it says: 'I'm lost...though I knew she was sleeping.'" The rest of us looked at one another in confusion. "Look, fuck it, I ain't crazy," Bobby slurred angrily. "You know what I'm sayin, dammit! Times ain't no fucking good. We all know it. I love you, but I know it's no good. So, like, we're either lost or just sleepin through this whole mother-fuckin mess, just lost or sleepin through the black-white stuff and the war of course, the war...we gonna die in this motherfuckin war, blown to bloody motherfuckin bits! We **ARE GONNA DIE**!" He dropped his head back down and his Afro seemed to cover him.

Kerry said suddenly, "Oh, I can not stand this; I just can not take it!" She, too, slurred her words now. "Everyone is talking like that, like Bobby. Every good time just turns into a depressing shit of a conversation these days—some heavy goddam shit that makes no fucking sense. I mean, what the fuck is Bobby saying? Does anyone know? I'm sick of it, just so goddam sick of it all!"

"You're right," Bobby said, barely lifting his head. "You're all right, and I'm wrong, and I'm drunk, and I am so fucking sorry." He stood, his head rolling more dramatically, "Let's go. It's no fun anymore, thanks to me."

"I swear to god," Kerry said, shaking her head, "this is unbearable. I HATE it! We are all so fucked!"

Bobby weaved toward the exit, and we followed.

CHAPTER TWENTY-ONE

The cold snowflakes stung, and the fresh air made me aware that I had also drunk too much. There was a faint pounding around my temples, a soft echo of a headache. I walked gingerly in the snow. Bobby slumped against the Chevy, shivering. We shoved him into the front seat. Fish drove, and I sat between Kerry and Donna in the back. Bobby jerked spastically as the car lurched forward.

"Gonna be sick, Fish," Bobby said, fumbling to open the window. I reached across the seat, rolled down the window for him, and shoved his head out. Snow speckled his Afro as he vomited loudly over the side of the car, moaning, "Sorry you guys, I'm sorry, it's all fucked up...typical college scene fucked because of me..." He vomited again and Kerry turned to face the opposite side of the car. The seams of Donna's tight blue jeans pushed against my thigh as I continued to lean forward, but even as Donna pushed lightly against me, I thought of Erica.

At the dorms, Bobby stumbled out and immediately fell into the snow-covered parking lot. His hair was dappled with vomit and snow. He struggled to stand.

"Can't walk," he said weakly. Fish and I hoisted him to his feet. "No no no fuck me you guys, you don't help my useless black ass." Bobby said. "Leave me here, lemme freeze out here, lemme sit in the rotten fucking snow and freeze...gonna be blown to pieces some day anyway."

I draped one of Bobby's arms around my neck, and Fish took another. "Come on, Bobby," I said, "you're going inside."

Bobby's feet dragged behind him, and then he suddenly stiffened and straightened up.

"Kerry! Donna!" Bobby called to the girls who walked behind us. "I am so sorry 'bout tonight! Bobby gonna make it up to you someday!" Then he dry-heaved with such force that Fish and I had to brace ourselves to keep him from pitching onto his face.

"Oh, my god!" Kerry screamed. "I just can not stand it! We **ARE ALL SO FUCKED**!" She increased her pace and walked quickly past us toward the dorm.

"Kerry!" Donna called.

But Kerry just waved her hands in the air and shouted, "I just can not stand it!"

Fish and I struggled to steady Bobby.

"Where are you going now, Mike?" Donna asked me, backpeddaling. "After I make sure Kerry's okay, I thought, you know, maybe you and I could meet up."

"I guess we'll take Bobby to his room."

Fish nodded.

"Will you come back down then?" Donna asked. "You know, once he's in bed, I mean."

"Uh, no, I don't think so," I said. "I'm feeling a little blitzed myself. Besides, it's kinda late."

Donna tilted her head sideways and pouted, trying to be cute but it just annoyed me. "Oh, Mike, come on. It's not that late. Are you sure you won't be coming back out?"

I slipped on a patch of ice and almost fell as Bobby leaned against me. "Goddamit!" I said, sounding harsher than I intended. "Yes, I'm sure."

"Well, okay then," Donna said, and she walked away quickly to catch up with Kerry.

"You sure you want to pass on that?" Fish said to me as we moved Bobby along.

"Yeah, hard to believe, but I am sure."

Bobby moaned miserably the whole way down the ramp to the dorm, through the lobby and halls and into his suite, which was located next to Bingham's.

Bobby's roommate, a mysterious African American guy named Andre Moon, wasn't in, but he had left his usual pungent residue of marijuana haze. Moon did more grass than the whole rest of the floor combined. Bobby gagged when he inhaled the sharp odor in the room. Fish and I dropped Bobby on his bed. I untied his high-top sneakers and threw them on the floor, and Fish pulled off Bobby's jacket and sweater. Bobby shook, goose bumps blooming on his cold glistening skin.

"Here," I said, grabbing a blanket, "help me roll up the poor S.O.B."

We wrapped Bobby in the blanket. Fish quickly mopped Bobby's Afro with a wet washcloth, but the dry vomit stuck in his hair. Bobby mumbled incoherently and then quieted, breathing heavily, steeped in alcoholic semi-unconsciousness.

"Let's go," Fish said, shaking his head while looking at Bobby.

We turned to leave and suddenly Bobby thrashed and sat upright.

"What do you want!" he screamed, his eyes wild.

"Nothing, Bobby, relax," Fish said.

"We just brought you in," I added.

Bobby calmed, rolling his eyes under heavy lids. "Oh," he said. "Leave me alone. I fuck up everything. I wanna die, I'm gonna die." He flopped his head down. "Something's all wrong, very wrong. I don't know what the fuck is going on."

His voice trailed off and suddenly he seemed sound asleep. Then I heard loud clapping behind us, and I turned to see Darrell Bingham leaning against the door just inside the room. He grinned wryly, a toothpick dangling from his lips, and applauded idiotically, flopping his hands around like a puppet out of control.

"Quite a show by Bobby Matson, my main, number one, favorite brotherman," he said, raising a fist in a mock salute and leaning forward so his ass bowed out.

"Fuck off," I said. My stomach muscles tightened.

"Toothpick?" Bingham offered, pulling two from his shirt pocket. Fish and I simultaneously gave Bingham the finger. "What happened to brotherman, anyway?"

"What do you think, genius?" Fish said.

Bingham pulled his toothpick from between his lips and then poked at his teeth. "Only one thing could do brotherman in like that," he said. "Too much o' de booze." He flicked his toothpick across the room, whipped out another one, and then said, "Mah main man be 'bout one dumb fuckin nigga cuz he don' know when to quit hittin de booze."

Feet shuffled just outside the door, and Andre Moon's vacant eyes struggled to focus on Bingham's face. Moon held a roach in a clip. He sucked deeply on it until the orange glow reached his lips.

"Shit, motherfuckers, I heard it, the magic fuckin word," Moon said softly as he exhaled and calmly placed the roach in his mouth, swallowing it slowly.

A good head shorter than Darrell, Andre looked up into Bingham's face and said, "It was you that said the magic word, you motherfucker."

Bingham leaned against the doorway smiling. He slowly lifted his fist again. "Say wha now mah brotha?" he said to Moon. Darrell pulled the toothpick from his mouth and offered it to Andre. "Pick, brothaman?"

"In your fucking eye, man," Moon said, standing on his tiptoes to push his chest against Darrell's.

"Andre, come with us," I said, but he ignored me.

Moon took one step back and threw a wild, arching punch that Darrell blocked by simply raising an arm. Then Bingham casually punched Moon squarely in the mouth; Moon reeled backward into the hallway and slumped against the wall, shaking his head and cupping his hand under his bleeding lip.

"Oh shit, shit, shit…" Moon moaned repeatedly, while Fish and I walked toward him.

"Christ, I feel like part of a fucking rescue squad tonight," Fish said to me as we slowly lifted Andre to his feet.

I heard a door close, and I knew Bingham had gone back into his own room.

"C'mon, Moon," I said. "It's been a rough night for you and Bobby."

Fish and I walked to the bathroom with Moon, whose lips were puffy and cut. Moon rinsed his mouth, spat repeatedly and angrily into a sink, and then looked at himself in the mirror. "Shit, I've got inner tubes for lips, man. Lookin pretty bad all-in-all," he said. He shook his head and faced us. "Might not even be able to toke for a while. But maybe I best try one little pal just to find out for sure." Moon's fat lips stretched into a quick painful grin as he pulled a joint from his jacket pocket. "Might just calm me down a little," he said, lighting the joint. "I'm gonna be all right. You guys just leave me here gettin my shit together."

Fish and I left him toking and slumped against the sink. We went back to our suite, and I realized it was only ten o'clock. I felt like I had been on an all-night binge.

"Nice idea you had about cruising, Fish," I said sarcastically.

"Okay, so it didn't turn out great." He kicked off his shoes and socks and started examining his toes while sitting on his bed. "At least it got your mind off that high school girl."

I sat at my desk and watched as the snow drifted steadily down. "Did it?" I said.

"It didn't?"

"No."

"So call her, you asshole." Fish rubbed viciously at his toes. "Hey, let me borrow your toenail clipper, will you?"

I fumbled around the desk drawer, found the clipper, and tossed it to him. Fish examined it skeptically. "Looks kind of dull," he said. "What's so great about this chick anyway?"

"Oh, man, she just, she's just got everything."

The wind swirled the snow around wildly outside our window.

Fish clipped with obvious difficulty. "Christ, it'd be easier and less painful just to pull my toenails off," he complained.

"She's just sort of natural…"

"Ah, a lot of those so-called natural types are just very well rehearsed at acting natural," he scoffed. "And this so-called clipper of yours really sucks."

I studied the odd-shaped mounds of snow in the distance. "A beautiful phony?" I said absently.

"Something like that," Fish said. "This natural thing is overrated anyway. What's it mean? No one escapes without warts or zits or hemorrhoids—that's all part of nature, too…Ouch! Son of a bitch! Look, I took a chunk out of what used to be my big toe." He stuck a foot into the air, pointing a reddened and slightly cut toe at me. "Damn! Do we have any bandages? Look, call her, and if she tells you to fuck off, go pay a visit to Donna. You know, man—best way to get over a girl is to get *over* another girl."

Fish hobbled around the room on the balls of his feet with his toes turned up in the air. He headed toward the door.

"Where are you going?" I asked.

"Down the hall to see if anyone has a band-aid so I can patch up this mess."

CHAPTER TWENTY-TWO

Fish closed the door, and I stared out the window. The snow had tapered. An occasional breeze lifted the fine flakes from our window ledge and whipped them into a small funnel. Soon, I knew, the snow would stop, leaving the landscape temporarily and beautifully altered. Inevitably, a thaw would come, the snow would melt, and grass, trees, roads, and buildings would look as if the mysterious white crystals had never touched them.

Impulsively, I picked up the telephone receiver and dialed Erica's number. The dull ringing sounded in my ear as I fought back the urge to hang up. I played with a paper clip that had been holding the syllabus for my writing class together. A man answered; her father, I guessed, I hoped. I spoke anyway.

"May I speak with Erica?"

"Who's calling, please?"

I told him my name and he said, "Mike? Just a minute."

I mangled the paper clip into a twisted line of metal. Why did he ask my name? Had she given him a list of people she would talk to? Was I on it? Was Bingham?

"Hello, Mike, are you there?"

It was Erica. I had been so deep into my own paranoia, I hadn't even realized she was on the phone.

"Uh, yeah, Erica?"

"Hi, Mike. How have you been?"

"Um...pretty good. How about you? How are things?"

I tossed the paper clip toward a trashcan. It hit the rim and dropped in.

"I'm okay, but I'm really busy getting ready for the party. Brian doesn't know a thing about it. He'll really be surprised. Will you be able to come? When I didn't hear from you I was afraid..."

"What party? Hear from me about what? I'm sorry, I..."

There was a long pause; then Erica spoke, her confusion evident: "Well, you know...or I thought you knew...the surprise party my family is planning for Brian. He's ships out next week and..."

Now it was my turn to sound confused: "I didn't know about any party. You never...I never heard you mention..."

"But Darrell Bingham was supposed to..." There was a silence on her end. Then Erica continued softly, "He was supposed to give you a sealed note from me. He had the balls to show up uninvited at Katie's the day after we went out with you two. We were busy packing for our ski trip. He pretended to apologize to her for running off with that waitress. He was so...so disgustingly condescending. While he was here, I wrote you a quick note about the party." She paused.

"You mean you didn't have a date with him?" I asked.

"*Me?* With *him?* You're kidding, right? Did you really think..."

"Well, I, hell, I don't know...I mean, he said..." My voice trailed off. I didn't like the way I sounded. I was thinking how Bingham had worked me, how he had made me doubt myself and Erica and whatever it was that seemed to be different about her. He had made me think that things couldn't work out the way I wanted them to simply because it was I who wanted them to work out that way. The truth, I realized in that moment, was that it wasn't really Darrell's fault—it was my own for not believing in myself. I just blurted, "Ah, hell, Erica, I'm sorry. But Bingham and I had a little disagreement and he's been avoiding me. So I didn't find out about the surprise party."

She told me the party was two days away—on Saturday. She even offered to pick me up, and I said okay. We didn't say much more because after I said I'd go to the party, she sounded happy but hurried. So I said I had to get back to work and we hung up. I immediately began to decode the entire conversation: friendly, warm tone (probably just my imagination); she really wants to see me (her first ten choices couldn't make it); she offered to pick me up (and I said yes, like an ass, because I have no wheels of my own— I should borrow Fish's car and drive out myself). I breathed deeply, leaned back in my chair and flipped on the radio. The Beach Boys sang about "fun, fun, fun" on ABC New York. I smiled stupidly to myself in my empty room.

Fish returned to the room with a band-aid wrapped around one big toe. "I swear, the more I see Bingham, the less I can stand him," he said. "I wound up having to go to his room for this band-aid. He comes to the door looking kind of preoccupied, and I catch a glimpse of Juliet Starlipper in the background hanging her bra on a chair—only saw her shoulder, unfortunately, no boobshot. He shuts the door, reopens it, hands me the band-aid and winks. What an asshole. But still, he's getting laid, and I'm here bandaging my toe. What an evening, an abortion really, just one big abortion of a night. Cruising gets ruined, poor crazy Bobby gets blind drunk, Kerry and Donna are depressed and disgusted, Moon gets punched out, I chop off a piece of my toe, you're in full mope, and Bingham, as usual, that schmuck has it all work out fine—he always comes out ahead, in there just screwing the night away. Bingham. You can't beat that guy, can you?"

I started laughing hard.

"You drunk asshole," Fish said, laughing at me. "What the hell's with you?

What's so funny?"

"Let's sing it together, Fish," I said through my laughter.

"What are you...? Sing what?"

"Our theme song, our goddam theme song. Come on...like the Beatles said, 'I'm a loooooooser .... I'm a loooooooooser...'" I shouted it loud, but I was laughing.

Soon Fish was shouting and laughing with me until our voices rang out throughout the entire floor. Yelling, filling the hallway, Fish followed me down to Bingham's room, shouting, "I'm a loooooooooooser ... I'm a loooooooooooser" at the top of our lungs outside his door until he opened it.

Darrell stood there in his underwear, and I screamed the lyrics in his ear, laughing wildly. He cursed us, and screamed back at us, and pushed us, but we were relentless, bellowing out of control, "I'm a looooooooser ... I'm a looooooooser" and then Bingham grabbed me, but Fish and I just kept laughing and screaming, "I'm a loooooooser... I'm a loooooooser..."

Bingham shook me hard, and my voice wobbled until, suddenly, I stopped shouting and punched him in the stomach so hard that his breath burst out in a gasp and he slumped slowly to the floor, moaning. I shouted several times into his contorted face as he crumpled, "I'm a loooooooser, I'm a..." but Fish had stopped shouting, and suddenly the room was silent except for Bingham's gasps and Fish and I breathing hard...and a muffled whimper like a punished child in hiding. I turned to see Juliet Starlipper softly crying in bed, wrapped in covers, her wide eyes staring fearfully first at me and Fish and then at Darrell, who was wheezing on the floor. She was whispering, "Don't... don't please don't" repeatedly, one hand holding her covers up to her chin and the other in front of her mouth. I started to say something—her palpable fear made me ashamed—but Fish pulled at my shoulder and said quietly, "C'mon, Mike, let's just go."

As I turned to leave, I noticed snow blowing furiously against the window in Bingham's room and the glass reflected Juliet's face—contorted, fearful, injured.

CHAPTER TWENTY-THREE

On the Saturday of Brian's surprise party, Erica was late picking me up. "She's forgotten," I said miserably to Fish. "I'm sure of it."

"Probably," he eagerly agreed.

I flicked him off and decided to kill some time by going downstairs to the laundry room, where I had clothes in the dryer. The laundry room always smelled of bleach, the perfect smell for a colorless room. Above the dryers was a bulletin board that usually had nothing at all on it except for the typical advertisement about who to call for the blowjob of your life, but this time as I pulled out my warm clothes, several items on the board actually caught my attention. The student group STEP had posted articles from magazines and newspapers about the various presidential candidates—or near candidates—and the organization's opinion of each.

The group favored McCarthy, though it expressed the hope that "his promises aren't as empty as his poetry." I imagined him writing an ode to the Soviet Union or appointing Allen Ginsberg as Secretary of State.

Beneath a photo of Robert Kennedy, pictured with his shirtsleeves rolled up as he walked amid an inner-city crowd of poverty-stricken blacks and Hispanics, STEP had written: "The man who feels guilt about his wealth seeks forgiveness from those he and his family have helped make poor." The comment seemed unfair to me. I thought, as I stacked my rumpled clothes into a laundry basket, how unfortunate it is that people are often stigmatized by a past over which they had no influence…and I wondered what Erica would think.

Hubert Humphrey smiled a particularly unflattering, witless grin from the bulletin board above a caption that read: "It takes more than a simple smile and the promise of happiness to rid the world of evil." Humphrey does always seem so damn happy, I thought, that he's hard to take seriously.

Finally, there was a large picture of saggy-faced Lyndon Johnson pasted above pictures of fire-gutted cities and dead soldiers. The caption below the pictures accused: "His 'War on Poverty' leaves millions searching through ashes for their homes; his **War on Vietnam** makes us criminals in the eyes of the world." And why, I wondered as I gripped the basket and waited for the elevator to take me upstairs, can't the leader of the land say "Negro" instead of "Nigra" on national TV, a pronunciation reminiscent of the racists who roamed my old high school in Virginia.

I returned to the suite and dumped the clothes on my bed.

"Still no trace," Fish said, taking exaggerated glances at his wristwatch.

"Cut it out, Fish," I said, exasperated. I sorted a couple of his shirts out from my laundry and flipped them onto his bed. "Look, asshole, if you ever see her, you'll know..."

There was a knock at the door, though it was half open. It was Erica. Unexpectedly, Katie was with her. I invited them in and introduced them to Fish in one of those awkward situations where, for a moment, everyone becomes preoccupied with their shoes or their watches. Fish's eyes widened after focusing on Katie, and he quickly ran his fingers through his perennially uncombed hair. Katie looked somewhat younger than she had that night with Bingham, but her eyes seemed brighter, as if she was amused. Erica beamed a smiling hello at me and touched my arm as her eyes flicked curiously around our suite.

"Jesus, Fish," I said to break the awkwardness, "it's a good thing we spent all morning cleaning in here. I wouldn't want these girls to think we were slobs."

Four sets of eyes glanced around at the haphazardly placed sweatshirts, jeans, underwear, books, and newspapers strewn around the room. Fish had once nailed about a dozen yarmulkes to the closet door to form a happy face that stared at us. A bumper sticker proclaiming "Brooklyn Dodgers Forever!" was stuck on the wall over my desk, and on my desk was a small photograph of a random Brooklyn fire escape that Erica stared at briefly, saying, "I like, I like." Then she said sarcastically in her semi-British, snobby accent, "Ohhhh, my, Katie, I do rather fancy the pop art here and the general ambiance, yes indeed." Then, returning to her natural voice, she said, "This actually looks a lot like my room."

"Sure," I said. Somehow I couldn't imagine that her room resembled our disaster area.

"If you don't believe her, you ought to visit it sometime," Katie said, teasing.

My face flushed slightly at the thought, and Erica's seemed to do the same. "Now that probably would *not* be very interesting," Erica said dramatically, rolling her eyes at Katie.

Katie browsed our record collection, and Fish carefully browsed Katie. She picked up an album by Tim Hardin and said, "I've heard of him, but I don't know where."

"It's Mike's," Fish said. "He collects all these guys no one's ever heard of. I'll put it on for you if you want."

"I'd like that," Katie said, staring at Fish.

"Tim Hardin wrote 'If I Were a Carpenter'," Erica said casually. She was the only person I had ever met who knew that fact other than myself; even Harry had not known it until I told him.

Fish, suddenly nervous, fumbled with the stereo but finally got the record on. He and Katie sat next to one another on top of one of the desks, Erica sat in one of the dusty Salvation Army chairs, and I sat across from her on the edge of my bed.

While the record played, the girls said their ski trip hadn't gone too well. I tried to hide my jealous pleasure. Erica complained about "a lot of commotion" but, she added, Katie managed to make everything a good time. Fish, suddenly hyper-animated, announced in a broadcaster's voice, "Ladies and gentlemen, coming to you straight from the potholes of the Jersey highways to the pristine slopes of Vermont, the world's first Joisy Ski Bunnies!" Katie laughed like it was the funniest thing she'd ever heard, and I asked Erica, as casually as I could, "So, uh, did you and Katie have to use your ski poles to fight off all the guys?"

Erica shrugged. "We weren't there to meet guys, just to ski and have fun," she said, dismissing my awkward attempt at prying. Then she nodded her head slightly and stared at me briefly as the Tim Harden song "Misty Roses" came on. I told Fish to turn it up. I said to Erica, "Hardin has a voice like a reedy old saxophone, but the words are nice."

"This is my favorite song on the album," she said.

I was surprised. "You've actually heard the album before?"

"I guess I bought the only other copy he sold," she said.

As she began singing softly with Hardin, Erica tilted her head so her hair hung slightly suspended. Then she pushed her hair back, revealing an ear, and I swear my body lurched involuntarily, as though her movement transmitted a subliminal prod. Hardin sang:

"You look to me like misty roses
Too soft to touch
But too lovely to leave alone..."

When the song ended, Erica smiled at me and again pushed her hair behind one ear. This time, I stood so quickly I think it shocked her because she laughed. I liked her smile so much, but I noticed again the slightly hard edges that always reappeared when her smile ended. She took me by the arm and said, "Are you ready to go? There are still quite a few things that I have to help my parents with at home." She squeezed my arm slightly and said in a half-whisper, "Come on," and led me out of the suite. "I think Katie wants to ask Dave something," Erica said to me in the hall.

"What do you mean?"

"Unless I'm very wrong, I think she's going to ask him to join us."

"You mean you think Katie and Fish…"

Erica chuckled. "Let's wait and see," she said, "but I think I could see something in their eyes."

She stood directly in front of me. We were alone in the hall. With the community bathroom just a few feet away, it was by no means the most romantic setting, but I could feel my face tinge with red again as I looked at her. Make a move, I thought. Hold her. Kiss her quickly.

"Erica," I said, stepping closer. She tilted her head a little. I moved faintly toward her lips just as a thunderous flush exploded from the bathroom. The surging sound of rushing water washed the romance out of the moment. We both laughed at that, and her eyes glistened.

Andre Moon stepped out of the john, puffing a joint. He spotted us, stopped, looked at Erica, then at me, then back at Erica. "Say, man," Moon muttered, "I mean, I'm buzzed, definitely, but even I can tell that is one beautiful girl, man."

He took a long drag, offered us a toke that we both reluctantly refused, and then Moon walked off, glancing back once to look admiringly at Erica again before disappearing in a haze of smoke.

Erica looked bemusedly at Moon, took my hand in hers, and led me back toward the room. "So tell me," I blurted out as we walked, "do you have about five or six hundred high school guys chasing you around?"

I said it jokingly, but I hoped to hear her response. Instead, she looked at me, then flicked her eyes downward, and started to respond flatly, "Look, Mike, let's not…" But I was saved from whatever embarrassment might lay ahead by Fish, who called out from the room, "Hey, Burns, can I wear your green sweater?"

"Why? Where are you going?" I called back.

Fish, with Katie on his arm, walked out of the room. He was pulling on his ski jacket over my green wool sweater. "I'm going with you," he said. "I'm one lucky Yid—I just made me a new friend."

As we left our building and walked in the cold toward the parking lot, I spotted a stack of heavy plastic cafeteria trays stuck in a mound of snow.

"Hey, wait, stop for a minute," I said, brushing the snow off of the trays. "Do you think these girls have ever 'trayed,' Fish?"

"Nah, they're skiers," he said, reverting to his announcer's voice: "Joisy Highway Ski Bunnies do not mess with cafeteria trays, Mike, come on, get real!"

Katie again laughed hard. Erica asked, "Why? What do you do with the trays?"

"We go traying," I said.

"What's traying?" Erica asked.

"Watch," I said, happy to demonstrate something Sally-Boy and I had actually done on icy Brooklyn streets, using trays from the bakery.

I walked a few feet away to the edge of the parking lot that rimmed a steep slope a couple of hundred feet long. I sat on the tray, digging my heels into the front, pulling my knees to my chest and gripping the thin edge with my fingertips. As I shifted my weight forward, the tray began to slide, and soon I glided rapidly on it over the snow. My hair flew back, and as I struggled for balance I saw pieces of sky and tree limbs and I heard voices, one that I thought was Erica's, shouting gleefully around me. And then I hit a rough spot in the snow, and the tray lifted slightly into the air. I lost my grip, spun, and was airborne. Of course, it was only for an instant, but it seemed so long—peaceful and long—as I glimpsed the sky and then the snow that rose slowly like a cold soft blanket to wrap around my face.

"Nothing to it!" I shouted, brushing the snow from my eyebrows. I was still smiling as I walked up the hill.

Erica knocked a clump of snow from my jacket. "Oh, it looks like such fun," she said. Katie and Fish were already sitting on their trays. Erica and I lined up behind them.

"On three, we all go," Fish said.

I glanced at Erica as Fish counted, and I saw her face tucked behind her knees and her legs folded beneath her tight jeans, straining slightly, gently as she slid forward, the wind catching her hair and lifting it into a blur as she started down the hill. Then I was close behind her, trying to focus as we bumped and spun. She lost control, screamed; I tried swerving but collided with her tray. Again, I floated freely for that instant that seemed like the clearest moment of my life. She rolled over, stopping face up, startled as she saw me approaching out of control, landing next to her, sliding toward her. I heard her laugh then, deeply, happily. She rolled in the snow like a child, turning her back for protection and ducking her head. I skidded on my side into her back where my weight pushed her deeper into the snow, and I came to a halt with my body flush against her, my face buried in her hair, now dampened with white flecks of snow.

For an instant, we stayed in that position, me wrapped around her like cellophane and smelling her hair and neck as we looked at the pure white-covered earth. There was no noise. Then, beautifully, from beneath me, Erica laughed the sincere, innocent laugh of childhood.

CHAPTER TWENTY-FOUR

I rode with Erica in her car; Fish drove his car with Katie riding by his side so he and I would have a ride back to campus after the surprise party for Brian. Erica and I were comfortably quiet at first as she drove past mounds of brown snow piled at curbsides.

"I guess we're out of things to talk about already," I said.

"I seriously doubt it," she said. "There's a lot I want to know about you."

"Like?"

"How about your major?"

"Obviously you want to make me uncomfortable right away," I said.

"Why do you say that?"

"Because I don't know my major. Pretty irresponsible, right?" I winced, expressing some honest guilt I'd been feeling.

"Shame on you, Michael," she teased, putting on her deep, authoritarian voice. Then she shifted quickly to her natural voice and said, "What are you considering?"

"Enlisting."

"No! Please tell me you're joking."

"Nah, I'm a coward."

"I doubt it, but you are evasive."

"That's because I don't know. I've considered English, poly-sci, and economics. I ruled out pre-med yesterday, nuclear physics last week, and the priesthood when I was about eleven and my cousin and I found out that priests are celibate; besides, I don't believe in prayer."

"Good reasons."

"Can't think of any better. Actually, I enjoy literature and writing, but my father may disown me if I choose it. 'What can you do with an English major besides teach?' he always says.

"But if you like it...doesn't that matter?"

"Not much, at least not to him. You know, he moved us out of Brooklyn when I was a kid so I would have more 'opportunity' as he always said. An English major isn't his idea of pursuing 'opportunity,' I guess. The truth is, I don't really know what I want to be when I grow up. If I grow up."

"Lit is my favorite subject," she said. "I love the worlds writers create. In so many ways, they're more real than reality."

"Lit's my favorite, too!"

"Since when?"

"Since you said it was yours!"

Erica shook her head and laughed probably more at my feebleness than anything else; after all, she had begun to talk about worlds created by writers, and I went right back to my sophomoric self. In the brief silence that followed, I could see that even behind the wheel, she was lovely and calm, even when facing things very much of *this* world, like the loose snow that spun up from the tires of trucks and spattered the windshield, or the rig drivers who rode past and craned their necks to get a second look at her. Still, although she was not intimidated by the rutted highways or frenetic Jersey traffic, there was always something, a tension around her mouth, lurking like a sniper in the brush.

"I can't wait to shut the door on high school and start college," she said, explaining that she and Katie had already been accepted at the University of Massachusetts in the fall and planned to room together. "I mean, so much of high school seems inconsequential or unnecessary...when you get the chance to study what you care about, it seems like you should satisfy yourself."

"You're right, but I do have guilt, like I should just do what my parents...my dad, especially...want me to do."

She was quiet for a moment, the said simply, "I guess."

We stopped at a red light. When it turned green, a truck coming from our left was cutting across the intersection. Since we were trying to turn left, which would have meant going around the truck, Erica waved it through. The truck driver, however, motioned for us to go. Erica stepped on the gas at the same time the truck driver did. Fortunately, they also slammed on the brakes simultaneously, the truck stopping inches from the side of the car. The now annoyed driver stuck his red face out of the window.

"Who's going, honey?" he shouted. "Me or you?"

Erica accelerated slowly, rolled down her window, and swung around the truck. "Me," she said calmly as she drove by, muttering, "Honey, my ass." Unruffled, she began talking again as though our conversation had never been interrupted. "You have all sorts of options still open, Mike. It's only your sophomore year."

I looked down the highway dotted with sad little truck stops and motels tinged the color of exhaust.

"I wish I could be so sure about the options," I said. "Sometimes I think I can see my whole life stretched out right in front of me like this road, bumpy and full of holes, but no option except to follow it."

"Well, Brian was definitely impressed with you."

"Brian? Really?" They had talked about me, I thought excitedly. "Obviously, your cousin is a man of rare perceptive abilities."

"Yes. He really is."

"What's his story anyway? Why the Marines?"

She said flatly, "He believes in it."

It sounded so simple. You believe, so you act. That was reason enough. Still, her voice sounded just short of carrying complete conviction, as if the word "but" was hovering like an unspoken shout.

"Do you believe in it, in his decision?" I asked.

She hesitated, then said, "I believe people have a right to their own beliefs."

"You're worried, aren't you?"

She nodded, said, "Of course..." and suddenly seemed in distant thought as we turned onto a side street of older homes surrounded by bare trees. She seemed to study the houses, then continued. "You know," she said softly, "Brian has never let me down, never lied to me, always helped me. Yes, I'll worry about him, but mostly I'm going to miss him."

Her face reflected the strain in her voice. We did not talk for the minute or two before we arrived at her home. Like a cat burglar, I stole glimpses of her while she was preoccupied. She watched the road; I studied her neck. She looked into the rear view mirror; I focused on the reflection of her eyes. She turned the wheel; I noticed her right blue-jeaned thigh lean reflexively in the direction of the turn. I breathed in deeply as though I was suffocating and she was a burst of life-sustaining oxygen. And, like oxygen, Erica offered strength:

You believe, so you act. You let people believe in their own beliefs. You seek acceptance but not by giving up your beliefs. Jesus Christ, I wondered, who's in high school here?

"Two more blocks," she said.

I glimpsed the mouth; the taut corners, I realized, were payment for something. There's a price for strength at any age; I had learned that on Brooklyn's streets from Sally-Boy. But the strength often comes, in part, from hiding something. Erica, I realized, was not so different in that way.

We pulled into her driveway, the snow piled neatly to the side. Her home was a split-level, more traditional than Katie's, but secure and comfortable looking. Fish and Katie pulled in behind us in the '62 Chevy.

"How's the old cougher?" I asked, patting Fish's car's hood.

"Reliable as ever," Fish said. He was proud of the car; it was sturdy, smooth-running. "You have to admit, Burns, it has never let us down."

"You can't ask for much more than that," Erica said, glancing knowingly at me.

I looked at her and smiled and slipped slightly on some ice that had built up on one of the flagstones leading to her doorway. I steadied myself by grabbing her arm tightly for a moment. Erica surprised me then by kissing my cheek.

CHAPTER TWENTY-FIVE

The bartender the Wakefields had hired kept nibbling at the fruit that people left in their glasses.
Pretty soon, every time any woman walked by, he'd
mumble something in what Erica later termed "extreme Jersey" and take on a very horny, pained expression. Eventually, he said he felt ill, and when he left, I
volunteered to tend bar, something I felt comfortable
doing from helping out the bartenders occasionally
at Silhouettes. Erica's father thanked me, and Erica
gushed that I had saved the party, so I stood behind
the bar in the family room feeling pretty smug.

From that vantage point I watched the rather odd
party, a party of harmonious contrasts, unfold. About

fifty guests spanned three generations: Brian and his fiancée and friends, his parents and their graying group of middle-aged executive types, and Brian's grandparents. It was a party for someone going off to fight a war, but Joan Baez, Simon and Garfunkel, and Bob Dylan songs played on the stereo. Taken separately, everyone and everything in the crowded room seemed like jagged, non-matching puzzle pieces, but put together, they all served a purpose of presenting a well-coordinated, cohesive picture. When I found myself leaning forward to hear people order their drinks, I realized the party had grown loud with a gentle, steady crescendo.

Brian said hello to me and walked around behind the bar to grab a beer for himself. Before he could return to his fiancee, Karen, however, he was cornered against the bar by two middle-aged men whose eyes seemed unsure whether they should reflect merriment or melancholy. The taller of the two men, who was hairy on every visible body part except the top of his head, put a long arm around Brian's shoulder and said, "I knew you would be a Marine some day, Brian. You had it in you all along. Your dad's brother, your dear Uncle Jack, would be proud too."

"Hello, Dr. Hawkins," Brian said as he tried unsuccessfully to maneuver away from having his back pinned to the bar. Brian turned toward me and said, "I'd like you to meet…"

He was interrupted when the other man, who wore heavy-rimmed glasses with lenses so thick the light red veins in his eyes seemed magnified into a network of rivers and tributaries, punched Brian in the stomach with his right hand. Brian tensed in time, but still let out a soft grunt.

"Pretty tough, pretty tight," the man with the glasses said without inflection. I noticed his left arm swung limply by his side.

"Are you kidding, Frank?" Dr. Hawkins said to the man. "Sure he's tight, in shape. He's a Marine, for cryin' out tears. All Marines kick ass! Right, Bri?"

"Oh, I don't know about that, sir," Brian said, looking self-conscious for the first time since I met him.

"Well, you're gonna do it, son, for us all and for old Jack McGee," Frank said. He looked at me and asked for scotch on the rocks. His magnified eyes had turned melancholy, and the red tributaries had grown plentiful.

"Damn right he's gonna do it," Dr. Hawkins said. "I'll have scotch rocks, too, son. Hey, Bri, you'll clean out those Viet Cong, just like they were a cancer up someone's ass."

"Cancer kills, unless you kill it," Frank said, grabbing the drink I handed him.

Brian just smiled at their comments. Frank rolled up his left shirtsleeve after taking a long pull on his drink. Dr. Hawkins chuckled: "Oh no, he's going to show his war wound. What's the saying? 'Old soldiers never die, they just bore others to death.'"

Frank's sleeve was all the way up, revealing a blue-pink, five-inch stretch of scar tissue where his biceps used to be. Black pockmarks dotted his forearm up to his shoulder as though someone had bored different sized drill bits into his skin.

"German grenade," Frank said. "Damn near blew my arm off. Still some shrapnel in there." He sipped his scotch and looked at Dr. Hawkins. "Thanks for the memories, right, Doc?"

"Ah, hell, Frank," Dr. Hawkins said laughing loudly. He scratched the tight skin across the top of his head and turned to Brian. "Frank forgets the good times, the friendships, the closeness..."

"No, I remember," Frank interrupted, pulling his shirtsleeve down with his right hand.

"Okay, then tell Brian where we first met up, Frank," Dr. Hawkins said.

"Outside Paris."

"Tell him *exactly* where."

Frank paused and his melancholy eyes peered at me and Brian from behind his heavy glasses. "In a farmhouse."

"Farmhouse hell!" Dr. Hawkins said, rubbing a huge hairy hand across his bushy eyebrows. He leaned toward me and Brian. "It was a whorehouse and not one of them ladies spoke English besides the madam,

and old Frank here was determined to bang every ma-
demoiselle in the place."

"Mission accomplished," Frank said without changing expression.

"Remember Peters?" Dr. Hawkins said, directing a
slight wink at Frank.

"Oh, sure. Tell these guys about him." Frank's voice
didn't change, but his eyes sparkled for an instant.

"Yeah, okay," Dr. Hawkins said. "This guy, a corpo-
ral named Peters...always horny, even hornier than old
Frank here...but one night Peters was sick and couldn't
make the trip with a group of us to the farmhouse. So
I go up to the door of the house and I knock—big
wooden door, heavy as hell. The madame, this huge-
titted older gal who could wrap those babies around
you and strangle you to death, she opens the door a
crack. She sees us and smiles and asks in that sexy
French accent, 'How many GIs tonight, monsieur?'" I
counted in my head and said, 'Let's see, there's six of
us without Peters.' She does a sort of doubletake, then
shrugs, and says all sexy, 'No peters, eh? Well, tell ze
men to grease up their sumbs and come right in!'"

Dr. Hawkins roared and pushed his hairy fist
against Brian's chest. Brian forced a laugh as he studied his beer. Frank made a noise that sounded like
a laugh, although his expression remained the same
and the redness in his eyes seemed to expand. Dr.
Hawkins, still laughing, looked at me for my reaction.

"Grease up their thumbs because 'no peters,'" I repeated stupidly through a strained laugh.

Somebody called Brian's name from across the room, and he used that as an excuse to say good-bye.

"Go ahead, Bri," Dr. Hawkins said, pushing his now empty scotch glass toward me and motioning for a refill. "See everybody tonight, you deserve it, Brian. You're a good kid. You're doing what's right, you know that."

Dr. Hawkins shook Brian's hand so hard it looked like he was trying to stimulate Brian's circulatory system.

"Thanks, Doc, I believe I am."

Frank, head down, slipped his empty glass toward me and tapped the rim. I poured him another.

Dr. Hawkins, still pumping Brian's hand, continued, "And it's not all bad either, kid. You're going to see people, get about as close to guys as you can get without marrying them." Then Dr. Hawkins turned to Frank. "He's ready for them, Frank. I know it. I've been giving him physicals since he was this high." The doctor turned an unsteady hairy hand down toward his waist.

"Thanks for coming, Doc, Frank," Brian said before walking away.

"And remember, Bri," Dr. Hawkins called out. "Clean 'em out just like I would a cancer."

"Cancer kills, unless you kill it," Frank muttered into his refilled glass.

Dr. Hawkins turned slowly toward Frank with his glass raised to about eye level. "To the old farmhouse," the doctor said.

"And to Jack McGee," Frank added.

The two men clanked glasses, and I saw that the flatness of melancholy had seeped into the doctor's eyes too, and I wondered about the man, Brian's uncle, a soldier named Jack McGee, whose name had popped up several times that night. Who was he? Where was he? The men walked away from the bar and mingled with the rest of the people, sharing stories with other vets, Dr. Hawkins' shiny head reflecting the light and Frank's left arm dangling uselessly by his side.

Their war was life itself for them, I thought—it was that way for my father and all of his friends, too. And we all owed them so much, because the war they fought made moral sense, had clear enemies, goals, boundaries. The people of that generation made their sacrifices out of expectation, certainly, but also out of honor and commitment and, most important, out of their personal belief that what they were doing was essential to sustain all that they loved. And because of that, as they talked about their war a generation later, it sounded genuinely beneficial and fundamental, just another part of growing up, like shaving or getting your driver's license or sneaking beers onto a fire es-cape. But the lingering pain of their war was evident in their eyes and in their stories and in the lasting reminders, like Frank's arm and their references to the mysterious Jack McGee.

Those who had returned alive made it all seem so worthwhile—they built sturdy homes of brick with neat rooms and equally sturdy foundations, as my father did for us so we could move out of Brooklyn, and their families reflected their homes, solid, strong, enduring, made to ensure security, to reinforce hopes, to protect. And I wondered, as I served drinks, when you lose someone, do things actually change, or do they remain the same for the family members of those who never return, those who are never seen or heard from again, whose lives now endure only in memory? Would they trade the security of now for the presence of the missing? I hoped the answer was yes—just as I was certain I would trade the present for Sally-Boy's return.

Brian was about to go off to a different war now for a different time, a war whose muddled purpose spurred anger, confusion, and violent disagreement among family members living in those sturdy post-World War II homes. I poured the people drinks and wondered how many of them recalled how they felt the night before they got shipped out. Did they think they'd be laughing and joking about it someday? I looked long and hard at Brian and Karen to see a crack in their composure, some weakness in their eyes, some uncertainty, but they remained completely gracious throughout the night, as though tomorrow would be just another day. They were entering the unknown, yet they showed nothing but the confidence bred by conviction. My stomach rolled a little as I realized that I was fearful...but they were brave.

CHAPTER TWENTY-SIX

Erica's father walked over to the bar and offered to relieve me, but I told him not to worry about it. He leaned over and half whispered, "Good thing, Mike, because I don't know how to mix a goddam thing!"

I liked him, a leather-skinned man named Warren who everyone called "Cap" because, in the early forties, he had captained the University of Massachusetts football team. He wasn't a big man, though, and I got the impression he probably made captain more because of his leadership qualities than an abundance of football talent. His eyes were about a shade darker than Erica's, and they were kind.

Erica came to the bar and asked me to get everyone's attention for a toast.

"You get their attention," I said, taking a sip of my second or third beer of the night.

"Come on, Mike, I'm not good at that," she said. She had been drinking rose' wine, at least two glasses, and the tint of the wine had settled in her cheeks. I hoped the shine in her eyes was from something other than the wine.

"Where are Fish and Katie?" I asked. I had seen them infrequently and, when I did, Katie was tugging the wide-smiling Fish around to meet people. On the rare occasions that I saw him, I called him "Mr. Grins" because of his big, pasty smile.

"They're around somewhere," Erica said. The redness deepened in her cheeks.

I leaned across the bar and asked with exaggerated secrecy, "You mean they slipped into a quiet room somewhere?"

"Why no, what a crude insinuation," Erica said, feigning insult. "I just mean Katie is out introducing him to more people, um, somewhere...I'm sure... maybe?"

I purposely reached too far for her nearly empty wine glass, so my fingers touched her wrist, and I slowly and gently stroked her hand. My gesture had been purposely ambiguous. I figured she could take it seriously or humorously, giving me an out either way.

Instead, she left me confused by looking directly into my eyes and smiling somewhat slyly. She leaned forward, her face just an inch or so away from mine, and I felt my own face flush as I thought she was going to kiss me. Instead, she whispered, "Now, Mike, please see if you can get everyone to..."

Just then, the noise level dropped noticeably, and for a moment, I feared that someone had fainted. Instead, practically every head in the room swiveled toward the stairway. A young man with a stocky, powerful build, straight, shoulder-length brown hair, and a full beard stood and quietly glanced around the room. He looked serious and intense, his expression contemptuous, yet amused.

"Who is it?" I asked Erica. I almost whispered.

"Tim," she said. "We didn't think he'd come."

Erica looked worried, but in the next instant she was by Tim's side. She kissed his cheek, but his expression didn't really soften. People began talking again, and soon Erica walked Tim across the room toward Brian and Karen. The two brothers shook hands and Tim hugged Karen, but his expression remained stoic. Katie and Fish were next to greet him followed by the McGees and Wakefields.

Erica angled Tim toward me, but someone distracted her, and he walked up to the bar alone. Up close, he looked even stronger and his brown eyes possessed an eerie uneasiness. Lips drawn tight, he seemed incapable of loosening his jaw even when he spoke.

"J.T.S. Brown and water," he said quickly. His eyes flashed at me and then darted away.

He was the first person of the night to ask for booze by a brand name. "Don't have it," I said. "How about another bourbon?"

His eyes snapped into focus with mine. A wave of intimidation rocked me, then quickly passed.

"Best goddam bourbon there is." He squeezed the words out of his tense mouth. "What kind of company is it that sends out a bartender without the best goddam bourbon there is?"

"Company? Oh, you think I'm employed to work here..." I started to laugh, but he never changed expression. "No, you see, the bartender got sick so I took his place. Actually, I think he got drunk from sucking on fruit from other people's drinks. I'm Mike, Erica's date."

Before I could extend my hand, Tim muttered, "Shit," and then spun around, his hair flying as he walked away without a drink.

I began straightening a few things behind the bar when Erica's father approached me again and said, "I think I can fake tending bar for the rest of the way, Mike. Erica will kill me if I don't let you out from behind this bar. Besides, she talked me into making the toast."

Cap carried a streak of sub-surface happiness in his features. He was vice president of sales and part owner, along with Katie's father, in a company that produced and sold cabin cruisers like *Happy Times* that I had seen in Katie's garage. He patted my shoulder as he took my place, and I could see the impact he probably made by using a similar gesture in a business deal.

I began looking for Erica amid the loud swirl of guests, but I bumped into Katie and Fish instead. They exchanged long glances at one another, and she kept leaning against him while they talked to other people.

"Hey, Mr. Grins, I see you're still walking around showing that big toothy one," I said, exaggerating the wide smile that was plastered on his face.

"How'd you escape from behind the bar?" he asked.

"My date, yeah, she's begging to see me. Uh, by the way, do you happen to know where she is?"

"Erica's over there, Mike," Katie said, pointing across the room. Erica was sitting on a sofa, still talking to Tim. Even from across the room, I could read her face, always full of expression. She was trying to draw Tim out. Her eyes would widen, she'd smile, and she'd reach out with a long, graceful arm and push jokingly against his sturdy shoulder. But his face remained taut.

A shrill whistle pierced the room. Cap sat on a bar stool with a beer held high and whistled again. "Thanks for your attention, folks," he said. Mrs. Wakefield, a slim, neat woman with a beautiful smile, stood next to him. Her name was Elizabeth, but Cap called her Betty, which he often bastardized playfully to "Biddy."

"Cap would like to propose a toast to our wonderful nephew, Brian," Mrs. Wakefield said.

Everyone raised their glasses, except for me. I was caught in the middle of the room with no drink and no one I knew around me. For an instant, I was stung by awkwardness. Then I felt Erica by my side, close, holding my arm and kneading her fingers gently into my biceps. I wanted to put an arm around her shoulders and squeeze her against me. Not here, I thought, not now. But soon.

"You can't toast without a drink, Mike," she said, holding her half-full wine glass between her lips and mine. "Share mine?" She moved the glass to my lips.

Brian and Karen stood with the Wakefields and McGees. Katie's mother clutched a tissue. Mr. McGee looked handsome and a little formal in his three-piece suit. He stood next to Brian, and in that moment before the toast, Mr. McGee looked thinner and older than he had all night. Fish and Katie stood with the McGee family, but Tim remained on the sofa where Erica had left him. He did not face the bar.

"Okay, okay," Cap Wakefield said. "I'll make this short and sweet."

The room quieted. I felt some discomfort at seeing Doc Hawkins and Frank standing side-by-side with their drinks at the ready, and I suddenly realized I still didn't know who the "Jack McGee" they had mentioned was. Even Mr. Grins was serious now. He turned his mouth down wryly when he saw me, and he pointed quickly at me and then at himself, and I knew he was thinking what I was thinking: This could be us some day soon. I focused on Brian...steady...strong... going off to war...look carefully now because...no, you can't think that way...think that way and you get confused...think about who he'll be fighting and why and where and nothing makes sense...but it does to him... he chose it, this guy who graduated Dartmouth, who makes miniature wooden ships, who has a family business and a fiancee waiting for him, he chose it, and we all have a right to our own beliefs...yes, you believe, so you act...you do what you have to do, you persevere like Morris and Tzipi Lieberman...and, like Shayna Lieberman, if she exists, you choose to work in the slums...and like Dad, who chooses to paint his own picture of the war...and like Sally-Boy who knew his time...

"A lot of us in this room were in the Corps," Cap said in a slow, deep voice. "We know the sacrifice, and we know the pride. And we take pride in seeing men like you, Brian, answering the call even in these confusing times. To be a great soldier, you have to have courage, strength, commitment, and—most of all— heart. The Marine slogan says, 'A few good men.' Well, in you, my nephew Brian, that's exactly what they are getting—a few good men. Brian, good luck, thank you, and *Semper Fi*."

Everyone burst into applause. Brian waved with one hand and hugged Karen with his other arm. Then, he said simply, "Thank you all. I appreciate you being here. I appreciate the chance to serve my country. And I appreciate all that my family has given me. Mom and Dad, here's something to remind you of all the happy times we've had, and *will* have, together." Brian reached into a canvas bag and pulled out the model of the *Happy Times* he had made with his own hands and gave it to his parents, who clutched it and then tearfully hugged him close.

Glasses clanged like the chimes of a clock, and long, silent swallows of drinks followed, and that led to a silence that grew quickly. Soon, people started to leave. Fish and Katie talked alone in a corner. Tim leaned back, still on the sofa, staring at the ceiling. The stereo was off for good now. Erica was saying good-bye to some people, when I heard Cap's voice behind me. He was talking to his wife.

"Biddy, I'm thinking of your brother Jack," Cap Wakefield said to the former Elizabeth McGee, who dabbed at her eyes with tissues. "It's twenty-three years. Hard to believe. Twenty-three years since Jack and the other boys of Easy Company fought at Iwo."

"Oh, I know, I know," said Erica's mother, the sister of Katie's father, Danny. "And it is so hard for Danny to see Brian going away. Brian looks so much like Jack in that uniform. Danny said to me earlier, 'Our brother is looking out for my son, Betty; I just know it.'"

"Of course he is," Cap said, shaking his head and holding his wife close. "Of course…"

They hugged and my mind jumped to the Iwo Jima Memorial in Arlington, Virginia, not far from where I lived. I recalled the time my father took me and Sally-Boy to see it during Sally-Boy's only visit to Virginia. Iwo Jima was the last stop on a tour of monuments that day, and it was the one that most impressed Sally. He just stood there staring at the bronze soldiers frozen in time, planting the flag at Iwo Jima.

"So what do you think?" my father asked after briefly explaining the heroics of Easy Company.

"Brave," I said in my youthful simplicity.

"Sally?" Dad asked. "How about you? What do you think?"

Even in that moment, Sally-Boy was filled with Brooklyn tough and that strange perception of events that often made his behavior and statements seem removed or peripheral to the moment. So he continued looking at the statue intently, and then turned to my father and said, "Lotta people must've helped them get to there."

"Well, yes," my father said, and he explained that many members of Easy Company gave their lives.

Sally seemed to think this over carefully, and when he turned and looked at me and my father, his eyes were red, and he said simply, "Uncle Kevin, it's the best thing I ever seen, the best, but it's sad—I mean, these men, these ones in the statue and the others… where are they, Uncle Kevin? Who will ever know about them?"

The party started to thin, and I helped Erica stack glasses behind the bar and thought how Jack McGee had died at Iwo Jima but now, a generation later, a nephew he had never met was leaving his family to fight another war against an enemy Jack McGee and his buddies in Easy Company never knew. And how a kid from Brooklyn's streets had been so moved by the statue and the story behind it that he said to me that night, "I seen that statue, Mikey, and now I gotta go home and make the deliveries for the *Panificio* and for One-Eyed Jimmy. What those guys done; what I do; it just don't make sense."

CHAPTER TWENTY-SEVEN

I followed Erica as she walked up a half flight of stairs toward the kitchen where the only light came from above the stove. Erica sat at the glass-top table, staring into her empty wine glass.

"Hi," she whispered. "I think I drank a little too much."

She wore a light blue blouse under a soft plaid jumper cut a couple of inches above the knee. Her legs were slender but firm with the long calf muscles of graceful athletes. The evening had left her hair somewhat mussed, individual strands slightly lost amid the dark fullness. The skin on one hand was wrapped tightly around the stem of her glass.

"I think a lot of people drank a little too much to-night," I said, sitting down in a chair next to her.

"You were so helpful, Mike. Thank you. I'm going to take you to dinner or something."

"I'll take 'or something.'"

She smiled. The yellow kitchen light softened the still-hard corners of her mouth.

"You really look nice tonight," she said, lightly touching the sleeve of the burgundy ski sweater I was wearing. "I like that color on you."

"Thanks. I thought maybe I was underdressed, all those guys with ties."

"No, you always look nice. I'll bet..." She paused and looked at me, then back at her glass, which she rubbed with long, steady fingers.

"Go ahead, Erica. Say it. I'll talk, if you will." For an instant, I thought maybe someone else had entered the room and had begun speaking, but the words were mine.

Erica shook her head slowly. Her eyes remained drawn to the glass as though it held an answer, or kept a secret

"Erica...look, I just..."

"No, Mike, it's too soon. It wouldn't be fair." She raised her eyes as if she had more to say, but she stopped and turned away.

"Too soon for what? What do you mean? I don't..."

The hard corners of her mouth turned downward sadly as she lifted a hand from the glass and placed a finger to my lips and then slid her hand back down the stem of the glass.

"Okay," I said, "this isn't the last time, is it? We'll have other times to talk, right? So whatever you want to do or whatever you want to talk about is fine with me."

"Yes, anything you want to do, or talk about," she said. I raised an eyebrow. "Well, almost anything," she added quickly. But she relaxed her grip on the glass, sighed, and ran a hand through her hair.

We sat alone quietly making small talk in the kitchen as sounds of the party steadily ebbed. People left, and Erica's parents went to Katie's house for a nightcap. Then Tim came into the kitchen to say good night to Erica, and she introduced us. He shook my hand quickly.

"The bartender, right?" he asked.

I nodded.

Tim kissed Erica's cheek. She hugged him and said, "Tim, don't worry."

"Yeah, sure," he said. "I won't, if you won't." He rested his head on her shoulder. Then, with an empty smile, he backed away. He turned toward me, flipping his hair off his shoulder with one hand, and asked, "Are you going to be a soldier?"

"Not anytime soon," I said.

"Not anytime at all, if you're smart."

He said good night and left, and I said to Erica, "He shook my hand like I had poison ivy."

"He's just so worried, so angry. Tim hates the war and all it stands for. He graduates in May."

"No deferments once he's out, not even for graduate school anymore."

"He doesn't know what to do."

Brian and Karen walked into the kitchen. We followed them to the front door. Erica hugged him tightly and said, "Take care, Brian." Her eyes filled with tears.

"Sure, sure," he said, smiling at her emotion.

"And write."

"I will."

"You won't."

"Well, I definitely might, I definitely sort of promise that I probably might."

She laughed, hugged him again, started to speak, and then choked back her words. She turned to say good-bye to Karen, and Brian shook my hand and *he* wished *me* luck...for what, I had no idea. I opened the front door. Erica turned her head away as Brian and Karen walked to the car. The night air felt good to me, but Erica shivered. She held tightly to my arm as we watched Brian and Karen drive off. Katie and Fish were alone in the garage, supposedly putting folding chairs and other party items away, but they were apparently able to perform those tasks in silence...and darkness.

"Can I get you something hot to drink?" Erica asked as we walked back to the kitchen.

"How about something cold instead?"

"What would you like?"

"Anything, just so it's non-alcoholic."

"Name it."

"Okay. Iced tea."

She opened the refrigerator door, looked around and said, "Uh, we don't have any."

"That's okay. I'll have hot tea."

"No. I'll make some hot tea for me and iced tea for me, I mean for you...iced tea for you."

Erica suddenly seemed charged with nervous energy. She swept her hair back over her ears and avoided my eyes. She hadn't looked directly at me since we had returned to the kitchen. The house was quiet; even the rare sound of clacking pool balls had ceased completely. Erica reached for the tea canister and clumsily removed about a dozen tea bags. Then she filled the brown teapot with water, and as she went to place the kettle on the stove, some of the water sloshed onto the counter. Her movements seemed awkward, and I was amused watching her. I leaned, half-grinning, against the counter.

"Is this your first time, Erica?"

"For what, the first time?"

"You know...making iced tea and all."

"Uh, Mike, this is going to sound weird but would you just sit down at the table? And don't, um, don't look at me, please."

"Relax, Erica. I'll have hot tea, too. It doesn't really matter to me. Hey, I'll drink ice water, okay?" I opened the refrigerator door and said, "I won't drink milk. I draw the line at milk. I had a cousin who said, 'Mikey, I'm tellin ya, milk is pee from the cow, that's what it really is—milk, it ain't nothin but cow piss.'"

She forced out a laugh and then closed her eyes tightly, her mouth tensing, then relaxing. "You're crazy," she said. She opened her eyes. "But you asked for hot tea, I mean iced tea, and I'll make it for you...the... iced tea. But just, please, Mike, sit down. God, look how many tea bags I've taken out! I'm hopeless." She shook her head at the pile tea bags on the counter. "Oh, I'm a wreck," she said.

She was stuffing the bags back into the canister and one broke open. "Look at me," she said, brushing the loose tea into the sink. She stood close to me but looked straight into the sink. Her movements were still slightly jerky, and as she turned on the water, it splashed all over her hands. I quickly grabbed a dishtowel and held it out for her. She thanked me, but when she reached for it, instead of letting go, I held it and playfully, but slowly, dried her hands for her.

"Let me do it," I said, giving her Crazy Stare and adding in a vampire voice, "I vant to help you, please von't you let me help you, you must let me help you." I wrapped the towel all around her hands, flipping it so it flew up in front of her face. Then I tied the ends together. Erica laughed, but the nervousness still showed behind her laughter. The kettle whistled.

"Oh, the water's ready," she said.

"How do you know this invormation?" I asked, still in Crazy Stare and vampire voice.

"Enough with those eyes and that voice, okay? The whistle—that means..."

"Really?" I said, exchanging Crazy Stare and vampire voice for overly sincere voice.

She looked at the ceiling in mock despair. "Okay, so I'm gullible. So take advantage of me."

"Oh, you do not have to beg me to do that!"

She shook free of the dishtowel. With the kettle in one hand, she bumped into the tea glass filled with ice cubes, almost knocking it over. Then she placed the kettle back on the burner.

"Wouldn't you like to sit down, Mike?" Without looking at me, she gestured toward a chair. "You'd be a lot more comfortable, really."

"No," I said, moving closer to her. The whole house was quiet. The only sound was the simmering steam of the water in the kettle. Erica's back was to me. I placed my hands gently on her shoulders.

"Mike...if..."

"Shhhh, relax." I spoke into her hair. "Come on. Look at me." She slowly lifted her head and for a moment held my gaze. Her eyes were so blue. Then she looked down. I stroked her arms lightly. "Take it easy. I'll just stand here and look at you. That's all."

"Why are you so nice to me, Mike?"

She still looked down, not into my face, but she raised her hands to my waist.

"It's pretty easy, you know, Erica."

I moved my right hand slowly to her cheek. My fingers seemed to blend into her skin, absorbed by the smoothness, melted by the warmth. I brushed her hair back so it fell lightly over her shoulder, let my fingers float down her flushed cheek to her chin, and lifted her face to mine. Andre Moon was not around this time to wash away the moment with a plunge of the commode handle, so her eyes, blue as swatches of an endless sky, drew me closer. The hardness vanished from her lips; our faces moved together. We kissed, just once, but a long kiss, and she sighed. Her hands slid up my back on the outside of my sweater. She pulled me toward her. My hands gently pushed against her shoulder blades and we held each other.

As I stood there holding her, feeling her full body against me, I couldn't help laughing to myself at the thought of how strange it all was—that whoever or whatever determines where and when our lives are headed must have chuckled at the fact that I was in New Jersey, sometimes called the "Armpit of the Nation," holding a girl two years younger than I, who was helping me see myself more clearly than ever.

The teakettle hissed quietly behind us, but it was not the mocking hiss I had heard from the diesel engines when I last left Washington. It was more like the soft sound of breathing, the sound of life itself.

CHAPTER TWENTY-EIGHT

The phone in our suite rang every night during the week after Brian's party. Whenever it rang, I jumped, anticipating Erica. Every time, it was Katie calling for Fish. I pretended to work while I listened to Fish, whose voice, with each hour-long conversation, grew richer and more charged with a scarcely contained giddiness.

"Sure, you know I do..." he'd say softly. "Terrible...Just for the weekend...Me and Mike, there wouldn't be anyone else here...I hope so, I hope you mean it...Different, just different...Yeah, exactly...me too, me too..."

I tried calling Erica twice that week. The first time there was no answer. The second time, Erica's mother answered and said, "Oh, hello, Mike. She's heading out the door now. Hold on."

Erica came to the phone and said, "Hi, Mike. I'm glad you caught me."

"Going out on the town?" I asked.

"Just to the library; always a big party there," she said emphasizing her sarcasm.

"Me too," I lied.

Fish was sitting across the room, and he turned his thumbs up when he heard me say that.

"Sorry I'm in such a rush," Erica said. "Things are kind of hectic at school."

"Yeah, I know what you mean." Fish raised a fist in salute. "I just wanted to know if you'd like to come up for the weekend. There's a Hell's Angels Party some group is throwing. Fish already asked Katie."

"I'd like to come, but I'll have to check and see what my parents say."

"Oh, I know," I said.

Fish tilted his head back and smiled.

"But I think it will be fine," Erica said.

"Really?"

Now Fish made smacking noises with his lips, and I made a grand gesture out of giving him the finger. He walked over to the dartboard hanging inside the utility closet in our suite and began pulling out the darts.

"Yes, it sounds great," Erica said. "I'll see what my parents say and call you back later tonight or tomorrow. Thanks again for all your help last Saturday."

"I enjoyed it."

Fish coughed loudly.

"And thanks for calling, Mike. I really have to run. I'll see you Friday."

"I hope so."

We said good-bye and hung up. Fish was filled with enthusiasm and brimming with bits of personal philosophy.

"This love thing is a lot like learning how to throw darts, when you think about it," Fish said.

"Oh fuck, here you go again. I think you're thinking too much," I said.

He fired a bullseye, as usual. "Let's throw to see who buys sandwiches," he said.

I said okay, knowing full well that it meant I would pay since I had never beaten Fish at darts. The many pockmarks in the door surrounding the board were almost all my doing. But Fish, the former high school quarterback, never missed the board, and he almost always nailed a bullseye. He threw several more right next to the first one. And suddenly, he was Fish the Philosopher, the Plato of Love.

"You know, Mike, when you first start fooling with girls and you're all groping and fumbling around, it's like throwing at that dart board. You're not quite sure if your aim is true, so you experiment. Once in a while everything clicks and it's bullseye! But there's always that worry that you can't hit it consistently, you know, like you're going to lose your control and that dart's gonna land smack in the middle of the wall. Then you have to start working toward the center again."

Another of Fish's darts found its mark.

We were both sitting in the tattered Salvation Army chairs. Fish slumped casually in his, which made his accuracy all the more amazing. He got up to collect the darts and total his score. Eight of the ten were in or around the bullseye. It was my turn to throw, and though I knew I should stand in order to improve my horrendous aim, I was going to try to take Fish on at his own game, so I just sat there and pretended to zero in on the target.

"It's not such a weird idea you have, Fish. We all go through that testing ground. I'm still going through it."

"Jesus, Mike, aren't you going to stand when you throw?"

I shook my head.

"No, no, Fish, my Screwball Philosopher, I am not standing. I'm just going to shoot from the hip. I might let all ten fly at once, might throw them backwards, might close my eyes and spin around in circles before I throw."

"Don't fuck around. The last time you got cute you almost hit Bingham, and he was sitting in his room."

"Listen, if I ever hit Bingham with a dart, I'm going to have the pleasure of taking aim beforehand."

My first dart landed in the upper right hand corner of the door, a good two feet from the perimeter of the board. I lobbed the second dart and it scraped the ceiling, turned downward and, incredibly, stuck on the top of the dartboard, parallel to the door.

"God almighty!" Fish bellowed. "I've never seen a shot like that! If you can do it again, I'll buy the sandwiches, no matter how few points you score."

"Forget it," I said. "There's only one shot like that in a person. I'm not even going to try it again. I didn't even try it that time, come to think of it. I'll win my sandwich fair and square."

I held the dart in front of me at eye level and aimed. Fish jumped behind me. My next two darts sailed into the outermost edges of the board.

"Now, according to the analogy you've been developing, Oh Great Dorm Philosopher, those darts indicate I've just held hands with a couple of girls."

"Yeah," he said from behind me. "Now let's see if you can use those to draw a bead on the bullseye and actually score a girlfriend."

My next dart hit the doorknob and fell to the floor.

"The problem," I said as Fish groaned, "is that one man's doorknob is another man's bullseye."

I threw the next two darts at the same time. One hit the board, the other tailed off and stuck in the door.

"I'm hot now!" I shouted. "Look out, mama, I'm drawing a bead! I can feel it! Bulls'-ass coming up! True love on the way!"

I threw hard and the dart sailed deeply into the door, quivering as it stuck. Then I stood with a leg on each arm of the chair. Fish made a dramatic leap over the top of his chair and hid.

"I wanna woman, I wanna woman, I wanna woman!" I shouted at the two darts in my hand.

I teetered, then caught my balance. I glimpsed myself in the mirror, saw my hair bouncing around my ears and neck. I puffed up my chest, yelled, "Gimmee woman, woman, woman!"

Fish cursed loudly from behind the chair as I made a dramatic wind-up, but instead of throwing hard I lobbed the dart gently. Too gently. It dropped harmlessly to the floor.

The phone rang and I still had one dart left. I knew who would be calling. So did Fish, so he answered. While Fish talked softly and confidently, I played with the last dart. His back was to me. I walked up to the board and carefully placed the dart deep into the bullseye. Then I counted my money to make sure I had enough to buy the sandwiches, and I got our ski jackets out of the closet.

When Fish hung up the phone, he wore a slightly dazed grin. "She's too much, Mike," he said. "Different, that's the only way to describe her...I don't care about anything else...it's just...just how I feel." He caught the jacket I tossed him, and he noticed the dart I had put in the bullseye. "You made one, Mike! Bullseye! Look at that! It's good luck. You'll see this weekend. Katie says Erica called her right after you two talked. She can come. They can't wait to get up here. See? Bullseye!"

"It'll be a good time," I said.

Fish didn't pick up the flatness in my voice. Why hadn't Erica called me back herself?

Fish, more animated and youthful than I had ever seen him, talked and I responded mechanically. Caught up in his own exuberance, he didn't perceive my doubts, though I could feel them creeping up slowly, distinctly. The knots in my stomach, the too loud laughter. He mistook the nervous energy and uncertainty that punctuated my conversation for exuberance of my own.

"I heard you schmoozing on the phone, Mike, don't kid me," he said, tying his shoes. "I know what was going on."

"What?"

"She's saying, 'I love you...I miss you...I want your body...I dream about you' and you're playing it so cool, 'Me too...Sure...I know what you mean.' Look, Mike, I know, because I do the same thing. When you're around and Katie's telling me those things, those are the same things I say." He slipped into his jacket. "Let's go. A couple of sandwiches, a couple of beers to celebrate."

"Celebrate?"

"Being in love, man! It makes me feel like telling the school, the war, the world to shove it, just the hell with everything else!"

My best friend continued to overflow with energy, talking, laughing, singing. He thought we were sharing, but I was envying. Like a parasite, I drew from his relationship with Katie to imagine how mine might be with Erica. He seemed sure; I knew I wasn't. Erica and I had shared one kiss, one sweet, confusing kiss, and then Katie and Fish had emerged from the garage, disheveled shells of themselves. He had said to me later, "We weren't in that garage saying a '*brucha*'...you know, a blessing...to one another." Fish was sailing, and I was bumping along for the ride.

As I turned off the lights to the room, I noticed the visible chill of frost that clung (was it permanent now?) to our suite window. Suddenly it struck me that everything on campus around campus and even around the world seemed cold. News was worse than ever with the war's ever-increasing intensity, draft calls going up, Harry dropping me a note warning me about my father's anger over my hair, Sally-Boy showing up everywhere in my uncertain mind. I seemed to live on ice where everything slipped and patterns changed, and where what I thought would hold my weight suddenly lurched to leave me stumbling, feet clumsily askew in a panic-stricken search for balance.

CHAPTER TWENTY-NINE

I was buying so I picked out a bar and grill, a gray place next door to an even more gray fast-food store. There were a million such grills along Jersey's bleak highways. Nothing in particular attracted me to this one other than the fact that it was on our side of the road. Neither of us had ever been there before, but Fish didn't seem to mind. We sat at the bar where the bartender, an elderly one-armed man with deep creases like smiles on his forehead and cheeks, greeted us. He wore a brown cardigan sweater over a white shirt. The sweater's bottom two buttons were buttoned, the rest were not, and the empty left sleeve was pinned neatly behind his back.

"Ham and Swiss?" he asked with a smile, making sure he had heard our orders correctly.

"Yes," I said. Fish nodded, looked at me, and said, "I'm going all the way over to the other side tonight, my man—doing the ham *and* adding cheese on top of the meat. Ain't nothing Kosher about FishJew!"

The bartender, who looked pleasantly confused by Fish's pride in violating Jewish custom, asked, "Wheat? Rye? White?"

"Rye," I said.

"Me too," Fish added.

"How 'bout I grill that bread?"

"Sure. Sounds good," Fish said. I agreed.

"Beer?" The bartender raised his eyebrows with this question and the creases along his forehead deepened.

"Two Bud draughts," I said.

He brought out two frothy mugs in his one hand. I reached to pay for them, but the bartender waved his hand. "Run a tab?

"Okay," I said. "Thanks."

Two men in their early thirties, slick mini-Elvises, shared a pitcher of beer and shot pool at a good-sized pay-to-play table in front of the bar's only window. Smoke hung thick in the shaded yellow light above the pool table. In a corner of the dark room, a balding man leaned forward and spoke intensely to a woman with teased gray hair. She wore a skirt that was so short and so tight that when she tried to cross her legs she actually had to push down on the bar stool to lift herself slightly. If she heard what the man was saying, she gave no outward sign; instead, she just puffed hard on a cigarette and kept trying to blow smoke rings by putting her lips in a circle and forcing the smoke through with a staccato push from her jaw.

A couple of other men sat at the bar and sipped beer while staring vacantly at the neat stack of liquor bottles lined up in front of a panel of mirrors. The men spoke to each other infrequently, yet there was a definite, quiet communication there, which the bartender participated in. They would all laugh suddenly, although I could hear no real conversation nor see any significant activity, just a mumble, a movement, a flick of ashes from a cigarette—all some sort of code that the three men good-naturedly shared.

Fish assessed the place quickly after we ordered, and then he said, "When you feel like I do, any place, even this place, seems friendly."

"This place is *my* place," I said. "It's warm and I like the guy behind the bar. *My* place!"

I looked at the lone window in the front of the bar, just beyond the pool table. There was no frost on it. I pictured Sally-Boy smiling; it was his kind of place too, a place where everyone in the bar no matter how old they were would be his friend almost instantly, and where he might whisper to me, "Whoa, I feel so good in here, Mikey, I wanna take a piece of it wit me and carry it aroun for good luck," and then he'd touch his chest with his fist like he did when he locked something inside himself. My mind slipped momentarily, and I was suddenly back on the fire escape with Sally-Boy, telling him, *"I met this girl, Sally, and she's different. The way I feel is different around her. But, yeah, everything is different now, it's all just coming together but coming apart at the same time. I don't know...I don't know, Sally. You're here, aren't you, Sally! In this bar! Here..."*

I actually looked around for a couple of seconds and then became aware again of Fish sitting next to me, glancing dreamily out the window. Fish had spent much of the ride from campus painting great fantasies about the upcoming weekend. Dutifully, I added a bit of color here and there until the picture of what we anticipated seemed almost real to me, too. But in the dingy surroundings of the small bar, he was silent at first. His face, which often reflected a caustic sharpness as he prepared for a wisecrack, now simply looked darkly handsome, softly reflective...and very young.

"I've got to ask you something, Mike," he said suddenly. "There's no one else I even want to ask. You know, my parents are crazy about Judaism. Good people, I love them, but I don't discuss feelings with them any more because the whole house erupts into fireworks. My mom, she panics if she thinks I'm getting serious about a girl, especially if the girl is *a shiksa*, and my father, hell, he is determined that I go to med school, which you know I am not the least bit interested in. My sister is younger and, so far at least, she's a model Jew in every way, so there is no way I am talking to her." He paused and looked a little embarrassed. "But you've got your cousin who's married, doing well, has a kid..."

"You want to know more about Harry?"

"No, but he's what, ten years older than you, so..."

"Yeah, about ten, but what the hell are you getting at?"

"Well, I was wondering if he ever talks to you about women, about knowing when, you know, it's the real thing?"

The smoothness of Fish's face broke into a light furrow of lines as he raised his thick eyebrows. I shifted uneasily in my seat, took a sip of my beer and said, "The real thing? What does that mean, Fish?"

Fish leaned forward smiling. "Okay," he said, "okay, I know it's crazy, but the thing is, I'm thinking about Katie all the goddam time. I'm ready to cash in everything for her, and I've only known her a few days, and she feels the same way."

"How do you know?"

Fish leaned back and straightened up, and suddenly I felt like a child about to be told something that is just beyond his comprehension.

"She's told me, that's how I know. We've talked about so much." He began to laugh. "What a basket case I am. It's great."

I clacked my mug against his and laughed. "Seriously, I don't know, Fish," I said. "Something strange is going on, that's for certain, but fuck if I know what it is. As for me and Harry, I doubt if he even thinks I'm old enough to fall in love—and he might be right about that."

We simultaneously took long pulls on our beers, and then Fish continued talking, clearly caught up in his own confusion.

"I hate to admit it, Mike, but I wish I could be more like you."

I expected sarcasm. I didn't hear it, though I wished I had, so I added it: "Fish, wishing won't make your cock grow."

"I'm serious, dammit, Mike."

"So am I."

"No, I mean it. You coast so well. No panic. You don't really lose control."

The bartender put two plates with our steaming, deliciously greasy sandwiches in front of us.

"Beers?" he asked, looking at our nearly empty mugs.

"Two more," I said, pushing our mugs across the ruddy bar toward him.

"I've lost control, Mike. I'm telling you, it's like this, it's…I'm just really in love with her."

I bit into my sandwich and was surprised at the warm fullness of it, a perfect blend of meat, cheese, and bread. The bartender put two more frothy mugs on the counter.

"Great sandwich," I said.

"You like it? Want mustard?"

He slid a jar of benign-looking brown mustard toward us. I slathered it on the outside of the bread with a knife. When I bit into the sandwich, my nostrils flared from the mustard's penetrating heat. I grunted in pain and quickly sipped the beer.

"Hot?" the bartender asked with a wrinkled grin.

"Great," I said to him, my voice slightly hoarse, and he smiled kindly. Then I turned to Fish, who was still absently spreading the fiery mustard inside his sandwich, and I said, "Bite into that sandwich, lover boy."

"It's weird how things work though, isn't it?" he said, continuing to apply the mustard. "Katie just shows up at the door one day and, *boom*, that's it. Suppose I had been out taking a leak or doing laundry?"

"That reminds me," I interrupted. "I've got clothes to pick up in the laundry room tonight. Remind me when we get back."

Fish didn't even acknowledge me. He finally stopped spreading mustard and was putting the bread back onto the sandwich. "Or suppose I had gone home for the weekend? I might have never met her." He bit into the sandwich, looked at it approvingly until the full force of the mustard finally hit. His eyes widened and watered, "Oh Jesus...!" He gulped his beer and waved a hand in front of his mouth. "Why didn't you warn me," he said laughing.

I laughed at my friend, and so did the bartender, who said, "Should I put a sticker on the mustard that says, 'Eat at your own risk'?"

"Nah," I said, "most people ignore those warnings anyway."

"Yeah," Fish said, wiping his nose and eyes with a napkin. "We just have to learn the hard way."

CHAPTER THIRTY

As we ate, I watched the pool players in the mirror, and I scanned the room again for Sally-Boy. They had ordered another pitcher and put another quarter into the table's coin slot. They lifted the plastic cover so they could rack the balls again. The two had a possessive air that said the table would be theirs for a long time.

"I want to play some pool," I said to Fish.

"Elvis One and Elvis Two are still playing," he said.

"So? I'm going to give 'em a little Brooklyn-boy talk, know what I mean?" I finished my sandwich, grabbed my beer, and swung down from the bar. I walked up to the pool table and said, "Hey, yous guys, yous wanna play for beer?"

"Sure," one said with a shrug. The other said, "It's your money, kid."

We agreed: Winners would stay on the table; losers would pay and buy the beer. The game was eight ball. They shot first. Helplessly, incredulously, Fish and I watched as the first shooter ran a string of phenomenal shots after the break until all he had left to drop was the eight ball. I looked out the window and saw a smattering of snowflakes floating to the gray sidewalk. I didn't want to go back out into the cold.

The shooter sipped his beer and rubbed a palm across the side of his grease-laden hair. He drew back his stick firmly, confidently. He nudged the white cue ball and it gently bumped the black eight ball, which then began its slow, deliberate journey toward the pocket. You can't escape certain truths, no matter how hard you try, I despaired, an eight ball rolling into the pocket means game over, just like the cold outside waiting to deaden feelings and thoughts and life itself. I cursed. Fish shrugged.

But then we realized that the cue ball hadn't stopped rolling. On the imperceptibly imperfect table, the white ball crawled after the black ball. It hung on the lip of the pocket and then disappeared from sight.

"Scratch!" I said, slapping hands with Fish. "Salvation is a cue ball with a mind of its own, man."

Elvis and Elvis wanted a rematch. We gave it to them. This time I broke. This time they never even got a chance to shoot. Disgusted, the Elvis twins left, so Fish and I racked up a game or two by ourselves.

A few more shivering people entered the gritty bar, their ears aglow. Once inside, they smiled, friendly, comfortable, red-cheeked. More challengers lined up for the rights to the table. But everything was so simple. I knew exactly what was expected of me in that small gray room on that exceptional night, the kind of night where you expect something good to happen— Sally-Boy might stroll into the bar; Erica might leave me an "I love you" message; Johnson might declare a secret truce has been reached.

Morris Lieberman would have liked the way I was looking at life in those hours of perfect pool. It was all so incredibly easy: I just stretched across the green tabletop, concentrated, tapped the cue ball squarely, and the shots rolled and plunked into the pocket. Sometimes I missed, but at least everything was clear. Immediate knowledge of success or failure. No midground. No waiting. Hope…right there in my own hands like a prize for me to grab.

The bartender brought us more sandwiches, ham and Swiss on grilled rye again.

"On the house," he said.

Every pair of challengers paid for the chance to play us. We drank for free, courtesy of our victims, for about two hours. Fish and I scarcely spoke, just a couple of guys caught up in our own cool, like me and Sally-Boy in our neighborhood. The gray bar with its pool table had become our sanctuary. No frost, no future, only warmth and times present. Our final challengers, the two men who had been sitting at the bar, quit in disgust and went back to their bar stools. There was no one left to play. The intensely talking man and the woman who tried to blow smoke rings were gone—probably long ago; I had never seen them leave. The bartender bought us one last beer.

"Always play so good?" he asked.

"Just a lucky night," I said.

With a sponge he stabbed at beaded water on the bar top.

"Good to have those nights once in a while, huh?"

"Yeah," I said, finishing the beer. Fish nodded. We put on our jackets.

"You just never know when and where something good's going to happen, do you?" the bartender said, smiling.

"Not really," I said, "but I'm going to start looking more often." And I thought I meant it.

"Well, son," he said with a sad smile, "that's a good way to be. Good night."

Smoke hovered low in the dirty bar as we opened the door to leave. We said good night to the one-armed bartender. Outside, the night air felt good when it stung my face.

We returned to Cunningham House a little before midnight. No one was at the desk, although it was supposed to be open until twelve. I remembered about the laundry; Fish decided to walk down to the laundry room with me.

"I'm too charged up to go to the suite yet," he said.

"You mean from playing pool, right?" I joked.

"Oh, right," he said, sliding down a metal banister. I met him at the bottom of the steps and we entered the laundry room together. "You know, I'd like to do Katie's wash, just to fool with her dirty clothes."

"God, someone save this boy..."

At first the noise from the laundry room sounded like a broken washing machine growling in protest, a raspy hum swelling and softening repeatedly. It was dark in the room except for a lone row of three dull light bulbs. Someone had tossed my clothes in a bundle next to my laundry bag on top of a dryer. Fish stopped talking to listen for the noise, but it had stopped suddenly. I shoved my clothes into my laundry bag.

No machines at all were running, but the low hum started up again from the furthest corner of the room. Fish slowly walked toward it, stopped short, and then there was a flurry of activity from a small space between the last washer and the cinderblock wall next to it. I first recognized the spaghetti-like hair of The Thatch as she slowly stood, straightened her blouse, and looked directly at Fish. She inched to the side, her blue-jeaned bottom sliding over the edge of the washer until she was completely free of the machine. And then Tomato emerged, his skin tinged a darker red than usual.

"Uh, I don't, um, see it back there," he said to The Thatch after eyeing me and Fish. "I'm afraid it's just, um, lost."

"Oh well," she said, primping her hair quickly and futilely. "Thanks for, uh, helping me look."

"She lost something," Tomato said to me as they walked toward the stairway and shuffled quickly up the steps.

"What she lost isn't behind the dryer," Fish said to me, rolling his eyes. Then he spotted the bulletin board. "Look at all this STEP propaganda. Nobody's good enough for them." He looked for my reaction; I shrugged but was surprised at his tone since in the past, whenever we had talked about war and politics, we had both seemed more aligned with the protesters. He said, "It says here they're organizing a protest against Dean Carmody. They want him to kick ROTC off campus."

I moved to the board and read a new notice accusing Dean of Academic Affairs Harlan Carmody of "insensitivity to students' rights" and demanding his resignation. There was also a new poster on the wall, this one showing a photograph of a burning Vietnamese village with its residents running in horror. The message read: "Support ROTC??? Then YOU support THIS!!!"

"Everyone's pissed off about something," I said, staring at the smoldering village.

"Not me," Fish said, walking away toward the stairs. "Right now, only one thing matters."

We got to our floor and the halls seemed oddly quiet, like someone had etherized the other residents. No odor of grass floated from Moon and Bobby's room and Bingham's room was empty of the sounds of music, TV, and moaning females. Our own suite seemed peaceful and comfortable in its typical disarray. I was tired, and I eagerly stretched out on top of my bed.

Fish picked up some darts from the desk and said, "Hey, the intercom message light is on." I didn't even move while he rang the desk. Tomato responded.

"Did I have a call?" Fish asked, speaking directly into the intercom.

"What did you say?" Tomato whined. "You know, it's after midnight and I'm not even supposed to be working..."

"Did I have a call?"

"Well, who are you anyway?"

"Dave Fishbein! Come on, Tomato!"

"Room?"

"409B."

There was a pause during which Tomato breathed so heavily I had a flash of The Thatch finishing what we had obviously interrupted in the laundry room.

"No, no messages for you," Tomato finally wheezed.

"Okay, but the light was on."

"Well, you don't have any messages."

"All right, but it seems strange..."

"It may seem strange, but I can't help it if there was no message for you! It was Michael Burns who had the message. Good bye..."

"Wait, asshole!" I yelled, jumping up from the bed. "I'm right here!"

"Well, I wish someone had said so," Tomato said.

"Just tell me the message, Tomato, will you?"

"Fine. Michael Burns. Erica somebody-or-other called three times. She can come this weekend. Good-bye!" The intercom clicked off.

"Bullseye, Burns!" Fish wildly threw a dart, but it missed the board and buried itself deep into the door. We looked at each other in shock. "What the hell is going on?" Fish said, starting to laugh. "Now *that* has never happened before."

"Well, there's a first time for everything, Lover Boy. How does it feel?"

"It feels like...like...I don't know!" Fish said, laughing hard now. "Fuck it! We make our own bullseyes, Mike! That's just what we do!"

CHAPTER THIRTY-ONE

"Satisfaction!"
"Satisfaction!"
"Satisfaction!"

A bare-chested drunk led hundreds of screams for "Satisfaction" at the Hell's Angels Party. His motorcycle roared as he revved it wildly inside the massive fraternity party hall. He shouted at the band, "PLAY IT, GODDAMIT! PLAY 'SATISFACTION' OR I SWEAR, I'LL ROLL RIGHT OVER YOUR GODDAM EQUIPMENT!"

His date—also drunk, also bare-chested—teetered while perched on the bike's handlebars, legs spread so wide that the bike's thick front tire appeared to roll out from her crotch. The band had already played "Satisfaction" at least four times, and as the crowd shrieked, the band tore into it again. People wearing skin-tight black leather clothing stomped around in engineer boots, swinging chains, screaming lyrics in slurred voices and attempted to dance while trying valiantly to hold their balance as the singer's voice crackled out of the speakers:

> "When I'm drivin' in my car
> And the man comes on the radio
> He's tellin' me more and more
> About some useless information
> Supposed to fire my imagination
> I can't get no...oh no no...no..."

Beer—gold and sudsy white—gushed freely from three kegs at one corner of the room. A guy with a black leather cap and a braided ponytail fired a pistol loaded with blanks, the signal for people to tear wildly at one another's clothing. They ripped shirts to shreds and then tied the strips above their biceps or wore them as headbands. Chains clanged, whips cracked; all of the materials of violence were there but were now mere parodies of terror, sources of fun instead of horror.

Erica danced in tight black jeans and a light blue T-shirt with a peace sign on the front. I wrote "Mike's

Chick" across the back in pink lipstick; she asked what I had written, and did not object when I told her. A black headband drew her skin tight along her forehead and pulled her hair back from her face. The hair on one side of her head was swept back behind an ear, revealing a small black earring. When she danced, her hair, frazzled slightly from the swell of body heat, swung from side to side. Sweating, we took a break from dancing and wandered toward the perimeter of the room, where some fraternity guys had set up various party games.

"Want to try any of these?" I asked Erica. I had to shout to be heard above the band and the crowd.

"Maybe some, but not that one." She pointed toward a sign that said "Kiss a Pig." In a small booth someone dressed as a policeman and wearing a pig's face sold kisses for a quarter.

The pig spotted Erica and beckoned to her. "Come on, make friends with a pig, honey," he snorted.

"No, thanks," she said, muttering, "honey my ass."

"I've noticed that you don't like being called 'honey,' sweetie," I cracked.

"How very observant of you," she said, smoothly transitioning to her mock sophisticated voice, "to notice that condescending males are not my favorite sub-species."

"Look, here comes Donna," the pig said. "She's gonna kiss me, right, honey?"

"Why not?" Donna said, looking at Erica and then at me. "At least this pig wants to be kissed."

The pig grabbed her, bent her backward and kissed her dramatically, while several people surrounding the booth grunted and squealed in approval.

"You gotta try this! Come on over!" A tall frat guy with a handful of darts waved to us. "Here's where you get back at all those pompous, hard-boiled fuzz you love to hate!" He stood inside a roped off area where for fifty cents you could throw three darts at a large poster of a state trooper. Circular bullseyes were drawn around his face, heart, and crotch. "Win a valuable prize, too!" the frat guy said. He held up a rubber dagger and a black water pistol.

"Who gets the money?" Erica asked him as he handed three darts to a girl smoking a cigar.

"Charity," he said.

"Which one?" I asked. "Your frat, right?"

He laughed. "No, really, a real charity, the PAL of New Jersey."

Erica looked at me, confused.

"The Police Athletic League?" I asked.

"Yeah," the frat guy said, "the cops didn't like the idea of this party, so we agreed to set up these games as charity. Hope they don't stop in!" he laughed. He handed a rubber dagger as a prize to the girl, who was now blowing smoke the size of clouds with her cigar. Two of her three darts had hit the poster of the policeman in the head. "So which one of you is gonna throw?"

"I will," Erica said. "I like the idea of playing for charity. Besides, I got a parking ticket the other day, so I have some aggression to release."

"Were you parking alone, baby?" the frat guy asked, as she dug fifty cents out of her jeans pocket.

Erica stared at him, her eyes widening as she slowly aimed a dart at his head and said so convincingly in one of her broken-English accents, "You vant I should throw this dart right into your pumpkin," that he squealed and put his hands in front of his face.

"Hey, no! What the fuck!"

Then Erica turned toward the poster and threw her first dart, which hit the poster but didn't stick, falling weakly to the floor.

"Pathetic," she said, dropping her accent. She turned to me. "Here, you try one."

I took the dart. "Look out!" I heard Fish's familiar voice bellow from behind me.

My dart sailed right between the figure's eyes, protruding from the bridge of his nose.

"Amazing, Burns!" Fish said. He and Katie stood next to us now with freshly filled cups of beer. "But tell the truth, you were aiming for the heart."

Katie, also dressed in black jeans and wearing a black leather vest that covered nothing but flesh on top, held Fish around the waist. Erica took the last dart and aimed at the poster. Katie said to her just as she released the dart, "Watch where you throw!" The dart arched in the air and seemed to skim the poster until it stuck straight up in the bullseye between the trooper's legs. "A one-track mind!" Katie shouted.

Erica, flushed with embarrassment, laughed as she hid her face for a moment in my shirt.

"A dagger *and* a water pistol for that shot!" the frat guy said. "That's about as big as a cop's gets, right, honey?"

Erica turned quickly, grabbed another dart, stared at him, and said, "I guess you do vant I should throw dart at you, right, Pumpkin Man? You no get that you not to call to me this 'honey' or this 'baby' shits?"

"Uh, I get it, I get it," the frat guy said, keeping his eyes fixed on Erica. He somewhat nervously handed me the prizes. "Hey, watch where she points that dart, man."

Fish and Katie walked back to the dance floor as the band, playing at ever-increasing volume, burst into "Good Lovin."

"No more games for me," Erica said with a smile as we walked toward another booth.

"Oh, come on," I said, lowering my voice to a purposely creepy whisper, "tell the truth, Erica, you were aiming for that exact spot."

She shoved me, then hugged me.

"Now you try this one," she said, as we neared something called "Bob for Knuckles." To play, you submerged your face in a large bucket filled with Purple Passion—a mixture of grain alcohol and grape juice—and tried to sink your teeth into a pair of floating rubber "brass" knuckles. If you emerged with a pair in your mouth, you kept them. "Go ahead," Erica urged, "try it."

"Why?"

"Because I want to see you with a wet head and a purple face."

I paid my fifty cents and plunged my face into the bucket with my eyes closed. I came up with a sticky head of hair, a purple face, no knuckles, and a mouthful of Purple Passion, which I made a big show of gulping down.

Towels were stacked on a nearby chair. Erica grabbed one and patted softly at my face. Then she dabbed at my head and flicked her fingers through my damp hair until bangs fell evenly across my forehead. She formed a rough part in the middle and swept the sides over my ears with her fingers, tilted her head slightly to one side, and suddenly kissed me hard, moving herself against me, pushing slightly, gently against my hips. She eased away, took my hand and walked toward the dance floor as the singer in the band shouted into his microphone, "Get on up here, everybody! It's Badass Dance Contest time!"

The band ripped into the familiar opening of "Woolly Bully," the gun exploded, and pieces of shredded clothing flew into the air around us.

"Oh yeah! Tear up those clothes because we've got a special contest for you!" the singer said while the band played behind him and dancers jerked as though the electricity that powered the instruments charged through them too. "Everybody knows a Hell's Angel is one badass sonovabitch, so we are lookin for the baddest, meanest, fiercest dance you can do—I mean dirty, nasty, foul, and ugly! I'm talkin obscene 'cause this is the Badass Dance Contest, and we've got two special badass prizes for the winners!"

He held up a jug of red wine and a quart of motor oil. The crowd screamed in approval and the house vibrated from the voices, the music, the feedback. People merged into one mass, writhing and jumping and rolling on the dance floor.

Erica surprised me with erotic moves that she added to her rhythmic twisting and, at one point, she turned her back to me and leaned forward, her ass against me, and then she spun quickly back to face me, her eyes big and soft, and she snapped her fingers to the pulsing music as I momentarily lost track of where I was and who I was.

The music drove on. No one was really eliminated by judges; instead, dancers just wilted and fell to the side as the band kept repeating verses of "Woolly Bully" until a circle formed around one couple rolling around on the floor, pulling hair, and biting. They "danced" as though they were fighting or being tortured and it was hard to tell if they were pretending. The guy, wearing a torn blue-denim vest and black pants that laced up the side, pulled out a blackjack and came so close to hitting his date that people screamed, and she responded by kicking at his crotch and, though she stopped short, I winced in anticipatory pain. They kicked and punched and sometimes made contact but always in time with the music, and the girl's black miniskirt repeatedly flipped up revealing a tiny pair of leopard-skin underpants as her date held her under one arm and bounced her off his hip. Then he slipped one arm under her knees and the other behind her head, cradling her in that position and furiously whirling her in circles, encouraged by the rest of us who had stopped dancing and now surrounded the dance floor.

"Okay, okay!" the singer finally shouted. "You're the winners! Hey, you guys WIN, I said! Hey goddamit, stop, STOP!"

But the couple continued though the only sound left in the speakers was continuous screeching feedback. Finally, the couple fell to the floor, heaving and gasping, the rest of us clapping and cheering wildly.

"Jesus, you talk about a couple of wild fucking heathens!" the singer shouted into his microphone. "Come on up now and get your prizes!"

The couple groped and kissed wildly as they walked toward the band. People cheered, the gun fired blanks, clothes ripped. "Wine and motor oil!" the singer said, handing the winners their prizes.

The girl immediately began chugging the wine, and her date opened the oil, poured some into his hands and massaged it vigorously into his stringy black hair. The blank pistol fired again and the guy ripped her shirt off and massaged blue-black motor oil on her nipples and breasts.

The couple slipped to the floor and a few others joined them there as they all sloshed around in the oil and wine. The band suddenly started rhythmically beneath the din with a deep, familiar pulse that people slowly picked up and echoed: "Tah dum dum...tah dum dum...tah dum dum...tah dum dum..." Couples hung tightly to one another, kissing and grinding to the deliberately long introduction to "My Girl," holding one another and swaying until the whole crowd was of one voice: "Tah dum dum...tah dum dum...tah dum dum..."

The singer finally began with a mellow, "I've got sunshiiiine on a cloudy day..." and the dance floor, tumultuous just minutes earlier, transformed into a sea of swaying, grinding bodies, whispering the wonderfully familiar words to the song.

I wonder if Smokey Robinson, when he composed "My Girl" for the Temptations, realized how his lyrics would free young men like me to venture into that vulnerable ground of honesty as we held our girls and whispered lyrics to them, as I did to Erica: "I've got so much honey, the bees envy me..." without fear of being laughed at for being corny because, after all, we were only drunkenly singing words to a song. Such safe, secure ground Smokey set up for us guys—after all, girls could take it personally or choose to believe we were just sing-along drunks.

But I know this: I cruised slowly around the dance floor with Erica and meant the words, at least in that simple moment of my then limited life in the innocence of my ultimately protected college scene—as removed from my fire escape days as I could possibly be—as I half hummed, half sang, "I don't need no money, fortune or fame..."

Erica held me closer then, and though I didn't know if it was the words that made her do so or just coincidence, I knew what I chose to believe, so I kissed her as the singer sang, "I've got all the riches, baby, one man can claim..." and Erica didn't back away. Instead, Erica Wakefield allowed my lips to linger again and then longer, kissing more deeply each time, until the song wound down, fading off into a repetition of the echoed words "my girl" until there was suddenly no song, and the feet along the dance floor slowed dream-like to a stop, and then there was no dance, only people standing still, or embracing, or sipping yet another beer, while those safe words hung in the air and entered the memories of those who shared the simple love of a moment.

CHAPTER THIRTY-TWO

We went outside for some air, and Erica put an arm around my waist. I slowly guided her to a bench in a small garden behind the fraternity house. I felt the vibrations of the music that had picked up again into something I strained to identify.

"'Let's Spend the Night Together,'" I said, recognizing the song.

"What?" Erica stopped walking.

"No, I mean the music, the song that they're playing now, 'Let's Spend the Night Together.'"

"Hmmm," she said, tilting her head as she thought, "that song was playing in the hamburger place we went to on the first night we went out together. I bet you don't remember, do you?"

"Oh, trust me, Erica," I said, "I do remember."

The air was cool, and the quiet of night was punctuated frequently with shouts from the partiers inside. Erica sighed. "What makes them so crazy?" she asked absently.

"Crazy times make crazy people."

"Yeah, that's it exactly," she said.

Her eyes looked like melancholy blue stars in the misty night. The moon was partially hidden by a string of smoky clouds.

"Are you okay?" I asked.

"Yes, yeah, it's wonderful. Really fun."

"We could leave this party, go someplace else."

"No, no, not at all. I just think maybe they're all trying to forget something, like when a little kid breaks a vase and starts talking real loud and fast to cover it up."

"Doesn't everyone try to cover the things they break?"

"I guess, but then you find out that you really can't, right? Things don't work that way." She turned her face away from me.

"What's wrong?" I asked.

In the shadows I saw her shoulders tremble slightly. I gently stroked her hair.

"Take your time," I said. "Things don't come easily for me either. Not actions, not thoughts, not words.

Like right now. I know what I want to say, but I don't want to sound foolish..."

She pushed closer to me. Her lips touched my neck so lightly I thought at first it was a gentle breeze. I continued in a whisper, "And sometimes, just when you're around, there are ways I want to act and things I want to do, but I don't know..."

Erica tilted her head back to look at me. She half smiled. She removed her black headband and put it around my head and flicked lightly at my hair.

"I like that look," she said with a smile and then added, "I just want to go slowly, Mike."

"I can see that, but why?"

"There's time, that's all." She moved inches away, but I was aware of more than physical distance now. "It can't work like this, not now."

My arm was still around her shoulders, but the position seemed awkward. Erica looked away, her eyes down, and I leaned over trying to read her face. My stomach was hollow, and I thought that I surely stank of beer. There was that terrible distance, even as she pressed her lips against mine and found my tongue with hers. This time, I was the one who pulled away.

"What are we doing, Erica?"

I couldn't control the needy voice that sounded like it squeezed out from my childhood. I was almost twenty years old—old enough to be considered an adult by most standards, old enough to be on my own, old enough to be drafted and counted on to uphold whatever honor the war was about, but I was dressed like a kid at a Halloween party and about to dissolve into a heap of emotions in front of a beautiful, mysterious high school girl. A powerful wave of panic swelled inside me.

"I'm sorry, Mike. Don't be confused, don't be anything, just hold me and keep me warm and then take me back inside and dance with me and make me laugh, make me like the rest of them."

"But you're not like them. You're...you're so different." The wave broke inside me, washed my thoughts and words together, and gently pushed them out. "I love you, Erica." A flat statement in the sharp air, a sentence I had never uttered to any other girl. Erica's eyes shifted downward again, but the words filled the hollowness inside me and, surprisingly, I relaxed. With rock music blasting in the background and the night air damp and thick and people somewhere being drafted and schoolwork hovering over me and Sally-Boy's disappearance a lingering obsession, I had admitted to Erica how I felt and nothing else mattered. Something was happening to me, but I didn't know what—I only knew what I felt, so I had said it.

Erica looked at me, started to speak, turned away and then said, "Take me inside now, Mike, please; let's go inside."

I stood quickly, startling her a little. She looked up. Light from the fraternity hall tinted her face a haunting yellow.

I asked softly, "What is it, Erica? Tell me, I don't…"

There were party sounds—the gun firing, the band's feedback, the frantic screams again for "Satisfaction." Erica reached up and took my hand, and I sat down beside her again on the bench.

"I just didn't want to meet someone like you now," she began.

I looked directly into her eyes, which reflected the flecks of light like a neon sign that practically spelled out a message that should have been obvious to me weeks ago.

I asked calmly, "Who is he?"

"Someone to forget," she said immediately. She put a hand up as if to stop me from asking anything else and then touched her forehead and lightly pulled her hair back behind each ear. The ground pulsated with the opening chords of "Satisfaction" again.

"Maybe it's just not such a good idea," she said slowly, "for people to tell bad things about themselves. Maybe we damage ourselves more that way; maybe talking about them just makes them linger."

"But I want to hear everything about you, not just this, but everything."

"But knowing might change everything," she said.

I nodded. "I know. But go ahead. Tell me."

She smiled quickly, hesitated, and then said, "It was just that I...I didn't really know about things. I was stupid. This guy, he was a senior in high school when I was a freshman. He took me out a few times and I was, well, a little impressed I guess." She stopped and studied my face; I focused directly on her pleading eyes. She continued: "He went to the Naval Academy right after high school, and I'd see him once or twice at parties when he'd come home. He wrote to me occasionally over the next couple of years. I thought about him quite a bit, but I figured I was just a kid in his eyes." She spoke steadily now, looking straight ahead into the black misty night. "Anyway, last spring he invited me to June Week."

"Impressive."

"You know about it, June Week?"

"Sure, the DC papers and TV feature it every year. All those Navy guys try to climb that monument— the Herndon Monument—that the officers have all greased up. Then there's the statue of Tecumseh painted different colors, pretty girls gawking at the Navy men..."

I stopped and shivered slightly.

"Mom didn't like the idea of me going, but my father, he's so sweet, so trusting, said, 'Sure, why not?' I went and I was, you know, I guess I was completely, stupidly flattered." Her grip tightened on my hand, and the corners of her mouth tightened too. "Then all last summer, we dated when he was around. I went to the beach with him for a week."

"Alone?" Did she detect the hollowness in my tone? I immediately hated my insecurity.

"With his family. We went everywhere together, did everything." Her eyes grew filmy, and she let go of my hand.

Then Erica looked at me as if she was searching for something. Somehow, from that look, I knew that my insecurity was insignificant, so I said, "It's okay, Erica. Just...just tell me whatever you want me to know...or not. It's up to you, Erica, really, we can go back inside...I have no right..."

"No," she said firmly, looking deeply into my eyes. "I want to tell you. I can't believe it, but I'm glad I do."

She adjusted my headband again. "I didn't sleep with him. Not in the summer." She studied me for my reaction; I remained composed. "But this past fall, I'd go down to Annapolis for football games. That's when it started. Then he'd come home. His house always seemed available. His parents travel a lot. We didn't see each other often, so when we did...It just seemed so difficult to get out of it, Mike. I knew I shouldn't, but I just did. And I was a little afraid—not of him, not physically, but afraid of my choices, that something didn't feel right, but I did it anyway. I stupidly, so very stupidly, did it anyway." She looked confused and sad, and she drew a deep breath and rested her head on my shoulder.

"Let's go back inside, Erica," I said. "You're shivering, and I've kept you out here answering questions too long..." Her head remained, unmoving, on my shoulder, so I continued, "What you did is nothing terrible; we get caught up, we get involved, we think we know someone, or we think we know what we want. It happens...it just happens. Come on, let's be like them," I motioned inside, "let's rock-and-roll, let's dance. It's okay, it's all okay."

I started to stand, and I knew that part of the reason I wanted to go back inside was because I did not want to hear any more—because I knew that if I heard more, I might find out what I didn't want to know, details that might torment me, facts I wasn't ready to face.

Noise began to grow again in the background. Three drumbeats...four...five in a row. Then the electric guitar, vibrating, and a long squeal from the speakers. The lead singer screamed something inaudible, followed by his clear urging: "Everybody daaaaaaance!"

A growing rumble of laughter like mortar fire exploding in the distance, and then kids shrieking, and the grunts of the motorcycle driver and his girl, now screwing in the dirt—all the sounds of young people celebrating a moment, not for any special reason other than that it was another moment that they were alive to celebrate. So I started to stand, to re-enter the frenzy, to go from one confusion to another, to grab a moment and to absorb whatever it offered and to say the hell with consequences. I started to stand, but Erica stopped me.

"You know there's more, Mike, don't you?"

"Yes, but maybe this isn't the time to tell it."

"I'll feel better if I can tell you."

"But my wanting to know shouldn't be your major reason."

"Well, it's equal to my other major reason."

"What's that?"

"Because I want so very much to tell you."

I sat back down, aware that I was about to enter a world much newer to me than those mysterious steps Sally and I used to take off the bottom of the fire escape and into the night. Erica kissed me long and hard amid screams and vibrating electric music and passionate groans from the earth nearby—things now as removed from us as the planets hovering light years away over our heads. Then Erica stopped shivering, sat up straight, and all of her features, including the corners of her mouth softened, as she quietly, calmly, and without tears told me about the abortion.

CHAPTER THIRTY-THREE

"*When the Dodgers left, that was it for me, Mikey, the start of the end of everything,*" *Sally-Boy was saying. He was doing chin-ups on the ladder rung that hung from the fire escape above us. "Last game at Ebbets— September 24, 1957—we was there, remember? Massimo took us. We cried like every other stupid little jerk in the stands. I pretty much stopped cryin after that, and now I don't cry no more, not over nothin. Cryin's a waste. Don't do any good. Dodgers leave, we cry, do they come back? No. Someone dies, we cry, do they come alive? No. How 'bout you, cuz? Do you cry?" He was finishing his second set of fifteen, and his biceps glistened in the moonlight. Before I could answer, he continued talking: "I stay strong, I don't cry, I pick my fights, I don't follow the Dodgers no more because they left us. They left Brooklyn, they left me, that was the beginning of the end of everything. Your turn to do chin-ups, Mikey. Gotta stay strong, cuz, gotta stay strong. Always. We stay strong, we don't cry!"*

A flare of yellow sunlight shone through our suite window and woke me. Fish was asleep as I left the room for class. Only three days had passed since the Hell's Angels party, but it seemed like a generation.

"Is it as warm out as it looks?" I asked Andre Moon, who was standing in the doorway, drawing on a pipe now nearly empty of grass.

He shrugged. "Say, man, damn if I know. I mean, is it as blue out as it looks, man?" he said, stuffing out the smoldering grass in the bowl with his fingers. "I ain't been out this morning either; just lookin at the world from my own little window, man. That's all we can do, right, man? Look out our own window."

I grabbed a nylon windbreaker and we walked out of Cunningham House together. I said, "Warm" as soon as we stepped into the sunlight. Simultaneously, Moon said, "Chilly." I unzipped my jacket. He pulled up his collar. Moments later, goosebumps sprouted on my arms, but Moon unzipped his jacket to the bottom of his chest. The sun played games by beaming the magical but chilling heat that sometimes comes in early March, the teasing warmth of new spring—enough to warm my hair but not my scalp; enough to make my back perspire faintly, but not my face; enough to incubate an idea, but not to hatch it; enough to make me look ahead, but not enough to help me forget the past.

Moon, in typical grass-induced abstractedness, said, "Say, my man, here we are each on our way to our own class, which is the ultimate purpose of our participating in all this college bullshit, right?"

"I guess," I said.

"Say, you have that writing class, my man. What will you write about today? Something to change the world? Something folks can get off on? Say, I have an idea for you, man—hit on this doobie doobie doo a couple of times before class and see if you don't write like ol' Sammy Clemens himself." Moon pulled a joint from his pocket, lit it, and toked.

I sucked in for one long toke and then handed it back, but Moon had already been distracted by noise from ahead of us. He tapped out the joint and put it back into his pocket and watched as members of STEP, dressed for summer in cut-offs and T-shirts and attaching firecrackers to balsa-wood airplanes, lit them and cheered as the planes exploded in mid-flight. Moon coughed and laughed uncontrollably as we neared the group.

"Say, dig 'em," he said, smiling through green-ish teeth. "Crazy fuckers, radical, man, through and through. They think it's July, like the motherfuck-ing weather's as radical as they are—that it jumped right from winter into summer." Moon coughed. "And dig those airplanes. Kaboom! Nothin but splinters. Kaboom! Kaboom! Kaboom! And Kaaaa-boooom! Crazy motherfuckers think they're going to change the whole world, man, and I say more power to 'em. Say, man, now there's something to write about: the crazy fuckers from STEP."

"Maybe," I said.

I was going to my Writers' Workshop lab, taught by the strange white-haired man I had seen in the Tombs on that snowy evening of cruising, but I knew I wouldn't write about STEP and their exploding airplanes. Somehow I had to write about what had clung to my mind for three days:

The solemnly secret trip to Manhattan Erica told me she had taken; the appointment Brian arranged and drove her to with Katie along for support; the stark apartment they entered; her fear of the procedure; the frowning but sympathetic female doctor who did not give her name; Erica's sadness over how easy it all was ("Like nothing ever happened. It's there, inside you, and then you leave and it's not there, it's gone...just... gone...just a light, lingering pressure.").

She had told me this in a steady stream of whispers, looking at me but not into me, her face showing vague confusion, her fingers involuntarily tightening around my wrist, as though she was taking my pulse to make sure I was alive.

Moon and I were just a few yards away from the balsa dive-bombers of STEP. He coughed out his laughter in explosive fits.

"Wild, wild stuff!" he marveled. "You gotta write about them. They are some strange characters these STEP-children. Say, I'll tell you a fact, too—they do some mean drugs, man."

Suddenly, the group spotted Dean Carmody walking in its direction. The students joined hands and started chanting: "Kill ROTC not children! No more ROTC!"

Carmody's head peeked turtle-like out of his topcoat. He hesitated momentarily and then passed near the group. Two STEP members launched lighted airplanes that glided by and exploded in slivers near the dean's feet. He froze momentarily, quickly composed himself, and glared at the group, which cheered and continued its chant.

"Dig that! Look what those crazy motherfuckers did there!" Moon said, his red-streaked eyes coming to life. "Say, maybe those crazy mothers have the right idea, man. Think radical, be radical, and pretty soon you're so used to it, radical seems normal—yeah, say, radical be as normal as bread on motherfucking butter."

Moon unzipped his jacket and took it off.

"What are you doing, Moon?" I asked.

"Gettin radical too, man. C'mon, let's go blow up some airplanes with 'em, show people how to shake some things up 'round here."

"Don't you have a sociology class?"

"Hell with it, man. All them people in it thinking they can relate to that great vast black sea of poverty by saying things like, 'Yo, brotherman, we solid.' I tell you, I've had it with that bullshit."

He rubbed his hands together and blew on them.

Another airplane exploded behind Dean Carmody as he walked away. He stopped and glared at the members of STEP like he was photographing their faces for his private file.

Without warning, Moon, who had moved to the edge of the group, shouted, "Say, what about some courses us black kids can get into, man?"

The STEP members cheered, and a few black members among them moved forward shouting their support of Moon's question. Carmody measured Moon coldly; from behind his thick glasses the dean's eyes became needles that attempted to pierce Moon's belligerence. But Moon said evenly, "Say, deano, you got a lilly-white fuckin curriculum here, bro. Me and the brothers ain't nothin but your guests, oh great white massa."

Another loud cheer rose from the group, and now a small but vocal group of black students from STEP stood behind Moon.

Dean Carmody turned his petite body toward the STEP members and let a thin, tight smile pull across his lips as he said calmly, "If you people wish to talk, make an appointment in my office—fourth floor of Hopewell Admin Building." He spoke shrilly, scarcely moving his lips, and then walked briskly away.

"Say, deano, 'us people' be takin you up on that!" Moon shouted. "Andre Moon gonna see you personally in the plantation house, massa, if yo' black secretary will let me in!"

Moon turned, scanned the cheering STEP members, put his arms around two of the black students standing next to him and shouted, "I'm gonna see him in his office! All you all ought to come with me! Blowin up these little wooden airplanes ain't gonna change shit, you hear? But if we go see massa and don't like what he has to say, we can fuck up more than these airplanes! Hear what I'm saying, STEP children? We can fuck him up good!"

The STEP crowd cheered and chanted, "Fuck him up! Fuck him up!"

"Let's go, Moon," I said, walking toward him. "You'll be late for class."

"Hell with class, Mike. I told you I ain't goin. Class don't mean shit."

"Suit yourself, Moon," I said and began to walk away.

A STEP member with a nearly waist-length beard put up his hand to Moon. They clasped in a soul handshake.

Moon turned toward me and called, "Say, Mike, why don't you stop writing about some motherfucking bullshit for that class, man. Stick with us. Let's go see deano together, get some change goin round here."

I shook my head. "Some other time, Moon."

"Typical college scene for you, right man?" Moon coughed out a laugh. The bearded guy scoffed at me.

"Yeah, Moon," I said. "Something like that." I walked away.

Moon was wrong about me, of course, because nothing seemed "typical" anymore. The sunlight was chilly. An unsettling irritation that spread like a nerve-wracking rash plagued the campus. The government had eliminated draft deferments for anyone not in school. Sally-Boy kept reappearing in my dreams, alternately settling me and haunting me. And a young woman had shown me that no one, no matter how beautiful, intelligent, insulated, and strong could escape the twisted atypical times.

Nothing was as it seemed to be, and nobody was who they seemed, or wanted, to be. Erica had been broken, though not unwittingly, and now she was rebuilding, determined to make unseen scars fade with time. So I now understood the hardness that lingered at her mouth like a tenacious blemish. Brian, the Ivy League Marine, arranged for the illegal abortion and paid the $200 cash for it, assuring Erica that no one would ever have to know other than her, him, and Katie. Erica had told me: "I felt everything slipping away and Brian steadied me. He took care of it all and then tried to convince me that I wasn't the awful person I thought I was. But I don't know…"

I was ashamed to admit to myself that, by confiding in me, I realized Erica knew more of life than I did. She and I were not equals, and it was more than the abortion that made me aware that we were on different planes of experience and depth—it was the whole relationship she had developed, the confusion she had felt, the inability to extricate herself until a potentially life-altering event had occurred…and the way that she was now thinking it through, examining her life, and moving ahead in the deliberate manner of those far wiser than others. And here I was, struggling to leave a fire escape behind.

CHAPTER THIRTY-FOUR

As I walked to my writing class, I continued to snap and unsnap my windbreaker in an unsuccessful attempt to adjust to the weather. A few more firecrackers exploded behind me, followed by loud cheers and Moon's loud coughing laugh. The deceitful sun promised that winter was over, but the chill lingered like a reminder that the past is always with us. It was her decision, Erica said, just as it was her decision not to tell Navy boy, just as it was her decision to have sex with him in the first place. ("I made the choices myself, good or bad. I made the decisions. All of them.")

Maybe I'd write about that, I thought, the choices we make or don't make, the control we have or lack. I looked forward to the class, though my father had said in a recent phone conversation that "a creative writing class doesn't sound very practical, Michael. Creative writing means writing fiction for free that no one else understands. And you know when creative writers get tired of starving they become journalists; then they get *paid* to write fiction no one else understands." And, of course, he added, "Your hair has been cut, right?" And, of course, I lied and said yes, a gutless response, but, nonetheless, the one I made.

I hadn't tried to convince him about the class. It wasn't your typical say-whatever-you-want, spill-your-guts-out, purge-me-of-all-my-psychological-hang-ups, won't-somebody-out-there-please-understand-me writing class. That wasn't tolerated by the white-haired Professor Everett Quinton "Willie" Staunton, writer-in-residence at Sinclair College for the 1968 school year. In fact, Professor Staunton's very first words to the class were delivered with a sneer as he entered the classroom on the second day the course met. His voice, distinctly Southern, was surprisingly clear for a man with a face so weathered and wrinkled from long exposure to the strong sun in his native Louisiana.

Professor Staunton had leaned his prune-like head to one side and said: "Want to know what I hate more than anything?" His head moved like a snow-tipped beacon, taking in the room with its sweep. "Printed puke! The spontaneous and helpless regurgitation of half-digested words of wisdom! The garbled and gurgling sounds of ill-prepared phrases! The retching and writhing spewing of fetid philosophies! The heaving of tales and terms and turned sentences! The burping belligerence of the would-be writer who thinks readers are salivating to digest every tainted thought he throws up! I pity the poor readers who open books only to have the pedantic pukings of would-be writers drip all over them, overwhelming them with their uncontrollable verbal vomit, repulsing readers to the point where they can no longer stand to have books around! Would-be writers with their projectile puking that drives the minds of repulsed readers to their ultimate death—to the insidious suffocating end inflicted by television, that video marvel that envelops the thought processes, chloroforms the senses, bludgeons the imagination, and, finally, ultimately, inevitably, sucks the whole person into a vast vacuum where only excesses prompt reactions—mass murders with hatchets bring a raised eyebrow... perhaps; auto chases ending in gnarled hunks of tons of metal scarcely warrant a pursing of the lips; tidal waves, hurricanes, fires, orgies, tornadoes, train wrecks, and wars elicit the classic verbal reaction of our times: 'Oh, wow!'"

Professor Staunton had stopped abruptly, his face a bright red ball, his jaw chiseled in anger, rage flickering in his icy blue eyes. No one in the room moved. Everyone looked either frightened or sick to their stomach. Staunton spoke again in a slow whisper. As he spoke, his voice grew louder but his features grew softer, more like a grandfather than the demon he had seemed seconds earlier.

"Give me printed puke in this class and I'll give you a raft of shit right back, my friends. Remember, language is a cracked kettle upon which we bang to make bears dance, when what we really want to do is move the star. The hell with the bears, my friends; let's try to move the stars!"

Someone pointed out after class that the business about the bears was really just a paraphrase from something by Flaubert, but I still worked hard to please Staunton. In every class he did something bizarre, always spilling out the language in some unique, albeit disgusting, way. He read to us dramatically from Twain, Hemingway, Fitzgerald, Nabokov, O'Neill, and others. Sometimes he cried and criticized; other times, he ranted and raved angrily. He meted out praise with an eyedropper and ladled out criticism from a bottomless pot. And once, after several people apparently complained to him in private that he never seemed satisfied with their work, he said to the class:

"I am not paid to be a sycophant. I will not praise mediocrity. I will not refrain from saying that slop is slop. I do not intend to coddle your feelings. I refuse to refer to your bleating as 'beautiful prose.' Most of what you have shown me so far is less appealing than spoiled milk. I accept that, and I plow through it gagging gallantly, making suggestions. Don't complain to me that I am too hard on you. It is I who should complain to you that *you* are too hard on *me*, that your attempts at metaphor spoil my dinner, your simplistic symbols give me nightmares, and your fractured emotionalism has ruined my sex life. Yes, even my new, young wife has complained."

He paused, waiting for reaction. There was, as usual, very little, although I noticed he stared at me briefly as I attempted, unsuccessfully, not to smile at his rant. He turned away from me and continued:

"Fortunately, all of you have provided me just barely enough well-written words, phrases, sentences, and perhaps even paragraphs to keep me from dying of starvation, being fearful of sleep, and suffering disuse atrophy to that part of my anatomy that is so necessary in holding a marriage together. For those saving glimpses of what may loosely be termed 'talent,' I assure you I am grateful."

After walking with Moon on that morning when I felt the first chilly warmth of spring, I sat in a seat toward the back of the damp classroom where the rays of sunlight split the windowpanes and washed over several desks. The sun, magnified through the window glass, heated my arms, shoulders, and head. Professor Staunton entered, the class quieted, and he began to ramble and shout, cursing us, cursing the war, cursing President Lyndon Johnson, reading passages from books and cursing them.

His voice grew distant, an echo to me. He was just sound locked outside, impersonal and meaningless like the distant screaming sirens Sally-Boy and I would listen to late in the Brooklyn nights. Heat had overtaken the chill, and my veins tingled. I wrote, filling the corners of my notebook with tiny cursive letters, my pen erupting with words, pulling my hand along with it. I felt out of control. Fatigue pulled at my eyes, and I was angry because I didn't want to grow tired; if I tired, I might stop, and if I stopped I might never start again, and then the questions would stay inside me and *they* would atrophy, and *I* would become impotent.

I suddenly realized that Staunton was sitting behind me. The class had ended, and the room had emptied. When? Professor Staunton apparently decided that if he didn't do something to get my attention he'd be ignored completely, so he coughed loosely; I felt his breath on my back.

"Young man, you fancy yourself a writer I take it?" he blustered when I turned to face him. "You wrote almost the whole time I talked today. Is that appropriate comportment?"

The edge in his voice surprised me. Still, I was half smiling. With creases from the corners of his mouth to the sides of his chin, he looked like a puppet. I didn't answer.

Professor Staunton continued, his voice growing louder. "I talked, I performed, but you felt you did not have to listen. And I have seen you laughing at me before. Why? What have you published recently that has made you an authority on the written word? Who or what has convinced you that you are so deep in the knowledge of writing that you can afford to ignore the direction provided by someone of my experience?" I heard his booming words, but they rocketed by me before I could feel them. "Let me see what you wrote; let me see what was so urgent that you had to write while I spoke."

Obediently, I handed him the papers. There were about ten sheets, with both front and back written on. The handwriting was terrible and I said, "You won't be able to read it, probably." My hand shook slightly.

"I will eat a light dinner," he said quickly. Then his tone changed, surprising me with its gentleness. He said, "Your hand shakes. Are you afraid of me?"

"No."

"Why not? I will probably hate what you wrote, and I will tell you it is revolting and disgusting."

"Then again, you might like it. I do."

"Yes, and perhaps someone might make perfume out of my feces."

I got up to leave. Professor Staunton's voice roared past my back. "You think I am too hard, don't you? You think I am cynical or maybe I am jealous of your so-called talent. You are afraid of me ruining your brilliant career as a writer!"

I shook my head. "No, Professor Staunton, I really don't think any of that," I said, looking back from the classroom door. Sunlight tinged his wrinkled skin the color of soiled newspapers.

"Bullshit!" The panes of glass on the classroom door vibrated with his resonance. "What do you think makes you so special?"

I stopped at the doorway and looked back at him. "Nothing," I said. "I'm not...special. It's just what I wrote—that's all, good or bad, it's me today, right now. It's just me. Today. Me. Now. That's all. Have a good day, Professor Staunton."

He nodded his head so slightly at first that I thought it was a nervous twitch. But with each nod his face made the change again, the red lines and angles of the demon transformed reluctantly to the glow of the grandfather. But still, when he spoke, his tone was caustic: "Then if we disagree about the eminence of your work, I have your esteemed permission to use this for toilet tissue, Mr. Burns?"

I chuckled and said, "That's fine, Professor. Because it's just me, today. Tomorrow, I may be some-one else. I've become someone else before." I waved, and walked out of the chilly classroom.

In the empty corridor, I saw a sign on a bulletin board advertising several upcoming parties, and next to that sign I saw a photocopy of an article from *STEP Words*, the underground student newspaper, with the headline "Thousands of Vietnamese Children Missing: The Untold Story of an Unjust War." I read of the thousands of children in Vietnam roaming lost in their war-torn country, and I looked at pictures of sobbing parents, and I felt myself shake slightly. Then I heard Sally-Boy behind me saying, *"Meet me on the fire escape tonight, Mikey, like we always did and let's just sit and look and see who can see the furtherest into the night, Mikey. I bet I can; I bet I can see more farther than you can, Mikey, and I can see more of everything than you can,"* but when I turned around, the corridor was, of course, still empty.

CHAPTER THIRTY-FIVE

Professor Staunton didn't particularly like what I had written, or at least that's what his comments indicated when I got the papers back, but neither did it appear that he had used them to wipe his ass. He said in his summary notes that the writing had given him "a mildly penetrating migraine that would have been more severe had I not already been viciously repulsed by someone else's work, making me somewhat numb to yours. The idea you write about, this theme of 'disappearance' is vaguely interesting in a creature as delectably attractive as the fantasy girl you have created and that strange, haunting boy. While the girl's hardness comes with the territory these days, is such a young woman also likely to possess the kind of sophistication you've described? And what extraordinary awareness she has—her deep insights about war and family! But flowers like her don't turn into weeds. And does anything really disappear? Isn't there always both a reason for the passing and a remnant that remains? And is that boy a permanently haunting menace? Even fiction needs reality, Mr. Burns. Remember, your reader is like a dog who doesn't know if the mound he sees along the curb is shit until he gets down and sniffs it."

But what I had written, of course, was mostly non-fiction.

So I wondered what you do when the truth itself is not believable. And why do we sometimes refuse to believe what we know to be true? Like the body counts from Vietnam each day in the paper, and the sight of the bodies themselves, the actual corpses floating down rivers, hauled off on trucks, stacked like human building blocks that appeared nightly on television. It was all so hard to believe, but it was right there for all of us to see...and then it wasn't.

One evening, as Walter Cronkite introduced film footage on TV with a warning about its graphically violent content, Darrell Bingham passed a gigantic bag of jelly beans around his room and said, as a camera panned the bloody results of an explosion in a Saigon cafe, "It only looks bad because the camera zeroes in on those mangled fuckers. If they swung the camera across the street, you'd see people just as normal as us."

"That ain't sayin much," Bobby Matson said, chewing a jelly bean, "considering that we all flock to your room to see this mess in color, and we all gonna die in that mess over there anyway. People gonna see our dead-ass selves on TV some day."

Even Fish, growing more detached every day, stretched to make sense of the truth by making the truth seem less real: "This is the only war ever where we see it like we would a baseball game—highlights, lowlights. They didn't use TV like they do now, didn't really even have it in the past. Imagine how the repeated highlights of Bataan would have looked, or Hiroshima, or Iwo Jima, or the camps where my grandparents suffered. It's hard enough for people to forget as is."

"Yeah, Fish, you right about all that...and suppose they had TV during the Civil War," said Bobby. "All that hand-to-hand shit at Gettysburg. But I don't know, man, I don't know if it's good to forget." He shook his head.

"Oh, but your people would be at the center of that one," Bingham said to Bobby. Darrell winked at us all.

"Why don't you cut that shit out, Darrell," I said.

Then we all stopped talking—remarkably, even Darrell Bingham—as on the screen an ancient Vietnamese woman, as small as a doll and as fragile as rotted wood, cried, her wrinkled face leaping out of the television to haunt us in the comfortable, color-co-ordinated suite. Her gnarled fingers slipped from the head of a corpse that was being pulled away, revealing mangled flaps of skin where her cheeks used to be. The camera zeroed in on the woman's sorrow-rutted face, and she seemed to morph into a grotesque mask of crisscrossed lines not foreign, nor recognizable, nor even human.

"Sick," Bobby said in a high-pitched whisper. "This war gonna get us all…all of us right here in this room. We all dead men."

"Grenades!" Darrell yelled, and tossed a handful of jellybeans at Bobby, who ducked and said, "Ain't funny, man…too real."

"This stuff on TV may be real, but it is terrible to show it," Fish said, looking around the room for support. "I'm telling you every war is brutal, but not every war settles down into your room or your home or a bar with you."

Moon prepared to light up. "Say, that may be true, Fish, my man, but that don't make what we see on the tube any less real. That old lady there, she feeling something, man, something real to her." He touched the yellow flame of a match to the paper and sucked in several times, the smoke pouring out in non-rhythmic streams as he spoke: "You see, it don't matter that we didn't see the Civil War on no TV sets or World War II or no World fucking War I—that's the one they called the War To End All Wars, right?—or Korea, which some people say ain't even officially ever ended… none of that stuff that happened back then matters." He drew in quickly a couple of more times and nodded his head toward the TV. "That there is what's happenin now, man, over in Vietnam, people dyin, and our chicken-shit Congress ain't even got the guts to call it a war, but you watch it, and there ain't no way to escape that fact that it is happening."

"If there's no way to escape, why do you blow all that pot, brotherman?" Bingham asked, tossing a jellybean into the air and catching it in his mouth. Darrell reached for the joint and, to my surprise, Moon gave it to him and then swept his arm around the room. We all took a hit or two and then Moon brought in a pipe and we all shared a couple of bowls, passing time, watching the news—bad and grotesque and frightening—and the more we smoked, the more we spun out our pot-induced philosophies and ironies and theories and promises, an isolated and lonely bunch of refried college boys watching the world go up in smoke, watching moments and people and pieces of ourselves disappear in a foggy blue haze.

The more I smoked, the foggier it got, the larger his face loomed over me from the corner of the fire escape, shaking his head in disbelief over what I had become.

CHAPTER THIRTY-SIX

I wondered a lot about a lot, and I wrote, and I talked to Erica on her visits to campus, trying to break down barriers that existed, barriers formed by a truth that I now knew, afraid to question what would happen once the barriers were down or if they could, in fact, be tumbled. I tried without really trying, because I noticed that when I was with her everything—school, the war, our relationship—seemed at once more intense yet less threatening than ever. Sexually we were deliberate—okay, slow, extremely slow—but by design, not because of lack of interest.

And the more intensely involved with Erica I became, the less Sally-Boy jumped into my thoughts...

Sally, The Fire Escape Philosopher, loved by all one day, gone the next...a disappearing reality.

At the same time, I watched Fish, unrestricted by barriers—or at least choosing to ignore them if they existed (and if you ignore them, does it matter in the immediate present whether they actually exist?), as he opened his daily letters from Katie and whispered nightly on the phone with her, sometimes five-minute long silences on his end (Was she listening to him breathe?).

After an hour he would hang up and stare silently before launching into his too familiar litany of love: "She's beautiful...sexy, too, trust me...really intelligent, incredible...almost nothing gets her, she's too smart and determined for that, my friend...she understands things...and, god, she's so sure of things, really confident...You know, I introduced Katie to my parents and they were polite, but I know they were thinking *shiksa* the whole time, like just because Katie is a non-Jewish girl makes her unacceptable. Bullshit!"

Sometimes he'd ramble about Katie's family's business: "Mr. McGee was saying at dinner last weekend that he expects a record season in sales this spring... The mid-sized cabin cruiser is the next major status symbol to distinguish the upper middle class or the lower upper class from the middle middle class...." Or Fish would pass along the latest news that Brian had sent home: "Not too happy about being stationed in

Saigon—wants more action, but, at the same time, says he wants to do more than fight...whatever that means. Just between us, he seems a little too philosophical for a Marine, don't you think? But, you know, he's already got it by the balls over there. Know what he did? His commanding officer sent a letter home telling about it...Brian saved some Vietnamese kid who got run over by an Army supply truck. Gave the kid mouth-to-mouth right on the street until the Medics got there. Brian never even mentioned it."

March howled through the Ides, each day bringing grisly new horrors. We plucked pistachios from a huge bowl in front of Bingham's color TV, sucking the sweet salted green nuts from their red shells, spitting the hulls into a wastebasket, fingers and lips stained blood-red with dye, we judged...and we theorized about the slaughter we were seeing:

Bingham: "Soldiers do what they have to do."
Bobby: "Overdo it just a little, maybe, bro? This war gonna kill us all; everyone in this fucking room."
Bingham: "Who's to say we overdo it?"
Moon: "What the hell, man, *we* are to say...I mean, someone gotta say somethin!"
Fish: "Stuff happens. It's war."
Me: "Does that mean it has to happen again and again?"

Bobby: "All them people bein mowed down every day, like the cows in that movie *Hud*."

Moon: "Yeah, but those cows had a disease, man; all that these people have is slanty eyes."

Bobby: "Sometimes that's all it takes to build the wall, right, brother?"

Moon: "Say, you got that right—slanty eyes, different religion, different language, diff...er...ent skin. Just about any goddam thing'll do if people want to hate bad enough. And one thing you can count—people sure enough want to hate."

We watched and thought and surmised and wondered and assured and speculated; to me, the world seemed increasingly littered with garish obscenities, human slaughter, human suffering, personal loss, vanishing youth:

The Erica I met that night with Bingham was gone; the night of winning pool was an innocent piece of history; my Bob Dylan story seemed juvenile; Sally-Boy was a lingering dream becoming less real than our fire escape; the Fish I knew was morphing into something unrecognizable before my eyes, his wild mass of hair suddenly neatly trimmed; ancient Vietnamese watched their culture explode; young servicemen returned limbless...or not at all...and we sat in the now-vulnerable room of a college campus and watched life change while we ate pistachio nuts and, eventually, washed their red stain from our fingers.

CHAPTER THIRTY-SEVEN

On the last weekend in March, a week before Spring Break, Erica and Katie came to campus on a Saturday with plans to stay overnight in Miller Hall, a freshman women's dormitory, and to leave on Sunday. While we waited for them to arrive, Fish uncharacteristically fidgeted until he finally suggested that we go downstairs and meet them in the Cunningham lobby rather than wait for them to come up to our room.

"Why?" I asked as we rode the elevator down.

He kept flicking his eyes nervously up at the floor indicator, as though he worried that the elevator would stick between floors. "I don't know," he said. "The room's a mess."

"Uh, it's not like they haven't seen it that way before, Fish. What's the real reason?"

The elevator door opened, catching Tomato and The Thatch in mid-kiss behind the intercom desk. They broke and began shuffling papers.

Fish and I sat in two plaid lounge chairs, facing one another. He picked at a cigarette hole in the material on the arm of his chair. He suddenly looked shy, rubbing his neatly cut curls and scratching at the hole and finally focusing on me with a half smile. "I don't want to sound offensive," he said.

"Jesus, Fish," I said, "you're starting to sound like Gary! What is it? Haven't I been giving you enough time to change clothes? Am I swearing too goddam fucking much? Look, asshole, you offend me by thinking you could offend me. Now what the hell's the problem?"

"Take it easy," Fish said, putting a hand up, as though he were trying to block my words. His back was to the intercom desk. Looking over his shoulder, I could see The Thatch sitting on Tomato's lap, holding a mirror in one hand while plucking at her jungle of eyebrows. The dexterity of those two amazed me. "I'd just like Katie all to myself this weekend, and I figure if we can split them up right here in the lobby, it will be easier to sort of go in our own directions. Is that okay with you?"

"Let's see...me, alone with Erica. I think I can stand it. But what's with you?"

"Look, you gotta understand, I don't mean…"

"I understand, believe it or not, I understand, so don't worry about it." Of course, I did not understand, but what I knew was that it was too painful to watch my friend grope for an explanation.

The desk telephone rang as an intercom buzzer sounded, causing Tomato to jump as if someone had stuck him with a pin. The Thatch's tweezers caught a piece of skin above her eye.

"Dammit," she shouted.

Tomato said, "Get the phone!"

The Thatch held her eye and said, "It's your job, you do it," but Tomato couldn't reach around her. The phone stopped ringing and the intercom stopped buzzing. Tomato sighed, licked his stubby index finger, and ran it over The Thatch's eyebrow.

"Here they come now," Fish said, nodding toward the ramp outside the lobby.

A breeze caught Erica's hair as she walked down the ramp. She saw me through the glass doors and waved. Katie saw Fish, and she blew him a kiss.

Erica and I set up a picnic lunch beyond the outfield fence of the campus baseball field. A game was underway, and all the players wore long-sleeved jerseys under their baseball shirts to cut down a slightly chilling breeze. A few spectators sat scattered in the small grandstands near the baselines, but the bleachers were more full than usual. Erica and I were stretched out just beyond the low, mesh outfield fence—close enough to see some of the action if we wanted, but far enough away to be undisturbed by the routine pop flies, ground balls, and bloop hits of the game.

I helped Erica spread the blanket, but I purposely yanked it in different directions to tease her.

She put her hands on her hips and sighed in mock exasperation. "Hand me that bag, NOW!" she said authoritatively.

We had bought a six pack of beer, a loaf of Italian bread, a couple of apples, some cheese and about four varieties of cold cuts at a deli just off campus. I sat between Erica and the bag.

"I can't reach it," I said. "You'll have to get it."

"Mike..." She tilted her head and reached out her hand to straighten a piece of my windblown hair, which was promptly windblown again.

"How about that bag? Don't you want it anymore?"

"Yes. Are you ready to hand it to me?"

"No, I still can't reach. And if you don't want us to starve, you'd better get the food quick."

"I say, you *are* an incorrigible child," she said in British, leaning across me.

I pulled gently on her arms and leaned back before she reached the bag. She stretched her body on top of mine. Her hair fell forward and her whole face was silhouetted by the blue sky, which matched her eyes. I felt the back of her jeans, snug and tight, the coarse denim clinging to smooth skin underneath. She outlined my face with her fingers. The wind blew in our direction, so we could hear the sounds of bat meeting ball, the gruff calls of umpires, and the noise of the small but excited crowd.

"It was another disturbing week, wasn't it?" she said.

"What do you mean?"

"The war, the news and all; it's so upsetting."

She sat up, reached into a bag and pulled out an apple. She studied it and rubbed it on her jeans, bit into it, and then held it out for me to bite.

"So what have you been doing with your days, Michael, besides going to class occasionally? I want to know all," she said in her mock interrogator's voice.

I sat up next to her, bit the apple, held it out for her, and raised an eyebrow. "Forbidden fruit means trouble ahead," I said.

"Just answer my question." She pointed a finger inches from my face.

"What was it again?"

"What do you do all day, Michael Burns? Answer... or else!" She pushed the apple toward my mouth. I fell back while taking a bite of it. She held it in my mouth and stretched out beside me, and then she spoke in some sort of German or Russian dialect: "I vill not remove de apple until you haf agree to tell me vat it is dot you do all the day. Do you understand this?"

From behind the apple, I mumbled agreement. She removed it.

"You're a hostile one," I said.

"And you are the tease and, um, how does one say? The procrastinator."

"Hmmm, 'procrastinator' is sort of a big word for a non-native English speaker, isn't it? I'm very suspicious of people who use big words and exhibit hostile tendencies."

"And I am the very—how do you say?—suspicious of the people who hide the things from the people they say they…feel close to."

"Having a little trouble following you, commandant," I said, "but I think we agree—we are very suspicious of each other."

Erica flopped onto her back, let out an exasperated sigh, looked up at the sky and rolled her eyes. I laughed and was vaguely aware of a growing noise from the baseball field. Suddenly, propping herself on one arm, Erica snapped her head toward me. "What do you do all day, Burns, no bullshit," she said quickly.

Now we sat face-to-face on the blanket. "Well, lately I write a lot," I said, mimicking her detective's tone.

She blinked. "You what a lot?"

"Write a lot."

"Really?"

"Right. I write."

She smiled. "That is rather counterintuitive, College Boy! What do you write?"

"All sorts of stuff."

"Poems?"

"Except poems."

"Short stories?"

"Well, not really. Not yet anyway."

"Then what?"

"What what?"

"Arrrgh!" she shouted in mock frustration as she jumped on me and stretched out on top of me. "I do, too, you know," she said.

"What?"

"Write. I do a lot of writing. Would you share yours with me sometime if I share mine with you?" Her tone had changed dramatically, and now as I looked up at her I saw something different, a need for closeness. She kissed me, then asked, "Has anyone else seen your work?"

"No, just my professor, and he hates it all equally. I'm not much of a sharer. But, yes, I'd like to show some of it to you sometime. I'd like you to see."

She rolled onto her back again. I propped my head on one hand. Wind blew cheers our way, and strands of her hair lifted across her face and onto my hand. I moved them back into place, tracing her face with one finger.

"Think of how hard it must have been for someone like Emily Dickinson," she said absently staring at the sky. "Such a private person with so much inside, yet no one wanted to publish what she had to say."

"Why not?"

"She was different, invisible really. And she was, of course, a woman."

"Did you write a paper on her or something?"

"No," she said. "I just started reading her work and then all about her."

I heard some cheering from the field again, but I wasn't going to turn and stop looking at Erica.

"Can I tell you something she wrote?" Erica asked. "I think about it a lot these days, with the news and all."

"You have one of her books with you?" I asked stupidly.

"No. I just liked it, so I memorized it. I don't know, sometimes I think about how many people never get heard from—they're here, they live, they do things...and then they're gone." Erica paused, a sudden catch in her voice gripping her words. When she continued, she sounded tired. "I guess that sounds strange, maybe even hypocritical knowing what you do about me."

"Not at all. Go ahead, Erica. Tell me whatever you want. You know a poem by Dickinson, and I want to hear it."

She kissed my forehead and said, "Okay, tell me if you like it, you know, if it makes sense today." Erica looked down shyly, a momentary glimpse in which I saw what she must have looked like as a child. Then she recited from memory:

> "'This is my letter to the World
> That never wrote to me—
> The simple News that Nature told—
> With tender majesty
> Her message is committed
> To hands I cannot see—
> For love of Her, Sweet countrymen—
> Judge *tenderly*—of Me'!"

I looked at the sky while she spoke and then continued searching it for a couple of minutes after she finished and wished nothing would ever change, that I would somehow stay almost twenty years old on a blanket with Erica, listening to her recite Dickinson from memory, and the same breeze would float by and push Erica's hair across my face, and we would be held together on the blanket permanently, like people in a painting, and that I might someday even introduce her to Sally-Boy.

But even then, even as she spoke Dickinson's lines, I knew that everything is tied to time and every second brings change; a breeze can push dust into your eyes; love begins or ends; peace explodes into tragedy; men and women spin helplessly into unknown worlds filled with jungles and strangers and frowning doctors and empty rooms and tunnels with no light at either end... and a fire escape that leads nowhere.

The cushion of Erica's voice fell away, and I heard something else—angry, hostile, fearful, dissonance blaring amid the harmony of the afternoon, coming from the baseball field, where something other than baseball was happening.

Erica looked toward the field. "There's some sort of fight," she said, as we both stood. She gripped my arm tightly.

We walked to the outside of the outfield fence together. There was, indeed, a fight of sorts, but not on the field. On the field, players stared at the stands behind third base. Even the home plate umpire stood with his mask off, knowing that something beyond his power was at hand. I squinted and strained to see a small man in a gray suit being pummeled. He was pushed to the ground, and when he lifted his head, I recognized him.

"Jesus," I said, "they're beating hell out of Dean Carmody."

The scuffling STEP group, about thirty people strong at that point, surrounded the dean and moved with him in our direction. The STEP member with the wild red hair and curly beard suddenly put the dean in a headlock, and the dean's arms dangled pitifully at his sides, flopping like a rag doll as he tried to maintain his balance. Two campus security officers pushed like slow awkward bears through the crowd, flinging students aside in an attempt to free the dean, but more students—STEP members and non-STEP members alike—jumped the fence and grabbed baseball bats and swung wildly at the rent-a-cops, clubbing some of them to the ground. The students cursed anyone who came near as they herded the surrounded dean in the direction of his office in the Hopewell Administration Building. They shoved him hard, pushing in our direction. I recognized many of the students, but with their angry faces and with the wind blowing their long hair wildly, they looked older, harder, and tinged with excitement, fear, and confusion. They hurried, and the wind swirled dirt and lime from the field in small funnels that danced alongside the crowd. They pushed closer to us and we heard them shouting, their voices raspy and tense: "Hurry up! Get the fucker moving! We got him! Lock the fucker up! We've got the sonuvabitch now..."

They passed directly in front of us, their shared anger propelling them, a girl elbowing me and Erica aside. The dean's eyes bulged, and purple veins swelled in his forehead. His glasses dangled from his shirt collar, then fell in front of me. I reached for them, but a boot came down crushing them in the dirt. I looked up into the face of a tangle-haired girl.

"Let the cocksucker go blind!" she shouted, waving her clenched fist in my face.

From behind her came a voice I recognized, shouting, "Say, we got our man, STEP-children, and we now gonna make this motherfucker face the facts...yeah, *all* the facts!"

It was Andre Moon, but he didn't see me. The crowd pushed by, and on the other side of the students I saw Professor Staunton, wearing sunglasses, leaning against a tree, nodding his head in approval as the longhaired young woman he had been with in the Tombs spoke into his ear.

I took a sweeping look around campus. In far corners I saw people who were unaware of what was happening. An incident can occur right behind you, or even in front of you, I thought, and you still might not know it's happening. A soldier blowing a kiss at a train never returns home, and only a handful of people ever know. A young woman lawyer fights for people in the depths of a deteriorating city, but not even the phone book carries her name. And how many people saw a determined young man running down a Brooklyn street one night, but had no way of knowing that he would vanish?

We followed the crowd. The STEP members and their captive dean disappeared inside the Hopewell Admin Building beyond the ball field. They shattered windows on the landing of each flight of stairs they ascended, huge chunks of glass violently gliding to earth and smashing gently into millions of jagged slivers.

Four flights up; four shattered windows. Within minutes they were in Carmody's office.

The umpires huddled together on the field and then dispersed to their positions.

"Play ball!" the man behind the plate shouted.

Mechanically, the players pounded their gloves and shook their heads clear and their muscles loose. Soon, the game continued because, well, that's what games do…they continue.

Erica dug her fingers into my arm. I held her around her waist.

"What do they want with the dean, Mike? What's going on? And how can they keep playing a game?"

I couldn't help wondering if the questioning, confused, almost pleading voice I heard was the same one Brian had heard several months earlier. I pulled her closer as we looked toward the growing number of students in front of the Hopewell Administration Building. Unlike Brian, I had no answer for Erica.

CHAPTER THIRTY-EIGHT

B y late evening, a thousand or more people, mostly students, ringed the admin building, shouting, singing, chanting, drinking, smoking. Some, like Erica and I, just watched, confused and curious. Tense state troopers gripped their nightsticks across their chests. A group of students from STEP dressed in tattered clothes eagerly worked the growing crowd, chanting and distributing mimeographed papers that stated their concerns and demands:

The repeated call to drop ROTC; more classes for minority students; a change in what it called the school's "narrow-minded, restrictive, exclusionary curriculum"; a demand that Sinclair College President

Avery M. Tolbert formally declare the school's opposition to the Vietnam War. Carmody had been apprehended, the paper said, because his university position "symbolized the bureaucracy's distance from the concerns, needs and ideals that best suit the students in particular and society in general. By failing to meet with students in good faith and by failing to recognize and revolutionize an antiquated academic structure, Carmody sanctions a curriculum and educational philosophy that is geared to support the War Machine, confine the intellectual growth of minorities, and imply, through inaction, the university's approval of countless atrocities in the most unjust war in the history of Ameri**K**a."

Packs of students periodically pushed against the police line and shouted at the cops, who restrained themselves at first. But as darkness deepened, everyone's patience thinned a layer at a time, like paint being stripped from a wall. The once-placid onlookers turned anxious as drugs, alcohol, and rumors circulated freely among them. Someone threw some firecrackers, and a state trooper squatted and put his hand to his pistol. The crowd jeered at him.

"Are you gonna shoot us, pig?" someone yelled. "Is that what you want to do? Kill, kill kill..."

And others picked up the chant, "Kill, kill, kill ..."

Rumors crackled rapidly across the network of students as though some unseen phone line connected us:

"Man, STEP has guns in there; there's gonna be blood..."

"The school told these fucking stormtroopers to end it quick, do whatever it takes to bust us up..."

"Hey, rumor is Carmody kicked, man, went down with a heart attack big time..."

"Fuck him! Hope he did croak!"

"STEP's ready for this, man, they got food, clothes, rubbers, they could start a whole fuck-in commune in there..."

Who knows the truth, I wondered, and would we recognize it if we saw it? The atmosphere in the crowd of students alternated between that of a huge impromptu party and one of desperate, smoldering anger. As the night wore on, the mood changed more frequently. Some of the more enterprising students sold beer, wine, joints, pills. A bearded and beaded photographer wearing a fringed buckskin jacket and a New York *Times* baseball cap snapped pictures, alternating between a camera with a zoom-action lens and one with a standard .35-millimeter lens. His girlfriend, dumpy and dirty, sold beer for fifty cents a can from a huge newspaper carrier's sack that said The New York *Times* on it.

I paid a dollar-fifty for some wine from a guy wearing a leather cowboy hat who was strumming a guitar while leaning against a tree. Erica and I decided to walk to the Mountain Hall about a hundred yards away. She was supposed to meet Katie later in the night at Miller Hall, but it was still early. Besides, neither of us had any idea where Fish and Katie were. So we left the admin building grounds and walked toward the Mountain, an old ten-story building used for classrooms. I knew it would be safe and quiet there, a good place to sit and talk and watch the world below.

From inside the Mountain the campus looked beautifully eerie in the darkness. A fine haze blurred the lights around the grounds. Large, black silhouettes of trees, outlined against the night sky, blended into the inky darkness. There were no lights on the small stair landing where we stretched out. I wanted to go to the top floor, the tenth, but both Erica and I heard passionate whispers from there as we ascended the steps, so we settled on the ninth-floor landing. With its cathedral ceilings, heavy wooden doors, and wavy glass windowpanes, the Mountain often loomed ominously over the campus, but now it seemed the perfect sanctuary away from the uncertainty that smoldered below. In the distance was the familiar rumble of trucks rolling along the highways of New Jersey. We were comfortably quiet for several minutes, sipping too-sweet wine out of a bottle, vaguely aware of an occasional pant from one flight up, or the muffled strained hum from the grounds of the admin building across the way, or the gnashing of gears from the heavy rigs on the distant highways.

"Someday I'm going to compose the 'New Jersey Symphony,'" I said to Erica. "I'm going to record gears grinding and horns honking, engines revving, tires squealing, and then I'll set it all to music."

"Sounds lovely," she said, smirking as she propped her head up on a folded blanket.

I stood and looked out the window. Images were distorted through the glass, some magnified, some reduced in size, some warped. "If you think it would be lovely, I'll do it," I said.

"Have you ever composed any music?" she asked.

"No, the 'New Jersey Symphony' will be my first. Do you know what instrument it will feature?"

"I'm afraid to ask."

"The *auto*harp."

She groaned. "I think you're overtired, Burns, and your mind is shot from standing at that window waiting for something to happen. Come here." She patted a spot next to her on the blanket. I sat and took another long pull on the wine bottle. It felt cool going down, but once in my stomach it caused heat to rise within me. I stretched out next to Erica on the floor and looked up into the blackness toward the ceiling.

"I liked your poem, the Dickinson one," I said absently. "I didn't tell you before because that's when all the shit started."

"I thought you might like it. 'Judge tenderly of me'; that's my favorite phrase. Please remember it."

"Okay, I'll try. Let me see: Judge...tenderly...um... for?...ME. Judge tenderly for me."

"It's *'of'* me, Burns. Please tell me you know that."

"I know that. I really do." I was aware that my eyelids suddenly felt oversized. Erica noticed.

"Are you tired?" she asked.

"A little." I strained to see the campus more clearly.

"It's bad out there, isn't it?" she said, motioning toward the window.

"I've never seen the grounds so crowded with so many different kinds of people. It's kind of inspiring in a weird way. I can't explain it."

"I know what you mean," she said, rubbing the back of my neck. "Inspiring but frightening, too."

"Yeah. And I don't have any idea how it will end."

We had a small portable radio with us, and I tuned in WABC in New York just in time to hear the final lines from Buffalo Springfield: "Stop, children, what's that sound/Everybody look what's going down...," so I told Erica my Bob Dylan story and said that I had never told it to anyone else. She listened intently to every word and when I was finished, she looked straight into my eyes and whispered passionately, "Mike, you know that's a story to keep for a lifetime; it's like a little letter for your world," and then she kissed me hard on the lips.

A slick disc jockey sailed through his spiel of non-stop chatter, but not even the hourly news broadcasts mentioned the campus incident just two hours down the New Jersey Turnpike. Erica and I talked and played and watched in the darkness, sharing sips of wine, listening to the music while stretched out upon the cool floor, bundled in ski jackets and each other. We pressed closer and closer to one another, the effects of the wine slowing every movement, taste, and sound. We spoke in scarcely audible whispers, sometimes one talking directly into an ear of the other. Spurts of impassioned mumbles came from the landing above. And from the Hopewell Administration Building grounds, cheers and music and occasional frightening screams grew steadily louder.

At one point, a police siren sounded, and there was loud commotion below, although we could not see anything specific happening. "What do you think, Mike?" Erica asked. "What do you make of it all? Where does all this anger go?"

"I don't know; I really don't. I hear the news and I can see almost every point of view. That's my problem—name a viewpoint, and old Mike Burns can probably see merit in it. For the war? Sure, I can see why we don't want Southeast Asia to go Communist. Against the war? No problem; I don't want to get blown away or see others get killed for a cause I'm not sure I understand much less believe in. For the government? Yeah, my dad works for it and it seems to try to operate in our best interests for the most part. For the press picking at the government? Definitely, like Thomas Jefferson said, I'll take a free press over a free government anytime, because I don't believe you can have the latter without the former...despite what my father would say. For ROTC? That's okay with me, it's a personal choice, kind of like what Brian faced. Against ROTC? Me too, since I can see where it is nourished by the 'war machine' concept. You know, I read something by Thoreau for my writing class, and it makes me wonder like Thoreau did—How long does a standing army remain satisfied with just *standing*? To me, it's confusing; to others it all seems so clear. It all just pisses me off sometimes, because, you know, I just have no idea..."

I didn't realize it but during my rant my wine-amplified voice had grown loud. I was lying on my back looking toward the ceiling through the blackness when Erica gently put a finger on my lips. She then rolled over on top of me and held my head in her hands, rubbing my temples with her fingers. I dropped my voice to a murmur: "I guess I sound pretty damn confused, don't I? That's because I just have no fucking idea..."

But her finger was back on my lips. Her thighs pressed against mine. She shook her head, whispering, "No, it's okay," and her hair brushed across my face. She paused, then whispered, "I never have understood how some people are always so sure they're right."

She kissed me.

"Well, I'm not."

"I know, I know, neither am I, and I'm glad you're not."

She touched my lips again with her finger. My hands moved lightly over her body and hers slipped over mine. I traced her eyes and lips with my tongue, a slow, sweet journey. We took off our jackets. I lifted her sweater, unbuttoned her blouse, and kissed her warm breasts. I held them in my cupped hands and watched her eyes close and her lips part in a smile. Her hand pressed slowly up my pants leg until she found me. Inside her jeans, I felt her smooth and moist; from mine, she pulled me and held her hand against me and moved it so slightly that I thought it might have been accidental. But then she moved her hand again, barely, slowly. And then again, and again, and I realized my eyes were closed. I opened them, and she was studying my face with tender eyes. She kissed me and made just the faintest movement with her hand as she continued to stroke me. Long, warm contractions extended down the insides of my thighs, and I uttered her name, but she just leaned forward and said, "Shhh, go ahead," and I glimpsed her face and surged warm and long against her hand. My eyes shut tight and my lips were taut, but they slackened with each declining pulsation, until my eyes opened slowly on their own, and I saw her passionate face, and she kissed me long and deep.

CHAPTER THIRTY-NINE

Hours passed, and we continued to talk and touch in the night, doing as much as we dared do, sharing love without actually making love and growing more comfortable together. The voice on the radio said it was two a.m., and we decided to leave. I drained the wine on the way to Miller Hall, kissed Erica good-night there, felt the cool night air against my head, which hummed slowly from the wine, felt the curious, definite pull of the crowd that crackled with a low, electric buzz in the black night, and felt the tension, scalpel-like, that seemed ready to cut through reason, age, cause, and purpose. I walked toward it, and somehow I knew I would, knew I must, knew that this was something that I had to know. The hum was a charge, a violent prod preparing to ignite a chaotic explosion. I listened with wine-laden hearing to people in the crowd, mostly people I didn't know, faceless people, but people with a cause, people with shared passion. The questions from the mix of people came repeatedly:

"What's happening in there?"
"Do you think the school will give in?"
"Is Carmody dead?"
"Who gives a shit?"

There weren't really answers, just an increase in the intensity of the hum and comments, ever stronger in their conviction:

"Stop the support of the fucking war machine!"
"We're gonna close this school up!"
"Gutless administration has no balls!"

Still I listened—an observer, taking it in, trying to make sense, seeing if I fit somehow. I talked little, bought one beer and then another from the photograper wearing the New York *Times* hat whose girl carried the *Times* bag. It was hot in the crowd, which tossed a non-stop volatile mixture of anger, frustration, hatred, and paranoia at the stone-like police whose faces now were rigid, heavy with fatigue, and whose knuckles grew white around the brown nightsticks. I was sweating. Another beer; it went down thick and warm and made my stomach rumble.

The crowd pushed and rocked. My back was toward the building; I turned to face it and, in turning, images blurred in and out of focus. So many thoughts, some floating, some darting. I was part of the crowd now, part of its hum, part of its rhythm, its life, washed along, bumping from person to person. And in the crowd, I was aware that I was finally part of something again, something very different from my Brooklyn childhood. Within the crowd, more movement, more force, more freedom; my hair was matted, still not cut, and I was proud of its length and that Erica liked it and, after all, it's only hair. I laughed with the crowd and spat with it and jeered with it and soon my head filled with the hum of it, an ever-increasing pitch and the faces mingled and blended with my thoughts.

I saw in my mind a soldier, a familiar young face, confused, grimy, stubble of a beard, tense, fears pushing little boy tears behind his eyes, and then...sniper fire. Where is it coming from? Run? Where? Is there pain? Does it burn? In that instant when you die and life flashes before your eyes, with a jolt, a pain, a fire, the ground coming up fast, not on me, but him—no, slowly, it must come up slowly while he remembers... What? A girl, maybe, a boat, a fire escape, a song, yes a song, of course a song, the music, full chorus, an odd rhythm, the rhythm of life ending slowly, the lyrics drawn out—

"I...can't...get...no
Sa...tis...fac...tion"

—slowly, the cold beads of sweat and piss and tears and all the questions floating up with the dirt:

What for, man? Why? Why me? Why you? Why now? What's left? What did I leave behind? WHERE IS HE???

And then the reality of the crowd overtook my thoughts: "Ain't this some shit, man, ain't this some shit though?" The voice came from a student pushed shoulder-to-shoulder against me; he grinned widely showing badly chipped teeth. Then, with a huge sucking noise, he dragged deeply on a joint, pulled it from his mouth reluctantly, grinned again at me through the smoke, and motioned toward me. "Take a good long slow blow, man," he said. And I puffed long and deep and he smiled, shaking his head again, saying, "But this is some shit, man, ain't it some shit, man, we are kicking *ass* tonight! They busted heads earlier, man—did you see it? Were you here? It's like we can't say nothin, like we don't have any voice, man, these fascist fucking pigs, man, but we are getting back now, we are going to fuck them up...gonna be some nasty shit coming down..."

Yeah, I thought, taking the weed again from the guy and sucking it deeply, it's some shit, shit that can lead to me being like that soldier, only here, alone, burning in the grass, wondering why, wondering...Did he have an Erica? Do I? Navy boy did, right? Come up for a football game, Erica; we'll watch it on TV. She loved it; I never asked you, but you loved it right, Erica? Blue-eyed Erica, sweet, long-haired Erica, gentle, gentle Erica. Was the light on? Did you smile? Did he see you?

Please let it sink, let it drown, let it fade, please... some things are best left unsaid, untold, now it will get deeper, an explosion not a wave, not flowing, not constant, just there, covered, bursting quietly and in time, in time, in time...What time? Now is the only time, and now slips away. Sally-Boy—slipped away, slipped off the fire escape, we were one in two, you and I, and you're gone and I still don't know why or where...where did you go, Sally, where do they go, the faces that just slip away, the old Vietnamese woman stinking and rotting, holding the leftovers of a face that slipped away, the faces of soldiers, the faces of children slipping away, the face of time running out, people disappearing, people we never know...

The hum of the crowd increased in pitch and grew into a chorus that included *my* voice, *my* fist clenched tight, raised high:

"Stop the war! End oppression! Stop the war! No more ROTC! Stop the killing! KILL ROTC, NOT BABIES!"

Sweat dropped from my face, poured down my back soaking my shirt, and my smell mingled with the smell of others. I unbuttoned my shirt, ripped a shred from it and tied it around my head to keep the sweat from my eyes. Amid a group of predominately black students, Andre Moon clutched Bobby Matson's waist. Bobby, unsmiling and weaving drunkenly, called out to me, "Hey Mike, you with us, man? You with the brothers? Best be, man, this war gonna kill us all!"

My voice was thick; I tried, and failed, at a smile, "Sure, yeah Bobby, you know..."

Moon interrupted, "Say, get this now, man, you either with us or you against us! Ain't no more time to be hung up in the middle. You either here to help us change or things are going to stay the same!"

I wanted to yell out, "I'm with you Moon!" but I paused, regrettably but, after all, that was me, it was what I did at the time, I was still in part a struggling, confused boy full of pauses—and in that instant Moon jumped onto a table and shouted and voices black and white alike started to echo agreement as he said, "Say, my people, you best believe things have got to change, no other motherfuckin way about it, brothers and sisters!"

People cheered and responded, "Right on, brother, tell 'em how it is!"

Moon's voice, resonant with emotion possessed incredible range, starting down deep, hundreds of years deep, and climbing to a shrill whine: "Things have got to change, motherfuck, things are going to change, goddamit, things are going to change, goddamit, 'cause we gonna take up the fight for ourselves, motherfuck, that's right, motherfuck, take up the fight for ourselves, motherfuck, we gonna see to it ourselves, goddamit, and we ain't waitin no longer, we ain't waitin no longer, we gonna see to it, goddamit, best believe we gonna see to it **now**! Say, this school run outta time, govment run outta time, motherfuck, see too many brothers starvin, see too many brothers burnin, goddamit, too many dying, too many children bein murdered, and we gonna see that the time is here for things to begin changin, the time is here, goddamit, the time is now, the time has come, **MOTHERFUCK, THE TIME FOR CHANGE HAS COME!**"

The cheers were deafening, and in my spinning head I heard the echo of my own cursing, shouting to be heard with the others, shouting until my throat ached, as I kept thinking there's no time, time's up, fuck time, burn time, torch time, war time, and I joined other students and sang with them: "battle lines being drawn, nobody's right if everybody's wrong"— sing it—"battle lines being drawn, nobody's right if

everybody's wrong"—soldier's face—"battle lines being drawn…"—no time…no fire escape…

A white light flashed, and for a moment I could
not see or hear and my mind went empty, but screams
and curses brought reality back into focus, the hum
exploding in thunderous jolts of sound and light, the
thud of fists, smell of tear gas, crack of nightsticks,
sharp in their dullness. I turned away from the building to run, but a state trooper ran up behind me, pushing a girl over, her face bouncing despite the cushion
of grass, her eyes squeezing shut and open in pain
and surprise. Beside her a boy bled from his forehead,
moaning like a hurt dog and the girl reached for the
boy, then grabbed the trooper around his ankle, her
face scratched, bleeding, she shrieked through tears,
"You fucker, you pig, you fucker, you pig!"

Someone shouted, "They're rushing the building!
Don't let the fucking pigs get into the building!"

An incredible deafening roar, a powerful surge, I
ran with the others toward the admin building, throwing rocks and cans and twigs—anything that would
move—at troopers who swung their sticks randomly, furiously. A nightstick cracked across the neck of
a student running in front of me; he moaned, staggered, fell. I tripped over him and stumbled to the
cool ground. I looked up to see a trooper's black boot
swing back in a short arc over the grass and suddenly, slowly, I realized it was aimed at me and with that

realization the boot sped forward in a blur toward my head. I raised my right arm for protection, but the thick boot caught me under the biceps, deflected hard off my right cheekbone, and drove me onto my back. My head rang, and I looked straight up at the trooper, spinning like a triumphant ogre above me, the plastic mask of his helmet hiding half his angry face, his gun glistening in its holster. He raised his nightstick high over his head, my stomach churned, and I muttered "no" in a sickly voice, a foreign voice. But the stick wasn't aimed at me. He swung instead at someone behind me, and the ground trembled as a body thudded, groaning, to earth. The trooper moved away, swinging, kicking, punching. I rolled onto my stomach, my right arm burning, my face swollen, my head spinning wildly as I vomited into the grass.

I don't know exactly how long I lay in the damp grass in my own pool of puke, but I heard student voices grow more frantic, their cries more frequent and high-pitched, like the rapid yelps of cornered dogs. I looked toward the building about thirty yards away. Police had the student charge under control now. Tear gas poured from the building and cops piled out of the main entrance, their gas masks making them look like a pack of storming alien invaders. They had about a dozen coughing, choking, vomiting students behind them.

Dean Carmody emerged, surrounded by a protective wall of police, a gas mask over his face. My head was clearing, and I felt some strength returning to my wobbly legs. I tried to stand, but could only rise to my knees. The lawn resembled a battlefield, not unlike the ones Walter Cronkite warned us about before showing them to us on TV. Students milled around, helping friends. Ambulance workers took care of the few injured cops first, then picked their way through the students.

The STEP ringleaders who had been in the building were handcuffed and shoved into a paddy wagon. Moon and Bobby were gone, somewhere, but I had no idea where. I stood, and my stomach did one quick flip, but my legs felt solid and the smell of tear gas was clearing, so I gulped for fresh air. Then I noticed cops handcuffing students who were either still on the ground or were being checked on by rescue workers. A cop approached the student I had tripped over, who moaned while still kneeling, and I heard the clicking of the photographer's lens as he aimed his camera and snapped pictures of the littered grounds. The trooper slapped the handcuffs on the kneeling boy in front of me and then spotted me, staring.

"You stay right there you, you little prick," he shouted at me.

The trooper pushed the boy's face down into the dirt, put his knee into his back, and looked at me from behind his mask. "Stay there, fucker," he warned. My face burned and my heart pounded hard as I stood frozen. The trooper looked down to snap the cuffs into place on the boy who writhed in pain from the trooper's knee in his back, and in that instant, I ran.

"Get back, you little sonovabitch, or I'll shoot your ass!" the trooper yelled.

But I ran, my legs churning in hard, meaningful strides, people blurring as I ran by, and the bullet never came for me. And as I ran, the night grew calm and comfortable and quiet until in the darkness, a safe distance away, I stopped and looked back at the building and the battleground. They looked small and serene and in the nighttime shroud, almost unreal. But I felt the swelling pain on my cheek and under my right arm, and I knew they were real. So I ran again. I ran long and hard and, for a while, to nowhere in particular, until in my mind I was laughing and elbowing Sally-Boy as we ran the Brooklyn streets at night to see who could go the fastest and "furtherest."

Eventually, I made it back to my empty room and fell into bed. Sleep came fast, spinning me into a mass of blurred dreams until a distant pounding caused explosions of light as I slept. In the slowness of sleep, I thought, "The guns, the guns, more guns..." The staccato pounding drew nearer and the colors lasted longer, grew wider behind my eyelids. "Sally! Nightsticks hitting heads, run, run, run, look out, Sally—get to the fire escape now..."

More pounding, but as I opened my eyes into night's shadows it sounded gentler, and I heard an urgent voice: "Mike, oh Mike, please, please open the door..." It was Erica; I knew it was her, but still I lay in bed, not reacting, instead puzzling over why the cool sheets were damp with my sweat. I suddenly bolted upright, smelled my own pot-and-vomit-tinged breath, and flicked on a small lamp. I glanced at the clock next to my bed, but for some reason couldn't make out the numbers—then I realized my right eye had swollen shut. Before Erica finished knocking again, I opened the door.

Erica spoke hurriedly as she rushed into the room without looking at me: "Mike, I got a phone call at the dorm. It's..." Then she stopped, noticing my eye for the first time. Her mouth opened silently and her face twisted in pain. She reached a hand to my bruised cheekbone and my ogre's eye. "Oh," she said, "oh, Mike, what happened? What's going on? What have they done to you?"

She untied the ragged headband I still wore, pushed my hair back, and held me. My right arm ached as I wrapped it around her. She came into the room. I closed the door. It was dark except for the lone beam of light from the lamp next to my bed.

"Tell me," she whispered, and as she moved to hold me, she touched my arm and I flinched. "What is it? What happened?" she asked. I sat on the bed and held up my arm for her to see. She pushed her head into my bare chest and wrapped her arms round my waist. Her hair swooped lightly across my shoulders. "Don't be hurt," she said. "Not you, not ever." Then she stood, and I saw that she was sobbing loud, choking on tears.

I said, "Don't cry, Erica...I'll be okay...Nothing's broken..."

She shook her head. "Okay, okay, Mike, okay... but...we have to find Katie, Mike, we have to find her, we have to," she said, shaking.

I held her face in my hands and pushed with my thumbs at the warm, streaming tears, but at my touch she sobbed with such sudden force that her body shook uncontrollably.

"Katie's parents called," Erica said. "It's Brian, oh Mike, it's Brian. He's dead, Mike. He's dead. He's dead. Oh Mike, Brian is dead..."

Erica's cry turned soft, but there was something in-human about it, and her arms grabbed and scraped at my back. Inside my head, a scream rang hollow and long, and I groped for the strength to comfort Erica by lightly kissing her lips and fingers but, mostly, her tears.

CHAPTER FORTY

A mound of rich brown early-spring earth was piled to one side of the flag-draped casket containing Brian McGee's body. I kept picturing how some mechanical device would drop the casket into the ground when we walked away, and then the cool dirt would tumble on top, and that would be it. Earth, giver of life, container of death.

And why was the day cloudless? Shouldn't nature be obliged to provide weather to fit the event and your mood? Not on that day—on the day we buried Brian McGee, a son, a brother, a cousin, a protector, a friend, a Marine—on that day, not even those stray white wisps that sometimes fleck the uppermost edges of the sky looked down. Nothing. Just blue, high and deep and endless. And the flowers lining the cemetery rows grinned widely, stretching their folds to greet the yellow sunlight, their roots sucking strength from the soil.

It should be raining, I thought.

But dogs sniffed at each other just beyond the cemetery fence.

It should be gray and cold.

But a bird pulled a worm from Brian's dirt and flew away.

It should be a day that forces you inside into some damp room, where wet windows fog over with every breath from the living.

But we stood amid growth and life, and I prayed with the rest of them—though even then I did not believe in prayer and wondered if anyone really did and if they did, how they could—and I glanced up at the terrible beautiful blueness and wondered why I wanted it to rain when I was so glad that it wasn't.

Tim McGee stood motionless next to the dirt that waited to cover his brother. Everyone else walked away, including Fish, who now huddled with the family, goatee gone, hair trimmed, one arm around Katie, the other around Katie's mother. Tim leaned forward, hair drooping onto the front of his suit jacket. I walked behind Tim toward the cars and noticed a tremble across his powerful shoulders. He glanced up quickly, saw me looking at him, and motioned for me to walk toward him.

"Bad looking eye," he said as I approached. I wore sunglasses that only partially covered the colors that, nearly two weeks later, still extended from my cheekbone to my eyebrow. "How'd you get it?"

We began to walk together, and Tim listened intently as I spoke, our hair swirling in the breeze, and then he stopped walking. He looked ahead at the cars preparing to return people home to their daily lives. I finished talking and stood next to him as we peered across the lush cemetery lawn at the cloudless expanse of blue and the white sea of stone slabs.

"Do you know?" Tim asked. "Did anyone tell you how it happened, how they got Brian?"

I had been told by a sobbing Erica, but before I could say anything, Tim spoke in a soft monotone:

"Walking down the street, busy street, heart of Saigon...Broad fucking daylight...He's with two other Marines, the three of them probably bullshitting about their girls back home or baseball or who knows what. Vietnamese kid just runs right up and stabs Brian in the heart, man, nothing said, no words at all, just one knife plunged with all his strength...One of the two other Marines wastes the kid with one bullet, man, boom, one bullet to the kid's fucking head. They say the kid was maybe thirteen." Tim shook his head and looked at me. His teeth were clenched just as they had been the night of Brian's going-away party. "I just hate it, Mike, I hate what happened to Brian, I hate what Brian did going to the war, and I hate what happened to that Vietnamese kid."

How could I justify it? "Tim, Brian felt he had to." But even to me, the speaker, the statement sounded shallow.

"But look..." Tim made a fatigued wave in an arc toward the people preparing to depart. Brian's fiancee, Karen, groped for composure, slumping against her father's shoulder. The McGees walked arm-in-arm, as if to help one another support the weight of their burden. Fish dabbed gently at Katie's face with a handkerchief. Erica's sorrow had pulled her face tight as though her tears had shrunk her skin taut against the bones. Her parents, who had struggled to contain their own grief in order to help comfort the McGees, looked haggard.

"Don't you see," Tim went on, "how bad it all is?"

When you are inexperienced at death, what do you say to ease someone's pain? What justifies a bullet in the brain, shrapnel to the lungs, a knife through the heart? What is the rate of exchange when the death of someone you love is cashed in for the lives of people you'll never know?

The group of starched, disciplined Marines who had performed the brief ceremony—folded flag, twenty-one gun salute, honor guard—drove away, their grim duty complete for that day. Other car doors slammed. Keys turned in ignitions. The living prepared to leave the dead. And walking with Tim, I realized that whatever pain I felt in my arm and eye and head from the trooper's boot would serve as a reminder that life had been kicked *into* me, and that whoever slashed Brian McGee's heart simply spread it among the rest of us.

"That must've been some wicked shot you took from that pig, man," Tim said.

I shrugged.

Tim turned his head back toward the hole in the earth which was shaded by a gently rippling canopy, and when he faced me again, he said in a near whisper, "The rotten fucking worst of it is, man, that I just couldn't talk him out of what he believed in."

Tim offered to drive me back to school. Erica joined us. It was a somber ride, death having reduced everything else to trivia.

"Seems like days since I've eaten," Tim said.

"It has been," Erica said.

I tried to remember the last time I ate a full meal; I couldn't. Then I tried to remember the last time I laughed; I couldn't.

Tim pulled into a dim diner. It might even have been the one where I had confronted Angie, the truck-driving pancake artist. I realized I had aged years in the three months or so that had passed.

We ate with surprising eagerness, but we were quiet, concentrating on our cheeseburgers and fries, passing ketchup and salt silently, sipping soft drinks and slouching wearily, as if the food that nourished us also reminded us of reality and therefore enervated us. Erica, sitting next to me, took bites and then leaned back against the vinyl-padded booth. Tim slumped across from us, his shoulders moving almost imperceptibly closer to the table as he ate. We made few sounds other than the clank of a fork or the rattle of ice in a glass. A ceiling fan clicked methodically, laboring to stir the stagnant air, which was heavy with a smothering humidity. Still we ate, savoring in silence a shred of lettuce, a slice of tomato, a corner of the fresh poppy seed rolls. Scarcely a noise, except the fan, constantly, laboriously marking time like a metronome, a slow definite pulse, with each revolution a reminder of things passing.

Tim finished first. He stretched, sat back in the cracked vinyl, and wiped his napkin firmly across his mouth and beard.

"I feel better now," he said. But when he looked at us his eyes seemed undecided about what to focus on. "Nourishment. Swallow food and your body goes back to feeling normal."

Tim's eyes darted around the gray restaurant and finally focused on the ticking ceiling fan as if it were an enemy. He rattled his ice around in his glass, and tilted it back toward his mouth, but the ice clung to the bottom of the glass for an instant before sliding quickly. Several cubes spilled onto Tim's lap and the floor. As he reached jerkily for his napkin, he toppled the ketchup bottle, which spilled a pool of red onto the table. Tim wiped angrily at his mouth and lap and then at the ketchup. Wadding his napkin into his fist, Tim slouched forward slowly, pounded hard, once, against the table, and put his hands to his face. For an instant, there was the kind of silence you might hear after waking suddenly in the black darkness of pre-dawn—silence thick and pregnant and fearsome; I thought that even the fan had stopped. But then I heard again its persistent click and Tim repeating in a wounded, high-pitched gasp, "Oh shit, oh shit, oh shit..."

Noiselessly, Erica placed her fork on her plate. I slid one of my hands across the seat and wrapped it around hers. She extended her other hand to Tim and touched one of his wrists. He clasped her hand, completing the circle, but he kept the fist with the napkin in it pressed firmly against his forehead, and his hair fell forward in layers as he trembled.

"Oh shit, oh shit, oh shit..." Tim's foreign, high-pitched voice continued into his wrist in rhythm with the clicking fan, until finally he said, "Oh my god oh god oh my god...he was my brother...and he's gone... he was my brother...gone...he was my brother..."

CHAPTER FORTY-ONE

Yes, life does go on, but as the number of people who make your life meaningful decreases, the intensity of your actions increases. I know it now; I felt it then, first after Sally's disappearance, then seeing and feeling the sorrowful impact of Brian's death.

Nothing seemed the same, as if the world, unable to cope with consistent and persistent abuses, staggered. The unusual became bizarre; the horrifying became expected.

Dust from the earth that covered Brian had scarcely settled when death again imposed itself as only death can—the intruder, the unstoppable force, appearing when and where and how it chooses.

Bingham's color TV, watched by four faces—two white, two black—carried murder into the false sanctuary of our campus. Andre just winced and toked extra long on a joint, but Bobby sat erect on the bed and muttered, "My mother must be dying herself, she loved King so much."

The crack of a bullet, the sound of grief; in my mind I heard one, but in reality I felt the other. And there was a hatred to the grief, hatred born of frustration, hatred that cast aside logic and fueled anger and sparked the instant of insanity that tells you to reject the past, forfeit the future, and grab the moment.

The vacuous white face of James Earl Ray, murderer of the Reverend Martin Luther King, Jr., stared at us from the TV screen, and Bobby sprang off the bed and without a word kicked Darrell Bingham's television set sideways. The picture tube smashed into a corner of the desk. Smoky blue sparks and thousands of shards of glass shot into the air as the set pitched forward and crashed to the floor. Bingham, enraged and cursing, instantly leapt at Bobby, knocking him backward over the desk. Bobby's skinny body fell against a custom-curtained window; Bingham charged at him. In one swift movement, Bobby ripped the curtains from the wall and flung them around Bingham's flushed face. Bingham struggled furiously but futilely to get free of the curtains, and as Bingham struggled, Bobby jumped from the floor to the desktop and kicked

Darrell in the back and then again on the top of his head. Bingham moaned and cursed from under the curtains, thrashing in confusion and muffled rage. Before I could get across the room, Bobby had jumped on Bingham's curtained back. With one hand, Bobby held the curtains tight across Bingham's face; with the other, he punched Darrell's head repeatedly.

"Cut it out, Bobby, cut it out!" I shouted hollowly as I reached for him.

But he punched and kicked and Bingham's cursing turned into a muffled hiss. Bingham was on all fours, the curtains still dangling over his head and upper body. I held Bobby's arms from behind, but he flailed his feet at Darrell, kicking wildly.

"Bobby, Bobby, Jesus Christ, you'll kill him!" I shouted, holding his wiry body.

"Let me go, you white trash motherfucker!" he said to me over his shoulder.

"Hey, it's me, Bobby" I said, shaking him, but in doing so, I inadvertently gave him enough room to slip free and kick Darrell again, his foot landing hard in Bingham's face. Darrell teetered sideways with a moan, and then Bobby wheeled to face me.

"Why you protect him, fucker?" Bobby shouted. "Motherfucker treat everyone like shit, even you. But you just like all the rest. You not only turn your white head on everything that's wrong, but if other whites are wrong, you defend them too!"

I slid past Bobby to get between him and Bingham. Darrell, disoriented, tried weakly to pull the curtains off.

"He didn't kill King, Bobby, and neither did I," I said, and again my voice and words sounded simple and inadequate. "You're my friend, Bobby. My friend."

Moon hadn't moved from the corner of the room, but now he spoke from behind a thick smoky haze. "You didn't fire the gun, man," Moon said, "but you didn't stop the bullet either, now did you, man? See, you a friend, man, but you a white friend, so you ain't ever gonna know exactly how things are."

I ignored Moon's comment, but even in that instant, I feared he was right. I pulled the curtains off Darrell's head. His eyes seemed to move independently of one another and blood ran from his nostrils down his chin and onto his neck.

"Shit, Bobby, you busted him up good," I said. "Throw me a towel."

"Fuck you, man. I ain't throwin nothing; not me. This is one black man that's through saying he's sorry. And look at you; you gonna tell me you never wanted to kick his motherfucking ass yourself?"

Bobby walked out of the room, and I called to him, "Bobby...Bobby, goddamit, listen to me."

Moon started to follow, but I blocked his way.

"Tell me, Andre," I said, "I want to know. I want to understand. Just tell me what you and Bobby ever did to help King live?"

Moon was silent for a moment, as if waiting for his pot-fried brain to process the question. But when he spoke, his voice was clear and tinged with sadness. "Say, don't you get it, Mike? I've lived black all my life, that's what I've done," he said, pausing to glance at the glowing roach between his fingertips. "Now that's something you can't ever do, man. People gonna be lining up by color more and more now, and me and you and that pathetic cracker on the floor over there, man...well, my man, we just don't match." He walked toward the door. "So long, my friend...my white, white friend."

CHAPTER FORTY-TWO

The Whisperjet shuttle from Newark to Washington purred through the cloud-streaked sky. I flew to Washington for Spring Break because the riots following the King assassination had made train and bus service sporadic. The airplane of convenience carried jet-set commuters who clutched briefcases like they contained life itself, while thousands of feet below us, life changed mutely as we passengers watched in silence.

We circled National Airport outside of Washington, DC, and with the Capitol dome as a backdrop we watched smoke billow steadily up toward us until it merged with the gray clouds and became indistinguishable from them. Look for the source of the smoke, see tiny people milling in the streets, their movements from thousands of feet above seeming as harmless as those of cartoon characters—watch windows break noiselessly, gracefully, and then the smoke pours upward like a great hazy river. Follow the smoke as it rises above the mass of mankind that is wrecking the slums that only someone who does not live in could call home—the "leftovers" Morris Lieberman had called them—follow the smoke as its trail widens above the grimy rooftops and blends with the sky, follow the smoke into the clouds, and, suddenly, smoke disappears and only clouds remain in the evening sky.

Moon and Bobby had been arrested before I left school for Spring Break amid campus riots over Martin Luther King's assassination. They were two of about fifty students—a mix of black and white, all mostly members of STEP—who terrorized the campus for nearly twenty-four hours, smashing cars and windows and attacking other students. I drove Bingham to the hospital in his A-H; he was treated for a broken nose and a broken rib and was kept overnight for observation of a possible concussion. His family swore out arrest warrants for Moon and Bobby, but police already hunted them as the campus came under siege.

Moon had been wrong—an odd combination of fear and trust rather than race had pulled many people together. Whites and blacks, both fearing violence from the other but also sharing a murdered dream, sought each other out, looking not for color but for trust. Moon, who had so often seemed humorous in his marijuana haze, now symbolized rebellion and possibly even danger; Bobby, always tight-roping the thin line between wild good times and insanity fueled by his incessant fear of death in war, fell increasingly toward anger.

"You know if they come around here, we may have to take them on," Fish had said to me in a call from Katie's home. I hadn't seen him in days; even the happy face made of yarmulkes on our wall was gone.

"Take them on?" I asked. "Who's coming for us?"

"Moon. Bobby."

"They won't bother us; they're still our friends," I said with more hope than conviction.

"Bullshit, too. The whole campus has to defend itself against maniacs like them. Even those few blacks who aren't militant are becoming targets."

"I know. But killing King has united them, and ignited them."

"It's bullshit, just so much bullshit, Mike! It's a bullshit excuse, and they know it. I mean, whites didn't rampage when JFK was shot."

"It's different, Fish. Totally different."

"How, Mike? How's it different besides color? Don't get me wrong, I understand civil rights. You *know* I do. But I don't support civil disobedience."

"What's happened to you, Fish?"

"What do you mean?"

"The hair...gone. The beard...gone. The war... okay. Defend ourselves...against friends. What's happened?"

"Look, things change, Mike. Let me ask you this: Why are you digging in? Growing the hair? Getting your face stomped?"

I thought about that, but all I could say was, "It's just different, Fish. That's all."

"Yeah. Exactly."

It wasn't until I was on the plane and following the smoke from the burning buildings up and down, and then, finally, focusing below so I wouldn't see reality dissipate into clouds, that I began to think of what I should have said to Fish, something that just a few years earlier, sitting on a Brooklyn fire escape, would never have entered my reality. The difference came fully to mind as the plane prepared to land, and I saw the noiseless fire engines and cop cars with their lights flashing and the tiny people running randomly like leaves detached from trees being blown across a field:

Fish, I should have said, it's not the same except in the sense of the tragedy itself. JFK led a nation of mostly confident, mostly comfortable people who, five years ago, confronted the discomfort of his death in the way they were taught was socially acceptable—through grieving. But King led a minority, Fish, a severely and historically oppressed minority, and he spoke for non-violence, and they believed him, loved him, followed him, but then he died from hatred, so the sins that he preached against were the very horrors that killed him, and the very horrors they have known all their lives. The people King spoke to and for are not the same comfortable people JFK symbolized—they are people who have experienced hatred and indignities daily, whose lives are different in so many ways from ours...that their reaction to this death, the death of their leader, their symbol of non-violence, was really their reaction to a lifetime of experiencing deceit.

Fish, I should have asked: Who ultimately pays the price for years of neglect, injustice, inequity? The answer is: We are finding that out now.

I should have said that, but I didn't then, didn't ever, but I remember thinking it clearly as the Whisperjet touched down lightly on the runway. The air-shuttle commuters clutched their briefcases, apparently unfazed. They cocked their eyebrows slightly, then smoothed out wrinkles that didn't exist in their three-piece suits. I grabbed my duffel bag filled mostly with dirty laundry and touched the still tender but fading remnants of the Jersey trooper's gift to my eye.

"Will your dad be upset about your eye?" Erica had asked me over the phone just before I left school for break.

"He'll be more upset about my hair. He'll figure I deserved the eye."

"Maybe he'll surprise you."

"He doesn't believe in surprises, which is another reason my hair will piss him off."

"Do you think you should get it cut before you go home?"

"Do *you* think so?" I asked, a little incredulous.

"Not if you think it's worth the tension you'll feel at home."

"Well, I don't want to cut my hair, and I don't even want to go home, but I have to. My dad and I have to talk. And I really want to see Harry."

"I'll miss you, Mike," Erica had said. And I had said the same, and it was certainly true...but the emotion I felt for Erica had started to blend into the mass of emotions I felt in general.

I walked out of the Whisperjet with my hair bouncing loosely over my jacket collar and just onto the top of my shoulders. I smelled the smoke that arose just a few miles away. Cities smoldered, a nation tensed, masses grieved, friends fought...and families argued over hair.

CHAPTER FORTY-THREE

During that Spring Break of 1968, I watched on TV as Washington, the Nation's Capital, land of the cherry blossoms, home to the President, Congressmen, lobbyists, and assorted other vermin, burned. The soot-filled air that hovered over the city did not foul my suburban home, but the angry symbol represented by the flames—the hatred, the injustice, the mistrust—seared fearfully and unmistakably into every living room.

The riots kept my father out of the house a lot because the Secret Service was on call. When he was around, we maintained a cautious distance, like two boxers trying to analyze each other's style before reaching back for the knockout punch. The need to spar with him angered me, but the truth is that what I feared more was the inevitable main bout. To delay it, I tried being the model son.

"I see the paint is chipped on the gutters, Dad, do you want me to paint them tomorrow?" I offered one night before bed.

"That's up to you. You're a busy, busy man, aren't you?"

"Not really."

"It's up to you."

So I painted the gutters.

I mowed the lawn.

I washed the cars, trimmed the hedges, re-sealed the driveway's asphalt surface. He acknowledged none of it.

My mother, on the other hand, lavished me with compliments as she became the official peacekeeping task force within our home.

"You've done so much in the few days you've been home, Michael; it's such a help to us," she said, spooning scrambled eggs into a dish for me one morning. "You're father's so busy, the work doesn't always get done. And you know me, I'm useless outside. Oh, I have Italian toast warming for you."

I played with a forkful of eggs and said, "I don't mind doing it, you know, Mom."

"Oh, we know it; we just hope you know how much we appreciate it."

She always spoke in the plural, saying "we" as though her statements represented my father's feelings, too. But I wasn't convinced he felt any of those things. I chewed unenthusiastically on my thick toasted-and-buttered Italian bread and moved the yellow pieces of egg around until my plate looked like a piece of abstract art. Call it "How Scrambled Eggs Imitate Life," I thought.

"What is it, Michael?" she asked. "Something's bothering you."

I moved the eggs around. The shape of the artwork changed, but not its message. "No, Mom, it's nothing."

"Come on, Michael. You think we don't notice, your father and me? You're too quiet. You've never been a moody person. It's not like you."

"I'm not being moody."

"I know, honey. It's all of this terrible news, isn't it? The assassination—it saddens us all. Such a good, noble man, that Martin Luther King, Jr."

"Yes, Mom, he was."

"It's awful, but we must learn a lesson from it, right, honey? Good is not always understood, and evil is never acceptable. Is it the assassination that's bothering you?"

"Sure, but no, Mom, really everything's fine. Look, I'm fine, perfect, *perfetto*."

"Then you're thinking of young Salvatore again, right Michael? Oh, honey, there was nothing you could do. Whatever he decided, he decided on his own. He'll show up someday. You'll see."

"No, it's okay, Mom. Sure, I think about Sally, but not like before. I'm okay."

My voice was false and we both noticed, so I tried a favorite ploy with her. I walked menacingly toward her, exaggerating everything I said, giving a slightly benign version of Crazy Stare.

"Okay okay, I'm in trouble, Ma," I said, full Brooklyn rising in my voice. "I'm, I'm flunkin out, an I owe these gamblers money, lots a dough, see, an I got a girl—no, Ma, it was two girls—pregnant." I backed her against the refrigerator and half shouted, "An it's all your fault for bringin me up wrong! You know, I'm depraved on account of I'm deprived."

"Oh you, just sit down and eat," she laughed, swatting a soapy sponge at me. "And don't give me those... those 'Big Eyes' you and Salvatore used to do. Your breakfast will get cold. And you better hurry. You're supposed to meet your cousin in Georgetown soon to talk about the summer job. Are you excited about it?"

"Sure," I said, "it'll be great."

"Now that certainly did not ring with enthusiasm. Don't you want the job?"

"Yes, I do."

"It'll pay well and, God knows, Michael, it sounds like fun. I mean, the beach? The ocean?"

"Yes, I want the job. It sounds like fun. Great."

She sat down across from me, sipped a cup of coffee, and studied me as though I were some kind of modern art made out of wrought iron or used car tires. Suddenly, a flicker of realization traveled across her face.

"Who's the girl, Michael?"

"What?"

"Who is the girl who has our Michael so knotted up?"

"What do you mean? I've got a million girls. Two pregnant, remember?"

"Uh uh. No, Michael, I see it now. Someone's got you, right? So even the girls at the beach don't seem so appealing. Oh, she must be something to have our Michael so serious."

"Yeah, you're right, you're right."

"See, I knew it! Is she nice? Italian? Can I see her picture?"

"Sure, Ma."

"Where? Show me."

I started searching through my wallet and my pockets, though I knew I had no photograph of Erica.

"Michael, what are you doing? Did you lose the picture? How could you?"

"Oh, don't worry Mom, you can still see her."

"What do you mean? How?"

The phone rang and as I got up to answer it, I said, "Simple. Just get this month's *Playboy* and turn to the centerfold."

"Oh you, you are just a disgusting boy...." she said in frustration.

I picked up the phone and it was Fish on the other end. My mother heard me say his name and she said, "Oh, is that your roommate, David?"

I nodded.

"You tell David he should come down with you next time. I'll make lasagna for you both."

I nodded again.

"My mom says hello," I told him. "I was just breaking it to her that I'm dating a *Playboy* bunny, complete with a furry little ass."

Trying not to laugh, my mother made a threatening noise from behind clenched teeth. I turned to her and said, "You ought to see Dave's girl, Ma. She was a *Playboy* reject." I turned back to the phone. "My mother says we'll meet really nice girls at the beach. The kind we can be proud to bring home to our lasagna-and brisket-cooking Mamas."

Fish didn't laugh. He just cleared his throat and said, "Yes, tell her I said hello."

"Sure, so how are you? Are people doing okay up there?"

"Well, yeah, you know, as well as can be expected I guess, given Brian's death and now Trenton being in flames."

"So why are you hedging like a drunk driver in the snow?"

"All right, Mike. Listen. It's about the beach, man. Have you talked to Harry yet?"

"No, I'm going to see him today. I'll get all the details ironed out for us." I heard empty silence on the phone and humming from my mother as she washed the breakfast dishes. "Why, Fish? Something you want me to…Oh shit. I get it. That's why you called, right? You're not going to the beach, are you?"

"No, Mike, I'm not."

"What the hell? Why the hell not?"

My mother heard me. "Your language, Michael!" she cautioned.

"No, Mike, look, don't get pissed off. Listen… just listen. Katie and I, we just need each other, especially now, you know, after Brian. We're too far along to go without one another for a whole summer. For any length of time." He paused, and then continued, "Mike, Katie and I have decided to get married."

I waited for Fish's familiar laugh, but it didn't come. I considered the setting, my mind racing back over the conversation; it wasn't right for humor.

"You're serious, aren't you?" I said. "Jesus Christ, what the hell will you do…money…school…your parents—I mean, Katie's not Jewish…"

I heard my mother, "Your language, Michael, please!" She was half joking, but when she saw that I wasn't responding, she grew serious and whispered, "Oh, there's a problem. I'm sorry. Can I help?"

I mouthed "thanks" and shook my head "no." "Fish, look," I said, "it's all the emotions, man. Shouldn't you just slow down a little?"

"Dammit, Mike, this isn't anything rash," he said, and I was aware that I was being scolded by my friend. "Sometimes you just have to go with what you know is right. And this is right. I'm going to finish school on time in two more years, and she's going to enroll at Sinclair in the fall. Our parents are getting used to the idea…well, sort of—mine didn't talk to me for two full days—I loved it—but then we all talked—my parents, her parents—like, all night last night. Katie and I—we mean it, and we didn't back down. The McGees don't really want her going away; they lost Brian already, and Tim's off in his own crazy world and no one hears from him anymore. They finally gave in and said if we really wanted to, we could live there and commute. So we're going to."

"And so, your parents, I mean, I can't imagine a world where they agreed to this?"

"No, they hate the idea, but I told them I was doing it with or without their blessing. My father wanted to throw me out immediately; I told him I didn't care if he did. My mother, she went hysterical, but they're both coming around, sort of. They both already seem to like Katie despite their best efforts not to, and once they get to know her even better and see how it's going to work out—that I'm not quitting school, that she's not getting pregnant—they'll have no choice, really. Accept her, Jewish or not, or lose me. It's that simple."

All I could do was mutter, "Jesus, you're really going to do it."

"Yes, Mike, we really are. I need to get control of things for myself. You'd do the same if the circumstances were the same."

His voice was different, clearer, more business-like, and he didn't seem even slightly aware of how condescending he sounded. He seemed rushed, the sound of someone ready to move on to the next topic, event, or stage of his life.

By comparison, my own voice sounded so immature. "What am I going to tell Harry?" I asked. "He needed two of us."

"Hey, I took care of that too. Tim might like the job. He needs the time away from home. Last time I talked to him, he said he thought you were cool; don't know where he got that idea, eh? He's an okay guy, if he'd just drop that radical shit. Of course, I don't even know if he wants the job, and if you really don't want him, I'll just tell him Harry had someone else in mind...that is, if Tim ever shows up again. Simple."

"Yeah, simple. Gee, thanks."

"Listen, Mike, before I let you go, don't make any plans for the week after exams, that's the second weekend in June. That's the big weekend. Actually, it'll be a small wedding—in Katie's house. But I want you to be the best man."

"A week after exams end?"

"Right, I'm not wasting any more time. Mr. McGee is giving me a summer job starting that week. Erica's going to stand up for Katie, so you have to stand up for me. After all, you're the one who got me and Katie together in the first place."

A confusing combination of frustration, jealousy, and anger pulled at me. I fought hard to control it.

"I'll see, Dave," I said. "But we were supposed to start work at the beach that very weekend, remember? All those plans? Parties? Hell, Katie could come down sometimes, and so could Erica. Don't you just feel like getting away from it all? I mean, it's too much, man, too much stuff happening."

"That stuff doesn't mean anything to me anymore, Mike. Think about it. You'll understand."

"I don't know...Everything's just happening so fast... When did you two decide all this?"

He paused, and when he spoke again, his voice had just a trace of youthful excitement to it, the voice that he had during that magical night of shooting pool.

"You won't believe it, Mike," he said. "That night of the Dean Carmody riots, remember how you and Erica found us walking toward the dorm, and you told us about Brian? Well, we had been up on the top floor of Mountain Hall, and we made love a couple of times right there…right on the top floor of Mountain! It was all so right, Mike. We were up there for hours, and that's when we decided. We could have lived there! We said then that we'd tell our parents that we wanted to get married. You just can't believe it, right? With all that bullshit going on that night on campus, we're up there making love and deciding on life, while you're getting shit-canned by a cop for hanging with hippies. And then, then you and Erica find us and tell us about poor Brian. Katie and I have talked about that night a hundred times, how all those things—such different things—were happening. You just can't imagine what it's like."

"Me? Shit no, I can't imagine, not me," I said, trying to contain my sarcasm as I realized how just one floor below Fish and Katie, Erica and I were talking, thinking, and slowly groping our way more deeply into one another's life.

"Michael, please," my mother said softly.

"Now, don't be pissed about the beach, Burns," Fish continued. "You'll be able to pick up girls without me…maybe." He laughed. "And you'll get along fine with Tim, assuming he reappears and is somewhat normal. Look, I have to go. Mr. McGee is giving me a series of orientations into the boat business; they start today. I'm going to learn how to sell the shit out of cabin cruisers, man, and maybe someday I'll run the whole business. Want me to say hello to Erica for you?"

"Sure."

"She seems to miss you, talks about you a lot. Maybe you should re-think going to the beach, Mike. Maybe you should stay up here near Erica. Life's short, Mike."

"Yeah, that's for sure, but I think I need the beach. Tell Erica I'll see her soon."

I stood by the phone after hanging up, feeling as if the eggs were re-scrambling in my stomach. My mother walked toward me quietly. I tried to smile reassuringly, but I couldn't. "Sorry about the language, Mom."

"Forget it, honey," she said. "I was teasing. I just don't want it to become a habit. Do you want to tell me what David said that's bothering you?" We sat down at the kitchen table. My mother was eager to hear. "I don't want you to think I'm prying."

"Ma, if I thought you were prying, I'd say so."

"You would?" She turned her mouth down, feigning hurt.

"Probably not."

"So what is it?"

"He's getting married."

"Michael, you never even told me he was engaged!"

Her big brown eyes expressed genuine surprise, and I found her comment wonderfully naive and refreshing. I began to laugh hard, so hard, in fact, that I couldn't stop. My sides ached·and my eyes teared as my mother said, "What's so funny, Michael?" and then she laughed, too.

Finally, I wheezed, "He wasn't ever engaged, Ma. It's a sudden thing. She's a high school senior."

My mother stopped in mid-laugh and put a hand to her mouth. "Oh no, is she preg..."

"...No, she's not, Mom."

"And you mean their parents are letting them? But they're still children. And David is Jewish, right? Is the girl Jewish?"

I shook my head, my laughter subsiding. "No, she's not Jewish, but they are both old enough to get married on their own."

"Oh, their poor parents!" she said, sitting down absently. All expression drained from my mother's sweet face. But, inside, she knew that all people have the right to make choices, like the choice she—as a young Italian woman—had made to marry an Irishman, and the decision she and my father eventually made to leave the Brooklyn neighborhood. Still, she also empathized with Katie's and Fish's parents.

So I just held her hands and said, "No, the parents don't really approve, but what do you do? Some people do things, Mom, they find themselves faced with certain situations and feelings, so they do things. They just...do. We all do...we all just do..." I stopped, embarrassed that my voice had cracked.

My mother quietly pushed away from the small wooden table. Her face quickly passed through a range of emotions, a soft, thoughtful consideration of something she did not seem to understand fully and then perhaps to a reflection on her own past. In that moment, I suddenly recognized my mother's beauty as she reached out and hugged my head briefly, tenderly. For some reason, it made me sad, but then she sighed, walked to the sink, and began to dry dishes. I picked up a kitchen towel filled with embroidered flowers in full bloom and helped her.

"So, what do you think about all of that?" I asked.

She raised her eyebrows, turned her palms up toward the ceiling, and said, "There are some things I don't completely understand, honey, but if they're happy..." She shrugged, looked warmly at me, and said, "Happiness is one thing I know I understand."

CHAPTER FORTY-FOUR

Silhouettes in the afternoon had the appealing quality of one of those clubhouses the East Side Kids used to escape to in their movies. Night would cover the scars, but in daytime, dust and cracks showed. Huge dark curtains were drawn back to let in light from M Street in Georgetown. Because of the riots several blocks away in the inner city, Georgetown was uncharacteristically empty, and I found a parking space across the street from the club. Police roamed the streets on foot and in cars, visible barriers of power separating the high society and wealth of Georgetown from the smoldering poverty of the rarely seen DC ghetto.

Harry talked on the phone in his office, a room filled with records and pictures of Bob Dylan, Woody Allen, the Kingston Trio, Joan Baez, and others all autographed personally to Harry:

"To Harry, the greatest ear in the business. Love, Joan."
"Harry, I got some 'harry burns' on my chest from groveling to play your club. All the best, Woody."
"Harry—don't think twice (you never do!), but it's all right. 'Zim.'"

Everyone in the pictures looked younger than I remembered. A large chart listing bookings for the next three months in black magic marker hung behind Harry's desk. He motioned for me to sit in an overstuffed leather chair that was partially buried under a stack of heavy boxes. I removed the boxes, sat, and Harry put his hand over the telephone mouthpiece and said, "Open a box and keep a record for yourself."

The box contained records by Stan Goetz, who was performing at Silhouettes at the time. The featured song on it was "Girl From Ipanema," and I hummed it over in my head:

"Tall and tan and young and lovely/ The girl from Ipanema goes walking..."

It reminded me of the girls I expected to meet at the beach in the summer, which reminded me of how much I missed Erica now, and probably would even more then—if I went.

Harry hung up and walked from behind his desk to give me a hug. He was slightly taller than I was, and he was a good twenty pounds heavier, but he was handsome and youthful enough that he almost looked like he could be one of my college classmates.

"Agents," he said, motioning to the phone, "they're hustling now, especially for folk singers. Rock-n-rollers are putting them on the run. Even Zimmerman's going more electric. You can pick up folk acts cheap, if you're not overanxious."

"Sounds good for business."

Harry nodded. "Yeah, things are good...if you don't count the fact that the riots have basically shut us down for a couple of nights. And the fact that perhaps the greatest minority voice in all of American history has been silenced. Not pretty at all." Harry smiled and flipped the hair hanging below my neck. "Cool hair, and that eye still has a little color to it. I heard about you bumping into a policeman's boot."

"Yeah, my mom and dad didn't seem to like it much. Not that my dad's even said a word to me lately."

"Hey kid, what do you expect?" Harry swiveled in his chair; he had a way of pushing a conversation to a new level and then quickly easing off. Then he'd come back minutes later to an even higher level. He slid an eight-by-ten-inch photograph framed in chrome toward me. "Have you seen this?"

It was a picture of my parents, plus Harry's African American wife, Sparrow, and their year-old son, Thomas (named after Harry's father, killed in World War II), with Peter, Paul and Mary. Mary had her arm around my father's shoulder, and Dad was flashing his great smile.

"I took it myself," Harry said. "I'm getting it blown up to poster size for your parents. Don't tell them. I think they'll get a kick out of it."

"Yeah, sure they will; it's a great shot," I said as I stared vacantly at it. "Little Thomas is getting big."

"Yeah, the little pisser is a handful, but fun. And Sparrow, she's just amazing with him. But this King killing; she is struggling. We've been to the protests together."

"I can only imagine how hard it is for the two of you."

Harry sat back down behind his desk and motioned for me to sit in front of it. "Yeah, things are bad. But let's talk about you. Let's have it, kid. What's happening? Your parents—they're worried about you, you know."

"I guess." I braced for Harry's leap to the next level.

"Listen, they're not so hard to please, even your dad. They're concerned, and you have to admit there's a lot out there to be concerned about. The drugs, the hippies, runaways, draft dodgers, dropouts."

"But Harry, tell me...what the hell have I ever done?"

Harry smiled and I blinked at it—it was the same great smile that my father had and probably his father did, too, the smile I tried imitating but couldn't master, the one where the lips slide open slightly sideways and reveal teeth in a burst of whiteness. You expect to hear a big laugh, but most of the time you just get the smile, and then you wind up providing the sound for the laugh. But I didn't provide the sound this time.

"You've been a saint all your life, I suppose?" he said.

I smiled back at him, but my smile seemed so paltry compared to his. He sat there, a success at age thirty, looking tan as always, because he and Sparrow so frequently ran off to Bermuda, the Bahamas, and Miami. Harry liked to talk, but he listened well, too. And his memory; Christ, it had to be the prototype for a supercomputer. I knew he was about to scan it at full speed and come up with one of my past misadventures.

"I guess you never disappeared for most of the night when you were, what, twelve? Remember? In Brooklyn? With Sally?"

"Sure, how could I forget, even if I wanted to? By the way, I was thirteen before Sally and I started disappearing...and you know it." But just because I remembered, and perhaps because I wanted to re-member, I knew good old Harry would want me to retell it. In an odd way, I wanted to walk through it all again.

"So tell me how it happened. I've heard a couple of versions but one thing they all have in common is that you and Sally-Boy finally showed up from god knows where and your dad reamed your ass out and Big Sal threatened Sally-Boy like the Mafia pal Big Sal turned out to be—a Secret Service reaming and a Secret Mafia reaming…not all that different, eh?" He laughed and then asked, "What the hell did you two do on the ferry all day and night?"

I thought about the unusual, wonderful weightless-ness of that night, the freedom, the delicious adven-ture of disobedience that I had shared with Sally-Boy. We started riding the Staten Island ferry around six in the evening, and we just kept going back-and-forth between Manhattan and Staten Island trip after trip.

"I don't know, Harry, you know, we were just rid-ing the ferry, talking, eating slices, looking at the Manhattan skyline lights, the people, all those faces, the Statue of Liberty," I said. It sounded odd when I said it, but it was the truth.

"The whole time?" Harry asked, raising an eye-brow. "I figured you guys picked up a hooker."

"No, man, I'm telling you, we were just talking, looking at the statue, people, faces, the skyline."

345

Harry swung around in his chair again and, without standing, he opened a portable refrigerator and pulled out two bottles of Lowenbrau. He lined the bottle tops on the edge of his desk and smacked them with the palm of his hand. The caps popped off simultaneously. He handed me a bottle.

"But why?" Harry said. "Why'd you just ride like that all night when you knew it meant trouble?"

I sipped the Lowenbrau and thought, but I had no plausible answer for my cousin.

"What the fuck, Har, what can I say? It just seemed peaceful," I said. "Kind of exciting. You know that the city's behind all those lights—there's all that turmoil in the city all the time—but from the ferry it seemed unreal, or maybe surreal. I don't know. And the Statue of Liberty looked kind of spooky tinged all green in the night." The musky smell of ferry spray came back clearly as I talked. "I wanted to go visit the statue, you know, walk inside her, but Sally-Boy always said, 'Nah, she smells like someone's pissed all inside her; she stinks like u-reen.' He didn't say urine, Harry, because Sally had that crazy way with some words—he said it, 'u-reen.'"

Harry smiled. "So you never got into the Statue?"

I shook my head, swigged the beer, and said, "So was that so bad, really, Harry?"

"Um, maybe the fact that you were missing until almost four in the morning was a factor in why your dad and Big Sal were so pissed." He smiled again. "Look, Mike, we all know you're not a bad kid…"

"Harry, please, no lectures, I just can't right now…"

Beads of sweat mysteriously appeared on my forehead. Harry stared at me and pulled slowly on his beer. I tried to see myself in him. In ten years, when I'm thirty, I wondered, will I be like Harry with a beautiful wife, a cute kid, a Porsche, a boat—maybe one I'd buy from Fish, one that we'd all go cruising in, me and Erica, Fish and Katie, and our kids? I'd seen Harry chat amiably after hours at the club with rickety old Congressmen and their wives or girlfriends, and I'd seen him cover up for Washington Redskins when a coach or the press called Silhouettes to see if some of the team's carousing players were around. A decade older than I was, and Harry wore his comfort with the world with clear grace and confidence. But looking ten years into the future seemed like looking at the hazy Manhattan skyline that night on the ferry with Sally-Boy, when the fragmented outline of skyscrapers made us wonder if they actually existed.

Sally-Boy had said, "It's like they're just pieces of one of them jumbo jigsaw puzzles I seen kids workin on in the park over on Knickerbocker Avenue— there's, like, about a million or two tiny fuckin pieces. Forget puttin them things together, it takes months, years maybe. Here, at least you know wit the ferry, the ferry's gonna put the puzzle together; like it goes back to the city and those buildings start fittin back together. But to put a jumbo jigsaw puzzle together myself? Forget it. Who has time to figure that shit out? Not me. And then you just bust it all up again and stuff it in a box like it's dead. What's the point?"

Where are you, Sally-Boy?

"Every time someone talks to you, it isn't a lecture, Mike."

"I know, I know. Look, I need the beach job. I need to get away."

"You got it. You know that."

"My roommate won't be going. I'll get someone else…"

"Really? What happened to Dave?"

"He's getting married."

"Oh, Jesus, he knocked someone up, huh?"

"No, no, he didn't."

"Really? Just like that? Getting married? How long has he known her?

"Couple of months. But they've been through a lot."

"Couple of months?" He shook his head, then shrugged casually and quoted Bob Dylan, "'Ain't no use to sit and wonder why, babe.' Well, go ahead and find someone you can have a good time with at the beach. Use the job right. Loosen up, kid. Are you coming tonight to hear Stan? He's smooth, soothing, it'd be good for you."

"Nah, I'm gonna spend some time at home, maybe clean out the garage."

"That'll make your dad happy."

I gripped my beer bottle tightly. "Goddamit, Harry, why is that the measure of everything I do?"

Harry looked at me; I felt myself shrinking. One of life's unalterable patterns had begun again: I get angry; Harry makes sense.

"You're missing the point, Mike."

"Oh yeah? Well what's the fucking point, Harry? Get to it, and let me the fuck out of here!"

Harry still wasn't angry. His eyes shifted from me to the paint-chipped ceiling, then back to me. "Look, kid, believe this if you don't believe any of the other horseshit you hear—things change. People change. The things and people that seem so important right now, they'll change in time and you will wonder why you didn't do things differently."

"But Harry," I stammered, "Harry, what the fuck am I doing that's so wrong? See this fucking eye of mine? Take a good look. I'm lucky that's all I got—that cocksucker cop who kicked me threatened to shoot me, Harry. He would have shot me, but I ran so fucking fast I disappeared!"

"Calm down."

I was sweating harder now, and my voice was increasing in pitch. "Well, exactly what are you telling me, Harry? What? When you were in school promoting concerts, winning elections, I suppose you had your eye on the future the whole time? I can't be you, Harry. I love you, you're like a brother to me, you helped me so much after Sally disappeared, but I can't *be* you."

Harry didn't budge, didn't change expression, just sat there looking handsome and tan and unflappable, a little god-like, but an unpretentious god despite it all. I slumped back in my chair and wiped my forehead.

"Hey kid, it's all going to be okay," he said. "Don't you see that it's all games? Being young, being in college, even work—all games. The trick is to play seriously in the right games, the ones that will help you, not hurt you."

"But how do you or my dad or my mom know which games are right for *me*, Harry? The fucker that put his boot to my face and threatened to shoot me in the back wasn't playing a game, was he, Harry?"

"Relax. Hey, you're a tough one today. Sally-Boy would be proud."

Something about mentioning Sally-Boy again, the kid I always loved—the kid who was tough and rough, an undereducated high school goofball, and yet thoughtful and smart and worldly in his own streetwise way—made me angry at Harry. I stood up, waving the beer bottle. "Please, Harry, please, please, please just fuck the Sally-Boy shit, all right!" I shouted. "I get the message! He ran! He's gone! He might as well be dust! He's nobody in everyone's eyes! But everyone forgets that Big Sal hangs with criminals beneath all his smiles and charm! My god, Harry, Sally-Boy had his reasons, whatever the fuck they were! So leave him the fuck alone, leave poor Sally on that fire escape where he was himself, where he was happiest! You did not really know him, goddamit, none of you did! And I am not him...so leave me the fuck alone too!"

I slumped back down and drained the beer and wished for another, but I didn't ask because I didn't want to have to stay and drink it.

Harry regarded me carefully and spoke softly: "Mike, you're a great kid. And Sally-Boy was a great kid too, but I guess he never figured out the angles, how to deal with life and turn it to his own advantage. That's not a criticism of the kid, but it's just the way it is—he approached everything the same way when everything's different. He never learned that."

"So is that it, Harry?" I asked. "Should I bend? About fucking what? And maybe, just maybe Sally *did* figure it out, and the fact that he's not showing up is *his* way of dealing with his own fucked up life. But you tell me, Harry, tell me what you want me to know, so I know what the fuck I do that's so wrong."

Harry was the picture of calm, the picture of the man who knows what he knows and knows how to figure out what he doesn't know. "Reassure your dad," he said calmly, looking straight at me. "Talk to him. Get your hair trimmed..."

"Oh shit, Harry! Hair? Is that it? Look, he's got his picture there with Peter, Paul and Mary! For Christ sake, he's practically sucking up to Mary's tit! Aren't they long-haired hippie types? But those things don't seem to bother him there. They're big successes, people who made the most of those 'opportunities' he's always talking about. He probably already has a copy of that picture sitting on his desk for all his fellow spooks to see. Just look at that smile of his."

"So that makes him what? A hypocrite? Is that what you're saying? You're wrong. He cares more than you will ever know."

"Shit." I dabbed my forehead with a cocktail napkin from Harry's desk.

Harry leaned across the desk toward me, and I prepared for the conversation to jettison to the next level. It did, but he spoke softly: "Think about it from his end, kid, how it makes him feel when you won't cut your hair to appease him, when you won't take advantage of a possible football scholarship, when you get your face half kicked in during a protest. What you see as personal expression, he sees as a direct challenge to his position as your father, and as a figure of the government that he's dedicated his life to."

I put the empty bottle on the desk and said quietly, trying hard to steady myself, "I've gotta go, Harry."

"Have you picked a major yet, kid?"

"Fuck you, Harry, you prick, okay," I whispered. I attempted to stand, but my shin banged into a box of records. "Motherfucker!" I shouted and kicked over the box so the records spilled onto the floor.

Harry pushed away from his desk and started laughing as I limped around the records, grabbing at my shin.

"Don't you laugh at me, you asshole!" I shouted. "It hurts, goddamit, it hurts, you goddam big asshole!"

"I know it does, kid," he said softly, still chuckling, "but it'll pass."

I rubbed my shin while Harry grinned, and I had an urge to stomp on all of the records in the box and crush them, but Brian McGee's face suddenly replaced Harry's just for an instant—Brian's kind eyes appeared for about the length of time that it takes a camera to flash, the eyes I saw when Brian showed me the model he had built of the cabin cruiser *Happy Times*—and I couldn't see Harry or hear him laugh any more. The beer rose up into my throat for an instant, and then Harry's face came back, and I stared at him to make sure it really was him. And then he hugged me, and somehow I laughed hard at myself smothered in his kind embrace.

CHAPTER FORTY-FIVE

When I arrived home from Silhouettes in the early evening, my father's long black Oldsmobile sat gleaming in the tree-lined driveway. Underneath the trunk there was, I knew, a false panel that covered a high-powered rifle. To my knowledge, he had never used it, but he knew how; the Secret Service required it as part of the training of all agents. My father never acknowledged the rifle's existence in any way, never spoke of it, never referred to it even obliquely, but we all knew it was there. A working rifle's power may be rendered dormant through non-use, but it is still potent, still alive and real, brimming with the potential to kill.

The rifle stayed on my mind as we ate homemade spaghetti, meatballs, salad, and bread. Mostly, I created more artwork with the red sauce, stringy noodles, and fragile meatballs. Like a skilled pilot, my mother successfully steered the conversation around the stormy controversy hovering between me and my father. But when she went to the kitchen to get coffee and dessert, the storm broke.

"Your hair is still not cut," my father said flatly.

"No but, Dad, it's just me trying to be stylish, that's all."

"Style you call it, eh?" He shook his head in disapproval, yet he was stylish and handsome himself with slightly thinning, neatly cut, mostly gray hair. "It's more than just style, and you know it. Admit it. It's a symbol, and one I don't care for."

"Dad, I'm not symbolizing anything with it except that I like the way I look. That's all."

"And I suppose you weren't symbolizing something by being at that rally where a cop had to stomp your face?"

"No, Dad, you don't understand. It just happened. And the cop didn't *have* to stomp my face."

Of course, I had already told my parents quickly and casually about that night and about Brian, but my parents knew me too well, and they both knew that it meant more to me than I let on.

My mother came in with a tray containing three coffees and three bowls of spumoni ice cream.

"Not too much for you, Kev," she winked, patting the smallest of rolls around my father's middle.

For a while there was only the sound of spoons stirring and sliding against the cool bowls. I thought it might be a good time to back off the previous conversation, so I said, "I have been dating a really nice girl."

My mother looked up from her coffee and beamed as she always did after learning something I had previously held confidential. "I *knew* it! What's her name, Michael?" she asked.

"Erica...Erica Wakefield."

"Sounds pretty, doesn't it, Kev?"

"Whose hair is longer, yours or hers?" my father asked, scooping out the last bit of ice cream from his bowl.

My mother looked at him. "Kevin, what is wrong with you?" she said. Then she turned to me and asked, "Where is she from, Michael?"

"Jersey, pretty close to campus."

"She commutes to school?" my mother asked.

"No, she's still in high school. A senior. She's going to University of Massachusetts next year."

"The younger girls, they like that hippie look, right?" my father said. He blew coolly on his hot coffee and waited for my reaction.

I backed my chair away from the table, but stayed seated. "Look, Dad, I'm not going to..."

"Kev, why are you doing this?" my mother interrupted. "He looks good, and can't you see he has things, this young woman, Erica, on his mind?"

My father firmly placed his cup onto his saucer, the tension in his grip causing coffee to spill like ink over the sides. "Looks good? Things on his mind?" he said sarcastically. He reached over and flicked at the back of my hair. "This doesn't have anything to do with those things. This is a statement, am I right, Mike? You are expressing where your sentiments are, right? No matter how wrong they are. Instead of maturing, you grow your hair long, put your fist in the air, yell, 'Power to the people!' right? Fly in the face of us all... the government, the 'system,' even the family. Name one thing wrong with your life or with us, something we haven't tried to provide for you. Are we not good enough *to* you? Not good enough *for* you? What is it? Don't grow your hair. Instead, act like a man is supposed to act and say it!"

I shook, unable to move, and my mother sat speechless at this unprecedented display of anger, this borderline rage coming from deep within a well that harbors the fear of change—irrational anger from a traditionally rational man, a man who kept a rifle hidden in the false trunk of his car without ever so much as mentioning it, a man deemed cool enough to deal with the press on behalf of a secret arm of the government, a man who never missed Mass, still ate fish on Fridays, took Communion weekly. A man who had completed his goal of moving us out of what he saw as the dangers of Brooklyn and to the opportunities of the Nation's Capital. Knowing that something could rip at him this way tore at me as though my insides were made of threadbare cloth.

But I sat there wondering where you back off and why you back off, and I realized that each step backward removes the chance to prove that the fears in the well are unfounded, irrational, unfair. So instead of backing away, I pulled my chair closer to the table. I looked directly into my father's eyes, and, for an instant, I could see myself.

"Dad," I said, "listen, it's nothing really, just hair... take it easy...I..."

"Take it easy? Take it easy? Dammit, Michael, you don't even know what you're doing, what you're saying or trying to say. You're just doing, not thinking."

I shook my head hard. "No, Dad, no, you're wrong, that's not fair," I said. "If anything, I overthink. I'm too slow to act. Sometimes, sometimes it's like I'm frozen by ideas..."

"He's right, you know, Kev," my mother said, again trying to pilot the conversation. "Michael's very considerate, very cautious, very thoughtful. What's wrong, Kev? Something else is bothering you. Tell us, please. This isn't like you."

He looked at her and attempted to compose himself with a kind of tense shake; then he leaned across the table and his eyes seemed to grab my face. For an instant, I felt like a child again.

"Why the hell did you go to that rally, Mike?" he asked.

There was a pause during which I considered backing off completely, returning to the comfort of apology and remorse, but instead, I decided to try to explain, as much for myself as for them.

"At first, I went just because it was there," I said, "but then it was, like, I don't know, like a rhythm that fits you perfectly, and nothing makes sense if you look at it in pieces but it all makes sense if you look at it as a whole. So it just made sense, not that I supported everything going on there, but a lot of it made sense."

"It made sense," my father repeated softly but tersely. "That's your explanation? It made sense? It made sense to think about a moment, when you have a whole life to live? It made sense?" Then he jumped up from the table so forcefully, the dishes rattled. He went into the den just behind him, repeating, "It made sense." He returned quickly with his black leather Secret Service-issue briefcase and pulled a red folder from it. "It made sense," he said again. "But the truth is you don't really know, Michael, and what's worse is what you might never know."

From the folder, one by one, face up, he placed six eight-by-ten black-and-white photographs in the middle of the table. They were close-ups of me, fist in the air in front of the Hopewell Administration Building, swigging a beer, handing the joint back to the guy who had given it to me, cheering while Andre Moon talked, me sprawled on the ground, and me running from the state trooper. The lower right hand corner of every picture bore the stamp "FBI File Photo" in big red letters.

I could feel the blood drain out of my face. My mother covered her mouth in horror at the pictures... and at me.

"You like these, Michael, eh?" my father said. "You look stylish, right? Maybe your girlfriend would like a copy? The cops would, you know, and they'd have them if it weren't for my buddy Phil Archibald at the Bureau—you know his son, Phil Junior, he played ball with you in high school and now he's the quarterback at West Point. Well, we keep in touch, the Service and the Bureau. So Phil calls me for lunch, and when we meet he says, 'Keep these, and if anyone asks, you didn't get them from me.' He tells me, 'Talk to your kid, Kevin, because if he shows up again at a protest, we'll have to start watching him.' Watching *my* kid! He watches *his* kid call plays for West Point! See, Michael? See what I mean when I say that you do not know what you are doing? They have files, thousands of them, kids they watch all the time. And sometimes, Michael, things happen to those kids and the people who support these rallies." He sat back now and sounded exhausted when he continued: "So don't go around making statements anymore—not with your hair, not in rallies, nowhere. If your face shows up enough, it could be a lifetime of trouble. Do you get it? Do I make sense?"

I stared at the pictures, the most clear and realistic images of me that I'd ever seen. But I didn't feel the shame my father wanted me to feel, though I did feel a fear similar to what I used to feel on those nights when I would walk behind Sally-Boy into his pitch black tenement and he would suddenly not be there. I knew with every step I took that I was closer to him leaping out at me in the dark. But what always frightened me more than Sally's inevitable leap was the fear of never knowing when it would happen. Now I looked at the red FBI file and thought how there's really no room for anything...no room for talk, no room for reason, no room for change, protest, choice, new leaders, new followers, new ideas, only room for what is powerful now, who is in power now, and how power exists now...

Suddenly, I stood with the pictures clenched in my hands.

"Do you know how they got these, Mom?" I asked.

She shook her head, her hands still covering her mouth in shock.

"Go ahead, Dad, tell her how your buddies operate, how this system you're so proud of works."

He looked away momentarily, then said, "It's not important..."

"Oh, it's not?" I interrupted. "Well, I think it is, and so do thousands of kids all over this country, so I'll tell her, I'll gladly tell her." I turned to my mother and continued, "They plant some photographer in the crowd carrying a canvas bag with the name of a newspaper on it; in this case it was the New York *Times*. The guy looks like a hippie. He shouts and curses and sings, drinks beer, smokes pot, raises his fist like the rest of us. And he sells booze and drugs to us. And then, after he's helped get everyone smashed or stoned or angry, after he's been part of it all, the chicken-shit sonofabitch takes enough pictures to fill hundreds, thousands of little files, right, Dad? Is he a hero to you and your pals? If they're capable of doing that, how do we know they're not capable of starting these things? Maybe it's the FBI that puts rocks and matches and gasoline into the hands of rioters, maybe they killed King and JFK, maybe they're behind the burning in Washington, L.A., Newark, maybe they took Sally-Boy...I mean, you said it yourself, 'Things happen to kids.' So tell me what you do to them? Tell me where they go!"

My voice filled every corner of the room. I slowly sat back down. My father was quiet, looking down at his cup. My mother broke the silence: "Michael, honey, that can't be, that's irrational."

"Mom, don't you see that it's more rational to me than Dad's complaints about how I wear my hair?"

"You're off base, Mike, and you know it," my father said, but the walls didn't ring from his voice.

"Why, Dad? Because J. Edgar Hoover didn't put his stamp of approval on my hair like he did on those pictures?"

"Michael," my mother said, "you know Dad is just looking out for you."

My father's face looked distinctly confused now, like he'd forgotten something he wanted to say, so I did what Harry would do and went to the next level.

"Don't you see, Dad," I said earnestly, "that I need to make my own choices, see the good and bad in things for myself, to live by using what you've given me as a guide but not as a map? I'm never going to consciously do anything that would purposely hurt you or Mom..."

"...or yourself?" he broke in softly, looking directly at me now, a slight quiver in his voice.

My mother stood up and hugged him.

"Or myself, Dad. But I need some room to choose, with your support, your willingness to at least listen. The stuff on campus, the war, some things need to change. Two of my black friends were arrested; they're through as far as the school is concerned, and maybe what they did was wrong but what caused it was more wrong. Will they 'disappear,' Dad? Will 'something happen' to them? My girlfriend Erica's cousin was a Marine, a classic, strong, model son who was stabbed in the heart, Dad, right on a street in Saigon…stabbed through the heart by a Vietnamese kid no older than thirteen. Some things have to change, and I don't pretend to know the answers, but I need to figure things out. And it's just not the time for me to say this is how I'll wear my hair for the rest of my life, this is going to be my job for the rest of my life, this is where I'll live forever…because, Dad, I just don't know."

The three of us talked late into the night, and when we finally went to bed, the chasm remained, but at least we could all see it now. My father, though his tone changed to the more controlled one of the man who lived on Lombardi-time, still wanted to pull me across to his side. But he was starting to see that if you pull too hard, someone's going to be sucked into that huge empty void—like Sally-Boy was and Brian was, as was anyone unlucky enough to encounter a madman with a loaded rifle.

CHAPTER FORTY-SIX

We could hear Professor Staunton approaching before he walked into the classroom, his drawl punctuated with profanity that rang through the corridor. When he stood in front of us, the entire class set aside conversations about the assassination of King, burning cities, and campus arrests that had occurred before and during Spring Break. Staunton walked in with the woman with waist-length hair I had seen him with inside the Tombs. Wearing a disheveled navy-blue suit, Staunton still looked somehow natural with the tall woman, who dressed in faded jeans and a fringed leather jacket.

He finished talking to her by saying, "We will see if they choose to act in response to his death or just to sit like steaming horseshit in the woods," and then without pausing for breath he turned to us, his face florid, his voice brimming with rage, and said, "You come to me each week to learn to write, to learn to use words in such a manner that you will become the new voice, the harbinger of truth, the one writer who makes a difference—who adds a blast of freshener amid the shit-befouled air that encases us. 'Make me great,' you are thinking, 'Make me immortal,' you bleat, 'Make me famous, make me loved, make me cherished, make my words the words people take to bed with them, cry to, screw to. Make me rich!' You dream of turning your words into cherished stories and books that will be passed from generation to generation, a kind of family trait like pigeon toes, baldness, heart disease. You never think that your manuscripts will wind up yellowed and lost amid your lives, which themselves will be fraught with lawyers, lovers, children, mortgages, groceries, insurance, installment purchases, and television shows. You know only the vigor and passion you put into your work now, you assume it will last forever, something like 'true love,' only you are making the mistake most common to lovers, dreamers, and writers—you can not expect last night's passion to persevere until next month, or next year, or beyond last night at all. Last night's dream is gone forever, no matter how warm or wet it was. It will never be captured again. Langston Hughes asks us if dreams deferred dry up like raisins in the sun or if they stink like fetid meat and, of course, he must know the answer is yes to both—we know both are true because we see those truths in people every day, people who dry up with their dried up dreams, shrivel with their emaciated love affairs—and yet Hughes tries to convince us that it is wrong to give up on dreams because if we do, as he puts it in another poem, 'Life is a broken winged bird that cannot fly.'

"So the same man who poses the question in one poem, 'What happens to a dream deferred?' warns us in another that without dreams our lives will not fly. If you are writers, you are dreamers by definition, so you must wrestle with Mr. Hughes's thoughts—some of you will, some won't, some will be haunted by dreams deferred, some will forget about dreams altogether, some will look around and dream of outrageously ostentatious houses—the measure of opulence today being size and amount whether in square footage of homes or horse power or number of cars—and exotic vacations and perhaps beachfront mansions and cabin cruisers.

"So many of you will be fickle to the dreams and words and passions that move you now, and by letting it all dry up or trading it all in, you will become vulnerable repeatedly to what we should have seen coming:

"The squeezing of the trigger of the rifle whose scope was focused on Martin's round black head, the assassin waiting, holding steady, calm, a horrifying distortion of Hemingway's grace under pressure, slowly focusing on the hairs that covered the epithelial cells drawn tight across the cranium that stored one man's extravagant and bold dreams—the perverted assassin turning his perverted dream into reality as he fired and felt the powerful kick of the rifle butt warm against his shoulder, and in the instant that he blinked from the explosion and smelled the acrid odor of gunpowder, he watched through his scope Martin's exploding head, while inside that broken head confused and gasping dreams now spun madly in milliseconds into blackness and then hurtled out the exit wound or dripped out of the entry wound.

"The assassin ended those dreams, betting that all of us will let them all dry up along with our own dreams, which we will trade in for comfort; in so doing, the assassin hopes to turn you all into assassins, murderers, killers, hypocrites. After all, he had the courage to act on his perverted dream and to gamble that we are not as courageous about pursuing dreams as he is. So what happens, I ask you, to a dream deferred and deferred and deferred and deferred…" Staunton repeated the word, banging his fists on the podium while we sat in a silence only death itself could duplicate, until, finally, after screaming the word "deferred" one more time, his voice cracked into falsetto, and the blue veins in his neck bulged like tree roots, and his face shone like a beacon, and he looked up, panting, into the face of the tall woman with the long hair, who was noiselessly crying, and extended his arms to her. She embraced him, his white hair touching just below her mouth.

When Professor Staunton spoke again, he held her around the waist, and she rested her face against his head, her hair spilling down the side of his face and over his shoulder. He gently moved her hair aside. His voice now was an almost piercing whisper, and he seemed to talk without moving his lips.

"My wife," he said, and at first I thought he was simply starting a new sentence, but then he repeated the words, "My wife, her name is Wakonda," and he squeezed the young woman to him and rocked sideways with her. She looked up shyly at us with her tear-swollen black eyes, and Professor Staunton went on, "Wakonda and I rode with Martin many times. We discussed his dreams with him; we shared his dreams. I first met my Wakonda in 1963 at Resurrection City in Washington. She is Sioux; she knows poverty. I am all southern aristocracy, part of a family made prominent by selling dark human flesh, part of a society so insanely frightened that it chose to make fear a motivator of life and then wondered why life left us so empty. There was so much love as Martin stood in front of Lincoln's statue and spoke to the sweltering, steaming mass of people about his dreams. Yet, do you know what the first thing I overheard some passersby say about it the next day? 'Why didn't somebody arrest them niggers who was bathin their feet in the reflecting pool?' That's what people were wondering...That's what so many 'enlightened' people wondered..."

Wakonda spoke into his ear. He nodded and then said quietly to her, "Tell them that, but after I say one more thing I think they must know."

"Yes," she said, "it is good for you to reveal to them what they must know."

Professor Staunton turned to us and now looked like the grandfather marionette I had seen him transform into earlier in the semester.

"All of us love words, but simply loving them doesn't mean we are comfortable with them, like with people," he said, smiling at Wakonda. "I admire you all for that, though I can not admire all of you for how you used, or, in some cases, abused, those words. When it comes to teaching writing, I can no longer spend time discussing voice, point of view, plot, agents, setting, conflict, character development—none of that is important, really. What is important is creating the dream as skillfully as you can, holding onto it, and passing it on to others. But if the dream itself is no good, all of the technical elements of writing provide little more than a shabby framework that can be destroyed by something much less powerful than an assassin's bullet."

It occurred to me, as Professor Staunton looked down, that he had just made the kind of speech a professor might make at the end of a course. But we still had several weeks left in the semester. The realization spread quickly across the classroom, and then Wakonda spoke while holding what looked like a letter.

"The university has fired my husband," she said evenly, in a voice filled with clear but subdued strength. "The firing is effective immediately, because of what university officials are calling," she read from the paper in her hand, "'conduct unbefitting a professor and subversive to the goals of the university.' They cite what they call 'repeated instances of meetings with groups of students from STEP, passively viewing the capture of Dean Carmody during the student riots, and inciting black students in the wake of the tragic shooting of Dr. Martin Luther King, Jr.' Inasmuch as Willie did not deny the charges—in fact, he proudly admitted his role—the university said it chooses to, quote, 'terminate our relationship with Mr. Staunton effective immediately.' They do add that the remaining amount of what the university owes Willie on his contract will be forthcoming. Willie and I will turn that money over to the leaders of STEP."

Applause built steadily, and I was one of the first students to stand and show support for the professor.

"Since you all put it that way," Professor Staunton said, smiling, "I'll even look at some of the putrid attempts at writing you people make in the future.

Actually, I hope you all realize I always have enjoyed reading your writing, despite my sometimes, shall we say, less than enthusiastic comments."

Wakonda interrupted a new round of applause, saying, "We are both actively involved in Senator Robert F. Kennedy's presidential campaign. Willie knows the senator and has met with him to urge his entry. We feel the senator has the vision, charisma, and honesty needed to redirect the course of America. If you would like to join us in our efforts, contact us at this number. We need the energy of young people in order to bring about change."

She wrote a phone number on the board. Then Wakonda, with Professor Staunton at her side, walked quietly out of the classroom. I wrote the phone number in my notebook, and then, out of nowhere, Sally-Boy's face appeared, and though I tried to blink it away, I was frozen by his dark eyes, the rusty odor of the fire escape, the innocence of a Brooklyn night, a shared cigarette, a moon slightly shrouded by a ribbon of cloud, and Sally staring into the blue-black, light-studded New York night, saying, *"Hard to believe, ain't it, that some people gotta die on a night like this, Mikey. It just don't seem right...but can't do nothing about it. They're just gonna die. I don't really like to think about it, but it's what happens. It's all around us. It's one thing we all do. We die."*

CHAPTER FORTY-SEVEN

E rica worked the phone next to me; she had immediately decided to join me when I informed her that I was taking up Prof. Staunton's and Wakonda's offer to volunteer with the Kennedy campaign. I took a break from calling and watched as she polled people on their feelings about Senator Robert F. Kennedy and the policies he stood for. In the dim overhead light of the formerly vacant New Jersey building that now housed the local Kennedy campaign office, Erica looked slightly older, a tense sense of urgency making the angles of her face look sharper, more mature. She spoke into the phone with such earnestness that she seemed oblivious to all else, sparking a twinge of

jealousy in me for which I felt both childish and surprised. She hung up the phone and made some nota-
tions on the survey sheet.

"What are you writing?" I asked.

"This last person, a Mr. Calvin Rent, was so rude.
As soon as I mentioned Kennedy, he cursed: 'That bastard. He's a Commie—they oughta throw him in jail...
at the least.'" She stopped writing, looked across the
gray metal desk at me, and then asked, "Should we
make one more call each tonight?"

"It's a little after ten; we better not. Staunton'll be
here to lock up and he said calls after ten are liable
to cause a backlash—people get grumpy and grumpy
people carry grudges."

"I just hate to end on such a bad note," she said, pe-
rusing the response sheet she filled out for Mr. Rent.

"Well, there have been a lot of positive responses,
too, haven't there, in the last four hours?"

Erica flipped back through the thirty or so sheets
she had filled out in the course of the evening. "Some,
but not a majority, and not that real, deep-rooted sincerity I've hoped for. It seems like every time we're
here, it's the same response."

She was right. Kennedy had formally entered the
race, but instead of a swelling of momentum, his campaign sputtered. So many people had expected him
to run, the public met his announcement with yawns
or, worse, with caustic comments about his political

opportunism. And Erica and I noticed the same disturbing thing—that those people who did react to Kennedy often expressed their opinions with frightening virulence. It was as if Bobby Kennedy, whose shaggy hair and big-toothed smile stared down at us from giant posters on the walls, offered choices so distinct that people either felt that his words echoed their thoughts, or that he forced their backs against a wall. The Mr. Rent Erica talked to clearly fell into the latter category.

"What do you think Rent's problem was?"

"Just so narrow-minded; no matter what I said, he kept coming back to the same thing."

"Let me guess—Kennedy's soft on blacks."

"Yes, but the big thing was Kennedy versus Jimmy Hoffa, like challenging the corrupt president of the Teamsters Union was a terrible thing."

"Well, there you go."

"I guess, but I can accept that he objected to Kennedy's conflicts with Hoffa, even if I can't agree with it. But Rent was so hateful, almost vengeful—not in a political way, not just, 'I wouldn't vote for him even if he were the only candidate running,' but 'How can that Mick hypocrite run if he's six-feet under, because that's where he oughta be.'"

"He said that?"

"That, and things like it, several times."

Erica thumbed through some documents that summarized Kennedy's position on various issues. We were supposed to refer to them if people asked specific questions.

"I hardly ever get to these issues, do you, Mike?"

"No, not often."

A door opened behind us. Professor Staunton and Wakonda walked into the room.

Erica asked me, "If a mind's made up at one point, can it ever be changed?"

Before I could answer, Professor Staunton responded to her question: "Most studies say no, so if you insist on being depressed, young lady, just keep thinking that each of your phone calls is fruitless, that every person on the other end of that telephone is standing there listening to you with about five percent of his consciousness while the other ninety-five percent is directed to something more significant than who will lead this country, something like television or bowling teams or whose rear end to kiss in order to climb the ladder to success."

"Do not depress them any more than they already are," Wakonda chided him, gently touching his shoulder. "Erica and Mike are two of our most diligent workers. They realized from the start that this kind of work would be frustrating."

"It's the irrational nature of what they say that scares me," Erica said intently. She leaned forward, her eyes narrowing. She fumbled absently with the policy summaries, and as she spoke, the Stauntons listened sympathetically to her confusion. "This man, this Mr. Rent, the last person I spoke to tonight, listen to his profile." She read from his survey sheet: "Catholic, four kids, oldest nineteen, youngest twelve, married twenty-two years. Right down the line, on paper, he sounds like a natural Kennedy supporter. But the Hoffa thing kept coming up, and then he talked about how his oldest, a daughter named Regina, is in a convent and even she hates Kennedy. I asked why, and all he said was, 'The man hurt me when he hurt Hoffa, and that's enough for my family.' He said his oldest son, a senior in high school, knows he has an obligation to fight to stop communism, so why should he vote for a candidate that's 'soft' on the Vietnamese? When I mentioned urban renewal, he cut me off and used every racial epithet imaginable. And he kept repeating how Kennedy couldn't run if he were dead."

Erica looked at all of us; we looked back at her in silence. I put an arm around her shoulders. Professor Staunton said, without conviction, "A crackpot, that's all, Miss Wakefield. Forget his venomous rhetoric, write it off as the ravings of a mind wracked by peristalsis. In fact, give me his survey and profile." Erica handed Professor Staunton two sheets of paper. He pulled out a cigarette lighter and touched the flame to them. An orange and black blaze soon erupted and Professor Staunton held the papers by one corner and watched the charred remains drop onto the desktop. "Now it is as if Mr. Rent never was."

As we put on our jackets to leave, the ashes of Mr. Rent's profile and survey swirled off the desk. Some of the ashes vanished, others remained hidden behind desk legs, and others scattered to the floor so they blended in with the tile and would eventually cling to the shoes of people walking by and be deposited elsewhere.

Erica and I left the office, and she handed me her car keys as we walked in the night.

"That Rent guy really upset you, didn't he?" I said as I unlocked her seven-year-old Volkswagen bug convertible. We climbed in. I toyed with the idea of putting down the top so we could enjoy the tingle of the late-April air, but Erica was still distracted, so I said, "It worries me, too, you know—the Kennedy hatred, the war, the draft—all of that."

Erica placed a warm hand on top of mine. She moved her face toward me and kissed me. "Hold me," she said. I wrapped my arms around her, and the tighter I held her, the harder she kissed me. We sat there for several minutes and then she said, "Let's go for a ride."

"Sure. I was hoping you could; I mean, it's Friday so I was hoping you might not have to go home right away. Aren't you and Katie going out shopping tomorrow for some wedding stuff?"

"Later in the day, yes."

"Are you sure your parents won't get upset if you stay out for a while. They've been really good about you working here every night. What time did you tell them you'd…"

Erica kissed me in order to stop my nervous talking. She reached behind her seat. "Look," she said, holding up a small overnight bag. I must have looked confused, because she said, professorially, "Now Michael, this bag does not contain my bowling ball."

"You don't have to go home tonight?"

"So perceptive."

"You don't have to go home tonight!"

I started the car and she turned up the radio, but just before driving off I said, "Wait a minute." I put the car in neutral and raised the hand brake. In unison we said, "Let's put the top down!"

"Hey, did we just say that together?" I said.

"Oh yes, my dear, oh yes, we certainly did," Erica said in a mock tone of extreme sultriness, as she unsnapped the top on her side just as I unsnapped it on mine, and then she helped me fold it back to let in the light of the moon and the stars.

The ride began as one of those pointless, destination-less journeys, where the exhilaration of promise is far more palpable than the comfort of direction. The highways seemed to clear for us; there were no other cars on the road as far as I was concerned. The little VW ruled the highways, humming along smooth-ly, easily turning seventy miles per hour, gliding over potholes, holding corners like Harry's Porsche. Erica reached over and pulled my hair out from between the collar of my windbreaker and my shirt. The night air lifted it, and I felt strangely free when the wind raised my hair, swirled gently beneath it, and tickled the back of my neck. Erica's hair was much longer than mine, but she gathered it at her shoulders, lifted it free of the car seat, and draped it behind her. The wind turned it into a burst of dark streamers that blended with the night sky.

Erica directed me to the parking lot of her high school, where we stopped on a small hill overlooking the dark football field and sat on the hood of the VW. She pointed up at the sky and said, "There's Orion and the Big Dipper and Cassiopeia." She named a few other constellations equally fast. "Do you see them?"

"No," I said. "I have to admit I've never been much good at that. I always figured to really see the constel-lations, you should be allowed to connect the stars, like in those dot-to-dot pictures kids have. Without the lines, I can't make out any shapes."

"Hmmm, really?" Erica said, kissing my cheek while I looked at the sky.

"Yeah, I'm afraid so. Disappointed?"

"No, relieved."

"Why?"

"Because I can never make them out either; I just wanted to see if you could!"

"Trick me will you!" I said laughing, and I pushed her just as she was leaning toward me. She lost her balance, and I reached for her, but as I grabbed her, we both slipped off the rounded hood. My feet hit the blacktop parking lot first, and Erica fell into me.

"Are you okay?" we said simultaneously.

"Hey, maaan, did we just say that, like, together, maaaan?" Erica asked in mock slang.

"Oh yes, we certainly did," I said. I leaned over and kissed her beneath some constellation or another.

CHAPTER FORTY-EIGHT

The night sped by in a benevolent blackness, not the threatening black so often filled with shadows, emptiness, and the unknown. This was night at its gentlest, the trustful night of breezes, promises, hope.

We stopped at a Dairy Queen, attracted by the huge yellow-cone-and-spiraling-white-ice-cream neon light. Our chocolate sundae arrived, and we took it to the car, where we took turns feeding one another. I would dip the spoon into the ice cream and syrup, gently place it to Erica's lips, and she would slowly lick it clean; then she would take the spoon, scoop with it, touch it to my mouth, and whisper, "What a big boy you are," tilting her head and dabbing at my chin with a napkin. When the ice cream was gone, we licked remnants of the sticky syrup and nuts from the inside of the plastic dish.

"Not a speck left; neat as can be," I said, inspecting the clean dish by holding it up in the moonlight.

"Not quite," Erica said. "You have a little ice cream left." She leaned forward and licked my lips clean.

From there, we rode smoothly, randomly northward under the stars. Then I had a thought. "Want to go for the ride of your life?" I asked.

"You mean this isn't it? If it isn't, then I definitely want to see what is."

I drove out of New Jersey, across Goethals Bridge, and onto Staten Island, the "other island" as Long Islanders like to call it. It was desolate, except for traffic passing through to pick up the Verazzano Bridge in order to reach Brooklyn, Queens, and Long Island. I pulled the VW off the main highway and followed instinct more than direction, winding the car along the perimeter of the island, occasionally passing dingy beaches that were once considered "day getaways" for wealthy city-dwellers, passing more neighborhood bars than there were neighborhoods, until finally I saw a rusty sign that said, "Ferry Terminal, Keep Right." I parked the car, walked with Erica through the canyon-like terminal strewn with winos, and we paid a nickel apiece to ride the Staten Island ferry, which she had never ridden before.

Through the black night, the flecks of Manhattan's lights grew as we approached the city, the ferry churning steadily through the water. Erica stood next to me along the ferry rail, and the fine spray settled in her wind-tangled hair. Though the air was not cold, the combination of wind and spray caused a tingling chill, so she tugged upward on the zipper of her light-blue windbreaker. The color of the windbreaker highlighted her blue eyes. They were soft, yet penetrating, and they seemed to look inside me and study me.

"Like the ride?" I asked about halfway across.

"It's really nice," she said.

"It's a little trashy, don't you think? The bums leave their paper bags around, see?" I pointed toward three tattered men with newspapers and shopping bags blowing around their ankles.

"It's fine. But the poor men are sad. It's like they're forgotten."

"Like leftovers," I said vacantly.

"Oh, that's so true, and so very sad. Leftovers. Discarded. Alone in all this beauty, all these riches."

"Yeah," I said, looking off the side of the ferry toward the Statue of Liberty. Even in the mist, I could clearly decipher the outline of the lady and her torch. Erica instinctively followed my gaze, as somehow I knew she would. I looked at her looking at the statue, and I heard the ferry's peaceful sloshing wake and soft humming engines. A little after three in the morning, I thought, and here, on this ferry, everything's in place.

"Did I ever tell you about my cousin Sally-Boy, the time we rode the ferry most of the night?" I asked, knowing, of course, that I hadn't.

"Sally-Boy?"

"Yeah, his dad's name was Sal, and no one liked calling him 'Junior,' so they nicknamed him Sally-Boy to distinguish him from his dad, who is, of course, Big Sal."

"I think I'd have stuck with Junior," Erica said with a chuckle. "But I'd like to hear the story."

And then, for the first time in my life, I talked about Sally-Boy to someone outside of my family or the neighborhood. The fire escape stories, clear and raw, just poured out of me to Erica, whose eyes never left mine and whose grip on my arm and then on my shoulders grew stronger as I spoke. I told her about me and Sally-Boy riding the ferry, about being the neighborhood Delivery Men, and then I told her more, things no one else knew—about the countless fire escape talks, and the times Sally and I would jump on the back of a moving ice cream truck, open the freezer door, and throw ice cream bars to younger kids in the neighborhood. Then we'd jump off while the truck was still moving and we'd tumble along the roadside to catch our balance and pick up any of the stolen ice cream bars that were left and eat them.

I told her about Sally's only visit to Virginia for a few days one summer when we saw the Iwo Jima Memorial together, and then how the time we slept in a tent in the woods near my house in Virginia, tough, city-bred Sally woke up just before dawn quivering, fear gripping his eyes, calling, "Mikey, Mikey, something's tryin to get in the tent," and when we looked, a chipmunk ran in. Sally shrieked in horror, so I laughed at him and he punched at me but not to hurt me…not at all… and we wrestled as I called him "Nature Boy" and we wound up laughing and cursing and exhausted. And I even told her about the Brooklyn twins—Tana and Marianna, friends of Sally's—who, when we were fourteen and they were fifteen, let us feel them up in the dark on the parking lot of St. Vittorio's Church on Myrtle Avenue, girls Sally knew from school, girls who knew what rubbers were. When Tana heard me talk with my disappearing Brooklyn accent, she laughed and said to Marianna, "Oh, he is cute, ain't he? He pronounces his 'r's even like when he says 'B*rr*ooklyn,' he says it wit the 'r' so you can hear it, not like 'B*vv*ooklyn' with a 'v' like we says it." And then she casually unbuttoned her blouse and said, "So, how do you like my b*rrrr*easts?"

I told Erica all of that and more and she listened so closely, eyes moist, hugging my arm, and soon the ferry banged into the dock in Manhattan—"I think the boat captains do that on purpose," I said, steadying her—but we didn't even get off the boat, just waited there until it chugged out again, and the next thing I knew the Statue of Liberty was on the other side of us, and the flecks of Manhattan lights slowly shrank behind us as we headed back toward Staten Island.

"I'm sorry I'm talking so much," I said.

"No, I love hearing it, Mike, it's such a piece of you. You love your cousin. Where's Sally-Boy now? Do you ever see him? Can I meet him someday?"

The Statue of Liberty was slightly behind us now, and I wondered if people really pissed on her, or if Sally just made that up. I could only see the statue out of the corner of my eye; if I looked straight ahead, all I could see was darkness.

"Nah, I don't ever see him anymore," I said, the quiver in my voice surprising me. "Sally disappeared, just vanished, the night before our seventeenth birthday. I was visiting him like I always did to celebrate our birthday, and we were sitting on the fire escape at night. We were just sipping beer, talking, wrestling a little, flipping matches and now that I've gone over it a million times, there was something different that night. He seemed to be telling me something. All of a sudden he got up and told me he loved me...never really said that before to one another. Then he jumped inside Big Sal's apartment, and I thought he went to the bathroom. But he never came back outside, and no one has heard from him since. He's never called me or written or anything. No one knows—not Big Sal, not Sally's stepmother, Capricia, not the police, no one. Just gone."

"Oh, Mike," Erica said, holding my arm tighter now, "how could that happen? Why? Do you have any idea?"

I shook my head and thought hard again about what I had already covered so many times. "No, no idea, but for a few months everyone kept asking me what I knew and what he had told me, because I knew him better than anyone, but he never...I mean, we talked about everything, did so many things together. Oh, occasionally he would say he was going to do something, that he wasn't going to be a 'Delivery Man' or own a bakery, but he never told me about an actual plan to leave. There was a rumor that a mob guy named One-Eyed Jimmy might have hustled Sally off somewhere so he wouldn't be drafted and could keep doing 'deliveries' for him."

"So Sally-Boy never said anything specific about what he wanted to do?" Erica asked, touching my face lightly.

I stared straight ahead into the black water, searching. "Nah. I mean, we talked about all sorts of silly stuff—firemen, police, outfielders for the Dodgers before they moved. And it was always, always *us*, together, always the two of us. But I guess, really, in that sense, he's no different at all from me right now. I don't know what I want to do, want to be, where I want to go, and he doesn't know where I am. All I do know is I'm here, and Sally, well, he's...somewhere."

"Someday, Mike, maybe he'll show up, just like that," she said, snapping her fingers.

"Yeah, well, I like to think so, you know, the phone will ring, or there'll be a knock on the door...and Sally'll be right there, talking tough, talking New York all cocky and crazy just like he always was...well, at least when chipmunks weren't threatening him."

I tried to smile for Erica, but I couldn't; my face felt frozen. I was so happy for the ferry's mist to hide the childish tears I felt welling, and then Erica went to hug me, but just at that very moment, the ferry's foghorn blasted. Erica jumped at the first blast, laughed, and settled comfortably against my chest and into my arms for the second and third blasts that followed. "He'll return," she whispered. "You'll see. He will. Someday, Sally-Boy will be back with you." I held her like that until the echo of the horn faded into darkness.

Manhattan widened as the ferry pushed further along toward the emerging outline of Staten Island. I motioned inside some sliding glass doors that led to rows of pew-like seats.

"In the daytime they sell food in there—soft pretzels, hot dogs, stuff like that," I said. Then I pointed to my left toward a large ship anchored and rimmed in bright lights. "Look, Erica! Look at the outline of that ship! Jesus, it's beautiful, isn't it? It's a shame the shine boys don't work at night."

"Shine boys?" she asked, turning her head toward the ship.

I didn't answer right away. I tried to determine what nation's flag the ship was flying. Then I looked at Erica.

"The men who shine shoes all day on the ferries. They carry their polish in these little wooden boxes, and they all look the same. They wear blue and they stoop over and have stubbles of gray beard. Most speak only Italian. You know, they've shined shoes so long their stubby fingers are permanently stained with old polish. Sally always had a soft spot for them. He always gave them whatever he could afford—fifty cents, a dollar—but he never had them shine his shoes. He said, 'Those guys, they come here from wherever, an all they got to show for it is the stain they ain't ever gonna get outta their fingers. You tell me how that's better than whatever they left behind, Mikey.'"

I clasped Erica's long fingers and looked back at the sparkling outline of the vanishing ship. "The shine boys probably never get to see a ship like that; I mean, even if they worked at night, they hardly ever get to look up." I touched my lips to the back of Erica's hand, but my eyes never left the ship's silhouette. "But then, the people on that ship never get to see the shine boys...I don't know who the loser is, do you?"

The brilliance of the ship's lights dissolved into blackness as night deepened around them. I had not identified the ship's flag—another thing in life I'd never know.

Erica didn't speak for a while. She just looked at me and then back toward Manhattan, which was now spread wide and looked vibrant, but distant. She sighed as if she had been crying, but there were no tears.

"What's wrong?" I asked.

She shook her head and then held me with both arms and said, "I wish we could just stay here. I wish this was all we'd ever have to do or see."

"Well, maybe if we wish hard enough the ferry will stop chugging toward shore."

Like children, we closed our eyes tightly for several seconds; then we opened them together.

"Still moving," Erica said.

"So do we give up on the wish?"

She ran her fingers through my hair and pulled it tight behind my neck.

"Never," she said, "because if you give up on a wish, then there's no chance at all of it coming true."

The ferry neared its slip. Behind us, Manhattan was reduced to an outline, an apparition speckled with lights that looked like misplaced stars, an unnamed or unrecognized constellation. Ahead lay the emptiness of the "other island" and the trip back to campus, a long ride that I knew would seem too short.

"Brace yourself; this ferry is going to bang into its slip," I said. "Like I said, these ferry pilots love to slam these tugs into the docks. A little burst of reality."

We gripped the rail tightly. The ferry's engines slowed and we awaited the imminent jolt of the docking ferry. It didn't come.

"A smooth ferry landing," I chuckled. "I don't believe it."

Erica flicked her tongue against my cheek. "Why not?" she asked, smiling. "Anything's possible."

We were mostly quiet on the ride back to campus, the wind whipping by and the sky very slowly lightening. Instead of driving onto the school grounds, I parked on a deserted hill in a neighborhood not far from campus, and we shared coffee from a large plastic cup. To the east, the hill overlooked a flat stretch of barren land, dotted with vintage Jersey car parts.

Erica riveted her eyes on the line the land made in the horizon. Absently, she asked in a voice slightly craggy from tiredness, "Do you think Kennedy can win?"

"Yes," I answered, though I immediately realized I sounded more certain than I actually was.

"Do you think he can make a difference? Stop the war? Bring things under control? Open up people's eyes to poverty?"

"I hope so."

"One hope at a time, I guess, huh?"

"Yeah…anything's possible, remember?"

She sat up quickly, yet even in the suddenness of her movement, she failed to seem awkward. I saw the glow in her face first, and then I followed the light out beyond the car, beyond the field, over the rusted car parts, and toward the horizon. The sun's narrowest beam—a delicate ribbon of palest gold—stretched silently through the morning's darkness.

Erica said, "Oh, this will sound so very very corny, Mike, but there's this verse from Dickinson I always wanted to say to someone special at sunrise."

"Ah, so I'm special?"

She kissed me. "It goes:

'The Sun—*just touched* the Morning,
The Morning—Happy thing—
Supposed that He had come to *dwell*—
And Life would all be *Spring*!'"

On a deserted hill, beneath a sky turning blue with morning, we again passionately did not make love, but Erica Wakefield and I loved each other through the sunrise.

CHAPTER FORTY-NINE

By early May, the pistons of the Kennedy machine were pumping powerfully, freely, and his every move was photographed, filmed, analyzed. It became clear that the man with the bothersome lock of hair and the voice that stabbed at you for attention and the policies that forced you to take a stand had the power to raise passion. More people were receptive to our phone calls, but, at the same time, the intensity of the vitriol also increased.

Erica and I worked often and late, our commitment to Kennedy reinforcing our growing commitment to one another. She would show up at the campaign office as soon as her high school classes ended daily, while

I worked there between my own classes and any free time I had. With Kennedy's surge, the office changed appearance. Curtains were installed, a sofa and some easy chairs replaced the old gray folding chairs, and senior staff members brought in coffee and food regularly. The number of volunteers increased steadily.

"Well, Wakonda, my lovely Wakonda," Professor Staunton commented wryly one afternoon as he surveyed the activity in the busy office, "we are a nation of front-runners, are we not? Everybody just loves to catch a ride with a winner." He smiled broadly and put an arm around Wakonda's waist. "Why, just a couple of weeks ago these people were as hard to find as ticks on a sheep dog."

"Not Mike and Erica," Wakonda noted. "They have been here since the office opened last month."

"Yes, but I sometimes wonder if the two of them wouldn't join a campaign for the anti-Christ himself as long as they could have a reason for meeting with one another."

"Do not listen to the professor," Wakonda said, placing a hand over his mouth. "He appreciates your work. Change can only come about through persistence at all levels. Hard work eventually erodes barriers."

Professor Staunton frowned, took his arm from Wakonda's waist, and raised both fists into the air. "Yes, but sometimes the barriers need to be exploded!" he shouted.

The office workers shook their heads and smiled at the professor's familiar outburst.

"Willie, I don't believe the senator would appreciate your word choice," Wakonda said gently. "He is, after all, a man who is committed to peace."

"He expects that language from me; he wouldn't know it was Willie Staunton talking if I didn't throw in some invective. I am his Director of Malicious Invective!"

"Such hostility!" Wakonda teased. "Control it, or your blood pressure will soar to heights even the eagle does not see."

Professor Staunton turned to me and said, "I love it when she talks Indian to me. Women are wonderful…" He stopped in mid-sentence and looked carefully at Erica. He squinted and moved closer to her. She blushed. A smile of recognition creased the corners of his puppet-like mouth, and he said to me while looking at her, his eyes wide with surprise, "It's her, isn't it? She's the one you've written about, that mixture of strength, beauty, and conviction, the one I told you couldn't exist! It's her! Well, I will be a sonuvabitch!"

Erica looked at me, confused.

"What I wrote was fiction, Professor Staunton," I said, a small truth, since there were no specific references to me and Erica in my writing.

He turned to face me squarely. "Yes," he said, "and there is no greater truth than fiction."

Later that day as we walked in the night outside of the campaign office, Erica asked me, "Mike, have you been writing about me...us? Did you write about... it?" She looked at me with a mixture of hurt and confusion.

"No, not specifically about you, Erica, and not about...that," I said.

"What then? What was it?"

"I've written about the individual power of choice, the importance of decisions, how people disappear, the confusion of not understanding these times..."

"Confusion?" Now her face turned warm and her eyes liquid.

"Yes."

She looked directly into my eyes, as if studying something she once knew that was morphing into something unknown. "We won't know each other forever, will we, Mike? Or will we?"

I felt my throat close as I swallowed. "I hope so, and I could lie, Erica, and say yes, I know for sure we will..."

"But that would be a fiction, in effect?"

"Yes."

She nodded, looked away, and then turned back toward me, kissed me, and smiled. "Then let's say it, let's say we will," she said, "because there is no greater truth than fiction."

CHAPTER FIFTY

Sally-Boy and I were on the fire escape one evening sharing a Schlitz, talking about a storm that was predicted for the next morning. He became even more animated than usual, looked at the clear sky, and said with great certainty: "When you get the clouds in the night, it's like they're sneakin up and hidin somethin. Then you start wakin up, and its thunder—it's like people wakin up scared and hate explodin in their heads. Boom! Then comes rain—it attracts the lightnin like some people attract the hate, and the lightnin is like the hate all pissed off and outa control. So when it storms in the mornin, hate just hangs in the air all day, little pieces of it zappin down on people. And it might zap down and smack you, you never know, you don't. And if it even hits someone near you, it can mess you up too. Storm in the mornin, I lay low all day. Too much hate, Mikey, too much hate."

So amid blue bolts of lightning and gray streams of rain, I fought back my juvenile apprehensions on a stormy Saturday morning in mid-May when Erica was late arriving at the campaign office. I ate one of the day-old doughnuts that were in a box next to the coffee pot. While the coffee brewed, I picked up a copy of the Trenton *Times* that had been pushed through the mail chute in the front door. The lead story was about Draft Board offices in Elizabeth, Camden, and Trenton being burned down during the night, all attacked in the same way—broken into, ransacked, firebombed. Most records were totally destroyed; the buildings themselves gutted. State police and the FBI vowed to capture and prosecute the "radicals" who committed the crimes. Three youths had been spotted near the Trenton office just prior to the early-morning fire; no positive identification yet.

The coffee pot groaned like a bloated animal until I turned it off and poured a cup. I burned my mouth on the first sip; immediately, a little piece of skin dangled from the roof of my mouth. I didn't feel bad about the Draft Boards—in fact, the whole idea of fighting the draft by force had a perversely thrilling appeal to me, somewhat like the appeal the campus protest had—and I thought it would be inspiration-al to see the damage first hand or to know that you had caused it. There was something comforting about knowing that such institutions were vulnerable to the very violence they represented.

Then I thought about the FBI, and I wondered if there were photographers outside of the burned build-ings, waiting for someone like me to grow curious enough to visit the charred Draft Boards; my curling hair on my shoulders and my tattered jeans would be all they'd need to bust me. The worst feeling, however, came from wondering why I doubted that I could ever be responsible myself for such a dramatic act. I could picture others breaking windows and climbing in, tip-ping over files and spilling out papers, crashing gaso-line-filled bottles against the wall and setting a match to it all—I could visualize it and philosophically cheer it, and maybe even risk visiting it for a quick look, but I could not see myself doing it, and I felt weak because of my lack of courage.

The rain had stopped, and the thunder rumbled further in the distance. I sipped more coffee and looked around the still-empty office. Kennedy's face stared at me, the latest picture showing the hair slight-ly trimmed for better appeal to middle-aged voters, the white teeth that might have benefitted from or-thodontics appealingly oversized in their imperfec-tion, and the contrasts his eyes reflected—vision and questions; hope and despair; force and kindness. His looks made me wonder again: What drives men to action, from thinking to doing?

Erica entered the office with her mouth set so hard that I immediately grabbed her shoulders and asked, "What's wrong?"

"You heard about the Draft Boards?" she whispered rapidly, urgently.

I nodded, placing the coffee cup on a table.

"It was Tim. Tim and some friends."

"Jesus," I said, the perverse thrill rippling down my back like an electric charge.

"He's hiding in my car right now. On the floor. He's scared. Canada. He wants Canada. He wants to run, to be safe."

I paused for just a moment—an instant in which I felt the present shift to the past—and then I knew what to do, so I went to the phone and called Professor Staunton's home. I was discreet—paranoid?—enough not to mention the Draft Boards specifically, instead talking about an assignment for class that was missing. Within seconds, he reacted knowingly. "Stop fretting now," he said. "Do you have a car?"

"Yes."

"Stand near it. I'll be right there, but I don't have a lot of time to review your essay."

Somehow—perhaps it was an insight gained from the deliveries Sally-Boy and I had made for One-Eyed

Jimmy—I understood that Professor Staunton had understood. Erica and I walked across the rain-soaked street in heavy, humid air. Tim slumped sideways across the back of Erica's VW, hunched down so he could not be seen from the street. His face looked not just tired but withered, as if he had begun to deteriorate. His once firm, bearded jaw now seemed scarcely capable of providing a foundation for words as he spoke with craggy weariness: "Can you help me, Mike?"

"I'll try."

"I didn't mean to get you or Erica involved, man, but the guys that worked with me on this, we all knew even before we did it that we wouldn't leave ourselves many options. We agreed we'd all head our own way. I didn't know who else to go to."

"We're going to help you, man, we're going to get you out of here." The voice was mine, and the strong tone of conviction suddenly fit me.

Erica squeezed my thigh.

Tim rotated his head slowly from side to side and rolled his shoulders, which now looked cumbersome rather than powerful.

"I never went back to school, you know, after Brian," Tim said softly. "I've just been drifting. I met these guys, some from Jersey some from Texas, California...drifters like me from all over. We showed up at rallies—New York, Philly, Boston. A lot of kids out there are getting beaten physically and defeated in every way. Some of us decided to fight back, take it in our own hands, right to the fucking heart of it all; the Draft Boards are visible and vulnerable. Besides, with the records destroyed, their system will be set back for months. We figure we bought some people some time."

"Fine for them, but now you're on the run," I said.

"People are dying for strangers, Mike. I don't mind leaving this country, but I want to say where I'm going and what I'm going for. Can you do it? Can you get me to Canada?"

My father's face quickly flashed into my mind, as did a glimpse of a photographer at a rally turning Tim's picture into an FBI file, but just as quickly I turned off those images and said definitely, defiantly, "Yeah, Tim, we're going to get you there."

Professor Staunton and Wakonda rode up to us in a new Buick sedan. Wakonda quickly, but casually, handed an envelope out of her window to me and then they sped off. Inside the envelope were directions to an address in Cherry Hill, New Jersey, and a house key. The note said that they would follow in about ten minutes and that we should use the key to enter the house.

We rode silently past South Jersey farmlands, the cloudy sky breaking slightly, the traffic thinning. At one point, Erica noted that I was speeding. "Careful, we don't want to get stopped," she said.

Tim slept, though his head rolled constantly from side to side. The address led to a dirt farm road, a private entrance with no house visible. We wound our way up the muddy trail until we finally saw a sagging farmhouse surrounded by potentially lovely, but now unkempt, shrubs and an array of colorful wildflowers. Tim awoke when the car stopped. Inside the house, the three of us discovered that it wasn't so much a house as a shell; it looked more like a church without pews. There were no walls to divide rooms, though there were some old kitchen appliances strewn along a countertop. The upstairs was equally barren, except for several scattered sleeping bags and duffel bags. We went back downstairs and waited. I looked out the window at the wild growth shimmering with wetness from the earlier storm.

Wakonda and Professor Staunton pulled up; this time, she was behind the wheel and they were in an old Ford pick-up. They walked into the house and Professor Staunton immediately said to me, "What do you know about the burnings?"

For a brief, paranoid moment, I hesitated, and Professor Staunton picked up on it. He smiled quickly and said, "You are correct to be suspicious in this fetid world, Michael, as you confront decisions about whom to trust. But you must decide now, because we haven't much time."

I gave him a quick summary and then introduced Tim.

"And you want Canada, son?" Professor Staunton asked him.

"Yes."

"You are certain?" Wakonda asked.

"I have no choice."

"You could keep running, turn yourself in, turn state's evidence against the others," Professor Staunton said.

Tim shook his head. "No. This country has left me no choice. Those are not options, any more than the draft itself is."

"If you go to Canada, you might never be allowed to return to your home," Wakonda said.

"My brother and a lot of other people aren't coming home for a lot of different reasons."

"Then you are *certain*?" Wakonda asked.

Now Tim looked strong again, the line along his jaw tight as wire. He nodded. "I can't think any more here," he said. "This country, I...I can't breathe in it any more. I can't even remember what it was like when I was a kid. It's like everything is gone. I don't know what happened to it all..."

"Michael, have you agreed to transport him?" Wakonda asked.

I nodded.

"I'm riding with you," Erica said firmly.

Wakonda looked at each of us in turn and said, "All of you understand what this means—Tim, you're dodging, and Mike and Erica, you are complicit. You all could go to jail if caught, you understand?"

We nodded, and Professor Staunton's face flushed with kindness. "There are courageous youth all over this planet, Wakonda," he said. He turned and faced Tim. "All right, son, all right, then. Let's get you ready. But you will all have to do exactly what we say, or the FBI will be on us all like maggots on a corpse."

Wakonda took over: "Go up the stairs. Look inside the duffel bags for a pair of fatigues and shoes that come close to fitting you. You will also find a shaving kit in the bag. Get rid of your beard. Then I will cut your hair—you must look like the Army. In the bag you will also find a billfold with a New Jersey driver's license and a military ID. You must check to make sure they match the nametag on your fatigues."

"How many times before have you done this?" Tim asked.

"About two hundred," Professor Staunton said.

"Not enough times to save enough people," Wakonda added.

"No more questions," Professor Staunton said firmly. "Michael, he'll need to get to the Catskills today. There are people who will be waiting. Are you ready?"

I nodded.

"I will give you directions," Wakonda said. "When you get there, Tim will have to change back into civilian clothes and use the civilian ID that is in the duffel bag. Tim, you must burn the military ID and give the nametag to the people you meet in the Catskills. You leave the fatigues with them too."

"How will they know I'm coming?" Tim asked.

"I will let them know," Wakonda said. "They know me. I know them."

"But can you use the phones safely?"

"We do not call directly to the place you're going; we speak a form of Sioux code," Professor Staunton said. He spoke rapidly. "We have people in straight positions who help us. We have our sympathizers, an entire network. But it is dangerous, and it requires silence and speed."

"After I get to the Catskills, how long before I'm in Canada?" Tim asked as he walked upstairs.

"Early tomorrow morning," Wakonda said.

"That is, if you are quiet, fast, and everything goes as planned, so you must get moving now," Professor Staunton said.

Wakonda went upstairs to check on Tim and to cut his hair. When Tim came down from changing into fatigues, he was beardless with his head practically shaved. Simultaneously, Erica and I looked at one another, an inaudible gasp passing between us.

Tim saw our shocked faces and said quietly, "I know, I look like him, don't I?"

Erica nodded. "Oh, Tim," she said, reaching for him, "I will miss you so."

He hugged her and closed his eyes so tight that the now-shaven skin stretched taut over his pointed cheekbones.

"Tell my parents..." Tim began.

Wakonda interrupted with unrestrained urgency. "No, no!" she said. "Erica can tell no one! Michael can tell no one! That must be understood and agreed to now, or else we can not go forward, we *will* not go forward. As far as Erica and Mike are concerned, Tim McGee has vanished. No one knows where he is. And as far as Willie and I know, he never existed. Tim, you are now," she looked carefully at his nametag and read, "Private First Class Adam Wright."

Tim looked at the tag, then with moist eyes at Wakonda. "Adam Wright...is he..."

Wakonda nodded. "But through you, he lives."

Erica made a soft straining sound that made me wonder if she was losing the last thread of her deep strength. She whispered to Wakonda in a voice now youthful and pleading, "But how will we know if Tim makes it safely after we drop him off? Who will tell us he's safe?"

"Sometimes, we do not know," Wakonda said, looking straight into Erica's sad eyes. "But we try, dear Erica, we try and we hope. From Canada, we hope word will be sent to the Catskills. If word is received in the Catskills, our people there will send back the nametag of Adam Wright. That is how we hope to know.

But sometimes…we never know…we just never know. Come…it is time now."

We stepped out of the house and into fickle beams of sunlight fighting through the rain clouds. A shiver, like electricity, ran down my back.

As I drove the VW north, we rumbled through sporadic lightning that touched off furious little storms, rain dripping through the convertible top in spots. Then, suddenly, the sky would open, and the road would dry, and traffic would speed up. Police cars seemed to be everywhere, but their drivers did not look our way, except for an occasional salute to Tim.

Just north of New York City, the world changes. You leave behind a city of some several million where human electricity constantly charges, leaping from race to race, linking culture to culture. In the city and the industrial towns of New Jersey, there is no single language, but many languages understood, or misunderstood, as one. People massed together vie for the same air and compete for life, extending an obvious warning to anyone who enters, a warning I knew well:

You fight for your fair, or unfair, share; you name it and claim it, and if what you want doesn't exist, you create it. You make it happen. Yourself. The bolder the better. Subtlety is for the meek, and the meek get their balls handed to them on a sterling silver platter rimmed with Christmas lights. This is the city. You can leave it behind, but it doesn't leave you behind. Ever.

But just north of the city, and just north of New Jersey's industrial-strength industrial stench, just beyond Paramus, the world changes into one of open spaces and other, different possibilities.

As I drove, my childhood blurred past, the sounds, the smells, the people, and I realized that my Brooklyn was becoming history to me.

Tim and Erica looked for cops, while I drove and looked at the wet greenness of forests and the orange glistening rocks set back in the hills. Traffic thinned with each northward mile that passed, and my ears popped lightly like a volume control knob on a radio, and the occasional swish of rain changed from soft to loud again as we rode. I looked into my rearview mirror and tried to picture what New York and northern New Jersey would look like from the heights of a mountain if it were possible to shrink the whole area and see it beneath me. But the mirror showed me nothing except the wet highway I had traveled.

"We're here, Tim," I said as we pulled into what looked like an abandoned resort called Wind-Woods.

"We're here," Tim repeated vacantly.

A green light came on in the office window. Wakonda had told us that Tim would have exactly one minute after the light went on to arrive in the office, or else he would find it vacant.

Tim clasped my right shoulder with his left hand. "Mike," he said, "if you ever need me...hell, well, I guess you won't know where to find me, but hell, I don't know how to thank you, man."

Then he turned to Erica whose face was firm and without the tears I expected. She kissed Tim's forehead. They embraced, and when I heard a sob, it came from Tim, not Erica.

"Hurry, Tim," Erica said firmly, "before the light goes out."

Tim stepped out of the VW and into a misty rain. He did not look back. We watched him disappear into the Wind-Woods office while the light shone through the spring wetness and a sharp flash of lightning ripped across the cloud-filled sky.

CHAPTER FIFTY-ONE

Exams, Fish and Katie's wedding plans, Presidential primaries—the busy spring turned hot as June approached. I went home before exams to pick up a pale yellow Mustang convertible Harry was loaning me to use for the summer. My plans were to go back to school, work in the campaign office, take my exams, go to the wedding, and then head for Virginia Beach...and try to get a clue about where my life was headed. But every time I thought about leaving Erica, I felt like something was disappearing into the night, another someone who would haunt my thoughts, decisions, directions.

During my overnight stay at home, my father made a passing reference to my hair, which was now pulled back neatly in a pony tail, but his comments were less caustic than in the past.

"Is Dad softening about my hair?" I asked my mother as she watered plants in the kitchen on the morning I was to drive back up to school.

"He's trying, Michael. You noticed, right?"

"Yeah, I did. But what changed? Why is he trying?"

"Michael, please. He loves you. He's proud of the work you're doing for Kennedy, too, because he says you are working within the system."

Just then, my father came into the kitchen dressed for work in a crisp gray suit, starched white shirt, solid blue tie. He had heard my mother. "Right system," he said, "wrong candidate."

"Come on, Dad, you must like Kennedy."

"Why must I?"

"Irish, Catholic, tough, smart, from New York..."

"Spoiled, opportunistic, inexperienced, hot-headed, not really a New Yorker."

"Once again," I said, "we see eye-to-eye."

He looked at me steadily, but kindly. I could smell the Old Spice. He said, "I am glad about the working within the system part, Michael. It's good to see. Maybe now you'll start believing again that the system is there for the good of everyone. That's why we keep an eye on things—for the good of everyone. I think you can understand that."

In that moment, I suddenly felt queasy as I wondered if somehow—maybe through his many covert contacts—he would find out about my trip to the Catskills. Tim's ID tag still had not been returned.

I drove back to New Jersey and went directly to the campaign office to meet Erica. It was the day of the California and Oregon primaries, and all of us who worked for Kennedy knew the importance of California in particular. When I arrived, most of the older campaign workers were settling in for a long evening of keeping track of returns.

"Do you want to stay here?" I asked Erica.

"No, let's go somewhere," she said. "The suspense in California will kill me."

Her voice had the sound of someone who has just stepped away from an argument, a tension I had heard more frequently lately. Her eyes looked confused at first, then quickly softened as she looked at me.

"Where?" I asked.

"I don't know. Surprise me, like that night on the ferry."

She tossed a duffel bag casually into the back seat, and we rode in the Mustang through Jersey Shore towns and stopped a couple of times to test the water with our bare feet. She carried a blanket under one arm. The beaches were still pretty empty; a few people dotted the shoreline, but only one lone surfer braved the water.

"There'll be a lot of kids out here tomorrow," Erica said, sliding sand over my feet with a bare foot.

"Why tomorrow?"

"A lot of proms are tonight. Prom tonight; shore tomorrow."

"Is yours?"

"Yes."

"Why didn't you tell me?"

"I didn't want to go."

"Why not?"

"It seems so pointless—a prom with all this other stuff going on. I'd rather be alone with you. I told my parents I'd be staying on campus again. That's why I brought the duffel bag."

"Oh," I said, slowly realizing the picture that was being created. "Good, good, I mean great. As long as, you know, you're not upset about the prom. Are Fish and Katie going? I hardly ever see him anymore."

"Yes, they are going, and no, I'm definitely not upset about not going." She paused, looking away for a moment before speaking again. "I love Kates, but I don't understand, I just don't see it. She was racing around all weekend getting ready—Brian dead, Tim missing, prom this weekend, wedding next weekend... oh god, listen to me, just listen to how cynical I sound. I hate myself for it. I'm not one to judge others, that's for certain."

"Why do you say that?"

"Well, you know, judge tenderly of me, Mike," she said steadily.

"Yes, but Erica..."

She rubbed her forehead wearily and said, "I just remember right after it was over how I felt this strange pressure inside me—sometimes I can remember it so vividly, Mike, I can still feel it. There's no mark, no scar, I'm whole, but there was this pressure and then... something was gone. It reminds me that people have their reasons, and those reasons are *their* reasons; I had mine. Kates has hers. I don't judge."

"I know, relax. Let's walk."

The water touched our feet for several blocks, and we spotted a small diner a hundred yards or so from the shoreline. We ate there, the only two customers in the place. Then we spread the blanket she carried on the sand, sat, and for a while didn't talk at all. Erica stretched out and the sun covered her. Sitting up, I turned away from her and sifted sand through one hand, then the other. I looked as far as I could across the ocean until I could see only that line against the sky. I felt Erica's hand on my back. She rubbed gently, then scratched lightly. Her eyes were closed. I kissed her eyelids and lay down next to her.

"How many times this summer will you repeat this same scene?" she asked.

"You mean at Virginia Beach?"

She nodded.

"Come on," I said. "I don't even like to think about it." I scanned some feuding sea gulls along the shoreline, then said, "What about you? There's the summer. UMass in the fall. Lots of people to meet, parties to go to."

She shook her head and put her arms around my neck.

"It won't be the same, it won't ever be the same," she said. "And UMass isn't so very far away, so who knows, right?"

I cupped her face in my hands and kissed her. We walked to the car and drove back to campus, not talking much, but touching a lot, sometimes squeezing hard as if we were trying to clutch a piece of something permanent. The campus was quiet. In the dorm lobby, Tomato whined to The Thatch that a move she had made in chess was illegal. The Thatch's only response was to sneer and sing, "You say tomato, I say tomahto; you say potato, I say potahto..." To which Tomato whimpered, "Don't you start that; now listen to me..."

We passed Darrell Bingham's room and could hear soft music and murmurs. He had returned to school in his A-H after a couple of weeks recuperating, and his life seemed to go on as always, just as he would expect. A few doors down, the room once shared by Andre Moon and Bobby Matson was locked tight as it had been since April. I never saw them leave, never saw anyone come to pick them up, but they were gone.

Upstairs, our suite was still a mess, a point Erica laughed at as she looked for a place to hang her jacket.

"Just put it on my bed," I said, as I turned away from her to look through the record collection. I put on a Simon and Garfunkel album, and when I turned back around, Erica was lying in bed with her jacket back on and her head propped up on my pillow.

"You said to put the jacket on your bed."

I lay down beside her. We started to undress one another tentatively, slowly removing one article of clothing at a time. She fumbled with my belt buckle and I laughed.

"Dost thou dare laugh at me?" she said in her British accent, but still fumbling.

I pointed out that I was only happy, and she smiled but then looked at me with her eyes angular and her face taut. "You know," she said, dropping her accent, "you've never really asked me much more about him. I'll tell you anything you want to know unless it's going to bother you."

"Right now, nothing bothers me," I said, unbuttoning her jeans.

"But it might later?"

"It might."

"Then I shouldn't tell, because it doesn't really matter now, does it?"

"Fine," I smiled, running my fingers lightly along the edge of her underpants.

"But what about you, Mike? You know, you've never told me about any of your past girls." She eased down my zipper.

"Okay," I said. "What do you want to know?"

"Just, I don't know, have there been a lot?"

"A few. None since I met you."

She had begun to reach around toward my hips to slide my jeans down, but she stopped.

"Really? No others since we met?" she asked.

I held her chin and looked straight into her eyes. "Of course, really," I said. "You are different. You are so different, I don't even know how to explain it to myself much less to you. I tried that time when I said I love you. I can't say that I understand it all."

"I know," she said. She leaned back a little onto one elbow, her full, youthful beauty emerging in front of me. "There's just been him, you know that, right?"

I realized that she needed to talk, and although I was almost literally bursting to actually make love to Erica for the first time, I softly encouraged her. "But you really felt something for him?"

"I thought I did. But I didn't know what I was supposed to feel. It's like...like I was being controlled by something invisible. I know now that it didn't feel like this, like it feels when you and I are together."

She slowly reached down and pulled off her jeans. Her eyes melted as my hand went over her thigh. "With him, all of a sudden, there was no excuse not to—at least in my terrible thinking at the time. There was the location and the time...and...and isn't that awful to say?"

Our jeans lay in a heap on the floor. I rolled her onto her stomach and kissed her bare back. "No, it isn't awful, but what about getting pregnant? That can be a big obstacle."

"He used something, except that one time. That time, he said he'd pull out."

"But he didn't?"

"No."

"Son of a bitch."

She whispered, "I never told him that I was pregnant, you know...because, well, there was no future there, I knew that, but still..." She turned her head to look at me as she groped for words. "It was me, Mike, it was me...I was stupid. I shouldn't have put myself at risk. I let him do it. So it had to be my decision."

I kissed her. "Erica, don't be so hard on yourself. It's pointless to blame anyone really, not you, not him. It was a moment in time. That's all."

She rolled onto her back and looked up at me. She eased my face against a warm breast. "You're so sweet, Mike."

And then I did something I never thought I would do. I backed away from Erica, this warm, half-naked young woman, and I said, "Let's stop. I don't think you're ready now. I don't want you to look back on this—on us—and say you were stupid or that you regret anything we've said or done or experienced together." I sat up on the edge of the bed.

Erica sat next to me. Neither of us spoke or touched one another for what seemed like hours, but must have only been a minute or two. Then she reached over and stroked my back with one finger. "What will happen to us?" she asked. "This summer? Next year?"

I looked straight ahead, afraid that if I looked at her I would lose the strength I needed to talk through this moment rather than just make love to her. "I'd be lying if I said I knew, Erica. I don't know." I realized as I said it that I sounded certain in my uncertainty, definite about my indecisiveness, and comfortable in my discomfort. So I went on. "I know I'll think about you and wonder about you, and I know you'll still wonder about me. But right now, we really can't say what it is that's different when we're together. In time, we might be able to, and then we won't wonder anymore."

"But it will take time, won't it?" she said with resignation, and I heard the confusion inside her rising. She twitched slightly as she moved one naked leg against mine.

"Yes, yes it will, Erica."

Suddenly she grabbed me by the back of my hair and said, "Oh, how I want to love you forever and ever, Mike," and then she kissed me hard, with a fierce passion that enveloped me, and she rolled back with me on the bed, and I felt her melt around me, and we made love. There were moments where she seemed to hold back, but then each time she let more of herself pour out, unfolding her body in bursts of coiled emotion that clearly, in her innocence, surprised her.

When it was over the first time, I lay with my face buried in her hair. All the world was quiet, save for our breathing.

And when it was over again, I smiled at her touch on my back. I wondered about nothing because for the moment there was only the moment—me, Erica, and the moment.

And hours later when it ended with the special strained beauty of exhaustion after the third time and the fierce youthful emotion of the fourth, the only other thought that crept into those moments was the picture of the line on the horizon where the ocean's vastness meets the endless sky.

We fell asleep tangled amid sheets, hair, and limbs.

We had the radio alarm clock set so we could awaken in time to see the sunrise, but the voice coming from the radio was too distant to be real. Before we had even fully awakened, I groped around, preparing to make love in semi-sleep. I rolled my eyes open for a glimpse of her face in the dawn light and wondered how many times people awaken from a dream only to find themselves still dreaming. But my dream wasn't the only reality. A deep voice from the radio brought my movements of love to a stop. I opened my eyes and saw Erica staring at the ceiling.

"Oh no, oh no," she said. "Mike, did you hear that? Did you hear it? Oh no, oh no…"

I sat up and cursed at what I thought I had heard and reached across the bed to turn up the volume.

The radio crackled and almost died out. I smacked it and cursed it. After all, we want our hardships clear, direct, forceful—a boot in the face, a knife in the heart, a bullet in the head, a leap off a fire escape.

The radio reception steadied, and the voice said, "The senator was leaving the ballroom of the Ambassador Hotel in Los Angeles..." and it picked up more clearly now "... went through the kitchen instead. There he exchanged handshakes and greetings with the kitchen help when a man, apparently one of the workers, we do not have an identification yet, fired a shot just inches away from the senator's head. The senator fell to the floor in a pool of blood while aides wrestled the gunman to the floor, reportedly breaking either the gunman's hand or arm in the process. Senator Kennedy apparently murmured something incoherent, but made no other movements or comments. Senator Robert F. Kennedy's condition is considered extremely critical. He is not expected to live. This sad event makes him another statistic in the insane violence that sweeps America, perhaps a commentary on society's..."

Erica and I, still naked from our night of lovemaking, stood and held one another. She cried with her face buried in my bare shoulder; I stared ahead into a mirror that reflected us holding one another, each groping the other's body, but our sorrow overwhelmed our sensuality and we slowly began putting our clothes on, listening, our belief suspended, our trust in life lower than our age. We stopped periodically to embrace, holding on to a piece of time that we knew we would never again share, and then we did what we knew we must do...we continued to dress in sorrowful silence.

The intercom suddenly switched on, then off, then apparently on again without Tomato knowing it because his whine was distant though clear: "It's my move, not yours."

And then The Thatch: "You say tomato, I say tomahto..."

CHAPTER FIFTY-TWO

A small group of weeping campaign workers sat around Professor Staunton in a corner of the campaign office. As Erica and I approached, I could see he cradled something in his hands. His face was flushed and his words slurred; he had been drinking. When he saw us, he held up a Kennedy poster. Red paint had been dripped across Kennedy's head. At the bottom of the poster, someone had painted the words, "Compliments of the friends of Jimmy Hoffa."

"There is no end to it," Professor Staunton said. "There will never be an end to it. We suffer once and then again and again and again. Hatred is in the air we breathe; it is what keeps us alive; it is what kills us all; it is what we worship; it is what we pray to; it is what destroys our soul."

Wakonda, who had been kneeling next to him, stood and held his head in her arms. She said to us, "This is another day of evil, but we must continue to find hope in our souls."

"But please, Wakonda, please help me; tell me what to hope for," Erica said.

Wakonda's kind, dark eyes focused directly on Erica's, and then Wakonda reached out, held Erica's shoulders, and said with soft but fierce commitment, "You can hope for the vision to live even as others die, Erica. You can hope for courage. You can hope for Tim. You can hope for the unborn and the newborn. You can hope for those you love and for those who you will love. And you can hope for yourself; we must all hope for ourselves."

Erica swallowed hard and nodded, but her eyes and voice remained unsteady. "Should we have heard by now, Wakonda?" Erica asked, her whispered words tinged with fear.

"Usually we know by now, if we are going to know at all, but no, we have heard nothing about Tim."

"But not always, right, Wakonda?" Erica said, eyes wide and filled with urging. "Not always? Sometimes you hear later, right?"

"Not always, Erica. Sometimes it takes longer. Cling to your hope."

Erica looked at me, full of youth, beauty, and pain, her words measured as if she were trying to keep from unraveling as she said, "Then I will continue to hope that someday it will arrive, the identification, the proof that he is alive. I can continue to hope for that. I can continue to hope that whatever is happening will all mean something. I can—and will—continue to hope!" She was almost shouting. She used no strange dialect to cover her pain, and she shook hard; I tried to steady her, holding her close as we walked to the car.

For the entire drive to her house Erica held her hands over her beautiful face, crying in sporadic, heaving sobs, blurting out in whispers a mantra, a repeated prayer, a confused contrition of sorts: "I'm sorry, I'm so sorry for everything I have done...I must hope...I must do better...I must be better...I am sorry for it all..." And she huddled against the car door, her knees against the backs of the hands that covered the face I could no longer see.

I pulled up in front of her house. Erica's face remained buried in her hands. She continued to struggle for self-control, but then she shook and made one final, high-pitched burst—a sound so deep and foreign that I can still hear it clearly, painfully, a sound like exploding glass that sent a shudder through me.

"It's okay, Erica," I whispered urgently. A pressure pulsed steadily like a drumbeat behind my eyes. "Time will take care of it all."

But she shook her head, which remained behind her hands, and said, "No, oh no, I don't believe that anymore. Time takes everything away; it gives nothing in return. It took Brian, it took Tim, it took Katie, it took King and Kennedy, and it took me and something from me, and it will take you, Mike, and us... it will, Mike, it will take us, it has taken us. But it gives nothing..." she struggled now, her voice husky with grief, "nothing in return. And yet...they tell us... to hope!"

I reached across the car for her, but she was somehow gone, outside, running to her house, both hands still covering her face.

I sat in the car and watched her go into her house and, suddenly, I heard my own voice muttering repeatedly in rhythm with the pounding behind my eyes, "Don't go...don't go ... don't go..." Then I realized her duffel bag was still in the car, so I grabbed it and started walking toward her house, knowing what I would do if she opened the door—comfort her, drive with the top down maybe to the ferry again, remind her of what she said earlier about hope, sit quietly with her at the shore, and then run away with her, the two of us together, removed from everything and everyone— just us and all the time in the world.

I stood in front of the door to her house and, at first, I did not knock. Instead, I listened and heard nothing, just the echoing pulse in my head, pounding against the perfect silence of the street, house, and sky.

"Don't go," I said softly into the door, my face flush against it, and then repeated it, "Don't go."

I listened, and in each beat between the pulse, I heard only the faint rush of a breeze—not what the breeze moved, but the invisible breeze itself. I heard nothing else from behind the door.

I looked up at the empty blue sky, and I wanted to fill it with an explosion, fill it with the powerful pulse bursting inside my head. I wanted to carry something somehow into the endless heavens and beyond the azure border that covers our dreams, so as I pounded with both fists on her door, I yelled repeatedly with an unfamiliar voice that emanated from somewhere in my past or, more likely, my future and erupted into the sky, "**DON'T GO, ERICA! PLEASE, ERICA, PLEASE DON'T GO! OPEN THE DOOR, ERICA! WE'LL GO FOR A RIDE TO THE SHORE, WE'LL RIDE THE FERRY, WE'LL...WE'LL BE TOGETHER ALWAYS! PLEASE...DON'T...GO!**"

My echo faded. Silence again engulfed me. I shouted again. And then again and again and again, until I tasted blood in my throat and spit it on the ground. Finally, I dropped her duffel bag on the steps and backed away from the house, looking for what I knew would never happen. It was so silent in front of the house that I believed that perhaps I had fabricated

Erica, that she was, in fact, fictitious and had never existed at all, that I had wandered onto the front porch of a strange house in search of a nonexistent girl.

I got into the yellow Mustang convertible, and as I rode to Staten Island alone with the top down, I tried to think of something—anything—I could believe in, to feel something—anything—that would last. But all I could feel was the June sun, and all I could see was empty sky, and, yes, in my desperation I talked out loud to him:

She's gone, Sally, she and her beauty and her thoughts and her funny voices, all gone, like you. Gone. Let's go back to the fire escape, Sally. Can we? Please, Sally? At least that remains. Let's sit there and see who can see the farthest—or "fartherest" as you say it—into the night. Let's see who can hear the most sounds in the darkness. Let's hang out at the Panificio, make deliveries in the early morning, peek at Angelina, go to the churchyard dances and meet girls and say stupid things to them and to one another, things that seem to matter but don't, things that we say just to say them, and let's see if you're still afraid of chipmunks. Let's grow to be old men together, like we always said we would, Sally-Boy. You remember, I know you do, we swore we'd always be near one another, always be there for one another. Talk to me like you do sometimes and tell me why it has all happened this way,

why we must not know, why there must be this...this
emptiness that can never be filled. And tell me, Sally,
what do we think before we pull the trigger or plunge
the knife or before we move our lives to the next height
or depth, before we reach the point where we can take
it no longer, where we know we have to change, have
to fight, have to love, have to...leave? How do we
decide, how do we know, Sally? How did you know
when it was time to leave the fire escape behind?

I kept it up all the way to the ferry, where I parked
the Mustang, paid my nickel, walked onto the boat,
and finally stopped talking out loud. But I did wait, as
always, to see if Sally-Boy would somehow answer. As
the ferry slowly motored through the waterway, I noticed the somber faces of others on the ferry; looked
at the Statue of Liberty and pictured people pissing
on it; gave a shine boy a dollar and said, "no shine";
breathed deeply and tried to steady myself as the ferry
banged into its Manhattan slip.

I briefly walked the downtown streets, where everything was eerily quiet; even the trucks seemed to
have their engines muffled, and cars floated by in
silence. I took the subway to my old Brooklyn neighborhood. I did not try to hide myself this time, but
no one seemed to notice me—no one seemed to notice anyone. I peeked into the *Panificio*; it was full, but
quiet. No arias on this day. No loud, Italian laughter.

No sign of One-Eyed Jimmy. I stood in the back and watched Angelina and Massimo work; Uncle Sal was not around, or maybe he was in the kitchen. I left, walked the nearly empty streets, thought about Sally-Boy, my fellow Delivery Man, started talking to him again, wondered how my life had changed, how we become different people, how pieces of us seem to disappear, how we go from trying to figure out life on a fire escape to realizing that there really is no way to figure it out.

Back on the ferry, I continued to wait for Sally-Boy to appear but, of course, he was not there, just people looking shocked, alien, muttering in disbelief of the latest assassination. And then the ferry hit the Staten Island slip with a jolt so hard that everyone, including me, lurched forward, groping at one another for balance. But I had no one to reach for, so I stumbled against the side rail and gripped it, barely keeping myself from falling.

CHAPTER FIFTY-THREE

Harry rescued me from myself that summer. So did Sally-Boy, in a way.

I blew off Fish and Katie's wedding and never heard a word about it. Sometimes I wonder if it ever actually happened, and, if it did, what it was like, how Fish's parents handled it, whether Erica was there. But over time, it's just another piece of the unknown to me.

Instead of going to the wedding, I drove the Mustang to Virginia Beach alone at night, top down, just me and a six-pack I drank on the trip. Sometime after midnight, drunk, I pulled up in front of the beach house Harry had rented for me and three other guys who were part of the "Silhouettes at the Beach" concert staff. I slept in the car until daybreak.

To this day, the weeks at Virginia Beach are just a speeding speck of my life steeped in drugs, fighting, and fucking. After the third time that I was thrown into a holding cell overnight and Harry had bailed me out again, my dad called to tell me he'd had it: "No more of these stunts, Michael. You're my son, and I love you, but I don't know you right now. No more college on my dime. You are on your own until you straighten out."

I couldn't pay for Sinclair myself, and my dad didn't want me living at home—and I had no desire to be there—so after the summer ended, I moved from the beach to Harry and Sparrow's spacious home in McLean, Virginia.

Harry gave me a job at Silhouettes, but the Draft Board was hot after me, and I was buying time until I could get into a college in the D.C. area and get a draft deferment. But working in a nightclub does funny things to you—after hours, everything you *shouldn't* do is so easy *to* do if you want to do it…and, believe me, I was willing. So it was just a matter of time before it had to happen. And it did…one morning around three.

After two hours of the post-work ritual of smoking grass, drinking shots, and having sloppy sex in a back room of Silhouettes, I drove, as I did every night, past Hickory Hill, Bobby Kennedy's McLean home, where his family still lived. I slowed down across from the driveway and looked at the haunting house shrouded with lovely trees illuminated beneath a full moon. A light flashed on in a window, so I stopped the car and cut off my headlights and just sat looking at the lone bright speck in the darkness, while draining the remains of a pint of Jack Daniels. Suddenly, a car sped up with several guys in it, and one of them shouted, "The only good Kennedy's a dead Kennedy!" A fiery glass bottle sailed out of the car and exploded in the driveway. An orange circle of flames and glass lit up the night as their car squealed away into the darkness.

I started the Mustang and raced after them, cursing, one hand on the horn so it blasted nonstop into the night's silence as I steered with the other hand. They ran a stop sign and turned, and I did the same, but my hand slipped from the horn and jerked the wheel. The Mustang swerved, skidded off the narrow road, and crashed into a tree.

Drunk, leg throbbing, pinned behind the steering wheel, shattered glass strewn in my tangle of hair reflecting the moonlight all around me, I lay unmoving and incredibly calm—calmer than I had felt in months—and I could still see the lone light shining in the Hickory Hill home and the swirling smoke from the small firebomb. Inside my head, I kept hearing a phrase Ted Kennedy spoke when he delivered his brother Bobby's eulogy, but I heard it in Sally's voice:

"My brother need not be idealized, or enlarged in death beyond what he was in life."

That one line echoed until red lights flashed overhead. Someone moved me. I screamed in pain.

"Watch his leg," one rescue worker said to the other as they lifted me.

"Oh shit! Nasty break...look at that pretty piece of bone sticking out," said the other. "That's gonna be a lifetime reminder of reckless behavior."

"They do it all the time; fucking Jack Daniels drinker this time," said the first worker, apparently finding my empty bottle of booze. "Why do they want to kill themselves?"

"So people will think they *were* something without ever actually having to *be* something."

"Well, this one's lucky," he said. Then he leaned over me and spoke directly into my face: "You're lucky, dickhead. Do you hear me, man? You're lucky, fuckface. Your leg'll heal. But if you're real lucky, it'll leave you with enough pain to remember." And just before I passed out, I heard Sally-Boy saying, *"See, cuz, it always changes; I knew my time, and now you know yours. It ain't ever gonna be the same, Mikey...not ever..."*

Sally-Boy was right, and so was the rescue worker, because I do remember, and I realize now that all those events are an essential part of me—remembering, changing, understanding, seeking contrition, learning how to persevere.

I got myself into a DC college, made up with my dad, trimmed my hair, avoided the draft (the severely broken leg helped; in fact, I still limp slightly, and then I got a great Draft Lottery number—Hey, wasn't that Lottery a fair deal? Hooray for me, but fuck the poor bastards born a minute too late or too soon!), and, eventually, I grew up to be, as the Kinks would say, "the well respected man about town," very similar to my ever-popular cousin Harry.

A kid from Brooklyn, I wound up just fine, I guess.

American fine.

Corporate fine.

Materially fine.

I played the game and won, climbing steadily higher on the corporate ladder...toward the end, I climbed just for the greed of it until I reached the pinnacle of my own nadir. I bought a cabin cruiser, named it *The Fire Escape*. My brilliant, beautiful wife, a science teacher who possesses all the qualities, and more, that I ever admired in a woman, worked with special needs students in DC's most rundown public schools...and she can actually identify one constellation from another! Our own kids are determined to be world changers— the son, a dedicated Peace Corps worker, the daughter, a graduate of the New School in New York who works with inner-city families (no, her name is not Shayna).

I never tried to run my kids' lives, the way my dad tried to run mine. All young people have their own secrets, stretches of pain and shame, doubt and confidence, weakness and strength—the stuff they keep inside and deal with...or not...that drives them to... or from...what they are...or what they want to be...or wish they were.

My kids watched me thrive in the deep morass of business, and I know they still wonder how I could possibly be the same longhaired freak they see in the couple of photographs I still have from when I was in college...or that smirking little kid in the one photo of me in front of the *Panificio*.

A couple of years ago, I turned my job over to one of those thirty-something's with round eyeglasses and pointy hair. Mr. Owl Eyes (apologies to F. Scott) made a speech on my last day of work, thanking me for whatever it was he thought I did—he was really just thanking me for moving out of his way. It reeked of the sellout world I lived in for so many years, but it was the world I somehow morphed into, grew to accept, and tried my best to use for good.

I bought my parents a place in Florida, and I sent them on cruises to different parts of the world, something about which my ever-grateful mother always would say, "Who would have ever thought that Anna DeRosa from Brooklyn would have this sort of life!" Mom still exercises daily, plays bridge, and stays busy with her friends in Florida, but Dad died a few years ago. A stroke landed him in the hospital as he finished up a round of golf at their country club.